THE WORKS OF STEFAN ZWEIG

PUBLISHED IN ENGLISH TRANSLATION BY
THE VIKING PRESS

MARIE ANTOINETTE
THE PORTRAIT OF AN AVERAGE WOMAN

JOSEPH FOUCHÉ
THE PORTRAIT OF A POLITICIAN

LETTER FROM AN UNKNOWN WOMAN

AMOK   CONFLICTS
(A STORY)   (SHORT STORIES)

VOLPONE
(A PLAY ADAPTED FROM BEN JONSON)

JEREMIAH
(A PLAY)

ADEPTS IN SELF-PORTRAITURE
CASANOVA · STENDHAL · TOLSTOY

THREE MASTERS
BALZAC · DICKENS · DOSTOEFFSKY

MENTAL HEALERS
MESMER · MARY BAKER EDDY · FREUD

KALEIDOSCOPE

KALEIDOSCOPE

thirteen stories and novelettes by

STEFAN ZWEIG

Translated by Eden and Cedar Paul

THE VIKING PRESS · NEW YORK

1934

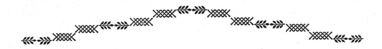

Foreword

The tales that follow spring from a period covering twenty years, and even though they always came into being between larger works I would not thereby say that my personal preference is for my more spacious productions. Conciseness has always seemed to me to be the most essential problem in art. To fit his destiny to a man so nicely as to leave no vacuum, to inclose him as irradiantly as amber does the fly and yet the while preserve every detail of his being has, of all tasks, ever been the dearest to me. And I wish nothing more than that in at least some of the stories here collected the reader may regard it as fulfilled.

STEFAN ZWEIG

177578

Gradually he became conscious
of the amazing kaleidoscope
presented to him by life.

—Stefan Zweig of Edgar in THE BURNING SECRET.

Contents

1. The Burning Secret   3

2. Moonbeam Alley   75

3. Transfiguration   95

4. Fear   155

5. The Fowler Snared   203

6. The Governess   215

7. Buchmendel   231

8. Leporella   263

9. The Runaway   293

10. The Invisible Collection   303

11. Impromptu Study of a Handicraft   319

12. Rachel Arraigns God   359

13. Virata or The Eyes of the Undying Brother   375

BIBLIOGRAPHICAL LIST OF CONTENTS

WITH ORIGINAL TITLES (IN ITALIC TYPE) AND, IN PAREN-
THESES, THE NAMES OF THE GERMAN VOLUMES IN WHICH
THE STORIES FIRST APPEARED.

1. The Burning Secret. *Brennendes Geheimnis.* (Erstes Erlebnis.)

2. Moonbeam Alley. *Die Mondscheingasse.* (Amok.)

3. Transfiguration. *Phantastische Nacht.* (Amok.)

4. Fear. *Angst.* (In a volume by itself.)

5. The Fowler Snared. *Sommernovelette.* (Erstes Erlebnis.)

6. The Governess. *Die Gouvernante.* (Erstes Erlebnis.)

7. Buchmendel. *Buchmendel.* (Kleine Chronik.)

8. Leporella. *Leporella.* (Kleine Chronik.)

9. The Runaway. *Flüchtling.* (Kleine Chronik.)

10. The Invisible Collection. *Die unsichtbare Sammlung.* (Kleine Chronik.)

11. Impromptu Study of a Handicraft. *Bekanntschaft mit einem Handwerk.* (Unpublished in German.)

12. Rachel Arraigns God. *Rahel rechtet mit Gott.* (Unpublished in German.)

13. Virata. *Die Augen des ewigen Bruders.* (In a volume by itself.)

KALEIDOSCOPE

The Burning Secret

A PARTNER

The engine gave a hoarse shriek as the express drew up at Semmering station. A moment of silence followed, during which the carriages rested in the translucent mountain air. The train belched forth a traveller or two, and swallowed down a couple of fresh arrivals. Peppery exclamations shuttlecocked to and fro. Again the locomotive uttered a raucous cry as it started off, dragging a dark serpent behind it, to disappear into the tunnel's maw. A healing peace once more pervaded the landscape, and the windswept atmosphere was good to breathe.

One of the men who had stepped out of the train was young, and of agreeable aspect. He was stylishly dressed and debonair, with an elasticity of gait which brought him to the cabstand well in advance of the other passengers. He engaged the solitary vehicle, and was conveyed without haste to the hotel he had selected. Spring was in the air. A few white clouds, glinting and glowing in the sky, such clouds as are seen only in the months of May and June, seemed to be playing at catch-as-catch-can in the blue, only to hide themselves from the observer's eye behind the scaling mountains, there to embrace and flee, to wave a lily-white hand, as it were, then to melt away into nothingness, reappear, and finally to settle down as night-caps on the neighbouring hills.

A restless, insurgent wind rustled among the lean and rain-drenched trees, so that their limbs groaned, and thousands of water-drops were scattered on the ground. Chill currents of snow-laden air descended from the peaks, until one caught one's breath in the keen, sharp atmosphere. The heavens and the earth were both in a yeasty ferment of impatience. The cab rattled along to the accompaniment of the leisurely trot of the horses and the silvery tinkle of the bells with which the harness was adorned.

On arriving at the hotel the young man's first move was to consult the list of guests. Not a name that he knew was to be found!

"What the devil have I come here for?" he communed. "No office could be worse than this lonesome place with not a soul for company. Obviously I am too early in the season—or too late. My vacations never seem to strike it lucky. Not a creature of my acquaintance among the whole bally lot of them. At least one or two women might have graced the list, so that I could have whiled away my one short week in a mild flirtation."

The youth, a scion of the minor Austrian nobility and employed in the Treasury, had decided to give himself this week's holiday, not because he was in need of a rest but because his colleagues were off on a jaunt and he did not see why he should not follow their example. Though by no means lacking in philosophical capacity, Baron Otto von Sternfeldt

was essentially of a sociable disposition, and was popular in
the circles he frequented. He found solitude irksome, soon
tired of his own company, and avoided every occasion for
being alone since he felt scant inclination to get to know
himself better. If his talents were to flourish, the warmth of
his heart to glow into a flame, and his natural high spirits
to find vent, he needed constantly to rub shoulders with
men and women. By himself he felt cold and lifeless, like a
match unlighted in a box.

He now wandered aimlessly about in the empty lounge, disconsolately fingering the papers and magazines; then he tried
the music-room and strummed a waltz on the piano, but
his fingers were stiff and clumsy, refusing to impart the necessary swing and rhythm to the tune. Utterly depressed, he
threw himself into an easy-chair, and stared out of the window. The evening was drawing in, and grey mist-wreaths
lurked among the pines. For a full hour, he remained drearily
watching the gathering shadows. Then he decided to go into
the dining-room.

Very few tables were laid; and he cast a hasty glance at
the persons sitting over their meal. Not a friend or an acquaintance to be seen! Ah, yes, over there was a face he knew
—but it was merely that of a professional trainer, to whom
he gave a nod. Women there were none; not a sign of anything worth the attention of a charming young gentleman
on pleasure bent. His vexation swelled into impatience.

Sternfeldt belonged to the category of those whose face is
a fortune; one took a liking to him at first sight. He was
always eager for new experiences, fresh adventures; he was
never taken off his guard, because he kept perpetually on
the alert to seize the skirts of happy chance; Cupid stood
ready at his elbow to give him a hint at the first approach
of amorous possibilities; he looked at every woman, be she
the wife of a friend or the chambermaid who opened his bed-

room door for him, with a searching eye which seemed to unclothe her. It is customary to call such men "women-hunters," and there is much penetrating wisdom in the appellation, for they actually do possess many of the instincts of the huntsman, passionately stalking their prey, enjoying the excitement of bringing the quarry to bay, and revelling in the spiritual cruelty of the kill. They are perpetually ambushed for the spring, and refuse to give up the chase until the game is theirs. Passion swamps their whole being; not the passion of a lover, but the passion of a gambler, which is cool, calculating, and dangerous. Some continue thus their whole life long, persistent adventurers in the field of "love," persons whose days are divided into countless petty and lustful episodes—a significant glance in passing, a suggestive smile, a touch of the knee to a neighbour at table—and the year is made up of hundreds of such days wherein sensuality is the main ingredient.

That evening, the baron found no one to take a hand in his favourite sport; and there is nothing so exasperating to the temper of a gamester as to sit with the cards in his hand awaiting the arrival of a partner. Otto asked the waiter to bring him a newspaper. His eyes ran down the columns and over the headlines; but his mind was elsewhere, and he read as though his senses were benumbed by drink.

Then a skirt rustled behind him, and he heard a clear voice say somewhat irritably and with an affectation of culture: "Mais tais-toi donc, Edgar!"

A tall, finely built woman in a silk dress passed, followed by a boy with a pale face and eyes filled with vague curiosity which seemed to caress his companion's form. The couple sat down at a table reserved for them. Edgar was obviously on his best behaviour, and yet the restlessness in his dark eyes betrayed his real feelings. The lady—and she it was who absorbed the whole of the baron's interest—was well groomed and dressed with taste. She was a type that the young man admired, being a not too buxom Jewess just past the prime but not as yet blowzy, a woman still capable of passion, though keeping her natural sensuousness veiled behind an outward decorum. At first he was denied a look into her eyes, for she kept the lids resolutely lowered; but he could contemplate at leisure the arch of her brows meeting delicately over her finely chiselled nose, which, though it betrayed her race, gave a noble grace to a clear-cut and interesting profile. Her hair was as abundant and feminine as the other charms of the flesh, and swept in opulent waves over her head. She possessed the assurance of a woman whose beauty has been the open delight of everyone with whom she has come in contact. Her voice was soft and low as she gave her orders to the waiter, and told her son, who was fiddling with his spoon and fork, to remember his manners and to sit still. Seemingly indifferent to what was going on around her, she appeared to ignore the baron's cautious scrutiny—though in reality her masked interest in him had been awakened by the fact that he was frankly interested in her.

The cloud upon the young man's spirit had dispersed, and his face was serene. Lines and wrinkles of annoyance were smoothed away, his muscles became taut, the blood flooded his skin and gave it renewed life, his eyes sparkled. Having many a feminine attribute in his nature, he responded to the presence of an attractive woman, as a woman responds to the presence of a man. Sensuous pleasure stretched his energies to the full. The hunter scented the game. His eyes challenged hers to the tourney. But she, though giving him a furtive glance, refused to look him in the face and thus to pick up the gauntlet. It seemed to him, however, that a hint of a smile might be detected flitting around the corners of her mouth. He could not be sure, and this excited him the more. What contented him was the fact that she deliberately

avoided his eyes. A good sign, he thought, for it might be interpreted as defiance and at the same time as embarrassment.
Besides, her preoccupation with the child was too meticulous,
and must undoubtedly be aimed at the onlooker. Nor was
her conversation with the lad quite natural; she seemed,
rather, to be talking at her observant neighbour. The forced
repose of her manner was, Otto felt, the mark of an initial
uneasiness.

His feelings were roused. The hunt was on. He lingered
over his meal, staring at the woman incessantly during a
full hour until at length he could have drawn every curve
of her face, while his eyes had secretly caressed each nook
and fold of her splendid body. A heavy shroud of darkness
had fallen over the countryside, blotting out the forest whose
trees continued to sob as though they were frightened children, for the rain-clouds were stretching eager fingers towards
them, grey and full of menace. Shadows had gathered in the
corners of the room, and an oppressive silence hung like a
pall upon the groups clustered round the dining tables. Sternfeldt noticed that the lady's chatter with her son became more
and more forced under the burden of this silence, became more
and more artificial and soon would have to cease. A test occurred to his mind. He got up, and, walking very slowly,
with his eyes glued on the window, he passed close to her
without giving her a glance, and disappeared through the
doorway. Suddenly, he reappeared as if he had forgotten
something and had come back to fetch it. She was caught
in the trap, for he found that she had been gazing with lively
interest at his retreating figure.

Baron Otto von Sternfeldt was enchanted at the success of
his ruse, and waited patiently in the entrance-hall. She soon
came out of the dining-room holding her boy by the hand,
fluttered the pages of some magazines as she passed the big
hall table, and showed a few of the illustrations to the little

boy. As if by chance, the baron, too, approached the table, pretending he wanted to read a paper but in reality that he might get another glimpse into those lustrous eyes, perhaps, even, say a word or two. . . . However, the woman turned abruptly away, not deigning to give him so much as a glance. She tapped her son lightly on the shoulder, saying with affectionate decision:

"Viens, Edgar. Au lit!"

A trifle crestfallen, Otto stared after her. He had fully expected to make acquaintance that very night. The postponement was a disappointment. And yet, it must be agreed, the situation was not lacking in charm. A zest had been added to the adventure. The incident goaded him to enhanced desire. He had to admit that a partner had come his way, and he could now play his hand.

FRIENDSHIP

When the baron stepped into the hall next morning, he saw the boy engaged in conversation with the two lift attendants who were showing him the pictures in one of Karl May's juvenile books. Since his mother was not present, it might be inferred that she was still engrossed in the cares of her person. For the first time, Sternfeldt took conscious notice of the child, who appeared to be about twelve years old, underdeveloped, shy, nervous, jerky in his movements, and possessed of a pair of dark, roving eyes. Like so many youngsters of his age, he gave the impression of being scared, as if he had suddenly been roused from sleep and placed in unfamiliar surroundings. He was by no means plain, but his face was still undifferentiated; the struggle between the man that was to be and the child that had been was hardly begun; his features were moulded but not finally set; there was no clear line, no striking silhouette, only a pale and somewhat

uncouth mass. In addition, being at the awkward age, his
clothes did not seem to belong to him; his thin arms and
frail legs were lost in the folds of jacket and trousers; he
lacked interest in his appearance.

The lad created a very poor impression. He was constantly
getting in the way. At one moment it was the hall-porter who
pushed him aside; at another he would be mixed up in the
revolving door. The outer world was unfriendly. But he tried
to compensate for this by futile and incessant chatter with the
hotel servants. When they had time they would endeavour to
answer his numerous questions, but would break off as soon
as possible and go about their business. The baron contemplated the boy, a compassionate smile curling his lips. Poor
child, he examined everything with curiosity, only to be fobbed
off with roughness. If another human eye caught his inquisitive look, he would cringe away, unhappy at being observed,
miserable that he had been detected in the act of investi-
gating. Sternfeldt was amused; he began to feel his interest
waxing. Then a thought struck him: why not make friends
with the lad and utilize this friendship in order to get acquainted with the mother? It was only fear that made the
youngster so shy. Well, a fellow could try. Unobtrusively he
followed Edgar, who had gone outside and was stroking the
soft nose of a cab-horse. Ill-luck dogged him even in this innocent pastime, for the cabby unceremoniously ordered him to
leave the beast alone. Ruffled and bored, Edgar was again re-
duced to standing about with his vacant expression of countenance, not knowing what next to be at.

The baron seized his chance, and said in a jovial voice:

"Well, young man, how do you like this place?"

The boy flushed, and looked up anxiously. He rubbed his
hands on the seat of his trousers in his embarrassment. This
was his first experience of a gentleman opening conversation
with him.

"Very much, thank you," he answered awkwardly, gulping down the last two words.

"You surprise me. I should say it was a rotten hole, especially for a young man such as you. What on earth can you find to do all day?"

The boy was still too flustered to find a speedy response. How was it possible that this stranger should take notice of a small boy about whom nobody ever bothered? He felt immensely shy and immensely proud likewise of what was happening to him. With an effort he pulled himself together.

"I like reading, and we go for walks. Sometimes we hire a carriage for a drive. I've been ill, and Mother brought me here for my health. The doctor said I was to sit about a lot in the sun."

As he spoke, an accent of self-confidence came into his voice. Children are invariably proud of their illnesses, for they guess that the danger makes them doubly important to their relatives.

"Yes, the sun is most beneficial for a young gentleman in your state of health. You ought to burn to a fine brown. But it's not good to be sitting about all day. A big boy like you would do better to go for rambles on his own, to be a bit uppish, and to play all kinds of pranks. It seems to me you are too obedient and well behaved. You look like a regular bookworm, always going about with a ponderous tome tucked under your arm. When I think of the young scamp I was at your age . . . Why, d'you know, every evening I came home with torn breeches; a terrible pickle I was in. No use for a man to be too good."

In spite of himself Edgar smiled, and on the instant his shyness vanished. He would have loved to respond to the baron's advances, but was afraid of appearing cheeky. How friendly this smartly tailored gentleman was! It was splendid to be talking on equal terms with him. The boy's pleasure in the encounter tied his tongue for very happiness. What would he not have given to find suitable words to continue the conversation! But his thoughts were in a whirl. As luck would have it, the hotel manager's Saint Bernard loped by at this crucial moment. Then it stopped still, came to sniff both boy and man, allowed itself to be patted and fondled.

"D'you like dogs?" the baron inquired abruptly.

"Very much. Grandma has one at her place in Baden, and when we go there on a visit he spends the whole day with me. It's topping. But we're only there in summer."

"I've a couple of dozen dogs on my estate, and maybe I'll give you one, a brown chap with white ears, little more than a puppy, but well trained. How'd you like that?"

The lad blushed with delight.

"Fine!" he exclaimed spontaneously. But then a revulsion of feeling overtook him, and he stuttered bashfully: "But Mother will never agree. She hates dogs about the house, they make so much work."

The baron chuckled, well pleased, for he had at length guided the talk on to the lady who interested him.

"Is your mother very strict?"

Edgar reflected for a moment, looked up at his new friend questioningly as if to see whether the stranger could be trusted, and then answered cautiously:

"No, can't exactly say she's strict. She lets me do anything I like just now because I've been ill. Perhaps she'd let me have a dog . . ."

"Shall I put in a good word for you?"

"Oh, golly!" cried the boy delightedly. "She'd be sure to agree. What's the dog like? White ears, did you say? Can he beg and retrieve?"

"He can do any and every trick you can think of."

It was tickling to Otto's vanity to watch the spark he had kindled in the youngster's eyes. All trace of shyness disap-

peared; and the child's spontaneity, no longer crippled by
anxiety and fear, bubbled up like a spring of fresh water. The
awkward boy had been replaced by a natural and exuberant
creature. If only the mother could prove similar to her son,
thought the baron. A score of questions were showered upon
him at this instant by the youth.

"What's it called?"

"Caro."

"Caro! Caro!"

Edgar seemed to revel in the word, and to be intoxicated
with delight at having acquired a friend so unexpectedly. The
baron himself was no little surprised at his easy conquest,
and decided to strike while the iron was hot. He invited
Edgar to go for a stroll, and the lad, who for weeks had hun-
gered after companionship, was in the seventh heaven of delight. He gave free rein to his tongue, responding innocently
to his new friend's subtle questions and assumed interest. It
was not long before the baron knew all he needed concerning the family: that Edgar was the only son of a Viennese
lawyer belonging to the well-to-do Jewish stratum. Plying the
boy with adroit questions, he further learned that the mother
was not particularly pleased with their stay in Semmering,
that she had grumbled at the lack of society. Moreover, it
would appear from the evasive answers given by Edgar that
Mother was not particularly fond of Father, so that Sternfeldt
surmised the situation to a nicety. He felt almost ashamed of
himself for extracting these scraps of information thus easily
from his decoy who, unused to finding anyone interested in
what he had to say, allowed himself to be inveigled into
confidence after confidence. Edgar's youthful heart beat quick
with pride, especially when, in the course of the walk, the
baron took his arm affectionately. It was an infinite delight
for the child to be seen in such company. Soon he forgot
his juvenility, and prattled disingenuously as to an equal. His

conversation proved him to be a bright lad, somewhat preco-
cious intellectually as is usual with sickly children who pass
a large part of their time among elders, and prone to like
or to dislike persons and things to excess. He seemed, so far
as his emotional life was concerned, to be unbalanced, feeling either hatred towards or passionate love for objects and
individuals. The golden mean did not exist for him, and his
tender face would at times become contorted with the excess of
his emotions. There was something wild and resilient in his
mode of expression which coloured his words with fanatical
ardour, and his gawkiness might possibly be explained as an
outcome of a painfully repressed anxiety at the violence of his
own passions.

The baron soon won Edgar's confidence. In half an hour
he held the child's warm and palpitating heart in his hand.
Children are so easily hoaxed, for grown-ups seldom try to
ingratiate themselves and when they do they catch the inno-
cents unawares. Sternfeldt merely had to think himself back
into his own boyhood, and the puerile conversation immediately seemed the most natural in the world. Edgar, for his
part, had by now quite accepted the elder man as a chum,
and very soon lost any sense of inferiority. All he was aware
of was that he had found a friend—and what a friend! His
relatives and friends in Vienna were forgotten, his pals with
their squeaky voices, their idiotic chatter, might never have
existed! They were submerged beneath this new and unprecedented experience. He had become an intimate of the stranger,
his wonderful friend; and he swelled with pride when, at
parting, he was invited to a further ramble on the morrow.
They separated as brothers; and this farewell was, perhaps,
the most glorious of Edgar's life. Children are so easily
hoaxed. . . .

Baron Otto von Sternfeldt grinned as Edgar ran off. An
intermediary had been found. The boy would doubtless re-

gale his mother to satiety with every word, every gesture, of this amazing rencounter. The woman-hunter preened himself upon the subtle compliments he had conveyed through the son to the mother. He had invariably spoken of her as "your lovely mother"—Edgar would do what was necessary; he, the baron, need make no further advances. The charming unknown would come to him. . . . Not requisite to lift a finger . . . The baron could muse over the landscape from morning to night, from night till morning. . . . A child's warm hands . . . he knew . . . were building a bridge between his heart and the heart of the woman he coveted. . . .

TRIO

As was clearly demonstrated a few hours later, the baron's plan proved highly successful. Intentionally he came rather late to luncheon; and the boy, who was already seated at table, sprang up to greet his new friend with enthusiasm. He plucked his mother's sleeve, whispered a few words in her ear, and drew her attention to the baron with hands and eyes. The lady reproved him for his unseemly behaviour, blushing the while and evidently put out of countenance. Yet she could not help glancing in the young gentleman's direction, and this gave her suitor an opportunity. He bowed respectfully—henceforward they "knew" one another, the necessary introduction had been made. She, in her turn, felt obliged to recognize his civility with a gracious nod, but for the remainder of the meal she kept her eyes glued to her plate. With Edgar it was otherwise. He was constantly spying in the baron's direction, and once even went so far as to address his newly found friend—for which piece of effrontery his mother reproved him smartly. So soon as luncheon was over, he was ordered to go upstairs and lie down. Edgar begged and prayed to be let off. In the end his mother per-

mitted him to take leave of the baron. The latter spoke a
few pleasant words to the lad, and Edgar's eyes glistened with
joy. Then, with a nonchalant air, the young man stood up,
turned towards the neighbouring table, and, addressing the
lady, complimented her upon having so intelligent and jolly
a little chap as son, and referred to the pleasant morning
he and Edgar had passed in one another's company. Meanwhile the boy stood by, blushing with delight. The baron
plied the lady with questions concerning Edgar's health, so
that in the end she was compelled to reply. Gradually, as the
barriers were broken down, the two elders engaged in a
lengthy conversation to which the boy listened entranced.
Then Sternfeldt introduced himself formally, mentioning his
name and title—to which, it would seem, the lady was not
wholly indifferent. Take it all in all, she was most gracious
in her manner towards her new acquaintance. Nevertheless,
she soon moved to withdraw, excusing herself from further
conversation because of her son's delicate health.

The boy entered a lively protest, saying that he was not in
the least tired, and was quite prepared to sit up throughout
the afternoon and far into the night. But his mother had
already proffered her hand to the baron, who deferentially
bent his head over it and kissed it gallantly.

That night Edgar slept badly. His brain was in a whirl of
ecstasy and despair. Something new had suddenly entered his
life. For the first time in his experience he had participated
in the destinies of fully grown persons. As he swayed between
sleep and waking he forgot his own childhood and deemed
himself an adult. So far, his existence had not been a particularly happy one, since he was an only child and his health
was constantly giving trouble. His parents had been the only
target for his affections, and they paid little heed to him. The
boy's other companions were the household servants. Thus
his feelings had been pent up to bursting-point, and at the

first chance were likely to overwhelm the object which seemed worthy of a great love. Edgar lay in the dark, happy but puzzled, wishing to laugh aloud and finding the tears streaming down his face. He loved his new friend more deeply than father, mother, or even God Almighty. An intense and passionate longing went up from his heart, and wove a glamour around the image of this fascinating companion.

"I'm certainly not worthy of his friendship," he thought. "A kid like me, barely twelve, all my schooldays before me, sent off to bed long before anyone else thinks of going . . . What can I ever be to him? What have I to offer him? . . ."

This torturing sense of inability to show his friend what he felt made Edgar miserable. Before, when he had chummed up with a schoolfellow, he had always been able to show his liking by the gift of a stamp from his album, or some other object dear to a youthful heart. But now things of the sort seemed idiotic, utterly valueless. How could he present such paltry tokens of affections to his new friend? What means could he employ to show his regard? He was tormented by the recognition of his immaturity. How rotten to be nothing more than a kid of twelve! Never had he so yearned to be grown up, to be big and strong, to be a real man.

These uneasy musings were interwoven with premonitions of an awakening manhood, rosy dreams which passed gradually into the realm of sleep. But even as he slept, a contented smile played about his lips. . . . Tomorrow he would see his friend again. . . . Had they not fixed it up for a walk together? . . .

At seven he awoke with a start. Had he overslept himself? Quickly he got into his clothes, and ran to bid his mother the customary good-morning. She was amazed to find him up so early. Usually it was all she could do to drag him out of his bed and get him washed and dressed in time for breakfast.

Before she could question him as to his unwonted behaviour,

he had already bolted from the room. Forgetting all about breakfast, Edgar prowled up and down the lounge till nine, eagerly watching the lift, determined not to miss his friend and the promised walk. . . .

At last, a little before ten, Baron Otto von Sternfeldt strolled unconcernedly into the hall. The tryst had long since escaped his memory. But when the boy rushed up to him and passionately recalled the previous day's promise, the baron proved affable, and cordially entered into Edgar's plan, smiling the while at so excessive a demonstration of friendliness. Linking his arm in that of his companion, he sauntered to and fro, quietly but firmly refusing to quit the hall immediately. He seemed to be waiting for someone, and scanned both lift and doors attentively. Of a sudden he stiffened. Edgar's mother sailed towards the twain with a smile of greeting. She fell in with the idea of a walk, and the three set out together.

This was far from being the treat Edgar had expected. He had reckoned upon a tête-à-tête, and was sorely disappointed. Biting his lips, the boy slouched sulkily in their wake. The promised walk, he thought, was his own special privilege. It had only been out of kindness that he had introduced his mother to this wonderful friend, but he could not conceive why he should share the baron's friendship with anyone. A dash of jealousy became intermingled with his loving adoration. He could not help noticing how attentive and considerate the man was towards this interloper. . . .

As the trio made tracks for the woods, the talk was almost wholly directed towards Edgar. His frail health, his paleness, were commented upon by the woman with loving anxiety, while the baron insisted upon the sprightly wit and pleasant ways of his "friend," as it pleased him to call the lad. This created an idea of his own importance in Edgar's mind, contributing to his sense of self-esteem—a dangerous feeling to arouse in a child's heart. Thus flattered, he regained his good-humour. Never before had people conceded him any rights. Now he felt he had been given his due. He was allowed to enter into the conversation on equal terms, instead of being told that little boys were to be seen but not heard. Moreover, he spoke of certain wishes he had long been forced to repress, and they were now given serious consideration. What was there to be surprised at that such treatment should make him feel grown up? Childhood with its artless dreams lay behind him, a relic of the past, discarded like a worn-out garment.

The lady invited Sternfeldt to share her table at luncheon. A casual acquaintanceship had ripened into friendship. Our trio was now in full swing, the voices of woman, man, and child mingling harmoniously together.

ATTACK

The hunter began to think that the time had come when he could bring his quarry to bay. A trio was not to his liking. Very pleasant as a temporary convenience doubtless, but it had served its turn and was not the object of his manœuvring. He knew that, as the saying runs, "two's company, three's none"—that the presence of a third party makes it necessary for Eros to wear a mask, that, except in a duet, loving words lose their tang and the fire of an onslaught is chilled. Throughout their conversation she must never be allowed to forget what he was aiming at. He was sure she had already understood. . . .

It did not seem to Otto at all improbable that his preoccupation with the lady would be crowned with success. She had reached an age when a woman may well regret having remained faithful to a husband she has never loved, an age when her mature beauty craves for one last acknowledgment, when a choice has to be made between the antagonistic forces constituted by motherhood and womanhood. Life, whose riddles had long since appeared to be solved, in this fateful hour poses a fresh question, and the magnetic needle of the will hovers between the hope of a final love-experience and quiet resignation. A matron has then to decide whether she is to live for herself or for her children, whether she is to be the devoted mother or the beloved woman. The baron, who credited himself with a profound knowledge of feminine psychology, believed he had struck up acquaintance with the lady precisely at the perilous hour when she would be obliged to decide the issue as between pleasure and duty. He noticed that in their talks she rarely mentioned her husband, who plainly could satisfy no more than the most superficial of her needs. She had expected marriage to give her an outstanding position in the world, but it had failed to do so; and, worse than this, her husband had little interest in their boy. A shade of melancholy and boredom veiled her lustrous eyes, darkening her life and blunting the edges of her sensibilities.

The baron made up his mind to set about his business of conquest without further ado, but he realized that he must not betray undue haste. Like an angler playing a fish, he wished to land his catch and at the same time to postpone the moment of netting, so as to be sure that his prey did not escape him. He would assume indifference, entice her into making the first advances; whereas in reality it was he who wooed her favours. Taking advantage of his social position, he resolved to treat her somewhat arrogantly so that she would feel her inferiority. It tickled his fancy, this thought that the glamour of an aristocratic name, the gloss of distinguished manners, would enable him to overcome her scruples and to clasp her beautiful body in his embrace.

The game was becoming an exciting one, and called for discretion. Otto spent that afternoon in his own room, well aware that he would be missed and his presence looked for.

Yet, truth to tell, this deliberate absence did not so much affect the lady, who hardly noticed it, as the boy, for whom it constituted a martyrdom. Edgar felt utterly lost, utterly at a loose end. With boyish obstinacy he waited, throughout the creeping, dreary hours, for a glimpse of his friend. To have sought other recreations would have seemed to him a betrayal. He haunted the passages and stairs, and, as evening approached, his heart was filled with anguish. He began to imagine that some misfortune had overtaken the baron, or that he had given unwitting offence to his big friend. Impatient and alarmed, the boy felt his eyes brimming over with scalding tears.

At dinner, Baron Otto von Sternfeldt received a warm welcome. Edgar sprang up to greet him, and, to the astonishment of the other guests and to the distress of his mother, flung his arms passionately round the baron's neck, exclaiming:

"Oh, where have you been? We've been looking for you everywhere."

Frau Blumental reddened with vexation at being dragged into the business in this tactless fashion. She called her son to order.

"Sois sage, Edgar. Assieds-toi!"

The child obeyed, but continued to ply his questions, so that his mother again reprimanded him.

"You must remember that Baron von Sternfeldt is his own master and can do as he likes. Perhaps he finds our society boring."

Admirable, thought Otto, she had included herself in the company, so that the reproach to her child became an indirect compliment to himself.

Our huntsman was again on the alert. He was indeed in luck to have thus easily found the spoor! With bright eyes, with a flush which brought the bloom on to his cheeks, he now talked easily and wittily. Like all strongly erotic persons, his eloquence grew as he felt himself appreciated by the object of his desire. He had a gift for anecdote and sprightly repartee which, after a couple of glasses of the champagne he had ordered in honour of the occasion, outstripped even his own expectations. Big-game hunts in India with an English nobleman—here, forsooth, was a splendid subject to captivate the interest of a woman for whom such exotic experiences were unattainable. Nevertheless, it was the boy who was the most impressed by these personal experiences, and not the woman. He sat enthralled, forgetting to eat or drink, lapping up every word that dropped from Sternfeldt's lips. Who could ever have hoped to meet in the flesh a hero of dangerous exploits, and to hear the account of adventures so enchanting? Tiger hunts, brown-skinned natives, Juggernaut cars crushing thousands of human bodies beneath their weight —of these Edgar had read in books. But he had never believed that such things actually existed. They had seemed no more than fairy-tales. Now they were proved to be true. Edgar's eyes could not leave his friend's face, or, alternatively, those marvellous hands whose fingers had pressed the trigger and had killed tigers. The boy hardly ventured a question, and, when he did, his voice trembled with excitement. His lively imagination quickly called up a picture of the baron perched aloft upon an elephant's back, sitting in a purple howdah, to right and left swarthy men wearing magnificent turbans; the tiger snarling and showing its teeth; the jungle; blood oozing from the elephant's neck where the great cat clawed. . . . Even more interesting narratives were in store, for Sternfeldt told of how old and well-trained elephants were used as decoys to entrap wild ones. Edgar's eyes sparkled. . . .

Then, shattering his magic world, came the voice of his mother, saying, as she glanced at her watch:

"Neuf heures? Au lit, Edgar!"

The boy went pale with alarm. Bedtime is for every child a bugaboo, for it implies a putting to shame, is a public demonstration that adults look upon a boy or a girl of tender years as an inferior, as a creature in need of more sleep than their Olympian selves. Doubly poignant was the disgrace of such an implication at so unique, so interesting a moment as that which Edgar was experiencing.

"Oh, Mother, do let me hear just one more story about the elephant who . . ."

He was ready to beg and pray for her leniency, when it dawned upon him that the role of suppliant little accorded with his new status as grown-up. Too late! His mother, brushing his request aside, said severely:

"Non, Edgar, il se fait tard. Monte. Sois sage. Je te raconterai toutes les histoires de Monsieur le Baron demain."

The child hesitated. Usually his mother saw him into bed. Still, he was not going to demean himself by begging a favour in front of this stranger. Not he! So Edgar merely asked:

"Promise, Mother, you'll tell me everything, you won't forget? All about the elephants . . ."

"Yes, yes."

"Tonight, when you come up?"

"Yes. Now run along with you."

How Edgar managed to bid them good-night without breaking down, he did not know. His throat ached with suppressed tears. Sternfeldt pulled a comical face which brought a grin to the lad's mouth, but he had to make quick tracks for the exit in order to conceal the sobs which could no longer be kept in check.

ELEPHANTS

Frau Blumental remained below in converse with the baron, but their talk was no longer about elephants and big-game hunting. After Edgar had vanished through the doorway, they were both troubled, embarrassed, and the conversation began to flag. Otto suggested they should transfer to the lounge. Here they found a quiet corner. The young man ordered more champagne; and, after they had sipped a glass or two, their oppression evaporated and the talk took a dangerous turn. Baron Otto von Sternfeldt was not handsome. His youthful appearance and manly bearing, his energetic, sunburned face, his short-cropped hair, and his sprightly manner were, however, undeniably in his favour; and these were the characteristics which exercised their spell upon the lady. She allowed her gaze to dwell upon this comely companion, and no longer feared to meet his eyes.

Gradually a certain boldness entered his speech, which ruffled her sense of security as if a hand had been laid upon her, palpating her body desirously, so that the blood raced up into her face and beat feverishly in her temples. Then she would be reassured as he flung back his head and gave vent to a boyish laugh, scattering to the winds as a childish joke any suggestion of sensuousness that might have lurked in his words. At times she thought it advisable to reprove him for his delicate effrontery but, coquettish by nature, she rather enjoyed the implication, and eagerly looked forward to his next move. The game caught her, too, in its meshes; and in the end she was led to follow his lead. Her eyes spoke flattering promises, her lips uttered encouraging words. She even allowed him to sit closer beside her, and she felt his warm breath upon her naked shoulder. Like all those who engage upon a game, they became so engrossed that they forgot the passage of time, and it was not until the hall-clock struck midnight that the woman rose in alarm.

Then only did she realize how far the young man's advances had gone. This was not the first time she had played with fire, but hitherto she had never permitted things to reach such a stage. With horror it was borne in upon her that she was no

longer fully mistress of herself, that something intangible
was slipping from her grasp, that her senses were in a whirl.
Her brain reeled, what with the wine, the momentary shock
of anxiety, the ardent talk. . . .

"Good night," she said hastily. "See you tomorrow."

Already she was stretching forth her hand in farewell. He,
however, was not inclined to let her get away so easily. He
retained her hand in his with gentle mastery, and bent his
lips to it ceremoniously. But the conventional act of politeness assumed ampler form as he kissed her slender finger-tips
and followed up his advantage as far as her wrist. When his
moustache brushed against the back of her hand, she shivered
slightly and a feeling of warmth invaded her being, anguish-
ing and ravishing at one and the same time. Again the tell-
tale blood coursed swiftly, setting her pulses throbbing.
Anxiety, senseless anxiety, deprived her of self-command,
and she wrenched her hand away from his grasp.

"Stay a little while longer," Otto pleaded.

But she was already half-way to the door, walking clumsily
with an excess of speed. He was more than satisfied at this
display of ungainliness, for it was a sure and certain sign
that the excitement he had wished to arouse was responsible
for her inelegant movements. For her part, all she could think
of was to get away as quickly as possible from this man who
might pursue and catch her. Yet another personality within
made her sorry that he did not follow. . . . What for years
she had hoped might one day happen might very well have
taken place at that perilous moment: an adventure. How she
loved the hazard that word implied. Often before she had
been on the brink, but always she had pulled up in time. Yet
she desired nothing better than to be swept off her feet by a
great passion. A mere flirtation seemed to her a paltry experience.

But Sternfeldt was too proud to seize the first favourable

opportunity. He knew that his victory was secured, so why take advantage of a momentary weakness, when a woman's mind was confused by liquor, to make a piratical onslaught and secure the prize? No, he must play fair; she should come to him of her own accord and when in full possession of her faculties. She could not escape him now, for the sweet intoxication had entered her soul.

As she got out of the lift, she pressed her hand upon her heart to stay its furious beating. She breathed a sigh that was partly one of relief at eluding a danger and partly one of regret that danger had not overtaken her. She felt dazed. With eyes downcast, swaying slightly like a drunken person, she groped her way along the passage to her room. Another sigh of relief as she felt the cold door-handle and turned it. . . . Safe at last!

With stealthy tread she entered, and softly closed the door so as not to disturb the child. Then she shrank back in terror. What was that, stirring over there in the darkness? She twitched all over in alarm, was about to cry for help, when a sleep-weary voice asked:

"Is that you, Mummy?"

"What on earth are you up to there?" she cried, switching on the light and running towards the sofa.

Edgar lay huddled up among the cushions, but as she advanced he sat up drowsily. Her first thought was that her child was ill, and had crept into her room for aid. But Edgar said sleepily with a note of reproach in his voice:

"I waited and waited for you to come, and then I went to sleep."

"What did you want?"

"To hear about the elephants."

"Elephants? What elephants?"

But even as she spoke she remembered her promise. Poor innocent, he had slipped into her room so confident that she would be true to her word and tell him about the baron's exploits, but she had failed him, and he had fallen asleep. . . . No, this was absurd, after all; extravagantly foolish. She was outraged. Yet at bottom she was angry with herself, feeling ashamed and guilty.

"Go to your bed at once, you young scallawag," she cried fiercely.

Edgar looked at her in amazement. What had he done to put her into such a tantrum? The child's bewilderment only served to infuriate her the more.

"I told you to go to your own room. Go, at once," she said savagely, feeling all the while how unjust she was.

Without a word, Edgar slunk away. He was desperately tired, and only dimly realized that his mother had broken her promise and for some unaccountable reason was angry with him. The mists of sleep encompassed his mind, and he was in no state to rebel. Every sensation was blunted by fatigue, yet he was alert enough to blame himself for having fallen asleep when it was so important to keep awake, "like a silly kid," he told himself reproachfully as he drifted off into the Land of Nod. Since yesterday morning his childhood had become detestable to him.

SKIRMISHING

It was Sternfeldt's turn to sleep badly that night. An interrupted love-adventure is not favourable to repose. A restless, dream-laden night made him regret not having seized the propitious moment. . . . The shades of sleeplessness and discontent still shrouded his mind when, next morning, he came down on his way to breakfast. The boy, who for some time had been lying in ambush, made a passionate assault, flung his lean arms round his friend, and volleyed forth questions. How jolly to have this big friend all to himself and not have to share his treasure with Mother! She did not need to tell him the wonderful stories, she had broken faith; the hero himself would give an account of those enthralling adventures.

The baron was put out. He found the child's constant spying most incommodious. The deluge of questions was intolerable. The passionate love bestowed on him by the boy was becoming a burden. It was a nuisance to have a twelve-year-old jackanapes perpetually at one's heels. What he wanted was to get hold of the mother before she had cooled off. How could this aim be realized if the child was always hanging around? Uneasiness germinated in his mind. Had he done wisely to arouse Edgar's tender emotions? Certainly it was going to prove difficult to free himself from this ubiquitous youth!

Still, it was up to him to try. He was expecting Frau Blumental to appear at about ten o'clock, and meanwhile he allowed the boy to besiege him with questions. They flowed over him like an avalanche, and he needed merely to put in a word here and there to keep the child happy. When the minute-hand was at the hour, he made as if he suddenly recollected an appointment, and begged Edgar to run over to the opposite hotel to ask whether Count Grundheim, the baron's cousin, had arrived.

Radiant that the message should be confided to his care, Edgar sped off to inquire. How splendid to be of use to his friend! Eager to carry out his mission worthily, the boy bustled along—to the inconvenience and surprise of other visitors. He was keen on showing how smart a messenger he could be, and took no notice of their exasperated stares. The porter informed him that Count Grundheim had not yet arrived, and that, indeed, the gentleman's coming had not, so far, even been announced. Edgar returned on winged feet, bringing the tidings—but the lounge was empty, the baron was nowhere to be found. No answer came to a knock at his friend's door. Dashing from hall to dining-room, from music-room to bar, he inquired from all and sundry whether they had seen Baron von Sternfeldt. Then he ran helter-skelter to his mother's quarters—but she, too, had vanished. Coming downstairs once more, he asked the porter, who told him that the pair had gone out together a few minutes earlier. The child was dumbfounded.

Edgar awaited their return with all the patience he could muster. In his innocence, he suspected nothing untoward. They'd only be gone a very short while, he was sure, for the baron would want to know whether Count Grundheim had come or not. Hour followed hour; and, as they did not return, the boy grew increasingly uneasy. Ever since the morning when this seductive stranger had entered his young life, he had been in suspense. The child mind is a fragile mechanism, and every passion leaves its imprint like a seal upon wax. Edgar's eyelids began to quiver, his face became wan. He waited and waited; at first patiently, but anon becoming more and more excited, until at last he burst into tears. Even now his suspicions were not aroused. He possessed so blind a confidence in his new friend that he attributed everything to a misunderstanding. A doubt entered his mind. Might he not have interpreted the message falsely?

At last they came back, and stood talking pleasantly in the hall just as if nothing unusual had happened. They did not seem to have missed him. Without asking for the answer to his message, the baron said:

"We thought we'd meet you on the way, Eddie."

Overcome with confusion at the thought that they had looked for him vainly, the child protested that he had run straight back along High Street. What direction had they taken? But Frau Blumental cut her son's indiscreet questions short, saying:

"There, there now! Children must not try to put their fingers into every pie."

Edgar went scarlet with mortification. It was the second time she had humiliated him in the presence of his friend. Why did she do this? What was the object of making him out to be the child he no longer felt himself to be? She must envy him so wonderful a friend, and had probably planned to capture the baron for herself. How mean! Yes; and it was she, doubtless, who had deliberately led Sternfeldt in the wrong direction. But he was not going to let her misuse him whenever the fancy seized her. He'd show her! He made up his mind not to say a word to her during luncheon, but only to address his friend.

This plan was difficult of execution. What he most feared happened: neither of them noticed his fit of the sulks. Worse still, they seemed to be unaware of his presence, though yesterday he had been the focus around which had concentrated their attention and interest. They talked over his head, joked and laughed as if he were non-existent. The blood welled up into his cheeks, he felt a lump in his throat which nearly suffocated him. Keenly aware of his impotence to create a more favourable atmosphere around his person, he sat mumchance while his mother stole his only friend away from under his nose. He would have given almost anything to have the courage to stand up and thump the table with his fist—just to make them realize that he was there. But he did not dare to assert himself. He had to be content with laying down his knife and fork, and refusing to eat. In this demonstration, too, he was foiled, for they were not aware of his self-imposed fast until the final course was being served. Then his mother inquired if he was not feeling well. "Ugh," he thought, "she's always fussing about my health. Otherwise she doesn't care a scrap." His answer was curt. "Not hungry," was all he said— and she appeared satisfied. Still they continued to ignore him.

The baron seemed totally to have forgotten his existence. Anyway, he never addressed a single word to the boy. Edgar's eyes burned with partially suppressed tears, and he was forced to adopt the childish subterfuge of wiping his mouth in order to mop up with his table-napkin the water which coursed down his face. At last the meal was over; and, with a sigh of relief, he pushed back his chair, prepared to rush away from the table.

While they had been eating, his mother had proposed an excursion to Maria-Schutz. "So she's determined not to leave me a minute alone with the baron," thought the child. But worse was in store. As Edgar was making for the door, his mother called him back, saying:

"Edgar, you'll be forgetting all you ever learned if you don't set to work on your holiday tasks. You had better stay quietly at home, and get on with your school-work for an hour or so."

Why was she set upon humiliating him before his friend, perpetually recalling him to the fact that he was a child? Edgar clenched his fists, and, turning on his heel, again made for the exit.

"Huffy? You take offence too easily, my son," she said, smiling indulgently. Then, addressing the baron, she added: "Do you find me too severe when I ask him to attend to his studies for an hour now and again?"

The baron's reply was like an icy morsel of steel plunged into Edgar's heart.

"Can't for the life of me see what harm a few hours' study could do."

Was it a plot to get rid of him? Were they leagued against him? Edgar's gorge rose.

"Dad said I wasn't to do any lessons while I was here," he declared. "Dad said I was to get well and strong."

The child's threatening aspect—or was it the reference to

paternal authority?—seemed to produce an effect upon his antagonists. His mother drummed with her fingers on the table, and stared out through the window. An oppressive silence weighed upon the trio. After a prolonged pause, the baron said with a forced smile:

"Just as you please, Eddie. It's not for me to preach; I was as lazy as you make 'em at your age, and failed in all my exams."

But Edgar was long past being in a mood to respond to such pleasantries. He looked up at Sternfeldt with searching eyes, as though he would fain have penetrated to his friend's innermost thoughts. What was happening? Something had changed. They were no longer the intimates they had been. Why? The child was too young to unravel the mystery. He lowered his eyes while his heart beat like a sledge-hammer. Doubt had entered his mind.

However, the mother relented, and said:

"All right, Edgar, lie down for half an hour. Then get ready to start. You shall come with us on the drive."

THE BURNING SECRET

"How account for the change?" mused Edgar, as the three of them rolled along in a hired landau. "Why are they no longer the same to me as they were? Mother avoids my eyes. I wonder why. Why is the baron always up to some foolery as if he wanted to amuse me? But I don't want to be amused, I want him to treat me as he did, man to man. They both seem to have got quite other faces. They don't speak to me as they did yesterday and the day before. Mother's lips are so red she must have painted them. She's never done that. And he's always frowning as though he were put out. But I can't remember saying a single word that could have been taken

amiss. Can't think of any reason why . . . Besides, they're
not behaving to one another in the old way. One could think
they were up to some game they were ashamed of. They're
hiding something, I feel sure. They're not talking naturally
as they did, and they don't laugh any more. There's a secret
they don't want me to know about. I must, at any cost, find
out what this secret is. Perhaps I know what it is already. It
must be the one people are always trying to hide from me;
the same as is hidden in books they forbid me to read, the
same as when we go to the opera and a man and a woman
hold out their arms to one another, hug one another. Then
there was that French governess who did not hit it off with
Dad, and was given notice and sent away. All these things
seem to hang together; but why, I wonder? Oh, if I could
only know, just get hold of the key to the secret. Then I
should no longer be a child, and have interesting things
hidden from me. It's a case of now or never. I'm going to
snatch their secret from them. . . ."

His brow puckered, giving his juvenile visage a quaintly
old appearance. The beautiful landscape might just as well
not have existed so far as he was concerned, for his whole
mental energy was absorbed in trying to unravel the enigma.
And yet the scene was an enchanting one. Mountains encircled with a ring of emerald trees, tender with their early
spring foliage; valleys filled with wisps of iridescent mists
dappled with golden sunshine. Edgar could only see his two
companions opposite him, lolling on the comfortable seat
of the carriage. He glared at them as though by the very
force of his concentrated stare he could extract the secret
from their eyes and hearts. Nothing is guaranteed to sharpen
the intelligence quicker than a passion-laden suspicion; nothing is better calculated to ripen the infantile mind prematurely
than the feeling that one is on the right scent without know-

ing what one is hunting. Children are often separated from
what adults call "the real world" by a tenuous partition which
a zephyr may blow down.

Edgar was convinced that he was nearer elucidating the
mystery than he had ever been before; the solution seemed to
be just under his hand. He was excited at the approach of
discovery, and the solemnity of the occasion made him grave
beyond his years. In his unconscious, he was aware that
he had reached the frontiers of his childhood.

The couple ensconced in the back seat sensed opposition
in the air without realizing that it emanated from Edgar.
The roomy vehicle had suddenly grown too small for the
three passengers. The intense scrutiny of the boy's dark eyes
made the two elders uncomfortable. They hardly ventured to
utter a word, to exchange a glance. They could not get back to
the gossamer-light tone of their previous discourse. No matter
what topic they started, the conversation soon flagged.

The woman was more sensitive to the child's mutism than
Baron von Sternfeldt. She was alarmed at Edgar's morose expression, and started back in disgust when she detected upon
the callow visage of her son the self-same grimace as that
which her husband made when he was put out. Never before
had Edgar shown any resemblance to his father. Particularly
at such a moment as this was she loath to be reminded of
her husband. The child sitting there huddled upon the tiny
seat seemed like a ghost, a reproachful guardian of her ways.
She felt conscience-stricken. Suddenly Edgar glanced up, and
looked her full in the eyes. Mother and son instantaneously
lowered their lids. For the first time in their life together they
were watching one another. This they both realized with
anguish squeezing their hearts. Up till now they had blindly
trusted each other; now a hedge of doubt and suspicion rose
up between them. A latent hatred invaded them, a sensation so novel that neither admitted as yet that it existed.

All three were genuinely relieved when the horses drew up in front of the hotel. The drive had been wretched from start to finish, but none of them was frank enough to say so. Edgar was the first to jump out of the landau. Frau Blumental, saying she had a headache, made straight for her room. The boy and Otto were thus left alone. After paying the driver, Baron von Sternfeldt strode off towards the lounge, passing close to Edgar without so much as noticing the child's presence. He had forgotten his little friend's existence, and left the poor lad behind as if such an insignificant creature was of no more concern to him any more than the coachman on the box or the horses harnessed to the carriage.

Something broke inside Edgar's head as that beloved and slender figure receded. Despair filled his heart at the thought that this wonderful friend had brushed past without a glance or a word. What could he have done to cause displeasure? The mantle of his newly acquired dignity slipped from his frail shoulders; he was no more now than a small and helpless boy, as childlike and immature as he had been yesterday and during all the years that went before. With hesitating footsteps, his legs quailing beneath him, he followed in the baron's wake, caught up the elder man who was about to engage in the revolving door, and stuttered:

"What have I done? Please tell me. Why don't you look at me any more? And Mother, too? Why are you and she always trying to get rid of me now? Am I a nuisance? Have I been naughty?"

Otto was alarmed at the tone of the child's voice; it troubled him strangely, and he felt moved.

"Eddie, you silly old fool, don't worry. I'm out of temper today, that's all. You've not done anything. You're a jolly little fellow, and I'm very fond of you."

He rumpled the boy's hair affectionately, but at the same time he averted his head so as not to look into those huge, im-

ploring eyes which were now brimming over with tears. The
game he was playing seemed to him paltry and unworthy.
He was ashamed of having wrought havoc with a child's
innocent adoration. That was a mean thing to have done.

"Run along now, Eddie. We'll meet again this evening on
the old terms, and this misunderstanding will be forgotten."

"And you won't allow Mother to send me to bed so early,
will you? Promise."

"No, Eddie, trust me. But you'd better be getting to your
room now. The dinner gong will be sounding soon, and we
shan't have washed and changed."

For the time being, Edgar was comforted. He felt quite
happy as he went upstairs. But soon his heart misgave him.
He had grown years older since yesterday, and an unknown
guest had taken up quarters in his mind: mistrust.

He waited. This was to be the ultimate test. The three of
them sat together at the little dining-table. Nine o'clock struck,
but Mother did not send him to bed. He became uneasy. Why
today in particular was she allowing him to sit up beyond his
wonted hour? Had the baron betrayed him? Bitterly did he
now repent having run after his sometime friend and put in
so urgent a plea. At ten his mother got up, and took leave
of the baron. Strange, but the man, too, seemed in nowise
taken aback by her breaking up the party thus early, and
made no endeavour to keep her as he had done before. The
child's heart beat to suffocation.

Now for the test, thought Edgar. He made as if he had
noticed nothing, and docilely followed his mother to the
door. Arrived there, he suddenly raised his eyes and caught
his mother in the act. She was smiling at the baron, an enigmatical smile, a smile of mutual understanding. So this was
the explanation of her early withdrawal from the dining-
room. The baron had cheated him. He was to be cajoled into

obedience so that they might enjoy one another's company unmolested.

"Cad," muttered Edgar.

"What was that you said?" inquired his mother.

"Nothing," he replied, between clenched teeth.

He, too, held a secret within his heart. Its name? Hatred, unbounded hatred for the two of them.

SILENCE

Edgar henceforward felt easy. His heart was overflowing with one undivided emotion: hatred, open enmity. He was now absolutely single-minded. Since he knew that his presence was irksome, he took a voluptuous pleasure in sticking to them like a leech. His energies were concentrated upon making their lives a burden to them. The baron was the first to feel the boy's fangs.

Next morning, when Sternfeldt passed through the lounge throwing a friendly "Good morning, Eddie," to the child, the latter did not look up but muttered a cold, hard "Good morning" in return.

"Mother down yet?"

Edgar remained buried in the newspaper.

"Don't know," he said carelessly.

The baron was surprised. What could this mean?

"Slept badly, Eddie?" he asked, facetiously.

"No," answered the boy curtly, and buried his head still deeper in the periodical.

"Silly young ass," murmured Otto, shrugging, and passing on his way.

War had been declared.

Towards his mother Edgar behaved with exaggerated politeness. A suggestion that it would be good for his health to

play a game of tennis was courteously thrust aside. A fixed
and rather bitter smile showed that he was no longer to be
duped by such ruses. With assumed friendliness he remarked:

"I'd rather go for a walk with you and Baron von Sternfeldt, Mummy."

He glanced up at her as he spoke, and noticed her embarrassment. At length she said:

"Wait for me here," and passed into the dining-room where
breakfast was served for her.

He waited; but as he waited distrust grew stronger within
him. At last he decided to go outside where he could keep
the front door under observation and all the other exits likewise. His instinct told him his enemies were likely to betray
him again, and he was determined not to be caught napping.
Books on Red Indians had taught him how to take cover,
and he crept behind a wood-pile. He chuckled contentedly
when, half an hour later, his mother came stealthily out of
one of the side doors with a superb bunch of red roses in her
hand, and, close at her heels, the baron, the traitor.

Both appeared to be in fine fettle, to be enjoying the fact
that they had given Edgar the slip, and could now relish
their secret together, without the boy's watchful eye perpetually upon them.

The moment had come for the young spy to act. He sauntered along the path towards the hotel as if he had not observed them, pretending he was engrossed in the bushes and
birds, giving them ample time to compose their features after
their initial surprise. Very deliberately the child drew nearer,
and, when a few yards away, lifted mocking eyes towards
them. Frau Blumental was the first to recover.

"Ah, there you are at last, Edgar. We've been hunting for
you all over the place."

"What a whopper," thought the boy, as the lie slid easily
off her tongue. But he kept himself in hand, and drew a veil

over the intensity of his hate. They stood in a bunch, not
knowing what next to do, each watching the other.

"Well, we'd better be starting," said the woman, nervously
plucking the head off one of the beautiful roses. Her sensitive nostrils quivered, and Edgar knew this was a sign that
she was angry. The boy did not move. He continued to gaze
indifferently aloft, into the blue firmament. At length they
passed onward down the path, and he followed. One more
endeavour on the baron's part.

"There's a tennis tournament this afternoon, Eddie. Don't
you want to be there?"

The boy looked at his interlocutor with unconcealed disgust, and did not deign to answer. He pursed up his lips
as if about to whistle.

His presence weighed upon the two elders. They walked
like convicts under guard. The child said nothing and did
nothing, and yet his presence became more and more irksome
as the minutes went by. He repelled their advances, their
essays at conciliation. His eyelids stung with suppressed tears,
his lips were drawn and sullen. Suddenly, feeling she could
bear this furtive observation no longer, the mother ordered
Edgar to go on in front.

"I can't stand your dogging my steps like this. It makes me
nervous."

Obediently, the boy took the lead, but every once in a
while he looked back to see if they were following, and
would wait for them to catch up with him if they dawdled
on the way.

His obstinate silence poisoned any pleasure they had hoped
to derive from this stroll, and his hostile eyes dried up the
words on their lips. Baron Otto von Sternfeldt did not venture to woo, and it was with impotent fury that he sensed
the woman slipping from his grasp as the passion he had been
at such pains to evoke cooled under the observation of this

nerve-racking and detestable child. Every time they started
to converse they became tongue-tied. In the end, the trio
wandered aimlessly through the forest, wrapped in a shroud
of silence, while the trees rustled above their heads and the
sound of their own footsteps beat upon the air. The boy had
successfully wet-blanketed their conversation.

A malevolent spirit had taken up its abode in the heart of
each one of them. But the child was armed and invulnerable;
he took a wild delight in the fact that he, whom they despised,
remained unscathed by their wrath. It was sheer delight to see
how mortified the baron was, how he resented such treatment. Edgar could guess the tenor of the curses that lay unuttered upon the man's lips; he knew that his mother's temper was rising; he realized that they would have given almost
anything to fall upon him tooth and nail, to get rid of him
by hook or by crook. But he gave them no occasion to treat
him harshly, behaving civilly, walking sedately before them.
His hatred had reckoned upon hours of this martyrdom, and
he was determined not to yield an iota of his advantage.

"Let's go back," said Frau Blumental at last, exasperated,
feeling she would have to scream if the tension continued.

"What a pity," rejoined her son placidly, "it's such a lovely
afternoon."

Both the elders noted that the lad was making fun of them.
But neither dared a rebuke, for the youngster's outward conduct was exemplary. In two days he had acquired a self-
mastery beyond his years. Not a sign could be read upon that
tender face. . . . Without further discussion the trio made
their way home. Alone in their suite, mother and son let fall
the mask of reserve. She threw down her sunshade and gloves
in a pet, thus revealing to Edgar's watchful eyes that her
nerves were on edge and that her emotions craved an outlet.
Nothing better, thought the boy, than that she should give
way to her exasperation. In order to provoke her he remained

fidgeting about in her room. She walked feverishly to and
fro, sat down, drummed with her fingers on the table, sprang
to her feet again.

"How untidy your hair is," she scolded. "Your hands are
grubby—wash them at once. It's disgusting to go about in
such a state. A boy of your age, too; aren't you ashamed?"

Edgar grinned as he betook himself to the bathroom. "She
can't stand my being with her," he reflected maliciously.

He knew now that they were frightened of him and his
relentless eyes, that they dreaded the moment when the three
of them were forced to share one another's company. Propor-
tionally as they grew uneasy, the boy grew happy and content.
They were defenceless against the child's tactics. Sternfeldt,
still hoping to gain his end, was furious, and determined to
pay the boy back at the first suitable opportunity. Frau
Blumental was fast losing control. It was a relief to her feelings to rebuke Edgar and find fault at every turn. "Don't
fidget with your spoon," she would say at table. "Where are
your manners? You are not fit to take your meals among
grown-ups."

The boy grinned, and continued to grin, with his head a
little to one side. He knew well enough what lay behind such
reproofs, and was proud at having provoked them. His expression was as calm and collected as that of a doctor by a
patient's bedside. Hate is an excellent master for teaching
the young self-discipline. A day or two ago Edgar would have
made scenes under such trying circumstances. Now he kept
silent and always silent, until they both squirmed under his
silence.

The meal over, Frau Blumental got up, and Edgar prepared to follow her in the most natural way in the world. She
turned on him with the irritation of a horse pestered with
flies, and said vehemently:

"Why do you cling to me in this silly fashion as if you were a baby of three? I don't want you constantly hanging around, d'you hear? Children should not always be with their elders. Go and amuse yourself on your own for a bit. Read, or do anything else you have a fancy for, but for heaven's sake leave me in peace. I'm fed up with you and your stupid, tiresome ways."

So he had got her to speak frankly at last! Edgar continued to grin, whereas the baron and she seemed at a loss. The woman turned her back, furious with herself for having given the show away to the child, while Edgar said complacently:

"Dad does not wish me to wander about here alone. Dad made me promise to be careful and to stick by you."

The word "Dad" seemed to exercise a paralysing effect upon the couple, and Edgar, therefore, took a fresh delight in stressing it. His father, he felt, must also have a place in this burning secret, must wield power over the twain from a distance, otherwise why should they look so distressed at the mere mention of his name? Without deigning to answer, the woman led the way from the dining-room. The baron followed. The boy brought up the rear, not humbly as an inferior, but with the air of a warder, hard, severe, ruthless. In fancy he held them on a chain whose links he could hear rattling and which was indestructible. Hate had steeled his childish strength. He, the innocent, was more invulnerable than they who were under the ban of their secret.

THE LIARS

Time pressed. No more than a few days remained of the baron's holiday, and these he wished to use to the full. Open conflict with an obstinate and determined child was unthinkable. The only way out of their dilemma was through flight. An ignominious surrender, undoubtedly, but what other al-

ternative could be found if they were to escape for a couple
of hours from the boy's tyrannical observation?

"Just run along to the post and get this letter registered,
there's a dear," said Frau Blumental affably to her son.

They were standing inside, while the baron was without,
engaging the services of a cabby.

Edgar took the missive gingerly. His heart misgave him.
Could this be another trap? Usually his mother sent the
porter on such errands. He hesitated and then asked:

"You'll wait for me, won't you? Where shall I find you?"

"Here."

"Honour bright?"

"Of course."

"Promise not to start without me."

This smacked rather of command than of supplication.
Fancy his ordering his mother about! Their relationship had
certainly altered considerably since the day before yesterday. . . . He scampered off with the letter and collided
with Otto as the latter was entering the hotel through the revolving door. For the first time since their estrangement the
boy took the initiative and addressed the baron:

"I'm just going to the post. Back in half a tick. Mummy's
waiting for me. Please don't start before I get back."

"Naturally we shan't," murmured Sternfeldt, squeezing by.

Edgar made for the post-office. Here he was held up by
having to wait in line for a considerable time. Then the gentleman in front had a dozen or more questions to ask. At last
came his turn. He did his business with the utmost dispatch
and rushed back to the hotel, the receipt fluttering between his
fingers. Just as he arrived, panting, within sight of the front
door, he saw his mother and the baron driving off in the cab.

Anger arrested his headlong progress. He felt like throwing stones after the retreating pair. They had eluded his vigi-
lance. How mean! What a beastly lie! He knew that his

mother fibbed occasionally. But that she should break her
pledged word—that was too much. His trust in her was shattered. Life had become an enigma. Words and promises were
no better than soap-bubbles; the merest prick annihilated
them. The secret must be a terrible one, Edgar thought, if it
made two grown-ups break faith with a child, if it made them
lie, steal away as though they were criminals. The books he
had read had told him of people who had cheated in order
to gain wealth or power or a throne. But what could these
two be after? Why did they try to elude him? What were
they endeavouring to hide behind this veil of lies? Cudgel his
brains as he might, Edgar could discover no solution. And
yet he felt dimly that if he could answer the riddle he would
find the "open sesame" out of the realm of childhood and
would enter the kingdom of an adult man. His fury at their
behaviour made it impossible for him to think clearly, otherwise . . .

The forest, the dark and silent forest, would furnish an
answer to his perplexities. He sought refuge in its cool shade,
gave free vent to his sorrow, allowed the tears he had so far
restrained to flow.

"Liars. Rotters. Traitors. Cads."

He felt that if he did not let go he would suffocate. All
the anger, the impatience, the inquisitiveness, the helpless-
ness, the treason of the last few days burst through the dam
of his childish controls and found relief in tears. But this fit
of unrestrained weeping closed the door forever upon his
childhood. The flood carried away all the trust, the love, the
reliance, and the respect which had so far been the essential
constituents of his life.

The boy who later re-entered the hotel was a changed being.
He was collected and purposeful. First of all he sought his
own room, and washed the traces of tears from eyes and
cheeks. Then he made ready for a settlement of accounts as

between himself and his two foes. This satisfactorily arranged, he was prepared to wait patiently for their return.

The lounge was full of guests when the culprits alighted from the cab. Two gentlemen were playing chess. A little coterie of ladies were chatting. Various other individuals were reading papers and periodicals. The child, alert, a trifle pale, had taken an armchair among these grown-ups. His mother and the baron were annoyed at meeting him so soon, and were about to proffer their excuses when Edgar cut them short with:

"Sir, I should like a few words with you."

The baron was nonplussed. He felt as though he had fallen into a trap.

"Yes, yes," he said, flustered. "Later, a little later."

But Edgar protested in a high-pitched voice, so that everyone could hear:

"No, I want to have a talk with you now. You've behaved like a cad. You told me a lie. You knew very well that my mother had promised to wait for me till I got back from the post. But . . ."

"Edgar," cried his mother, rushing towards him.

All eyes were now concentrated upon the trio, and the child, feeling that his hour had come, continued:

"I say it again so that everyone may hear. You lied, both of you—and that's a mean thing, a caddish thing to do."

Baron Otto von Sternfeldt went white under the barrage of eyes. Frau Blumental seized her son by the arm, saying hoarsely:

"Come, come up to your room at once or I'll spank you in front of all these people. . . ."

Edgar had by now quieted down. A pity, he thought, that his excitement had got the better of him. He felt annoyed with himself, for he had intended to keep more than usually calm while challenging the baron, whereas in actual fact his anger had overmastered him. Avoiding any display of haste, he now turned towards the lift in order to seek his own quarters. His mother, embarrassed by the scrutiny of so many quizzical eyes, was stammering:

"Please excuse his execrable behaviour. . . . I'm awfully sorry. . . . After all, he is no more than a child. . . ."

She detested scandal or even the lightest breath of gossip associated with her name, and she knew that the situation needed the utmost tact if she was to come out of it unscathed. To save her face, she was careful not to beat a hasty retreat, but inquired whether there were any letters for her. Then, calmly and deliberately, she made her way to the lift and went to her room. Nevertheless, she was aware of the fact that her withdrawal was accompanied by giggles and malicious whispers.

A serious situation invariably took her unawares and made her anxious. She recognized that in the circumstances she had been remiss, and she dreaded a confrontation with her child. So she loitered on the way. Edgar had donned a new visage since yesterday, a visage which paralysed her. Fear counselled her to have recourse to gentleness when dealing with her son. She realized that, if the issue was forced into the open, Edgar would prove the stronger. . . .

Opening the door quietly, she found the boy sitting in her room. There was no sign of fear in the eyes he raised to the encounter; there was not even inquisitiveness. He appeared to be absolutely sure of himself. Assuming her most motherly manner, she asked:

"Edgar, what could you have been thinking of? . . . You made me blush. A child has no business to behave so outrageously to a grown-up person. You'll have to ask the baron's pardon. . . ."

"No," he answered indifferently, gazing at the trees outside.

This involved her in a quandary. Nevertheless, she continued valiantly:

"What's up, Edgar? You are so changed I hardly recognize
you. You have always been such a sensible and well-mannered
boy that it was a pleasure to be with you. And now, all of a
sudden, you behave as if you were possessed of the devil.
What's your grievance against Baron von Sternfeldt? You
seemed very fond of him, and he has been so kind to
you. . . ."

"Yes; but that was merely to get to know you."

"Nonsense," said she, much perturbed. "What maggot's got
hold of you?"

"He's a liar and a cad. Everything he does is calculated
beforehand. He is a vulgar beast. He wanted to get to know
you and thought that the easiest way was to be civil to me,
and to catch me by promising to give me a dog. I don't know
what he has promised you, nor why he is so friendly towards
you. But I'm certain that he hopes to get something out of
you, Mummy. He's a rotter, a liar. You need only look at
him to know what kind of beast he is. I hate him, yes, I hate
him for his lies, his caddishness, his——"

"But, Edgar, you must not speak like that . . ." she protested, while her heart told her that the child was right.

"You'll never make me believe that he is anything but a
cad. Can't you see it for yourself? He's afraid of me. Why
should he be? He tries to hide his real motives from me.
Why? Because he knows very well that I see through him,
that I know him for what he is—a cad."

"It's not fair to say such things; really, it's not fair."

Her mind had become a blank, and she could only reiter-
ate the words "it's not fair." Panic seized her, but whether on
the baron's account or on the boy's, she would have found it
difficult to decide.

Edgar was well aware that he had made an impression.

He was tempted to lure her to his side and thus acquire a comrade to share in his hatred. He went over to where his mother was, put his arms round her, and said gently:

"Mummy darling, can't you see for yourself that he's a rotter? He has succeeded in changing you, in making you angry with me, because he wants you for himself alone. I'm sure he means to cheat you. Whatever he may have promised, he won't give—of that I am certain. Don't trust him, Mummy. He's cheated me, and he'll cheat you. He's a rotter, and no one ought to trust him."

The child's voice broke on the last words. It seemed as if she herself were speaking. And yet she felt ashamed to acknowledge that this youngster was right. She tried to maintain her dignity, as so many adults do, by assuming a lofty tone.

"Children are not the best judges in such matters. They don't understand. This is no business of yours. All you have to do is to behave like a little gentleman . . ."

The tenderness vanished from Edgar's countenance. He drew himself up, and said:

"Very well. You can't say I failed to warn you."

"So you are determined not to apologize?"

"Yes. Absolutely."

They stood facing one another, and the woman felt that her authority was at stake.

"As you will, Edgar. You will have your meal served here. You will eat alone. And I shall not allow you to share our table until you have made suitable excuses. I'll teach you your manners. You'll not move from this room until I give you leave. Understand?"

Edgar grinned. This sardonic smile seemed to have become part of him. But he was vexed with himself for having warned her (who was just as flagrant a liar as the baron) against that "vulgar beast's" advances.

Meanwhile the lady had slammed the door behind her without a glance in his direction. She was awed by the child's wrathful eyes. He had become uncanny, he knew too much, far more than it was desirable for him to know and to hear. He seemed to be an embodiment of her own conscience, a reproach and an admonition. Edgar had always been a plaything, an ornament to her life, a sweet and lovable object. Occasionally, it is true, he had proved a bit of a burden and a nuisance; but, taking the rough with the smooth, she had enjoyed his company, and their lives had run placidly side by side. For the first time the child had set up his will in opposition to her own. A breath of hate was now part of their relationship.

Yet even at this moment, as she made her way downstairs, she could hear the boy's tender voice raised in warning against the man she was about to meet. She was unable to silence the inward monitor. As she passed a mirror on the landing, she stopped and contemplated her reflexion. For long she looked at herself, deep, deep into her soul. Then she became aware of a smile playing about her lips, of her lips rounding themselves to pronounce a particular word—in the circumstances a dangerous word. Still the voice sounded within her; but she shrugged her shoulders as if shaking off an incubus, cast a bright glance at the answering image, smoothed her skirt, and marched off to her fate with the determination of a gambler staking his last gold piece upon the hazards of the game.

SHADOWS IN THE MOONLIGHT

A waiter brought up Edgar's supper on a tray, made the boy as comfortable as possible, and then withdrew, closing the door behind him and turning the key in the lock. "Insufferable," thought the boy, springing to his feet. To be bolted

in as though he were a wild beast was too great an indignity.
Could his mother really have brought this degradation upon
him? His mind darkened as he meditated.

"I wonder what can be going on down there while I'm
caged in this room. What are they talking about? Will their
secret be disclosed, when I'm not there to share it with them?
It's awful to feel there's a secret in the air, always when I'm
with grown-ups. They shut me out, especially at night, and
talk in whispers if I drop in and take them unawares. I feel
I'm on the track of their secret, and yet I just miss guessing
what it's all about. This isn't the first time I've tried to understand. Those books I sneaked from Dad's table and shelves!
Only the trouble was that even when I had read them from
cover to cover I never understood what they were driving at.
There's something that escapes me every time. How Emma,
our parlourmaid, laughed at me when I begged her to explain a passage! Oh, I think it's dreadful to be a child, full
of curiosity and not daring to ask questions. Grown-ups
merely grin, and look down on a fellow as if he were a fool.
But something tells me I'll soon know everything there is to
know. I'm not going to give in until I do. . . ."

He strained his ears to catch a possible footstep. But only
the breeze murmured in the foliage, swaying the branches
and breaking the moonbeams into a thousand facets of light
scattered among the shadows.

"They must be up to something they are ashamed of, otherwise why should they trouble to tell me such idiotic lies? I
expect they're having a good laugh at getting rid of me. Never
fear, my turn will come. I've been a silly ass to allow them to
lock me in. Ought to have stuck to them and never let them
out of my sight. Grown-ups aren't very clever at hiding what
they are doing, and they'd be sure to give themselves away
before long. They fancy we children go to sleep, and they
forget that we know all kinds of dodges so as to overhear

what they say and see what they do. We're not so stupid as
they imagine. When Aunt Clara had a baby two months
ago they pretended to be ever so much surprised. But they
had known about its coming ages before, and I knew too,
because I heard them talking. This time also I'll find out what
Mother and the baron are hiding. I wish the doors were transparent so that I could watch them when they thought no one
could see. I wonder if it would be a good move to ring for
the chambermaid? She'd have to unlock the door to ask what
I wanted. Then, before she knew what I was doing, I'd slip
out. . . . No, better not. That might give me away and show
the servants how meanly I'm treated. No one must know, it
would hurt too much, I couldn't stand it. But tomorrow . . ."

A woman's laugh floated up to him on the spring air. Was
that his mother? It might well be. She had plenty of reasons for
being gay. Had she not locked him up, small and defenceless
as he was, got rid of him, thrown him into a corner like a
bundle of dirty clothes? Stealthily creeping to the window, he
peered out. A couple of girls were strolling by with their
young men—no one else.

As he leaned on the sill, he noticed how close the window
was to the ground; and, before he realized what he was
doing, he had taken the plunge and landed in a bed of flowers. The slight noise he made passed unnoticed. He was free.
Now he could go and spy upon his foes. In two days, this
attitude of spying had become second nature to him who
hitherto had been so candid and innocent. Careful to avoid
making a sound, he prowled round the hotel, his heart beating furiously lest he should be discovered. Here was the
dining-room. With the utmost precaution he pressed his face
close to a window-pane. The pair were not there. He passed
from window to window, not daring to enter the building in
case he should stumble upon them in a passage or on the stair.
He failed in his search and was in despair. Then, of a sudden,

he saw two shadows issuing from a side door. He ducked so
as not to be discovered. Yes, it was his mother accompanied
by the inevitable baron. "Just in time," thought the boy.
"What are they talking about? Wish this rotten wind wouldn't
make such a row among the trees!" His mother laughed
audibly. He had never heard her laugh like that; it sounded
shrill, a trifle excited; most peculiar. Though Edgar felt
alarmed at this unusual mirth, he was likewise reassured for,
if she felt merry, there certainly could be no immediate danger
threatening her. Nor could the matter the twain had in hand
be anything of grave importance. Why, then, were they at
such pains to hide it from him? Edgar felt rather disappointed
at the thought that the secret was not something big, and
worthy of the trouble he was taking to unravel it.

Whither could they be going at this hour of the night?
High up in the sky a strong wind must be blowing for the
clouds were racing by, obscuring the moon. So dark was it
at times that one could not see the path, and then all at once
the earth was radiant with clarity, and a silver sheen lay on
leaf and blade. How strange, how eerie was the interplay of
light and shade—like a nymph unveiling and veiling her
beauties ere you could feast your eyes on her nakedness. Again
the moon shone out, and Edgar saw two silhouettes—or,
rather, one only, so closely were the couple walking together
—making towards the forest. Why? Whither? The wind was
busy among the firs.

"I'll follow," thought the child. "They'll never hear my footsteps in such a din."

Thrice blessed wind thus to muffle his movements! He slid
from tree to tree, from shadow to shadow. Thrice cursed
wind thus to muffle their words so that he could not hear
what the enemy was talking about. If he once caught the
subject of their conversation, he felt convinced that the secret
would be his.

Unconcernedly, Frau Blumental and her cavalier went on their way, little suspecting the presence of a spy in their wake. They were entirely happy, and were lost to everything but the splendour of the night and their own growing interest in one another. How could they know that every step they took was dogged, and that eager eyes were watching them with hatred and curiosity?

Suddenly they stopped in the middle of the path. Edgar pressed his frail body against a tree. He gasped with anxiety. "Suppose they turn back, and Mother doesn't find me in my room? She'll guess I've been watching her, and then she'll be so wary that I shall never discover their secret." Happily at that moment the clouds scurried by, the moon shone, and the clearing was flooded with light. The boy saw that the baron was trying to entice the lady into a smaller and darker path which led up a little ravine. Edgar's mother seemed to be saying "No," but Sternfeldt urged her to consent. Why? What did he want of her? The books Edgar had read told of "murders under cover of darkness," of "abduction," of crimes innumerable. Could the baron be planning to kill her? Then here was the explanation, this was why Sternfeldt had wanted to be alone with Mother, this was the reason he had induced Mother to turn the key on her own son. Should he seek help? Should he cry, "Murder"? He could not utter the syllables, for his lips were parched with excitement. So intense was his emotion that he found it difficult to keep his footing. He swayed; and, in order to steady himself, seized hold of a branch. It snapped with a loud report.

The two swung round in alarm and stared into the gloom. Edgar stood motionless, hardly daring to breathe. The silence of death lay upon the forest, for neither wind nor creature stirred. Then the woman said:

"Let us turn back."

How scared she seemed. The baron, too, was frightened,

and fell in with her wishes. Linked in a close embrace they retraced their steps, slowly, engrossed in their own thoughts. Edgar, profiting by their absorption, ran on all fours through the undergrowth, and arrived breathless at the hotel. Turning the key, he entered his room, undressed, and got into bed. He lay quiet for a while, recovering. Then he got up and went to the window, determined to witness their return. They must have walked very, very slowly. At long last he saw their shadows. They looked ghostly in the moonlight. Was the baron really a murderer in disguise? And had he, Edgar, prevented the bloody deed by breaking a dried and rotted branch? Again the moon shone brightly. Edgar had never seen an expression of such rapture on his mother's face before. But the baron looked wooden and disappointed—probably because his wicked scheme had come to naught, thought the boy.

As they drew near to the hotel they wrenched themselves apart. Would they glance up? No! "They have quite forgotten me!" Then with a mixture of triumph and bitterness Edgar muttered: "But I haven't forgotten you. You may fancy I am asleep or that I simply don't exist at all. Just wait; I'll show you how mistaken you are. I'm not going to let you out of my sight until I have snatched your secret from you. I'll keep awake all right."

The two stepped into the doorway. Again their shadows were united to form but one dark patch. Then the moonlight invaded the courtyard, until it looked like a field of untrodden snow.

A MIDNIGHT TUSSLE

With a catch in his breath, Edgar withdrew from the window. He was terribly shaken. Never had he been so near to discovering the riddle. Excitement, adventure, murder, be-

trayal, these had been no more than tales a boy reads of in
books, dream events, unreal, unattainable. Now, of a sudden, he felt that this awful world of risk and enterprise had
roped him in, had made of him a participant. He was alarmed
and pleased at so unexpected an initiation.

"I wonder what kind of a man this is who has come into
our lives. . . . Can he really be a murderer? If not, why does
he want to lure my mother into dark and lonely places?"

Something terrible seemed impending, and yet the boy did
not know what steps to take in order to avert the evil. Of one
thing he was certain: Tomorrow he would write or wire to
his father. But might not that be too late? Who could tell
what would happen this very night? Mother had not come
up to her room; she must still be with that wretch. . . .

Between one door and the other of their rooms, which were
in suite, was a small lobby. Here Edgar ensconced himself,
determined not to miss his chance of hearing whatever happened in the corridor. At length he heard their steps. He
strained every nerve to catch what they were saying and doing.

How slow they were—just as though they were climbing
a mountain, not in the least as if they were making for their
rooms, tired, after a pleasant evening together. They were
constantly stopping and whispering. The boy trembled with
mental torment. He would have given almost anything to hear
what they were saying. Still, he knew they were coming his
way. But, oh, how slowly! Now he could hear the baron
pleading. Now his mother's voice saying: "No. Not tonight. No."

Edgar shivered. Every step that brought them nearer to
him caused him fresh agony. Then he heard the detested
voice pleading:

"Please, please. Don't say no. You've been so adorable the
whole evening. . . ."

And his mother, frightened, on the defensive, answering:

"I dare not. No, really, not tonight. I beg you, let me go."

Again Edgar wondered what the baron wanted her to do, and why his mother was so alarmed. Now they came to a standstill opposite the door behind which the child was lurking. He could hear them so clearly that they might have been in the same room with him.

"Come along, Mathilde, do! Please, please."

His mother sighed; her protests became weaker. Hullo! What was happening? Frau Blumental did not enter her room, she passed along the passage. What did this mean? Why were they no longer talking together? Was it possible that the wretch had gagged her and was now in the act of throttling her?

Maddened with alarm, the child opened the door—only a crack, but through this he could see what was going on. The baron had his arm round his mother's waist and was cajoling her into acquiescence. She seemed to be nothing loath. Arrived at Sternfeldt's door they stopped.

"Now he's going to commit the crime," thought the boy, his head filled with reminiscences of penny-dreadful stories.

Banging the door behind him, he stampeded down the passage and butted in upon the lovers. His mother drew abruptly aside, alarmed by the sudden onslaught. Then she drooped as if in a faint, and was caught in the baron's arms. At the same time, the baron became aware of two small fists pummelling his face, bashing his lips against his teeth, and nails scratching him like a cat's claws. The alarmed woman quickly took to her heels, while the man hit back at his assailant before grasping who it was.

Edgar was only too conscious of the fact that his puny strength could not hold out against the vigorous onslaught of a man in the prime of life. Nevertheless, he determined to do his best, and at least to show the intensity of his hatred. He banged away with all his might, his lips set firm, his teeth clenched. By now the baron had recognized the spy, and gave the lad a generous drubbing. He was furious at having his holiday ruined by this tiresome young monkey. Edgar suffered without uttering a sound. The struggle continued for several minutes in the dimly lighted passage until Sternfeldt, growing aware how ludicrous was this encounter between a man and a child, tried to seize Edgar by the nape and hold the boy at arm's length. Feeling that he would be overpowered by the man's superior strength and longer reach, the youngster turned savagely and clenched his teeth in Sternfeldt's right hand. A low growl issued from the baron's throat, he relaxed his grip, and before he could recover his presence of mind Edgar was back in his own room and had bolted the door.

No one had been aware of this midnight affray. All were asleep. Everything was as still and silent as the tomb. Otto wiped the blood from his hand with a handkerchief. He peered uneasily into the dark recesses of the corridor. Not a soul to be seen! And yet, up there, was there not a light, flickering in the draught, and a low, mocking laugh?

STORM

"Was it all a terrible dream?" Edgar asked himself when he awoke next morning. His head ached, and as his eyes travelled down his body he saw that he had gone to sleep in his clothes. He jumped up, and ran to the looking-glass. There he was confronted with a pale, drawn face, tousled hair, a red swelling upon a smudgy forehead. With an effort the child collected his thoughts, trying to remember what had happened. Yes, he had come to fisticuffs with his enemy, out there in the passage, sometime after midnight; had then rushed back to his room; had thought of decamping; had been overwhelmed by fatigue; had thrown himself on to his bed without undressing; and had fallen into a restless sleep, full of nightmares and the stench of freshly spilled blood.

In the garden below he could hear the sound of footsteps on the gravel; voices floated up to him; the sun was high in the heavens. It must be late. He consulted his watch, but found it had stopped. In his excitement he had forgotten to wind it up. Curiously enough this uncertainty as to the hour disquieted him more than anything else. He quickly undressed, washed, and dressed himself again. Then he went downstairs, feeling slightly guilty and very much disturbed.

He found his mother sitting in the dining-room over her breakfast. Alone, thank goodness. It was a relief not to have to look upon that hated countenance. . . . But Edgar was not quite sure of himself as he stepped up to the table and wished his mother "Good morning."

She gave no response, continuing to stare fixedly out of the window. Her face was very pale, deep shadows lay around her eyes, and her delicate nostrils quivered as they invariably did when she was greatly moved. Edgar bit his lips. Her silence puzzled him. Did she know who had attacked Otto von Sternfeldt in the passage? Had he seriously damaged the baron? Doubts assailed him and tortured him. Her sightless, staring eyes alarmed him even more profoundly; he was afraid to move lest they should suddenly be turned upon him; he drank his coffee and ate his roll with as little movement as possible so as not to attract her attention. He thought she must be exceedingly angry. A quarter of an hour went by, while he waited for something to happen. Not a word was spoken. Then, still behaving as though he were not present, his mother got up and went out. What was he to do? Remain sitting at the table, or follow her? In the end, he decided upon the latter course. She continued to ignore him, so that he felt more and more humiliated. He lagged behind, not knowing whither to go. In the end, he went up to the

suite he and his mother occupied—but found the outer door
locked against him.

Yesterday's hardihood had completely disappeared; he
had not a notion what to do. Perhaps he had acted badly
when he fell upon the baron tooth and nail. Could they be
preparing some terrible retribution or a fresh humiliation? He
was convinced they were concocting a plan, setting a trap
for unwary feet. There was a feeling about those two as
when a storm is brewing and flashes of lightning speed from
cloud to cloud. This burden of misgiving weighed heavily
upon his spirit throughout the morning, and it was a very
small and diminished Edgar who finally presented himself
at the luncheon table.

"Good day," he said, once more endeavouring to break the
silence which hung like a threatening cloud over his head.

She looked through him, and again made no answer. Edgar
now recognized how terribly angry she was, so angry, indeed, that she did not venture to speak. Never had he roused
her to such a pitch of exasperation. The boy's heart sank;
he was genuinely frightened. Hitherto when she had scolded
him it was, rather, an affair of the nerves than of the emotions, a summer storm that was quickly over and followed by
an indulgent laugh. Today he felt that he had stirred her
to the depths, had aroused something wild and untamed in
her nature, and he trembled in face of the forces he had un-
leashed. Hardly a morsel of food could he swallow; his throat
was dry, his lips were cracked. His mother seemed unaware
of his desperate plight. But when the horrible meal at last
came to an end and they rose from table, Frau Blumental
turned casually to her son and said:

"Come to my room, Edgar. I wish to have a few words with
you."

No threat in her voice, thank goodness! But, oh, how icy
and aloof was her demeanour. Her words fell over Edgar

like a cold douche and made him shiver. His defiance oozed
away. Like a whipped cur, the child followed his mother in
silence to her room.

She prolonged Edgar's martyrdom by sitting for a while
without uttering a word. Through the open window came the
joyous laughter of children at play; but Edgar's heart beat
to suffocation. Frau Blumental, too, was ill at ease, avoiding
her son's eyes even when she began to speak to him.

"I don't intend to tell you what I think of your conduct,
Edgar. The mere thought of it horrifies me. You will pay
for the consequences. But you are certainly not fit to mix with
grown-ups and sensible people. I have written to your father
and told him that your unruly behaviour needs stricter disci-
pline than I am able to provide. I have suggested he find you
a tutor, or that he send you to a boarding-school where you
will be taught your manners. That is all. I myself shall not
bother about you any more."

Edgar's head sank on his breast. He knew that this was only
a prologue, and that worse was in store. Frau Blumental
continued:

"You will have to apologize to Baron von Sternfeldt. . . ."

The boy trembled; but she was adamant, and refused him a
moment's pause for a protest.

"The baron left this morning and you will write him a letter to my dictation. . . ."

Again Edgar made as though to speak, and again his
mother went on precipitately:

"Not a word! Sit down. There is a sheet of paper and a
pen. . . ."

Edgar looked up at her. He read decision in her hard eyes.
Never had she looked like this. He seated himself at the
table, took up the pen, and bowed his head low over the
paper.

"Date it. Done? Leave a line. Good. Now write, 'Dear

Baron von Sternfeldt.' Comma. Leave another line. A little to
the right, begin, 'I am sorry to learn that you have left Semmering,' two m's in Semmering. Got that? Very well. Continue the sentence, after a comma, 'and that I cannot say
good-bye to you personally but only by letter'; hurry up, no
need to write as if you were doing a copy. Full stop. 'Also,
I want to ask your pardon for my unseemly conduct last
night. Mother told you that I am convalescent after a severe
illness and am easily overwrought. That makes me do things
for which I am very sorry afterwards. . . .' "

The bowed back straightened; Edgar turned round, defiance blazing up anew.

"That's not true; I won't write . . ."

"Edgar," cried his mother threateningly.

"It's not true. I've done nothing to be sorry for. I've done
nothing naughty for which I need beg anyone's pardon. All I
did was to run to your side when you called for help."

Her lips blanched; her nostrils quivered.

"I called for help? You're crazy."

Edgar sprang fiercely to his feet.

"Yes, you did, out there in the passage, last night, when he
caught hold of you. 'Let go of me. Leave me,' you said so
loud that I could hear the words quite plainly from my room."

"You are lying, my poor child. The baron and I were not
in the passage. He merely saw me to the landing."

Such a brazen falsehood took the boy's breath away. He was
stunned, looking at her with scared eyes, and stammering:

"You . . . were . . . not in . . . the passage? And he . . .
did not . . . take . . . hold . . . of you? Forcibly . . . against
your will . . . ?"

She laughed; a cold, dry laugh.

"Must have been dreaming, my boy."

This was too much for Edgar. He knew that grown-ups
lied, that they used funny words to express what was not

true, told fibs, had recourse to strange ambiguities. But anything as bold-faced as this he was utterly unprepared for.

"And is this huge bump on my forehead also a dream?"

"How am I to know what other young jackanapes you've
been fighting with? Come now, I don't want any back-talk
from you. Sit down and write."

She had gone very pale, and was making a great effort to
remain calm.

But Edgar crumpled up; a last faint ember of credulity
and trust in his elders was quenched. How could anyone
trample on truth so ruthlessly? He would not believe that a
monstrous lie such as this could go unscathed. He rallied
his forces, became cool and collected and bitter. An ironical,
bantering, and sarcastic tone entered his voice.

"So I've been dreaming, have I? All that happened in the
passage, this bump on my forehead—just a dream! And of
course you and he did not go for a walk in the moonlight.
Neither did he try to get you down a small, dark path in the
forest. Oh, no, nothing of that is true, is it? But did you
really fancy I was going to allow myself to be locked into
my room like a naughty child? Not such an ass. I know
what I know."

He looked her squarely and pertly in the face, and this
saucy expression cowed her for a moment. It was dreadful
to see hatred gleaming from the eyes of her only child. Then
her anger broke loose.

"Enough! Write what I tell you, immediately—otherwise . . ."

"Otherwise what?" he demanded peremptorily.

"Otherwise I'll beat you as if you were in very fact a little
child."

Edgar stepped close up to his mother a jeering and challenging laugh issuing from his mouth.

Her hand was already raised and came down in a resounding smack upon his head. He uttered a yell of rage and surprise. Then, like a drowning man whose ears are buzzing, whose hands vainly strive to find some flotsam whereon to cling, he struck out blindly. Something soft and yielding encountered his fists. Again he struck, this time upwards towards a blanched face. A cry . . .

The scream of pain brought him to his senses. What had he done? Something terrible, something unforgivable. He had struck his mother. Frightened, ashamed, disgusted, he wished the floor would open and swallow him up. He must get away from those horrified eyes. Away . . . away. Edgar stumbled towards the door, down the stairs, through the hall, into the forest. Oh, to get away, far away! He rushed along as if pursued by a pack of hounds giving tongue.

REVELATION

At length Edgar halted. His limbs, his body trembled so violently that he had to support himself against a tree. His breath came quickly and spasmodically. What was he to do? Where could he go? Impossible to remain here, almost within sight of the house which had been his temporary home. He was forsaken, helpless. The world was a harsh and unfeeling place. Even the trees which but yesterday afforded shelter from the sun and had clustered round him in brotherly affection, now stood aloof and looked down grimly. The unknown lay ahead of him. His loneliness amid the vastness of nature filled him with dread. Such solitude could not be borne, he must go somewhere and find a companion. He dared not seek out his father in Vienna, for Herr Blumental was a martinet and would insist upon Edgar's prompt return to Semmering. This thought was intolerable. Better by far to be alone and to journey forth into the unexplored. He felt as if never again could he look his mother in the face without remembering that he had struck her with his fist.

But what about Grandma? She had always made much of him—such a kind old lady. Invariably she had been on his side when he had got into trouble at home. He could hide in her house in Baden until his parents' anger had cooled off. From there he would write a long letter, begging Dad and Mummy to forgive him. All the pride had seeped out of him. He felt very small and helpless in the midst of this huge and antagonistic universe, and wanted nothing better than to become once again the child he had been a few days ago.

How did one get to Baden, he wondered. Pulling out a shabby purse which was his inseparable companion, he extracted a gold piece that had been given him for his birthday. How he had polished it every day with his grubby handkerchief, until it shone and shone again! He had never been able to make up his mind to spend it. Like a little sun it was. Lovely. Bright. Beautiful. Would it suffice to pay for his railway fare? Often and often he had travelled by train! Yet never had it entered his head to inquire how much a journey cost. For the first time in his short life he was up against reality. Things he had taken for granted apparently possessed a value of their own and could not be had for the asking. They needed to be paid for in hard cash. A short hour ago he thought himself so wonderfully clever, knowing all there was to know. But there were hundreds of problems and secrets that were a sealed book to him. He realized his shortcomings now. More and more did the sense of humiliation master him as he made his way to the station. Often and often he had dreamed of setting forth into the world to win his laurels, to become an emperor, a king, a famous soldier, a poet. Now that he had finally realized part of this dream, he felt exceeding small, and, as he fixed his eyes on the station building, his mind was wholly preoccupied with the question: "Shall I have enough to pay for my ticket?" The shining rails ran away into the infinite; not a soul could be seen on the platform or in the waiting-room. Edgar tiptoed up to the ticket office and asked softly and modestly how much it would cost to go to Baden. A pair of surprised eyes looked through the little hole, and smiled not unkindly at the timid youngster.

"Half fare, or a whole?"

"Whole," stammered Edgar, every atom of conceit punched out of him.

"Six crowns."

"Please give me a ticket."

He shoved the shining treasure across the diminutive counter, picked up ticket and change. The piece of cardboard spelled freedom. He thrust the silver coins into his pocket, and listened well satisfied to the muffled clinking as they rattled together.

Only twenty minutes till the train was due. Edgar crept into a doorway, so that no one should catch sight of him. A few passengers trailed in and wandered aimlessly about the platform. They failed to notice the runaway, though he himself felt as if all eyes were upon him. A whistle in the distance came as an immense relief to his suspense. Here was the train destined to convey him right away into the world. It was not until he had already stepped into a first-class carriage that he noticed he had been given a third-class ticket. So there were differences between travellers, he thought. Another initiation! His neighbours, when he had rectified his mistake, were a couple of Italian workmen, with calloused hands and rough voices. They had slung their tools on to the rack, and were sitting relaxed and listless. "They must have been working very hard," mused the child, as one of them nodded off to sleep. "I suppose they earned money for what they did. How much, I wonder?" Money, then, was a thing one had to earn, that one was not automatically provided with. So far Edgar had taken his comfortable circumstances for granted, and had never given a thought to those abysses of misery which beset him on either hand. There were professions and trades to be followed, incomes to be earned—so many secrets he had never even noticed. He had learned much during his hour of solitude; and, as he cogitated these problems yet further and gazed at the fleeing landscape through the window, greater and greater illumination came to him. Gradually, amid his gloomy anxiety, something seemed to grow up and to blossom as he became conscious of the amazing kaleidoscope presented to him by life. He had run away because he was a coward and had been scared: true, but through his poltroonery he had come to taste the sweets of independence, he had come into contact with a reality he had hitherto completely ignored. Was he himself not just as great an enigma to his father and mother as the world had been to him? Quite possible. He saw with a new vision, as if manifold veils had been torn away from his eyes, as if the inside of things was being revealed to him, as if the secret of secrets was being disclosed. Houses flew past as though borne on the wings of the wind. Who were the people dwelling inside all these cottages and farmsteads, Edgar wondered. Were they rich or poor, happy or unhappy; were they full of uneasy longing as he was; did they want to know everything; were the children, like himself so far, merely playing with life? At the level crossings, the switchmen with their little flags were no longer the puppets he had always thought them, toy men, objects set up at those particular spots by chance. Edgar understood now that they had a function to perform, that they were fulfilling their destiny, had entered upon the struggle for life. The train gained in speed as it wound its way down the valley, leaving the high mountains behind. The contours were softened with the tender green of springtime. Only once did the fugitive look back at the high country he had left. The hills were blue, misty, distant, unattainable. As they receded more and more, and were swallowed up in the late afternoon fogs, it seemed to him that he had left childhood behind for ever in those remote and austere regions.

BEWILDERING DARKNESS

When at length he stood alone on the platform at Baden, watched the signal lights, and realized that night was upon him, his more hopeful and cheery mood petered out, and he felt an immense desolation descending upon him. While daylight lasted he had been surrounded by human beings; there were all manner of interesting things a small boy could do, sit on a bench and watch the passers-by, wander along streets looking into shop windows. But what was going to happen when everyone withdrew behind closed doors, when they retired to bed, went to sleep, while he, feeling guilty of wrongdoing, slunk about the empty streets, unwontedly alone and forsaken? He must seek shelter at once, not a minute to waste; of that he was profoundly convinced.

Without casting a look to right or to left he made a beeline towards his grandmother's villa. It lay back from the road in a garden, sheltered by shrubberies and covered with ivy and other creepers. It peeped out white within its framework of green, a friendly, old-fashioned abode. Edgar looked over the hedge, feeling almost like a stranger. Nothing stirred, no lights shone from the windows; Grannie and her guests were probably sitting over their coffee on the lawn to the rear.

He already had his hand on the bell-pull, when an alarming thought entered his mind. So far his resolve to ask his dear Grannie for shelter had seemed quite natural to him.

But suddenly he had a doubt. What excuse could he furnish
for his unexpected arrival? How was he to answer her inevitable questions? He saw in fancy the old lady's look of surprise when he told her that he had run away from his mother.
Besides, he would have to confess having hit his mother, and
the enormity of this crime weighed heavily upon him. A door
banged. He started violently, and panic seized him. Suppose
someone came out and caught him loitering! He scampered
off, hardly knowing where his legs were taking him.

Arrived at the town-park gates, he came to a stop. Here it
was very dark, and no one was to be seen. Perhaps he could
find a vacant seat, sit down quietly, and think over the situation undisturbed. He slunk along a deserted alley-way. The
trees looked ghostly in the dim light of the lamps, but farther
on, up a little hill which he climbed, everything lay in darkness, the mist-laden gloom of a spring night. A solitary couple
or two sat absorbed. He passed quickly by, for he wanted to
be alone. But no solitude was to be found. Whispers could be
heard coming from the shadowy depths of trees and bushes,
borne upon the wind, mingling with the rustle of leaves and
grass-blades; stealthy footsteps sounded along the paths, a
sigh, a low laugh, mysterious, voluptuous. Did these murmurs
come from human beings or from the beasts? Nature seemed
wrapped in sleep, and yet all things were astir. A ferment
of living matter was at work, disquieting in the extreme to a
highly strung child. Could it all be part of the springtime?

Never had he felt smaller and more impotent, as he huddled upon a bench and tried to think out what he should do,
and how explain his flight. But he found it impossible to con-
centrate his thoughts. In spite of his best endeavours, his ears
were always pricked to catch the sound of those mysterious
voices issuing from the gloom. The darkness was terrible
and perplexing; yet how enigmatically beautiful! This rustling and soughing, this whirring and allurement, did it ema-

nate from animals or from men? Or was it merely the breeze
among the boughs? Edgar listened. Yes, it was the wind shaking the leaves. . . . No, it came from that couple over there,
held in a tight embrace. Man and woman. They had strolled
hither from the glare of the town, in order to be alone in the
darkness. What were they up to? If he could only find an
answer to that question he would find peace, and his tortured
mind would be at rest. Two people, but so closely pressed
together as to form but a single shadow—just as it had been
with his mother and the baron. . . . So the fateful secret
clung to this place too? Footsteps drew nearer; a soft gurgle
of laughter could be heard. Suppose this approaching couple
should catch sight of him? He cowered farther back into the
darkness. But they did not see him. They passed quietly by,
wrapped in one another's embrace. Edgar was beginning to
breathe freely once more, when they stopped, pressing their
faces together, and a sigh of content escaped from the woman's
mouth. The man spoke a few rapid words. Edgar felt horribly frightened, and at the same time he thrilled with an
unknown pleasure. A minute later the gravel crunched beneath their feet; the pair were swallowed up in the shadows.

Edgar's pulses beat furiously, and a sense of solitude gripped
him. He longed to hear the sound of a friendly voice; to feel
an affectionate hug; to see a lighted and familiar room, people
he knew and loved. The uncanny darkness of the night had
sunk into his very marrow. He would burst if he did not
shake himself free.

Home! Home! A warm and lighted room! Persons he
knew! All would be well, then. Nothing bad could happen
if he were once with his own people. They might scold him
or even beat him, he did not care so long as he had no more
to dwell in darkness and solitude.

Hardly knowing what he did he ran on and on, till again
he found himself in front of Grandma's house, with his hand

ready to pull the bell. Through the curtain of greenery, he
saw that the windows were alight; in imagination he pictured
the familiar rooms, and their occupants. This proximity was
a pleasure; and if he still hesitated to ring, it was merely to
revel in his happiness, in the knowledge that he was near to
those he loved and who loved him.

A shrill voice behind him brought him back to earth.

"Master Edgar, why, here you are at last!"

It was his Grannie's housemaid who had come out for an
airing. She ran up to the boy and gave him a hearty embrace. The doors, magically, swung open, the dogs dashed
down the drive to bark a welcome, people were coming from
the house with candles and lanterns, voices of mingled alarm
and delight sounded in his ears, a friendly tumult of noises,
shapes of persons he knew. . . . His grandmother, who
hugged him tight, and, behind her—could he be dreaming?—
his mother. Abashed, trembling, on the verge of tears, the
boy stood stock-still, not knowing which way to turn or what
to do. Was he frightened? Or was he happy?

THE LAST DREAM

Yes, it was his mother. Through inquiries made at Semmering station, she had traced the direction of his flight. She had
wired to her husband in Vienna, to Grannie in Baden. He
was expected. Why had he not arrived? Frau Blumental, taking the express, had outstripped him. They led him in subdued triumph to the sitting-room. True, he was scolded;
but the scoldings did not wound him, for in the eyes of those
that scolded he saw nothing but joy and love. Even their
assumed anger could not last; it fizzled out almost before the
reprimand had been made. Now Grannie was hugging him
again, and crying over him. No one reproached him. Wonderful! He felt as though he were a prisoner of love. The

maid pulled off his thin coat and muffled him in a warm shawl; asked him if he were not hungry, or if there was anything she could bring him. He had hated being looked upon as a child; but now he revelled in the bliss of being cared for. The arrogance and presumption of the last few days vanished.

The telephone buzzed in the neighbouring room. His mother answered the call. "Yes . . . Edgar's come . . . it's all right . . ." Why was she not furious with him, he wondered. Her dear eyes caressed him with a strange expression. His immediate impulse was to disregard all the coddling his Grannie and his Aunt Bertha were lavishing upon him and to throw himself into Mummy's arms, to tell her how sorry he was, to promise anything she liked. He got up. But Grannie asked in alarm:

"Where are you going, pet?"

Anxious, were they, if he so much as moved? They fancied he was running away again. So he had given them all a jolly good fright? How could he ever make them understand that no one regretted this flight so much as he?

They served him an impromptu supper. Grannie sat by him, and never took her eyes off him. She and Auntie and the maid formed a loving circle round him. The warmth of their affection solaced him marvellously. But why was his mother not present? He felt uneasy at her absence. If she could only guess how utterly crushed he was . . .

A carriage drew up outside. Grannie left the room. Amid a medley of voices, he recognized his father's. Auntie and the maid had also gone out into the hall. Edgar was again alone, and again he was frightened by solitude. His father had always treated the boy with the utmost severity, and had made himself feared. Now Edgar listened to his father's voice on the other side of the door. He appeared to be excited, and spoke in loud and angry tones. Grannie and Mummy seemed to be using their best endeavours to appease him. Resolute footsteps approached. The door opened.

Herr Blumental was a very tall man, so that Edgar felt as tiny as a doll when he was asked, in a harsh voice:

"What possessed you to run away and give your mother such a fright, you young scoundrel?"

The man was genuinely angry; but Mummy came in directly behind her husband. Her face was in shadow so that the boy could not take his cue from her and, therefore, did not answer.

"Well? Lost your tongue? What was wrong? Own up, don't be afraid. There must be some reason for running away. Anybody hurt your feelings?"

Edgar hesitated to reply. Anger and pique revived in him. Should he justify himself? He raised his eyes and looked at his mother. She was still in her husband's huge shadow, but the boy saw her make an unwonted gesture. She slowly raised a finger to her lips, and her eyes implored silence.

The child's heart warmed. He understood that she was begging him to keep her secret. How proud and happy he felt that she should ask him this service. Pulling himself together, he said:

"No, Dad! I was having a lovely time. Mummy was ever so good to me. But suddenly I felt I had to do something thoroughly naughty. So I ran away."

Herr Blumental looked at his son dubiously. He had expected anything but this, and was disarmed by so abject a confession.

"Well," he answered, "if you're sorry, there's no more to be said. Another time I trust you will reflect before behaving so rashly." He gazed kindly down at the boy and his voice took on a softer tone. "You're looking a bit pale, but you've grown a lot since you left home. Don't be up to any more childish pranks. You are no longer a kid, and must try in future to be reasonable. . . ."

Edgar gazed fixedly at his mother. There was a gleam in her eyes he had never seen before, they were moist and bright, while round her mouth played an elfin smile which seemed full of gratitude.

He was now sent off to bed, but he felt no resentment, neither did he mind being left alone once more. His head buzzed with thoughts. All the suffering of the last few days was swallowed up in the freshness and delight of this first real experience, and he looked forward undauntedly to further encounters with reality. The trees without soughed and swayed in the wind, but he was not saddened by the noise. Life was rich and manifold; he had seen it naked before him, bereft of lies and subterfuges, full of a perilous beauty. Hatred for persons or things seemed to him now a childish stupidity and misapprehension. Even the baron, his enemy, shared in the boy's exuberant gratitude, because it had been through this false friend that the door into a wonderland of the emotions had been opened.

He lay in the dark, contented, proud, and happy. Sleep had almost enfolded him, when he became aware of someone moving softly in the room and of a hand gently stroking his hair. Tears dropped on to his cheek . . . and, without a word, his mother kissed him fondly. Not until many years later did Edgar understand the full meaning of these tears and kisses. They were a vow that henceforward Mummy would devote all her energies, all her love to him; that there would be no more adventures in her life; that she had said farewell to the pleasures of the flesh. She was grateful to her child for saving her from a futile and unworthy liaison; and, in a bitter-sweet compunction, she pledged herself to her boy's service. Though Edgar could not, child that he still was, grasp the significance of all this at the time, he nevertheless felt that it was glorious to be loved so much, and he surmised that in some incomprehensible manner such love was inextricably interwoven with the major secret of life.

After she had withdrawn and closed the door behind her, Edgar felt her presence and the warm glow of her lips upon his cheek. As he gradually dropped off to sleep, he drowsily wished he might often feel the pressure of soft lips against his own. A final and confused vision of the last eventful days swept before him; fate turned the pages of the Book of Youth; the child fell asleep, and the profound dream of life began to unfold itself.

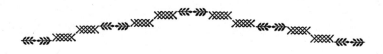

Moonbeam Alley

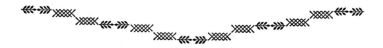

Stormy weather had delayed the ship, so that the evening was far advanced before she came to port on the French coast. Having missed the train which was to have carried me farther on my journey, I had a whole twenty-four hours on my hands. How could I best while away the time, marooned as I was in this unknown coast-town? There did not seem to be much doing. Melancholy strains of dance music issued from a dubious-looking haunt—not particularly attractive, I thought. The alternative would be to spend the interlude in desultory converse with my fellow-passengers. In the dining-room of the third-rate hotel where we put up, the air was thick with the smell of burned fat and tobacco smoke. Besides, it was an ill-kept and dirty place, its filthiness rendered all the more intolerable since for many days now I had enjoyed the pure ocean breezes and felt the salt, sweet taste of sea-spume upon my lips. I decided to go for a stroll along the broad main street leading to a square where the local band was giving a concert. It was pleasant to allow oneself to be carried gently along by the stream of idlers who, having done their work for the day, were taking the air after a wash and brush-up followed by a cozy meal at a provincial fireside. After a while, however, the jostling of the crowd and its empty laughter vexed me sorely; I found it exasperating to be gaped at because I happened to be a stranger in their midst; the physical proximity of so many unknown human beings was nauseating in the extreme.

The voyage had been far from calm, and the movement of swelling waters was still in my veins. Under foot, the earth seemed to be heaving and rolling, the whole street and the skies swayed like a see-saw. I felt giddy and, in order to escape, I ducked my head and plunged down a side street without taking the trouble to decipher its name. This led me into an even narrower thoroughfare, where the din of music and mob was muffled almost to extinction. One street opened out of another like the anastomoses of arteries and veins. They were less well lighted the farther I withdrew from the central square, which was brightly illuminated with arc-lamps. Overhead the stars could be distinguished, now that my eyes were no longer dazzled by the glare. How dark the intervening spaces of heaven appeared as I gazed upward!

This must be "sailor-town," quite near the harbour, for my nostrils were tickled with the stench of rotting fish and seaweed and tar, with the indescribable odour issuing from badly ventilated houses wherein the air remains stagnant until it is swept away by a health-bringing gale. Such twilight as hung over these alley-ways was healing to my mind. It was delightful to be alone. I slackened my pace, studied the narrow streets, each of which was different from the others, being here coquettish or amorous, there wrapped in inviolable peace. All, however, were dark, and filled with the soft murmur of voices and music which arose from nowhere in particular, but

from unseen springs deep within the houses. Doors and windows were tightly shut, and the only lights were red or yellow lanterns hanging from a porch at rare intervals.

I have a special predilection for such quarters in unknown
towns, these foul market-places of the passions, filled with
temptations for men who sail the seas and who turn in here
for a night of pleasure, hoping to realize their dreams in one
short hour on land. These places are obliged to tuck themselves away out of sight in the less "respectable" areas of the
town, because they tell a plain tale which the smug and well-
built houses of the elect hide behind a hundred veils. Tiny
rooms are crowded with dancing couples; glaring placards
lure into the picture-houses, square-faced lanterns twinkle in
doorways and beckon unambiguously to the passer-by.
Drunken voices clamour from behind the red-curtained windows of drinking booths. Sailors grin at one another when
they meet, their eyes are greedy with expectation, for here
they may find women and gambling, drink and display, adventure that is sordid or worth the risk. But these allurements
are discreetly housed behind drawn blinds. You have to go inside to find them out, and the mystery only serves to enhance
the lure. Similar streets and alleys exist in Hamburg and
Colombo and Havana and Liverpool, just as in these cities
the broad avenues and boulevards where the wealthy for-
gather are likewise to be found, for the upper stratum of life
and the lower bear a close resemblance everywhere in the
matter of form. These disorderly streets are strange vestiges
of an unregulated world of the senses, where impulses continue to discharge themselves brutally and without rein; they
are a gloomy forest of the passions, a covert full of manifestations of our instinctive and animal existence; they stimulate
by what they diclose, and allure by the suggestion of what
they hide. They haunt our dreams.

A sensation of being trapped in this maze overwhelmed

me. I had chanced to follow a couple of cuirassiers who, with
swords clanking along the uneven pavement, were taking a
stroll. Some women on the booze in a bar shouted coarse
jokes as the pair sauntered by; shrieks of laughter, a finger
knocking on the window, an oath from within—and then the
men went on. Soon the ribald mirth grew so faint that I could
barely catch the sound. Silence closed round me, a few windows were dimly lighted, the watery moon shone through the
mist. I breathed my fill of the stillness, which was almost uncanny, seeing that behind it lurked a universe of mystery, sensuousness, and peril. The silence was a lie, for it covered the
accumulated filth of a whole world. I stood listening, and peering into the void. All sense of the town, the street, its name,
and even my own name vanished; I was cut adrift, my body
in some miraculous way had been taken possession of by a
stranger, I had no activity in view, no reason for being where
I was, no relationship to my surroundings—and yet I was
acutely conscious of the seething life that beset me on all
sides; it flowed through my veins as if it were my own blood.
Nothing that was happening was doing so on my account,
though everything was germane to myself. An inexpressibly
delightful feeling that I was not a participator was accompanied by the conviction that I was in for an experience which
would bore down into the deepest springs of my being—a feeling which, whenever it comes to me, suffuses me with a pleasure that emanates from communion with the unconscious.

As I stood thus expectant, listening into the void, a voice
came to me from a distance, muffled by intervening walls,
but unmistakably singing in German. A simple melody, indeed; the "Schöner, grüner Jungfernkranz" from Weber's
Freischütz. A woman's voice, badly trained, but German,
yes indeed, German. Strange to hear one's own tongue in so
out-of-the-way a corner; and friendly, homely, at the same
time. Poorly as the air was sung, it held a greeting from

the land of my birth. Who can speak German here, who can
be moved to hum this innocent refrain? Straining my ears
against house after house, I reached one where there was a
glimmer in one of the windows, and the shadow of a hand
silhouetted against the blind. All doors were shut, and yet
invitation to enter was to be deciphered on every brick and
lintel. Nearer and nearer I approached the sound. This was
the house! I hesitated a moment, and then pushed my shoulder against the door, having drawn aside a curtain which
shielded the interior from draughts. On the threshold I encountered a man whose face was reddened by the hanging
lamp, and was livid with fury. He scowled at me, murmured
an apology, and thrust past me into the alley. "Queer customer," thought I, gazing after him. Meanwhile the voice
continued singing; clearer than before, it seemed to me. I
boldly entered.

The song was cut off sharp, as with a knife. A terrible
silence compassed me about, giving me the impression that
I had destroyed something. Gradually my eyes grew accustomed to the dim lighting, and I found that the room was
scantily furnished with a little bar at one end, a table, a couple
of chairs—obviously a mere waiting-room for the true business of the establishment which went on in the background.
Nor was it difficult to guess what the real business was, for
along a passage there were many doors, some of them ajar,
leading into bedrooms in which beneath deeply shaded lamps
double beds were to be discerned. A girl was seated on a
bench leaning her elbows on the table; she was heavily made
up, and appeared extremely tired. Behind the bar was a
blowzy woman, slatternly and fat, with a second girl, a rather
pretty lass, at her side. My good-evening fell flat, and was not
echoed back to me for a considerable time. It was eerie to
have stepped into this silence of the desert, and I wished to
get clear away. Yet, since there did not seem to be adequate

reason for absconding, I took a place at the table and resigned myself to the inevitable.

Suddenly remembering her business in life, the girl got up and asked me what I wished to drink, and I recognized at once by her guttural pronunciation of the French words that she hailed from Germany. I ordered beer, which she fetched and brought to me, shuffling her feet in slovenly fashion, thus betraying even greater indifference than did her lack-lustre eyes. Following the custom of such haunts, she placed another glass next mine and sat down before it. She raised her glass with a nod of greeting in my direction, but she gazed through and beyond me. I had a good look at her. A beautiful face still, with regular features; but it had grown like a mask, since the inner fires were quenched. There was a touch of coarseness about it, the skin and muscles were lax, the lids heavy, the hair unkempt, and two furrows had already formed on either side of the mouth. Her dress was disorderly, her voice husky from too much smoking and beer-drinking. Here undubitably was a fellow-mortal who was weary unto death, and who only continued living out of long-established habit. Embarrassed and horrified, I asked her a question. She answered without looking at me and scarcely moving her lips. I guessed that my coming was unwelcome. The elder woman behind the bar yawned prodigiously, the younger girl slouched in a corner, as if waiting for me to call her. If I could have got away, I should have done so precipitately. But my limbs were like lead and I sat on, inert, chained by disgust and curiosity, for, to speak frankly, this indifference stirred me strangely.

The girl next me suddenly burst into a fit of shrill laughter. Simultaneously, the flame of the lamp flickered in a draught of cold air coming through the open doorway.

"So you've come back," said the girl in German. "Creeping

round the house again, you mean skunk. Oh, come along in—
I shan't do you any harm."

I turned first to the speaker whose mouth seemed to be
spewing forth fire, and then to the door. Slinking in was the
individual who had scuttled away on my entry. He was a
cringing creature, holding his hat in his hand like a beggar,
trembling under the douche of words that had greeted him,
writhing beneath the torrential flow of mirthless laughter, and
rendered even more uneasy by the way in which, from behind
the bar, the hostess was whispering to the girl.

"Go and sit down beside Françoise," the young woman
said hectoringly. "Can't you see I've got a gentleman customer?"

She spoke to him exclusively in the German tongue, while
the hostess and the younger girl split their sides with laughter though they could not understand a word she said. The
man was evidently a habitué.

"Give him a bottle of champagne, Françoise, the most ex-
pensive brand," she yelled mockingly. "And if it's too dear for
you, my man, you've only got to stay outside and not come
bothering us. You'd like to have me for nothing, I know,
and anything else you could get without paying you'd grab.
Ugh, you filthy beast."

The tall figure crumpled under the lash of this tongue.
Like a whipped cur, he sidled up to the counter and with a
trembling hand he poured the wine into a glass. He evidently wanted to look at the slattern who was abusing him,
and yet he was unable to lift his gaze from the floor. The
lamplight caught his face, and I saw before me an emaciated
visage, with damp locks of hair sticking in wisps on the brow.
His limbs were slack, as if broken at the joints. He was a
pitiable object, devoid of strength and yet not wholly lacking
in a kind of vicious courage. Everything about him was

askew; and the eyes he raised for a flash did not look straight, but were shifty and full of a wicked light.

"Don't bother about him," said the girl to me in her ponderous French and seizing me roughly by the arm as though she wanted me to turn away from my contemplation. "It's an old story between him and me. Doesn't date from yesterday!" She bared her teeth like a vixen ready to bite, and snarled: "You just listen to what I tell you, old fox. I'd rather fling myself into the sea than go with you. Got it?"

Again the sally was applauded by shouts of laughter from behind the bar. The pleasantry seemed to be a joy which was daily renewed. Then a horrible thing happened. The younger wench put her arms round the man in simulated affection and caressed him tenderly. He winced under her touch, and glanced at me, anxious and cringing. At the same moment the woman next me threw off her inertia as if she had just awakened from profound sleep, and her countenance was so contorted with malevolence, her hands trembled so violently, that I could bear the scene no longer. Throwing some coins upon the table, I rose to go. But she detained me, saying:

"If he's bothering you, I'll chuck him out, the swine. He's jolly well got to do what he's told. Come, let's drink another glass together."

She pressed up against me with assumed ardour, and I knew at once that she was playing a game in order to torment the man, for she kept on glancing in his direction out of the corner of her eyes. Disgust filled me when I saw how, with every endearment she lavished upon me, the poor wretch shrank together as if branded with a red-hot iron. I could not take my eyes off him, and I shivered when it became evident what a storm of rage, jealousy, and desire was brewing within him. Yet every time the girl looked towards him, he ducked his head in fear. She sidled closer, and I could feel her body quivering with pleasure as she pursued her wicked game. The scent of cheap powder and unwashed skin was sickening, and in order to keep her at a distance I took a cigar out of my case. Before I had time to light it, the girl was screaming.

"Here, you, bring a light, and be quick about it."

It was horrible to make myself a party to her machinations by allowing the man to serve me, and I made what haste I could to find a match for myself. But her orders had already whipped the poor devil into activity, and he shuffled up to the table with the necessary kindling material. Our eyes crossed, and in his I read abysmal shame mingled with pusillanimous bitterness. This look touched a brotherly chord in me and made me vibrate in sympathy with his humiliation. I said in German:

"Thank you, Sir; but you should not have bothered."

I offered him my hand. He hesitated for a moment, then my fingers were squeezed between his bony fists. Gratitude shone from his eyes during the second he fixed me, but soon he lowered his puffy lids. Defiance made me want to invite him to sit with us, and I had probably made a gesture of invitation for, ere the words dropped from my lips, the woman had said harshly:

"Back to your place, at once, and don't come bothering round here again."

I was nauseated by her strident voice and her whole demeanour. Why should I worry my head about this repulsive harlot, this weak-minded wench, this sewer of beer and cheap scent and tobacco-smoke? I longed for a breath of fresh air. I pushed the money towards her, stood up, and, when she tried to detain me with her endearments, I moved resolutely towards the exit. I could not participate in the humiliation of a fellow-creature, and I made it clear to the girl that her charms had no attraction for me. An angry flush spread over

her face and neck, fierce words trembled on her lips; but she
did not speak. She merely turned to the man and looked
at him so meaningly that with the utmost speed he sought to
do her unspoken bidding. His fingers shot down into his
pocket, and he drew forth a purse. He was evidently frightened at being left alone with her, and in his excitement
fumbled with the opening. I guessed that he was not accustomed to spending money freely, he had none of the generous
way of a sailor who flings his coins carelessly about. This man
was used to counting his money carefully, and to testing the
pieces between his fingers before paying them away—as he
now paid for his champagne.

"Look how he's trembling because he has to part with some
of his beloved pence," she cried tauntingly, stepping nearer to
him. "Too slow, I tell you. Just wait till I . . ."

He shrank back in fear. When she saw how frightened he
was, she shrugged her shoulders and said jeeringly, and with
an indescribable expression of disgust on her face:

"I'm not going to take anything away from you. I spit on
your money. It is all counted beforehand, I know; never a
farthing too much must be allowed to leave your purse. But,"
and she tapped him on the chest, "what about the bit of paper
you've so carefully stitched into your waistcoat lining?"

His hand went to his side as if he were seized with a spasm
of the heart. Having felt the place, his face, which had gone
ashen pale, resumed its normal hue and his hand dropped
away again.

"Miser," she screamed.

At this the martyr turned, flung the purse and its contents
into the younger girl's lap, and rushed out as if the place were
on fire. At first the girl gave a shriek of alarm, then, realizing
what the man had done, she broke into peal upon peal of
piercing laughter.

The woman stood for a moment rigid, her eyes sparkling

with wrath. Then her lids closed, and her body went limp.
She looked old and tired. A forlorn and drooping figure
swayed before me.

"He'll be weeping over his lost money, out there. May
even go to the police-station and tell them we've stolen it. Tomorrow he'll be here again. But he won't get me, no, that
he won't. I'll give myself to anyone who offers, but never to
him."

She stepped up to the bar and gulped down a glass of
neat brandy. The wickedness still glinted in her eyes but it
was misty now as if shining from behind a veil of tears. My
gorge rose as I looked at her, so that I could find no compassion in my heart.

"Good evening," I said as I took my leave.

"Bon soir," answered the hostess, without a glance in my
direction.

Shrill and mocking laughter followed me into the street.

As I stepped forth into the alley, it seemed to me darker
than ever, closed in by the starless sky and the night; but soon
the pale moon shone down again, bringing me infinite alle-
viation. I took a deep breath, and the horror left me. Now I
could once more relish the amazing tangle of human destinies; and a feeling of beatitude, akin to tears, filled me at
the thought that behind every window fate was waiting, that
at the opening of every door an experience was ready for the
taking, that the multitudinous happenings of this world are
ever present for those who choose to observe them, that even
the foulest hovel is bursting with newly generated life like
dung filled with the larvæ that will become shining beetles.
The unsavoury encounter was no longer repulsive to me. On
the contrary, the suspense it had produced in my mind now
relaxed into an agreeable sensation of lassitude, and my sole
desire was to convert my adventure into beautiful dreams. I

cast a searching eye up and down the narrow street, wondering which direction would lead back to the hotel. A shadow fell across my path.

"Beg pardon, Sir," said a familiar whining voice in my native tongue, "but I'm afraid you will have some difficulty in finding your way out of the maze. May I act as guide, Sir? Your hotel, Sir?"

I gave him the name.

"Yes, Sir, I know it, Sir. Will you allow me to accompany you, Sir?" he asked apologetically.

A shudder crept over me. It was horrible to have this slouching, ghostlike creature walking by my side, noiselessly, as if on stockinged feet. My perception of the gloom in the alleyways of the sailors' quarter, the memory of my recent experience, were spontaneously replaced by a state of confused reverie. I knew that my companion's eyes still held the same meek expression, that his lips still twitched nervously, that he wanted to talk. But I did not wish to rouse myself from the inertia of mind which enfolded me, in order to take any active interest in the fellow. He hemmed, words choked in his throat, and I felt a cruel pleasure in not coming to his aid. Repulsion at the recollection of that dreadful woman spread through me like a miasma, and I was glad the man's shame should be wrestling with his spiritual need for explanation. No, I did not help him; but allowed a heavy curtain of silence to hang black and awesome between us. My footsteps rang out clear and youthful in contrast to his muffled and aged tread. The tension between his soul and mine grew stronger every minute. The silence became strident with unspoken words. At last the string, stretched to breaking-point, snapped, and he blurted out:

"You have . . . you have just witnessed a strange scene. Sir. I beg you to forgive me, Sir, if I refer to it . . . but it must have appeared very peculiar to you, Sir, and you must

think me a ludicrous fellow, but you see, Sir, that woman
. . . well, she is . . ."

He had got stuck again. His throat worked. Then, in a
very small voice, he said hastily:

"She's my wife, Sir."

I must have shown surprise, for he hurriedly continued as
if wishing to excuse himself.

"That is to say, Sir, she was my wife, five, no four years
ago, at Geratzheim in Hesse where I have my home. Please,
Sir, you really must not think badly of her. It's probably my
fault that she has become what she is. She was not always
thus. But I . . . I teased and plagued her. You see, Sir, I
married her in spite of her abject poverty. Why, she had
hardly a chemise to her back, nothing, nothing at all. Whereas
I am well-to-do, or, rather, I am comfortably off . . . at least
I had a pretty competence in those days . . . and I was, perhaps—she is right—I was thrifty . . . yes, I was thrifty even
before our great misfortune. But you see, Sir, my father and
mother were so, and the whole family a bit on the stingy
side. Besides, I worked hard for every penny I earned. She was
fond of pretty things, and, being poor, she had nothing but
what I gave her. I was constantly reminding her of this. Oh,
I know it was wrong of me—I've had time to learn that since
the catastrophe—for she was proud, very proud. Please don't
run away with the idea that she is naturally of such a disposition as you witnessed this evening. Far from it, Sir; that's
all make-believe. She hurts herself in order to make me suffer, in order to torture me, and because she is ashamed of
her own doings, of her present mode of life. Maybe she has
gone to the bad, but I . . . I refuse to accept such a notion . . .
for I remember how good, how very good she used to be, Sir."

His excitement made him pause, both in speech and walk,
while he wiped his eyes. I looked at him in spite of myself.
He no longer appeared to be a figure of fun, and I was no

longer annoyed by his constant repetition of the obsequious "Sir." The energy he had put into phrasing his explanation had transfigured his countenance. We started forward again, and he kept his eyes downcast as if reading his story printed upon the pavement. He sighed heavily, and his voice took on a sonorous tone very different from the querulous sound I had come to expect from him.

"Yes, Sir, she was good—good, and kind to me as well— she was grateful for having been raised out of her misery. I knew how thankful she was . . . but I wanted to hear her say so . . . always and always again . . . I could not listen too often to the verbal expression of her gratitude. You see, Sir, it is so wonderful to feel that someone considers you to be better than you really are. I would willingly have parted with all my money just to hear her say those few words, everlastingly renewed . . . but she had her proper pride, and she found it increasingly difficult to acknowledge her debt to me, especially when I made a claim upon her in the matter and almost ordered her point-blank to pronounce the words I longed to hear. . . . And so, Sir, I insisted that she ask me for everything she wanted, for every dress, for every scrap of ribbon. . . . Three years I tortured her thus, and her martyrdom grew worse as the time went by. And believe me, Sir, it was all because I loved her so desperately. I loved her proud bearing, and yet I wished to humiliate her. Oh, fool that I was! I pretended to be vexed when she asked for a hat, or any other trifle she took a fancy for; while all the time I was in the seventh heaven of delight at being given an opportunity to gratify her—and at the same time to make her eat humble-pie. In those days, Sir, I did not realize how dear she was to me. . . ."

Again he stopped, and reeled in his gait. He had forgotten my existence, and spoke henceforward as if in a hypnotic trance.

"I only discovered how greatly I loved her on the day—
the accursed day—when she begged me to give her something
to help her mother out of a difficulty, and I refused. It was
an insignificant sum. . . . I had actually put the money aside
for the purpose . . . but I longed for her to ask me again . . .
and then, when I came home I found a letter on the table
and learned that she had gone. . . . All she wrote was:
'Keep your damned money. I'll never ask you for another
penny.' That's all. Nothing more. I was like one demented
for three days and three nights. I had the river dragged and
the forest scoured; indeed I paid hundreds over to the authorities in the hope of discovering her whereabouts. I even confided my troubles to the neighbours—but they merely laughed
me to scorn. No trace, no trace at all. Months later, I learned
that someone had seen her in the train, accompanied by a
soldier . . . a train going to Berlin. That very day I went
to the capital, leaving my business to take care of itself. Thousands did I lose in the process. My farm labourers, my manager, my . . . oh, everyone profited by my absence to line
his pockets. But I assure you, Sir, I remained indifferent to
these losses . . . I stayed a week in Berlin .   . and, at last,
I found her. . . ."

He panted slightly, and then continued:

"I assure you, Sir, I never said a harsh word to her . . . I
wept . . . I knelt before her . . . I offered her anything she
pleased. . . . She would henceforward be the mistress of all
I possessed—for I had come to realize that life without her
was impossible. . . . I loved every hair on her head, her
mouth, her body, every part and particle of her being. I bribed
the landlady (she was, in fact, a procuress, what they call a
'white-slave trader') generously and thus managed to see poor
Lise alone. Her face was like chalk; but she listened to me,
oh, Sir, I believe she really listened to me as if pleased, pleased
to see me. But when I began to speak of the money it was

necessary to pay—and after all, Sir, you will agree that we were obliged to discuss such practical issues—she merely called her fancy-man on to the scene, and the two of them laughed me out of countenance. I did not lose sight of her, Sir, but returned to the charge day after day. The other lodgers told me that the cur had left her, utterly unprovided for. So I sought her out yet again; but she tore up the notes I gave her, and the next time I came—she was gone. Oh, Sir, you can have no idea of what I did to trace her. I followed her for a year, paying agents here and agents there. At last I discovered that she had gone to Argentina . . . and . . . and . . . that she was in . . . a house . . . of ill-fame. . . ."

Again he hesitated, and the last two words seemed to stick in his throat. His voice became sombre as he went on:

"At first I could hardly believe my ears . . . then I reflected that I was to blame, I, only I, because I had humiliated her. And I thought how terribly she must be suffering, she so proud, as I well knew her to be. I got my solicitor to write to the consul out there, and I sent money. But she was not to be told from whom it came. The sum was more than sufficient to bring her home again. Soon I got a cable that the scheme had worked, and that the boat would reach Amsterdam on such a date. Well, so great was my impatience that I got there three days too soon. When I saw the smoke in the distance, it seemed to me I could not wait till the ship slowly entered port and came alongside the quay. At last I caught a glimpse of her at the tail of the other passengers, hardly recognizable at first, so heavily was she made up. When she saw me waiting for her, she blanched even under her paint, and tottered so that two sailors had to support her. No sooner had she stepped on to land than I was at her side. I could not speak, my throat felt so dry. She, too, said nothing, and did not look at me. I motioned to a porter to carry the luggage, and we started for the hotel.

Suddenly she turned to me and said . . . oh, Sir, if you could
have heard her voice, so sad, I thought my heart would
break . . . 'Do you want me still as your wife, after . . . ?"
I could only clasp her hand. . . . She trembled violently, but
spoke no more. I felt that now all would be well. . . . Ah,
Sir, how happy I was. When we got to our room, I danced
for joy, I knelt at her feet babbling out the most absurd
things—at least I fancy my words must have been rather
funny, for she smiled through her tears and stroked my hair—
hesitatingly, of course. Her endearments did me good, my
heart overflowed. I rushed up and down stairs ordering
dinner—I called it our wedding feast. I helped her to change
her dress, and then we went down and ate and drank, a merry
meal I assure you, Sir. She was like a child, so warm and
affectionate, speaking of our home and how everything would
start fresh. . . . Then . . ."

The man's voice became rasping, and he made a gesture
as if he were strangling someone.

"Then . . . the waiter . . . a mean and vulgar cur . . .
believed me to be the worse for drink because I laughed so
much and had carried on in such a boyish fashion—and all
because I was so happy, oh, so happy. . . . Well, I paid the
bill and he, as I said, thinking me drunk, cheated me out of
twenty francs in giving me the change. I called the fellow
back, and demanded my due. He looked sheepish, and laid
the money by my plate. . . . Then . . . quite suddenly . . .
Lise began to laugh. I stared at her perplexed . . . and her
face was completely changed . . . mocking, hard, angry. 'The
same as ever . . . even after our wedding feast,' she said
coldly—and yet her voice was full of pity. I cursed myself for
having been so particular . . . but I tried to laugh the matter
off. . . . Her gaiety had disappeared . . . it was dead
and gone. . . . She insisted upon being given a separate
room. . . . I was in a mood to grant every request . . . and

lay alone, open-eyed, through the night, thinking what I
should get her on the morrow . . . a handsome gift, that
would show her I was no longer stingy . . . at least where
she was concerned. Early next morning I was abroad . . . I
bought a bracelet . . . and took it to her in her room . . . but
she was no longer there . . . she had gone . . . as she had
gone before. I looked round for a note . . . praying it would
not be there, yet knowing that it would inevitably be awaiting
me . . . and there it was, sure enough, on the dressing-table
. . . and on it was scribbled . . ."

He hesitated. I stood still, looking into his martyred face.
The man bowed his head, and whispered hoarsely:

"She had written . . . 'Leave me in peace. You are utterly
repulsive to me.' "

Our walk had led us to the harbour; and, in the distance, the
silence was broken by the roar of the Atlantic breakers on the
coast. The vessels, their lights shining like the eyes of huge
animals, swung at their anchors. A song floated to me from
afar. Nothing was very clear. I seemed to feel presences
rather than see them. The town was sleeping and dreaming
an immense dream. By my side I distinguished the ghostly
shadow of the man growing uncannily large and then dwin-
dling to dwarfed proportions in the flickering lamplight. I was
not inclined to speak, or to offer consolation, or to ask questions. The silence stuck to me, heavy and oppressive. Suddenly he seized my arm, and said quaveringly:

"But I'm determined not to leave this town without
her. . . . After many months of search I found her. . . . I
am invulnerable to the martyrdom she is putting me
through. . . . I beseech you, Sir, to have a word with her . . .
she refuses to listen if I speak . . . I must get her to come
back. . . . Oh, won't you tell her she ought to? Please, Sir,
have a try. . . . I can't go on living like this. I can't bear any
longer to see other men go in there, knowing she is giving

herself to them, while I wait in the street till they come down again, laughing and tipsy. The whole neighbourhood knows me by now, and the people make mock of me when they see me waiting out on the pavement. . . . I shall go mad, but I must keep my vigil without fail. . . . Oh, Sir, I do beg of you to speak to her. . . . You are a stranger, I know, but for God's sake, Sir, have a word with her. Someone from her own country might influence her in this foreign land."

I wished to free my arm from the man's convulsive grip. Loathing and disgust alienated my sympathies. When he felt that I was trying to get away, he flung himself on to his knees in the middle of the street and clasped my legs.

"I conjure you, Sir, to speak to her; you must, you must— or something terrible will happen. All my money's gone in tracing her, and I'm not going to leave her here . . . not alive. I've bought a knife. Yes, Sir, I've got a knife. I won't let her stay here; at least not alive; I could not bear it. Oh, speak to her, Sir, I beg and pray you to have a talk with her. . . ."

He crouched like a maniac before me. At that moment two policemen turned into the street. I dragged him violently to his feet. He looked at me blankly for a moment, and then said in an utterly changed voice:

"Take the first turning on your right, and the hotel is about half-way down."

Once more he stared at me with eyes wherein the pupils seemed to have melted away into a bleak, white void. Then he vanished.

I hugged myself in my coat, for I was shivering. I was tired; and sleep, a kind of drunken sleep, black and feeling-less, claimed me. I wanted to think, to turn these things over in my mind, but sleep was ruthless and would not be put off. I got to my hotel, fell on to the bed, and slept like an animal.

In the morning it was hard to disentangle dream from

reality, and something within me urged me not to try and find out. I woke late, a stranger in a strange city, and visited a church far-famed for its mosaics. But my eyes were blind to such sights. The night's adventure rose vividly before my mind, and unconsciously my feet sought that alley-way and that house. But such thoroughfares do not become alive until after dark. During the daytime they wear cold, grey masks, and it is only those who know them well who are able to recognize one from another. Search as I might, I did not find the street I wanted. Weary and disappointed I returned to the hotel, followed by pictures that were either the figment of a disordered brain, or the remembrance of reality.

The train was scheduled to leave at nine o'clock that evening. I felt sorry to quit. A porter carried my bags to the station. Then, at a crossing, I recognized the street leading to that house. Telling the man to wait a minute, I went to cast a final glance at the site of my adventure, leaving the fellow smirking in a knowing way.

Yes, here it was, dark as last night, with the moonlight shining on the window-panes, and outlining the door. I was drawing nearer, when a figure emerged from the shadows. I recognized the German cowering on the threshold. He beckoned for me to approach. But mingled horror and fear made me take to my heels. I did not wish to be delayed, and to miss my train.

At the corner I turned for another look. As my eyes fell upon the poor devil, he sprang up and made for the entry. He pushed the door open, and a piece of metal shone in his hand. Was it money or a knife-blade that glittered so treacherously in the moonbeams?

Transfiguration

In the autumn of 1914, Baron Friedrich Michael von G., an officer in a dragoon regiment, was killed in action at Rawaruska. Among the papers in his desk at home was found a sealed packet which contained the following story. The relatives of the deceased, judging by the title and by a fugitive glance at the text, regarded it as a first attempt at fiction, and handed it over to me for examination, with authority to publish it if I thought fit. My own belief is that it is not a work of fiction at all, but an account of actual experiences. I therefore publish it as a human document, making neither alterations nor additions, but concealing the author's identity.

It suddenly occurred to me today that I should like to write an account of my experiences during that queer night, so that I might be able to survey the whole course of events in their natural sequence. Ever since this fancy seized me, I have been dominated by an inexplicable impulse to pen the record of my adventures, although I doubt whether I shall find it possible to give an adequate impression of the strangeness of the occurrences. I have no artistic talent, no practice as a writer. My only attempts at authorship have been one or two humorous trifles written during my school days. I do not even know whether a special technique has been worked out in such matters; whether the aspirant to authorship can be taught the best way of producing a coherent account of the succession of outward things and their simultaneous reflexion in the mind. I am even dubious whether I shall be able to fit the meaning to the word and the word to the meaning, and thus to secure the balance which has always seemed to me characteristic of the style of the successful novelist. However, I am writing only for myself, and with no thought of making intelligible to others what I myself find it difficult enough to understand. My aim is merely to settle accounts, as it were, with certain happenings in which I was strongly interested and by which I was greatly moved—to look upon these happenings as objectively as possible. I have never told the story of the incidents to any of my friends. I was withheld from doing so, partly by my doubt whether I could make them understand the essence of what occurred, and partly because I was a little ashamed at having been so profoundly affected by a chance happening. The whole thing was no more than a petty experience. And yet, even as I write these words, I realize how difficult it is for the prentice hand to choose the right words; I understand how much ambiguity is implicit in the simplest syllables. When I describe the experience as "petty," of course I mean this only in a relative sense, in contrast with the mighty and dramatic experiences in which whole nations and manifold destinies are involved; and I also use the term in a temporal sense, seeing that all the adventures I am going to relate took place within six hours. Nevertheless, for me personally, this experience, however petty, insignificant, and unimportant from a detached and general viewpoint, was so momentous that even today—four months after that queer night—I am still burning with it, and burning to tell the story. Daily and hourly I turn over the details in my mind, for that night has become, as it were, the axis of my whole existence; everything I do and say is unconsciously determined by it; I think of nothing else; I am always trying to recapitulate its sudden happenings, and thus to ensure my grasp of them. Indeed, I now realize what was still hidden from me when I took up my pen ten minutes ago, that my sole object in writing this account of the incidents is that I may hold them fast, may have them so to speak concretized before me, may again enjoy their rehearsal at once emotionally and intellectually. I was mistaken when I said that I wanted to settle accounts with these memories by writing them down. The fact is that I want to have a livelier picture of what was all-too-fugitive at the time when it was lived through; I want a warm and breathing picture of them, which will make them real to me for ever. Not, indeed, that I am afraid for a moment of forgetting that sultry afternoon, or the queer night that followed. I need no memento, no milestones, to mark my course during those hours. Like a sleep-walker, I move with an assured tread through those memories, whether of the day or of the night; I see the most trivial details with the clarity proper to the heart rather than to our fallible intellectual memory. I could sketch on this paper the outline of every leaf in the green spring landscape; and now, in autumn, I can still fancy myself smelling the soft and pollen-laden odour of the chestnut blossoms. If, therefore, I write this record, and thus recapitulate those hours, I do so, not in fear lest I should forget them, but in sheer delight at the recapitulation. And when I attempt to describe the exact succession of events, I shall have to keep a tight hand on myself, for whenever I recall them I am seized with a kind of intoxication, an ecstasy of feeling, so that I find it hard to steady the flow of memories, and to keep the incidents from becoming merged in a motley confusion. So passionate, still, are my impressions when I recall that day, June 8, 1913, on which I took a cab. . . .

Once more I feel the need to curb my pen, for I am startled when I note the ambiguity of words. Now that for the first time I am trying to write a connected account of what took place, I realize how hard it is to give a fixed presentation of that perpetual flux we call life. I wrote that "I" did so and so, that "I" took the cab on June 8, 1913. But the very pronoun is ambiguous, for I have long ceased to be the "I" of that eighth of June, although only four months have passed since then; although I live in the house that used to belong to that "I," sit at his desk, and hold his pen in my hand. I have long since become distinguished from the man of that day, and above all on account of the experiences I am about to describe. I see him from without, dispassionately and with an alien eye. I can describe him as I might describe a friend or companion of whom I knew a great deal, but who was an essentially different entity from myself—one of whom I could speak, one whom I could praise or blame, without feeling for a moment that he had once belonged to me.

The man I then was differed but little either in externals or internals from other members of his class—from the people who, without any overweening sense of pride, are wont to think of themselves as "good society." I was thirty-five years old. My parents died shortly before I came of age, and had left me fairly well off, so that there was no question of my having to earn a livelihood or of having to carve out a career for myself. Their death thus relieved me of the need for making a decision, which had been worrying me a good deal. I had just finished my university studies, and it had become incumbent on me to choose a profession. Family connexions, and my own leanings towards a tranquil, secure, and meditative life, had made it likely that I should enter the higher civil service; but I was my parents' sole heir, and I found that my means would now enable me to lead an independent existence and to gratify all my wishes. I had never been troubled with ambition, so I decided to spend a few years seeing life, and to defer the possibility of taking up some more active occupation should any prove sufficiently enticing. Ultimately, I remained content with this life of watching and waiting, for I found that, since my wishes were modest, I coveted nothing I was not able to get. In the easy and pleasant life of Vienna, which excels all other capitals in the charm of its promenades, its opportunities for idle contemplation, its elegance, and its artistry—all combining to form a life which seems a sufficient end in itself—I forgot to think of more strenuous activities. I enjoyed all the pleasures open to a rich, good-looking, and unambitious young man of family: the harmless tension of mild gambling, sport, travel, and the like. But soon I began to supplement this sort of existence by the cultivation of artistic tastes. I collected rare glass, not so much out of a special fondness for it, as because it was easy to acquire connoisseurship in this restricted field. I adorned the walls of my rooms with Italian engravings in the rococo style, and with landscapes of the Canaletto school, sometimes getting them from dealers, and sometimes buying them at auctions where I luxuriated in the gentle excitement of the bidding. I made a point of attending performances of good music, and frequented the studios of our best painters. Nor were successes with women lacking to round off my experience. In this field, likewise, impelled by the collector's secret urge (which ever denotes the lack of sufficient occupation), I enjoyed many memorable hours, and gradually became a true connoisseur. On the whole, my time was well filled, and my life seemed a satisfying one. I grew increasingly fond of this lukewarm and easy-going atmosphere of days that were always interesting and never agitating; and I was rarely moved by any new desires, for, in these peaceful surroundings, trifles brought me sufficient joy. The successful choice of a necktie, the purchase of a fine book, a motoring excursion, or an hour with a woman, would brim the measure of my happiness. An especial delight to me was the fact that my existence resembled a suit perfectly cut by an English tailor, in that there was nothing unduly striking about it. I believe my friends liked me well enough and were always glad to see me. Most of my acquaintances regarded me as a lucky fellow.

I really cannot remember whether this man of an earlier day whom I have been trying to describe also regarded himself as a lucky fellow; for now when, thanks to my crucial experience, I demand of every feeling that it shall have a deeper and more adequate significance, the appraisement of my earlier feelings has become almost impossible. But I am certain that I was not unhappy in those days. Practically all my wishes were gratified, all my claims on life fulfilled. But the very fact that I was accustomed to get all I wanted, and to make no further demands of fate, had as its inevitable sequel the growth of a sense that life was a rather flaccid affair. Unconscious, or half-realized, longings were at work. Not genuine wishes, but the wish for wishes; the desire to have stronger, less perfectly controlled, more ambitious, and less readily satisfied, desires; the longing to live more fully, and perhaps also the longing to suffer. By too admirably designed a technique, I had cleared all resistances out of my path, and the lack of resistances was sapping my vitality. I noticed that desire stirred in me less often and less vigorously; that a sort of stagnation had ensued in my feelings; that I was suffering (how can I best phrase it?) from a spiritual impotence, from an incapacity to grasp life with all the ardour of passion. Let me mention some little signs which first brought this lack home to me. I noticed that I often had no inclination to go to the theatre to see some noted performance; that I would order books about which everyone was talking, and then leave them uncut for weeks; and that, though I continued, automatically, to enrich my collections of glass and pictures, I no longer troubled to find the proper place for new acquisitions, and no longer felt any particular pleasure when I at length happened upon some object of which I had long been in search.

But the first time when I became fully aware of this transitional and slight decline in mental energy is still clearly present to my mind. It was in the summer. Simply from that strange disinclination to exert myself, and from the failure to be attracted by any new possibility, I had remained in Vienna. At this juncture I received a letter from a woman with whom I had been on intimate terms for three years, and with whom I honestly believed myself to be in love. The epistle was long and impassioned—it ran to fourteen pages. She told me that she had recently made the acquaintance of a man who had become all in all to her. She intended to marry him in the autumn, and must therefore break off relationships with me. She had no thought of regretting the experiences we had shared; the memory of them was a delight to her; the thought of me would accompany her in her new marriage as the sweetest thought of her life hitherto; she hoped that I would forgive her for this sudden decision. After the circumstantial opening, she went on to adjure me not to despise her, and not to suffer at being thus cast off. I was to make no attempt to hold her back, nor was I to do anything foolish as far as I myself was concerned. I was to seek consolation elsewhere; I was to write to her instantly, for she would be consumed

with anxiety until she heard from me. In a pencilled post-
script she added: "Don't do anything rash! Understand and
forgive!"

The first time I read this letter, I was simply surprised at
the news. But when I reread it, I became aware of a certain
sense of shame, which, as I realized its meaning, rapidly increased to a feeling of positive alarm. For I could not detect
within myself any of those strong and natural sentiments
which my mistress had anticipated. There was not a trace of
them. Her communication had caused me no pain. I had not
felt angry with her, nor had I dreamed for a moment of any
act of violence against either her or myself. Such coldness was
so strange that it could not but frighten me. I was to lose one
who had been my intimate for many years; a woman whose
warm, soft body I had clasped in my arms, and whose gentle
breathing I had rejoiced to hear when she lay beside me at
night—but nothing stirred in me at the news, I had no impulse to resist, no longing to reassert my conquest. My emotions showed not a sign of that which her instincts had led
her to expect as a matter of course from a real man. This was
the first thing to make me fully alive to the process of stagnation within me. Or, I might be said to be drifting, rudder-
less, on the surface of a stream. I knew that there was something dead, something corpse-like, about this coldness. There
was not, as yet, the foul odour of corruption; but there was
the hopeless apathy of waning life, the apathy of the moment
that precedes bodily death and the consequent obvious decay.

Thenceforward I began to watch this remarkable stagnation
of feeling, as a patient watches the progress of his disease.
Shortly afterwards, one of my men friends died. An intimate
of my childhood's days passed out of my life for ever. At the
graveside I asked myself whether I was truly a mourner,
whether I felt any active sense of loss. There was no such
feeling. I seemed to be made of glass; to be something through

which things became visible, without forming part of it. However earnestly, on this and similar occasions, I might strive to feel, however excellent the reasons I might bring forward to convince myself that I ought to feel, there was no response from within. Men were lost to me, women came and went; and I was myself moved by these movements as little as one who sits in a room is moved by raindrops on the window-pane. There was a transparent partition between me and the immediate things of life, a partition which I had not the strength to shatter.

Nevertheless, this clear realization brought, in the long run, no anxiety in its train; for, as I have already explained, I was indifferent even to the things that touched me closely. Sorrow itself was no longer sharp enough. My spiritual lack was no more perceptible to my associates than the sexual impotence that is revealed only in the intimate hour is perceptible to a man's ordinary associates. In social life I often aroused astonishment by an artificial fervour, by a parade of emotional interest designed to conceal my inward apathy. To all appearance, I continued to live the old, easy-going, unhampered life. Weeks and months slipped away, and the months slowly lengthened into years. One morning I noticed in the glass that my temples were tinged with grey, and I realized that my youth was preparing to take flight. But what others term "youth" had departed from me long ere this. The loss of youth was not particularly distressing to me, for I had not valued it immoderately. I had no special interest even in myself.

Thanks to this apathy, my days became more and more monotonous, despite all outward differences in occupation and incident. They followed one another in an undistinguished series, growing and then fading like the leaves on a tree. Nor was there any distinguishing mark about the beginning of the day I am about to describe. It seemed one just

like another. That morning, June 8, 1913, I had got up rather
late, for a lingering memory of my school days always inclined me to lie abed on Sunday morning. After I had had my
tub and had glanced at the newspapers, I was lured out-of-
doors by the warmth of the day. As usual, I strolled down
Graben, nodding to acquaintances and exchanging a word
with one here and there. I dropped in at a friend's house to
luncheon. I had no engagements that afternoon, for I liked
to keep Sunday afternoon free, and to dispose of it when
the time came as fancy might dictate. When I left my friend's
house and crossed the Ringstrasse, I had a lively sense of the
beauty of the sunlit town, and was delighted with its charm
that afternoon in early summer. Everyone looked cheerful.
People were rejoicing in the Sundayfied aspect of the gay
thoroughfare; I was myself struck by many of the details,
and especially by the contrast of the spreading green foliage
with the asphalt of the pavement. Although I walked this
way almost every day, the sight of the crowd in its Sunday
best came upon me as a surprise, and involuntarily I began
to long for more verdure, more brightness, and an even more
diversified colouring. I felt a curiosity to see the Prater, where
now at the close of spring and the beginning of summer the
great trees stood like rows of giant green-liveried footmen on
either side of the main alley way thronged with carriages—the
huge trees silently proffering their white blossoms to the
smartly dressed loiterers. Being wont to yield to such trivial
impulses, I hailed the first cab that passed, and told the driver
to take me to the Prater.

"To the races, Herr Baron?" he asked with polite alacrity.

This reminded me that today was, indeed, a fashionable
race-day, when all Vienna would turn up to the show. "That's
queer!" I thought, as I stepped into the cab. "A few years
ago I could not possibly have forgotten that this was race-
day!"

My forgetfulness made me realize, like an invalid who has to move an aching limb, the full significance of the apathy with which I was afflicted.

The main avenue was almost empty when we arrived. The racing must have begun some time before. Instead of the usual throng of carriages, there were only a few isolated cabs rattling along at top speed. My coachman turned half-round on his box to ask whether he, too, should whip up. But I told him to drive quietly, as I was in no hurry. I had seen too many races and race-course frequenters to care whether I arrived early or late. In my lethargic mood I enjoyed the gentle swaying of the cab, which gave me the sensation of being cradled in a ship. Driving slowly, I could get a better view of the lovely chestnut blossoms, from which the petals were dropping here and there to become the sport of the breeze, in whose warm eddies they were tossed for a while until they fell to join those that already flecked the ground with white. It was agreeable to me to close my eyes and breathe this spring atmosphere, and to feel that there was no reason for pressing onwards towards the goal. I was disappointed when the cab drew up at the entrance to the race-course. I was half inclined to turn back, and to be content with another hour's cradling, this pleasant afternoon. But here I was at my destination. A confused uproar came from the course, like the noise of a sea surging within the enclosure. The crowd from which this noise came was not yet visible to me; and involuntarily I was reminded how at Ostend, when one is walking from the lower part of the town up any of the little side alleys leading to the esplanade, one can already feel the bite of salt in the air and hear the murmur of the sea before being greeted by the view over the grey expanse where the waves thunder on the shore.

The uproar showed that a race was actually being run, but between me and the course was a motley crowd shaken as

if by a convulsion. All the phases of the race were betrayed
by the varying moods of the onlookers. This particular race
must now be well advanced. The horses could no longer be
galloping in a bunch, but must be strung out along the course,
with a keen competition for the lead; those who were watching that which I could not see were giving tongue in their excitement to the name of this horse or that. The direction of
their heads showed me which part of the track was now the
centre of interest, for all had their eyes fixed upon a spot to
me invisible. The cries from thousands of throats united into
a single clamour growing ever louder, filling the whole place
and rising into the impassive heaven. I looked more closely
at the faces of a few individuals. They were distorted, almost
frenzied; eyes were fixed and gleaming, lips compressed, chins
thrust out, nostrils working. To me, a dispassionate observer,
the sight of this uncontrolled intoxication was at once ludicrous and horrible. On a bench near by was standing a
smartly dressed man, whose face was doubtless amiable as
a rule, but now he looked like one possessed by the devil. He
was thrashing the air with his walking stick, as if flogging
a horse, and his whole body was imitating the movements
of a man riding hell-for-leather. His heels beat rhythmically
on the bench as if he were rising in stirrups, and with the
stick in his right hand he continued to flog the void, while
in his left hand he was gripping a white betting slip. Everywhere I saw these white slips; they showed up like flecks of
foam upon the noisy flood. Now several horses must be passing the curve neck and neck, for their names were thundered
like battle-cries by various groups of persons who would have
been overwhelmed by their delirious excitement but for this
outlet in shouting.

Amid the frenzied uproar I was as unmoved as a rock
amid the breakers, and I find it difficult to give a precise account of my sensations. Pre-eminently, no doubt, I was struck

by the utter absurdity of so much excitement, was inspired
with ironical contempt for the vulgarity with which it was
displayed. But I had unwillingly to admit that there was a
spice of another feeling; that I was not free from envy of
such ardency of passion, and of the vigorous life which the
passion disclosed. What, I wondered, could stir me like this?
What could throw me into a fever of excitement, could make
my body burn, could force me to utter such involuntary
shouts? I could not think of any sum of money that could
move me so keenly, or of any woman who could stir my
feelings to such a pitch. There was nothing in the world that
could thus fire my dead emotions. If a pistol were at my
head, a moment before the trigger was pulled, my heart
would not throb as the hearts of these thousands and tens of
thousands were throbbing because of a handful of money.

But now one of the horses must have been close to the win-
ning post, for from a myriad throats came, ever louder, the
cry of one name, the sound breaking at last into a roar. The
band began to play, and the throng scattered. One of the races
was over, one of the contests decided, and the tension relaxed
into a lively animation. What had a moment before been an
ardent integration of passion, broke up into groups of individuals, laughing, talking, and hurrying to and fro. The mask
of maniacal excitement gave place to a tranquil expression.
Social groups were crystallized out of the undifferentiated
mass which, so recently, had been united by the passion for
sport. I recognized acquaintances, and exchanged greetings
with them, but most of those present were strangers to me
and to one another, and they contemplated one another civilly
but indifferently. The women appraised one another's dresses;
the men looked ardently at the women; the well-bred curiosity, which is the chief occupation of the idle rich class, was
at work once more; people sampled one another in point of
smartness, and looked to see who was present and who had

stayed away. Though they had but just recovered from their
frenzy, they were now in doubt whether this interlude or
the racing itself was the main purpose of their social encounter. I strolled through the crowd, well pleased to breathe
its atmosphere, for it was, after all, the atmosphere of my own
daily life; I enjoyed the aroma of smartness that emanated
from this kaleidoscopic medley—but still more enjoyable was
the gentle breeze from the meadows and the woods which
from time to time stirred the white muslin dresses of the
women. Some of my acquaintances wanted to talk to me;
Diana, the pretty actress, beckoned to me from where she was
sitting; but I paid no heed. I did not want to converse with
these fashionable folk. It would have bored me to see myself in their mirror. All I desired was to study the spectacle
of life, to watch the excitements of the hour—for, to the non-
participant, the excitement of others is the most agreeable
of spectacles.

A couple of handsome women passed me, and I looked
at them with bold eyes (though inwardly unmoved by desire), amused to note in them a mingling of embarrassment
at being thus regarded and pleasure at attracting my attention.
In reality, they had no particular charm for me. It merely
gratified me to simulate an interest, and to arouse their
interest, for with me as with so many whose passions are
lukewarm, my chief erotic enjoyment was to arouse warmth
and uneasiness in others rather than to feel the stirring of
my own blood. Thus, as I walked up and down the enclosure, I glanced at the women and received their glances in
return, with no sentiment beneath the surface of things, and
but mildly titillated by the sheer pleasure of the sport.

Even this palled on me ere long. I passed the same people
again and again, and grew weary of their faces and their gestures. Seeing a vacant chair, I sat down. A fresh turmoil was
beginning to animate the concourse, a restlessness was in-

creasingly apparent among those who passed by. Obviously
a new race was about to begin. This mattered nothing to me.
I sat musing, and watched the smoke-wreaths from my cigarette, watched them disperse as they rose into the blue sky.
Now came the real beginning of that unprecedented experience which still influences my life. I know the exact instant,
for it happened that I had just looked at my watch. The
hands, as I saw, glancing lackadaisically, were exactly over
one another; it was just after a quarter past three on that
afternoon of June 8, 1913. I was looking at the white dial,
immersed in childish contemplation of this triviality, when
behind me I heard the laughter of a woman, the bright and
somewhat agitated laughter I so dearly love in women—laughter that issues from the burning bush of voluptuousness. I
had an impulse to turn my head that I might see this woman
whose vocalized sensuality had broken in upon my careless
reverie like a white pebble thrown into the dark waters of a
stagnant pool; but I controlled the desire. An inclination
for a harmless psychological experiment, one I was fond of
performing, held the impulse in check. I did not wish to
look at this laughing woman yet; I wanted to set my imagination to work upon her, to equip her in my fancy with a
face, a mouth, a neck, a swelling breast. I wanted to picture
the whole living and breathing woman.

She was close behind me. Her laugh ended, she began to
talk. I listened attentively. She spoke with a slight Hungarian
accent, quickly and vivaciously, enunciating the vowels with a
rich intonation like that of a singer. It amused me to fit the
speech into my fancy picture, to add this to all the other details. I gave her dark hair and dark eyes; a rather large
and sensuously curved mouth with strong and very white
teeth; a small and finely chiselled nose, but with wide, sensitive nostrils. On her left cheek I gave her a patch. In one
hand she carried a riding switch, and flicked her skirt with

it as she laughed. She continued to speak, and each word
served to enrich my fancy picture with a new detail. She
must have small and virginal breasts; she must be wearing
a dark green dress fastened with a diamond clasp, and a light-
coloured hat with a white plume. The picture grew plainer
and plainer, and I felt as if this stranger woman, invisible
behind my back, must be brightly imaged in the pupils of
my eyes. But I would not turn round. Some stirrings of desire were interwoven with my vision. I closed my eyes and
waited, certain that, when I opened them and turned to look
at her, the reality would confirm my fancy.

At this moment, she stepped forward. Involuntarily I opened
my eyes—and was extremely annoyed. It was all wrong.
Everything was different, maliciously different, from my
fancy picture. She was wearing a white gown instead of a
green; was not slender, but deep of bosom and broad of
hip; there was not a sign, on her plump cheeks, of the patch
I had expected; the hair that showed from beneath her
helmet-shaped hat was auburn instead of black. None of the
details were right. She was handsome, indeed—strikingly so;
but, my psychologist's vanity being pricked, I was loath to
admit the fact. I looked at her almost malevolently; and yet,
in spite of myself, I recognized her wanton charm, perceived
the attractive animalism of her firm but soft contour. Now
she laughed aloud once more, showing her strong white teeth,
and it was plain to me that her ardent and sensuous laughter
was in keeping with the pervading luxuriance of her aspect.
Everything about her was vehement and challenging; her
well-rounded figure; the way she thrust out her chin when she
laughed; her penetrating glance; her imperious nose; the hand
with which she held her sunshade firmly planted on the
ground. Here was elemental femininity, primal energy, deliberate witchery, a beacon of voluptuousness made flesh. Standing beside her was a dapper and somewhat wizened army

officer, who was talking to her in emphatic tones. She listened to him, smiled, laughed, made the appropriate responses. But this was mere by-play. The whole time she was drinking in her surroundings eagerly. She drew the notice, the smiles, of all who passed by, and especially of the males among them. Her restless glance wandered over the grand stand, lighting up from time to time as she recognized an acquaintance; then, still listening smilingly and yet indifferently to her companion, she gazed to right and to left. But her eyes never lighted on me, for I was hidden from her by her squire. This piqued me. I rose to my feet, but still she did not see me. I moved nearer—now she was looking back at the grand stand. Resolutely I stepped quite close, raised my hat, and offered her my chair. She glanced at me in some surprise; her eyes twinkled; her lips formed themselves into a caressive smile. With a laconic word of thanks, she accepted the chair, but did not sit down. She merely rested her shapely hand on the back of the chair, thus leaning forward slightly, to show off her figure to better advantage.

Annoyance at my false anticipations had been forgotten. I thought only of the little game I was playing with this woman. I moved back to the wall of the grand stand, to a spot from which I could look at her freely without attracting too much notice. She became aware of the fixity of my gaze and turned a little towards me, but inconspicuously, as if it had been a chance movement; not repelling my mute advances; answering them occasionally in a noncommittal way. Unceasingly her eyes roved from point to point; nothing held her attention longer than a moment. Did she smile with any special meaning when her glance rested on me? I could not feel sure, and the doubt irritated me. In the intervals, when the flashlight of her errant gaze met mine, her expression seemed full of promise; and yet she indiscriminately countered the interest of everyone else in like manner, simply, it would seem, to

gratify her coquetry; just as at the same time she appeared
to be giving due heed to her friend's conversation. There
was something saucy in this ostentation. Was she a confirmed
flirt? Was she stirred by a surplus of animal passion? I drew
a step nearer, for I had been infected by her sauciness. I no
longer looked her in the eyes, but deliberately appraised the
outlines of her form. She followed the direction of my glance,
and showed no sign of embarrassment. A smile fluttered
round the corners of her mouth, as if at some observation of
the chattering officer, and, nevertheless, I felt sure that the
smile was really an answer to me. Then, when I was looking
at her foot as it peeped from beneath her white dress, she,
too, looked down carelessly, and, a moment later, as if by
chance, lifted the foot and rested it on the rung of the chair,
so that, through the slit of her directoire skirt, her leg was exposed to the knee. At this moment, the smile with which she
looked at her companion seemed to have an ironical or quizzical flavour. It was obvious that she was playing with me as
unconcernedly as I with her. The boldness and subtlety of
her technique aroused in me an admiration that was not free
from dislike; for while, with a deceitful furtiveness, she was
displaying to me the charms of her body, she was fully responsive to the whispered conversation of her gallant—was
playing with us both at once. I was soured, for I detested in
others this cold and calculating sensuality, precisely because I
was aware of its incestuous kinship to my own conscious
apathy. None the less, my senses were stirred, though perhaps
more by aversion than by desire. Impudently I came still
nearer, and looked at her with frank brutality. "I want you,
you pretty animal," was the message of my unveiled eyes; and
involuntarily my lips must have moved, for she smiled somewhat contemptuously, turning her head away and letting her
skirt drop over the exposed limb. But, a moment later, her
dark and sparkling eyes had resumed their tireless roving.

She was my match; she was as cool as I. We were both playing
with an alien fire, which was nothing more than painted
flame, but was pretty to look at. This sport was a pleasant
pastime to while away a dull hour.

Suddenly the alertness of her expression vanished; the
sparkle in her eyes was dimmed. Though she continued to
smile, an irritable fold appeared at the corner of her mouth.
I followed the direction of her glance, to see a short, thickset
man, whose clothes hung untidily on him, hastening towards
her. His face was moist with hurry and excitement, and he
was nervously mopping it with his handkerchief. Since his
hat was awry, one could see that he was almost bald. (I pictured to myself that beneath this hat his scalp was beaded
with sweat, and my gorge rose against the fellow.) In his
bejewelled hand was a sheaf of betting-slips. He was bursting with excitement. Paying no heed to his wife, he began
ot talk loudly to the officer in Magyar. Obviously, he was a
devotee of the race-course, probably a horse-dealer in a good
way of business, for whom this sport was his one ecstasy, a substitute for the sublime. His wife must have murmured some
hint to him (she was manifestly annoyed at his coming, and
her elemental self-confidence had vanished), for he straightened his hat, laughed jovially, and clapped her on the shoulder with good-humoured affection. She bent her brows
angrily, enraged by this conjugal familiarity, which was peculiarly vexatious to her in the presence of the officer and
perhaps still more in mine. Her husband apparently said a
word of excuse, and then went on speaking in Magyar to
the officer, who answered with a complaisant smile. Subse-
quently, the new-comer took his wife's arm, fondly and perhaps a trifle humbly. It was plain to me that his public display of intimacy was galling to her, and I could not quell a
sense of enjoyment at witnessing her humiliation, which
aroused in me a feeling of amusement tinged with loathing.

But in a moment she recovered her equanimity, and, while gently pressing her husband's arm to her side, she shot a sarcastic glance at me, as if to say: "Look, I am his, not yours." I was both enraged and repelled. I had an impulse to turn on my heel and walk away, to show her that the wife of such a vulgarian had no further interest for me. And yet her lure was too powerful. I stood my ground.

At that moment came the signal for the start, and instantly the chattering crowd was seized as if by a general contagion. Everyone rushed forward to the railings. I restrained myself forcibly from being carried away by this rush, for I wished to stay close by the woman. Perhaps there might be an opportunity for a decisive interchange of looks, a handclasp, or some other advance, and I therefore stubbornly made my way towards her through the scurrying throng. At the very same instant, her fat spouse was hastening in the opposite direction, in search of a good place on the grand stand. Thus moved by conflicting impulses, we came into collision with such violence that his hat was dislodged and fell to the ground. The betting-slips that were stuck in the band were shaken out and scattered over the turf, looking like red, blue, yellow, and white butterflies. He stared at me, and mechanically I was about to apologize. But a malicious imp closed my lips, and made me look at him provocatively without saying a word. For a brief space he endured my gaze, though unsteadily, his face flushing with vexation. But soon he wilted. With an expression of alarm which almost moved me to pity, he turned his face away, appeared of a sudden to remember his betting-slips, and stooped to recover them and to pick up his hat. His wife, furious at what had happened, looked at me scornfully, and I saw with a secret pleasure that she would have liked to slap my face. I continued to stand with a nonchalant air, looking on with a smile and making no motion to help the corpulent fellow who was groping about in search of his betting-slips. In his stooping posture, his collar stood away from his neck like the feathers of a ruffled hen; a roll of fat projected from the red nape; he coughed asthmatically each time he bent forward. The ludicrous spectacle forced another smile from me, and the wife could hardly contain her anger. She was pale now instead of red; at length I had made her show genuine feeling—one of hatred, of untamed wrath. I should have liked to prolong this spiteful scene indefinitely, to go on enjoying thus callously the spectacle of his laborious attempts to retrieve his betting-slips. A whimsical devil seemed to have taken possession of me, was giggling in my throat, and longing to burst out into open laughter. I wanted to prod the grovelling mass of flesh with my stick. Never could I remember having been so overpowered with malice as now when I was triumphing at the humiliation of this audacious woman.

But by this time the poor wretch fancied he had recovered nearly all his slips. Really, he had overlooked one of them, a blue one, which had been carried farther than the rest, and lay on the ground just in front of me. He was still peering about with his short-sighted eyes, squinting through the eye-glasses that had slipped down his perspiring nose, when the spirit of mischief moved me to prolong his misery, and I slyly covered the blue slip with my foot, so that it would be impossible for him to find it while I maintained the same posture. He went on hunting for it, grunting to himself as he counted and recounted the coloured strips of paper in his hand. Certainly there was still one missing! Amid the growing tumult he was bent on returning to the search, when his wife, who with a savage expression was evading my quizzical glance, could no longer bridle her impatience.

"Lajos!" she called to him suddenly and imperiously.

He started like a horse at the sound of the bugle. Once again he looked searchingly at the ground. I seemed to feel the hidden slip tickling the sole of my foot, and I could hardly refrain from open derision. Then he turned submissively to his wife, who with ostentatious haste led him away to join the tumultuous crowd.

I stayed where I was without the slightest inclination to follow them. As far as I was concerned, the incident was closed. The feeling of erotic tension had given place to an agreeable serenity. My excitement had quite passed away, so that nothing remained beyond a healthy satiety after my sudden outbreak of impishness—nothing, beyond an almost arrogant satisfaction with the success of my coup. In front of me the spectators were closely packed, stirred with increasing excitement. In a dirty, black wave they were pressing on the railings, but I was bored with the races, and had no inclination to look at this one. I might as well go home. As I moved to put this thought into execution, I uncovered the blue slip which by now I had forgotten. Picking it up, I toyed with it in my fingers, uncertain what to do with it. I had a vague thought of restoring it to "Lajos," for this would give me an excellent chance of making his wife's acquaintance. However, I instantly realized that she was of no further interest to me, that the fire of this adventure had cooled, and that I had relapsed into my customary indifference. A combative exchange of glances with Lajos's wife had been quite enough for me; the thought of sharing a woman with that gross creature was unappetizing; I had enjoyed a transient titillation of the senses, and this had been succeeded by a feeling of agreeable relaxation.

Taking possession of the abandoned chair, I sat down at ease and lighted a cigarette. The little flame of passion had flickered out. Once again I was listless; the renewal of old experiences offered no charm. Idly watching the smoke-wreaths, I thought of the promenade at Meran where, two months earlier, I had sat looking at the waterfall. At Meran, too, there had been a continuous roar that left me unaffected, an un-meaning sound had passed athwart the silence of the blue-tinted landscape. Now the passion of sport was attaining a fresh climax. The foam of fluttering parasols, hats, and hand-kerchiefs rose above the black wave of humanity. The voices of the throng condensed once more into a single cry. I heard one name, shouted exultantly or despairingly from thousands of throats: "Cressy! Cressy! Cressy!" Once again the noise ceased abruptly, as when a violin-string snaps. The band be-gan to play, and the crowd to break up into groups once more. The numbers of the leading horses were displayed on the board, and half-unconsciously I glanced at them. The win-ner's number was seven. Mechanically I looked down at the blue slip in my hand. On this, likewise, was a seven.

I could not but laugh. The worthy Lajos had backed the winner! My fit of spleen had actually robbed the fat husband of his money. The sense of impishness revived; it would be interesting to learn how much my stirring of jealousy had cost him. For the first time I scrutinized the betting-slip at-tentively. It was for twenty crowns, and for a "win," not simply for a "place." If the odds had been heavy, the slip might now be worth a good deal of money. Following the urge of curiosity, I joined the crowd of those who were hurry-ing towards the pay desk. I took my stand in the queue and soon reached the window. When I presented my ticket, two prompt and bony hands (I could not see the paying-clerk's face) thrust across nine twenty-crown notes in exchange.

At this moment, when the money was actually offered me, the laughter stuck in my throat. I felt extremely uncomfort-able, and involuntarily drew away my hands for a moment, lest I should touch another man's money. I should really have preferred to leave the blue bank-notes lying on the counter, but hard on my heels were other winners, eager to handle their gains. What could I do but reluctantly pick up the

notes? They seemed to burn my fingers as if they had been
blue flames, and I should have liked to shake off the hand that
held them. I suddenly realized the ignominy of my position.
The jest had become deadly earnest; had developed into something quite incompatible with my position as a man of
honour, a gentleman, an officer in the reserve. I hesitated to
give what I had done its true name. The notes in my hand
were not simply treasure trove; they had been obtained by
fraud, they were stolen money.

There was a clamour of talk all round me, as the people
streamed up to the paying-clerk's window and passed on with
their winnings. I stood motionless, still holding the unwelcome notes. What had I better do? The first and most obvious
thought was to seek out the real winner, to make my excuses,
and hand over the money. But how could I do this? Above
all, it would be impossible under the eyes of the officer who
was the wife's companion. There would be a scandal which
would certainly cost me my commission as a lieutenant in
the reserve; for even if it might be supposed that I had accidentally picked up the betting-slip, to draw the real owner's
winnings had been a dishonourable act. My next idea was to
crumple the notes into a ball and throw them away, but in
such a crowd someone was sure to see what I did, and the act
would arouse suspicion. Yet I could not dream of keeping the
money; or of putting it into my note-case until I could give it
away to some suitable recipient. From childhood onwards I
had had impressed upon me a keen sense of what was fitting
in money matters, and the handling of these notes was as unpleasant to me as the wearing of a dirty shirt would have been.
Somehow, anyhow, and quickly, I must get rid of the con-
taminated pieces of paper. Looking around me in hopeless
perplexity, in vain search for a hiding-place or for some un-
watched possibility for disposal, I noticed that a new line had
formed of persons on the way to the window. This time, those

in the queue were holding, not betting-slips, but bank-notes. Here was the way out of my difficulty! Chance had brought me this money, and I would commit it to the winds of chance once again; I would thrust it into the greedy maw of that window which was now ceaselessly swallowing up new stakes in the form of silver coin and notes. Yes, yes, there was the path of deliverance.

Impetuously I pressed forward towards the window. Now there were only two backers in front of me. The first was already at the totalizator when it occurred to me that I did not know the names of any of the horses. I listened to the conversation of those standing near me.

"Are you going to back Ravachol?" asked one of another.

"Rather," came the answer.

"Don't you think Teddy has a good chance?" inquired number one.

"Teddy? Not an earthly!" replied number two. "Teddy's no good. You take my tip."

I grasped at the casual information. Teddy was no good; Teddy could not possibly win. All right, I would back Teddy. I threw down the money, and backed for a win the horse whose name I had just heard for the first time. In exchange for my notes, I received nine red-and-white slips. Even these were disagreeable to handle, but they did not burn my fingers as the greasy notes had done.

I drew a breath of relief, feeling now almost carefree. I had got rid of the money, had shaken off the unpleasant results of my adventure. The matter had become once more what it had been at the outset, a mere joke. I returned to my chair, lighted another cigarette, and blew smoke-rings with renewed content. But this mood did not last. I was restless, got up, walked about, and then sat down again. My agreeable reveries were over. A feeling of nervous irritability had taken possession of me. At first I thought it must be because I dreaded a

fresh encounter with Lajos and his wife—but how could they
dream that the new slips were really theirs? Nor was it the
restlessness of the crowd which disturbed me. Indeed, I found
myself watching the passers-by to see if there were any movement towards the barrier. I stood up again and again to look
for the flag which is hoisted at the beginning of each race.
Yes, I was certainly impatient. I had been seized by the fever
of expectancy. I was looking forward to the race which was
to close the unseemly incident for ever. A man came by with
a bundle of sporting papers. I beckoned to him, bought one,
began to search its columns, and, amid a wilderness of strange
jargon and tipsters' hints, I at length discovered "Teddy,"
learned the names of his jockey and his owner, and was informed that his colours were red-and-white. Why should these
details interest me? Angrily crumpling the newspaper, I threw
it away, stood up, and sat down again. Suddenly I had grown
hot; I wiped my face; my collar seemed too tight. Was the
race never going to begin?

At last the bell sounded. The crowd rushed to the railings,
and to my extreme annoyance I found that this bell thrilled
me as an alarm thrills one who is awakened by it from sleep.
I jumped up so eagerly that I overturned the chair, and I
hastened—nay, I ran—forward into the crowd, gripping my
betting-slips tightly. I was terrified lest I should be too late, lest
I should miss something of the utmost importance. Roughly
shouldering my way through, I reached the barrier, and seized
a chair on which a lady was about to seat herself. She was an
acquaintance, Countess W., and her amazed and angry expression made me aware of my bad manners and my frenzy.
But with a mixture of shame and defiance I ignored her, and
leapt on to the chair in order to watch the field.

In the far distance, across the turf, I could see the eager
horses, with difficulty kept in line by the little jockeys on their
backs, who from here looked like harlequin puppets. I tried

to make out the colours of my own fancy, but my eyes were untrained to this sport. Everything flickered strangely under my gaze, and I could not distinguish the red-and-white. Now the bell rang for the second time; and, like seven coloured arrows shot from a single bow, the horses sped along the course. It must be a wonderful sight for those who can contemplate it unmoved, with a purely æsthetic pleasure; for those who can watch the slender race-horses in the gallop which seems almost as free as a bird's flight. But I recked naught of this. My one longing was to make out my own horse, my own jockey; and I cursed myself because I had not brought my field-glasses. Though I tried my hardest, I could discern nothing beyond a flying clump of coloured insects. At length the shape of this clump began to alter; at the curve, it assumed the form of a wedge, point foremost, while one or two stragglers were tailing off from the base of the wedge. The race was fiercely contested. Three or four of the galloping beasts were still in a bunch, now one and now another head and neck in front of the rest. Involuntarily I drew myself up to my full height, as if by this imitative and passionate tension I might hope to lend them an added speed.

The excitement of those around me was increasing. The habitués of the race-course must have been able to recognize the colours at the curve, for the names of some of the horses began to detach themselves from the confused shouting. Close by me, one of the onlookers was wringing his hands in his excitement. Now a horse forged a little ahead, and this man stamped, shouting with a raucous and triumphant voice:

"Ravachol! Ravachol!"

The colours worn by the jockey on the leading horse were blue, and I was furious that the animal I had backed was not to the front. The strident shouts of my neighbour, "Ravachol! Ravachol!" became more and more offensive to me. I was enraged, and should have liked to aim my fist at the great black

cavity of his yelling mouth. I trembled in my wrath. From
moment to moment I felt more capable of some preposterous
action. But one of the other horses was pressing the leader
hard. Perhaps it was Teddy, perhaps, perhaps—and the hope
aroused new ardour. Looking at the jockey's arm as it moved
rhythmically, I fancied that the sleeve was red. It might be
red; it must be red! Why did not the rascal use his switch
more vigorously? His mount had nearly overhauled the
leader! Half a head more. Why Ravachol? Ravachol! No, not
Ravachol! Not Ravachol! Teddy! Teddy! Go it, Teddy!

Suddenly I pulled myself together. Who was that shouting
"Teddy! Teddy!" It was I shouting. In the very midst of my
passion, I was startled at myself. I tried to maintain my self-
command, and for a moment a sense of shame overpowered
my excitement. But I could not tear away my eyes, for the two
horses were still neck and neck, and it really must be Teddy
that was thus overhauling the accursed Ravachol, the Ravachol I loathed with all my might—for from everywhere there
now came a roar of "Teddy! Teddy!" The clamour infected
me, after my brief moment's awakening. Teddy must win,
must win. Now, in very truth, he was leading by a span; then
by two; then by a head and neck. At this moment the bell
rang, and there was an explosive shout of jubilation, despair,
and anger. For an instant, the longed-for name seemed to fill
the heavens. Then the uproar passed, and from somewhere
came the strains of music.

I was hot, I was dripping with sweat, my temples were
throbbing wildly, when I stepped down from the chair. I had
to sit for a while, till the swimming in my head abated. An
ecstasy such as I had never known before took possession of
me; an idiotic delight at the answer Fate had given to my
challenge. Vainly did I try to persuade myself that I had not
wanted the horse to win, that my sole desire had been to lose
the money. I put no trust in my own persuasion, and I soon

became aware of an overmastering impulse. I felt drawn in a
particular direction, and I knew whither this impulse led me.
I wanted to see the concrete results of my victory; I wanted
the money in palpable form; to feel the blue bank-notes, lots
of them, crackling between my fingers. A strange, an alien,
an evil lust had taken possession of me, and I no longer had
any feeling of shame to prevent my yielding to it. I hurried
to the pay-desk. Unceremoniously I thrust myself forward
among those who were awaiting their turn at the window,
elbowing other impatient winners aside, possessed by the urge
to get the money into my hands.

"Bounder!" muttered one of those I had pushed out of my
way.

I heard the insult, but ignored it in the fever of my impatience. At length I was at the window, and my fingers closed
greedily upon a blue bundle of notes. I counted them over with
tremulous exultation. My winnings amounted to six hundred
and forty crowns. I snatched up the bundle and left the window.

My first thought was to venture my winnings once more,
to multiply them enormously. Where was my sporting paper?
Oh, bother, I had thrown it away! I looked round for the
chance of buying another, only to notice, to my stupefaction
and alarm, that everyone was streaming towards the exit, that
the windows of the pay-desks were closed, that the flags were
being furled. The day's sport was over. The last race had been
run. For a second or two I stood rigid. Then a fierce anger
surged up in me, aroused by a keen sense of injustice. It
seemed so unfair that when all my nerves were aquiver, and
when the blood was rushing through my veins with a vigour
I had not known for years, the game should be played out.
But I could not cheat myself into the belief that I had made
a mistake, for the crowd grew ever thinner, and broad stretches
of trampled turf had become visible amid the few remaining

loiterers. Gradually realizing the absurdity of my tense expectation, I, too, moved towards the exit. An obsequious attendant sprang forward. I gave him the number of my cab. He bawled it through his hands, and in an instant my driver whipped forward from the waiting throng. I told him to drive slowly down the main avenue. My excitement was on the wane, was being replaced by an agreeable lassitude. I wanted to rehearse the whole scene in my thoughts.

At this moment another cab drove past. I glanced at it without thinking, but promptly turned my eyes away, for in it were the woman and her corpulent husband. They did not notice me. But at sight of them I was overcome by a disagreeable choking sensation, as if I had been found out. Their nearness made me uneasy.

The cab moved along quietly on its rubber-tired wheels, in line with the others. The brightly coloured dresses of the women made these cabs look like flower-laden boats sailing down a canal with green banks bordered on either side by chestnut trees. The air was balmy, the first breath of the evening coolness was wafted across the dust. But the agreeable pensiveness came no more; the sight of the man I had swindled disturbed me, it blew upon my ardours like a chill draught. With sobered senses I reviewed the episode, and found it impossible to understand my own actions. How could I, an officer and a gentleman, have done such a thing? Without the pressure of need, I had appropriated another's money, and had done so with a zest which put my behaviour beyond the possibility of excuse. I, who an hour before had never transgressed the bounds of good form, had now actually become a thief. As if desiring to frighten myself, I passed judgment on myself by muttering, in time with the rhythm of the horses' hoofs:

"Thief! Thief! Thief! Thief!"

How shall I describe the strange thing that now befell? It

seems so inexplicable, so amazing, and yet I am convinced
that my memory of it is perfectly accurate. Every instant of
my feeling, every pulse of my thought, during that brief period,
comes back to me with supernatural clearness. Hardly any
other happening throughout my thirty-five years of life is so
vivid. Yet I scarcely dare to record in black and white the
absurd succession, the preposterous seesaw, of my sensations. I
do not know if any imaginative writer or any psychologist
could depict them in logical order. All I can do is to sketch
the sequence faithfully.

I was muttering to myself "thief, thief, thief." Then came a
strange pause, a vacant interval, in which nothing happened;
in which—how hard it is to explain—I merely listened, listened inwardly. I had formulated the charge against myself,
and now it was time for the accused to answer the charge.
I listened, therefore, but nothing happened. I had expected
that this name of "thief" would frighten me like the crack of
a whip, would overwhelm me with shame; but there was no
such response. I waited patiently for a few minutes, leaning
over myself, so to speak, that I might watch the better (for
I was convinced that there must be something astir beneath
this obdurate silence). Feverishly expectant, I waited for the
echo, for the cry of disgust, indignation, despair, that must
follow so grave an accusation. Nothing! There was no answer!
Once more I repeated to myself "thief, thief"; quite loud this
time, in the hope of awakening my conscience, which seemed
to be rather hard of hearing. Still there was no answer. Suddenly, in a lightning flash of awareness, I realized that I was
only trying to feel ashamed, but was not in the least ashamed;
that somewhere in the secret recesses of my being I was proud,
was elated, because of my crazy deed.

How could this be? I was now positively afraid of myself,
and tried to ward off the unexpected realization; but the feeling I have attempted to describe was irresistible. There was

no shame, no indignation, no self-contempt. This current of
strong feeling was joy, intoxicating delight, which flamed up
in me because I realized that during those few minutes I had
for the first time been genuinely alive once more after the
lapse of many years. I rejoiced to know that my feelings had
merely been paralysed, and were not utterly dead; that somewhere beneath the smooth surface of my indifference volcanic
passion must still be raging; and that this afternoon, touched
by the magic wand of chance, the volcano had erupted. In
me, in me too, in this fragment of the living universe that
passed by my name, there still glowed the mysterious and
essential fire of our mortal life, which breaks forth from time
to time in the vigorous pulses of desire. I too lived, was alive,
was a human being with evil and ardent lusts. A door had
been thrust open by the storm of this passion; an abyss had
been riven in me, and with a voluptuous giddiness I gazed
into the unknown profound with a sense of terror and delight. By degrees, while the cab gently conveyed my entranced
body on its way through the respectable concourse, I climbed
down step by step into the depths of the human within me,
incredibly alone in this silent descent, lighted on my way by
the flaring torch of my newly enkindled consciousness. What
time a thousand others were laughing and chattering around
me, I was seeking within myself the human being I had so
long lost sight of, was traversing years in the magical course
of reflection. Long buried memories surged up from the cob-
webbed recesses of my mind. I recalled that, in my school days,
I had stolen another boy's pocket-knife, and remembered how,
while I watched him hunting everywhere in vain and asking
all his comrades if they had seen his knife, I had been animated with the same impish joy I had felt this afternoon.
Now, at length, I could understand the strange intensity of
some of my love experiences; could understand that my passion had only been distorted but had never been completely

suppressed, by the social illusion, by the dominant ideal of
gentility. Deeply hidden within me, as within others, there
had continued to flow all the time the hot current of life. Yes,
I had lived, and yet had not dared to live; I had kept myself
in bondage, and had hidden myself from myself. But now
the repressed energy had broken loose; life, teeming with ineffable power, had carried me away. I knew that I was still
alive. With the blissful confusion of the woman who first feels
her child quicken within her, I perceived the reality, the irref-
ragable truth, of life germinating within me. I felt (I am
almost ashamed to use the expression) that I, the man who
had been fading and dying, was blossoming anew; I felt the
red blood coursing through my veins, and that in these fresh
blossoms there would grow unknown fruits both sweet and
bitter. The miracle of Tannhäuser's blossoming staff had come
to pass in me—on a race-course amid the tumult of a thousand idlers. I had begun to feel once again. The dry staff was
sprouting, was thrusting forth buds.

From a passing carriage a man hailed me, shouting my
name—obviously I had failed to see his first and quieter salu-
tation. I was furious at being roused out of the agreeable state
of self-absorption, the profoundest reverie I had ever experienced. But a glance at my acquaintance recalled me to my
ordinary self; it was my friend Alfons, an intimate of my
school days, now public prosecutor. The thought flashed
through my mind: "This man who greets you so cordially has
now power over you; you would be at his mercy if he knew
what you had done. Did he know, it would be his duty to
hale you out of this cab, to tear you away from your comfortable existence, to have you kept behind bars for several years,
in company with the scum of life, with those other thieves
who have only been brought to the sordid pass of prison by
the lash of necessity."

But this was no more than a momentary uneasiness. The

thought was promptly transformed into an ardent feeling, a fantastic and impudent pride, which made me sample almost scornfully the people within my range of vision: "If you only knew, the friendly smile with which you greet me as one of yourselves would be frozen on your lips, and you would contemptuously give me the cut direct. But I have been beforehand with you. This afternoon I broke away from your cold and petrified world in which I was one of the wheels running noiselessly in the great machine, one of the idle wheels. I have plunged into an unknown abyss; and in this one hour of the plunge I have lived more fully than in all the sheltered years in your circle. I do not belong to you any more, I am no longer one of your set; I may be on the heights or in the depths, but never shall I return to the dead levels of your philistine comfort. For the first time I have felt all the thrill that man can feel in good and in evil; but you will never know where I have been, will never understand me. Never will you be able to pluck the heart out of my mystery!"

How can I describe all that I felt while I was thus driving, to outward appearance a man of fashion, quietly exchanging greetings with those of his own order! For while my larval form, the semblance of the man that had been, continued thus to recognize sometime acquaintances—within me there was surging so intoxicating a music that I had to keep a tight rein on myself lest I should shout in my exultation. There was such an uprush of emotion that it aroused a sense of bodily distress. Like one who is gasping for want of air, I pressed my hand on my heart and sensed its painful throbbing. But pain and pleasure, alarm, disgust, or concern, were not isolated and detached feelings. They were integrally fused, so that the sum of my sensations was that I lived and breathed and felt. It was the simplest and most primitive of feelings, one that I had not experienced for ages, and it went to my head like wine. Not for a single instant during my thirty-five years had I had such an ecstatic sense of being alive.

My driver pulled up the horses, and the cab stopped with a jerk. Turning on the box, the man asked me whether I wanted to drive home. Emerging from my reverie, I glanced up and down the avenue, astonished to note how long I had been dreaming, how the intoxication of my senses had swallowed up the hours. Night had fallen; the tree-tops were whispering in the breeze; the cool air was fragrant with the scent of the chestnut blossoms. The silvery moon could be glimpsed through the foliage. It was impossible to return home, impossible to go back into my customary world. I paid the driver. As I was counting out his fare, the touch of the bank-notes sent a kind of electric shock running up my arm; there were still vestiges of the larval personality, which could feel ashamed. My dying gentlemanly conscience still stirred within me, but none the less the touch of the stolen money was agreeable, and I was spendthrift in my delight. The cabman was so effusive in his thanks, that I could not but smile as I thought: "If you only knew!" He whipped up his horse and drove off. I looked after the cab as from shipboard a voyager will look back upon the receding shores of a land where he has spent happy days.

For a little while I stood musing. Then I strolled across towards the Sacher Garden, where it was my wont to dine after driving in the Prater. No doubt this was why the cabman had pulled up where he did. But when my hand was on the bell of the garden gate of this fashionable open-air restaurant, I had a counter-impulse. I did not want to go back into the familiar world. The idle chatter of my social equals would dispel this wonderful, this mysterious fermentation—would tear me away from the sparkling magic of my afternoon adventure.

From somewhere in the distance came snatches of music,
and the crazy sounds drew me, as everything with a lure in
it drew me that day. My mood made it delightful to follow
chance currents. There was an extraordinary fascination in
thus drifting amid the crowd. I fermented with the ferment-
ing mass; all my senses were stirred by the acrid fumes of
mingled dust, tobacco, human breath, and human sweat.
Everything which till recently, till yesterday, had seemed to
me vulgar and plebeian, and consequently repulsive, everything which I had been sedulously trained to avoid, had now
become the goal of instinctive desire, as if for the first time
I realized my own kinship with the animal, the impulsive, and
the ordinary. Here, in the purlieus of the city, among common
soldiers, servant girls, and vagabonds, I found myself inexpli-
cably at ease. I breathed this new air exultantly; rubbing shoulders with the crowd was pleasant; and with voluptuous curiosity I waited to learn whither my drifting would lead me. As
I drew nearer to the Wurstel Prater, the blare of the brass
band grew louder; it coalesced with the monotonous sound
of orchestrions playing harsh polkas and riotous waltzes, with
strange noises from the booths, outbursts of coarse laughter
and drink-sodden yells. Through the trees I caught sight of
the roundabouts whirling amid their glare of lights. I drank
in the whole tumult. The cascade of noises, the infernal medley, was grateful to me, lulled me. I watched the girls on the
switchback, their skirts blown out by the wind; heard them
screaming in a way characteristic of their sex at each swoop
of the car. There were butchers' lads roaring with laughter
at the Try-Your-Strength machine; touts standing at the doors
of the booths, making monkey-like gestures, and doing their
best to shout down the noise of the orchestrions. All this
mixed confusedly with the manifold movements and clamours
of the crowd, drunken with the cheap intoxication of the brass
band, the flashing lights, and its own warm tumultuousness.

Now that I had been awakened, I was able to enter into the life of these others, to share in the ardours of the great city, in its riot of Sunday amusement, its animal-like and nevertheless healthy and impulsive enjoyments. Through my contact with this tumultuous life, with these hot and passionate bodies, some of their fervour was transmitted to myself. My nerves were toned up by the acrid aroma; my senses wantoned amid the tumult; I had that intangible but sensuous ecstasy which is inseparable from every strong pleasure. Never before, perhaps, had I thus been in touch with the crowd, had I thus grasped humanity-at-large as a massed power from which pleasure could flow into my own separate personality. The barriers had been broken down, so that my own individual circulation was now connected up with the blood current of this wider world. I was seized with a new longing to overthrow the last obstacles between myself and this wider life; I was filled with an ardent desire for conjugation with this warm and strange and teeming humanity. With a man's lust I lusted after the flesh of this titanic body; and with a woman's lust I was ready to accept all its caresses and to respond to its every lure. Yes, at length I realized it, I loved and I longed to be loved as when I had been a boy first growing into manhood. I craved for life; for union with the laughing and breathing passion of these others, to be bone of their bone and flesh of their flesh. Enough to be small and nameless in the medley, an infusorian in the slime of the world, one tiny fragment of vigorous life among the myriads. Enough, so long as I was in and of that life, moving with others in the circle, no longer shot away like an arrow animated with an isolated energy and moving towards some heaven of separateness.

I am well aware that I was drunk. All the influences of the environment were at work in my blood: the clanging of the bells of the roundabouts; the lascivious laughter of the women when gripped by their male companions; the chaos of music;

the rustling of the garments. My finger-tips and temples were throbbing. I had a fierce urge to speak, to break the silence of many hours. Never had I such a longing for human intercourse, as here among this surging crowd, of whom nevertheless I was not yet one. I was like a man dying of thirst upon the ocean. The torment of my own separateness increased moment by moment, while I watched strangers, who were strangers also to one another, coalescing into groups and breaking up again like globules of quicksilver. I was filled with envy when I saw young fellows making girls' acquaintance in one moment, and walking arm-in-arm with them the next. A word while on the roundabout, a glance in passing, sufficed; the strangers entered into conversation, and perhaps separated after a minute or two; but meanwhile there had been a union, an intercourse of thoughts and feelings, such as my soul craved.

Here was I, a man at home in the best society, with a certain reputation as a conversationalist, one who knew all the rules of the social game—yet I was timid and abashed, was afraid to accost a buxom servant wench lest she should laugh at me. I lowered my eyes when anyone glanced at me, eager though I was to begin a talk. My desires were far from clear to me, but of one thing I was convinced, that I could no longer endure to be alone, consumed by my own fever. Still, no one greeted me, all passed by unheeding. Once a lad came near me, a boy about twelve years old in ragged clothes; his eyes shone with the reflex of the lamps as he stared longingly at the whirling wooden horses. There he stood open-mouthed. Having no money to pay for a ride, he was perforce content with the next best thing, with enjoying the shrieks and laughter of the fortunate riders. I constrained myself to walk up to him and ask (why did my voice tremble and my tone ring false?):

"Wouldn't you like to have a ride?"

He stared up at me, took fright (why? why?), flushed scarlet, and fled without a word. Not even a bare-footed urchin would accept a little pleasure from me. There must be something extraordinarily repellent about me—such was my thought. What else could account for my inability to become one with the crowd; for the way in which, amid the turbulent waters, I was as detached as a droplet of oil?

But I would not give in; I could no longer bear to be alone. My feet were burning in my dusty patent-leather shoes; my throat was parched. Looking to right and left through gaps in the crowd, I could see islets of green on which there were tables decked with red cloths. Here, on wooden benches and chairs, tradespeople were seated, drinking beer and smoking cigars. This seemed attractive. Strangers hobnobbed here, and there was comparative quiet amid the turmoil. I went to one of these oases, and scrutinized the groups till I spied a table at which there were five persons—a fat, stocky workman, his wife, two merry girls, and a little boy. Their heads wagged in time with the music, they were chaffing one another and laughing, and their cheerful faces were good to see. I raised my hat, touched a chair, and asked if I might sit down. Instantly their laughter was frozen, and there was a moment's pause in which each of them seemed to be waiting for one of the others to answer. Then the mother, though discountenanced, murmured:

"If you please."

I sat down, with the feeling that my arrival had put an end to their unconstraint. A deadly silence now brooded over the table. I did not dare to raise my eyes from the red check tablecloth, on which salt and pepper had been freely spilled; but I realized that they must all be eyeing me stealthily, and it occurred to me (too late!) that my appearance was quite out of keeping with a beer garden of this character. My smartly cut suit, my tall hat, the pearl pin in my dove-grey necktie,

the general odour of luxury I exhaled, had sufficed to dig between me and my table-companions a chasm across which
they glared at me with confusion and hostility. The silence of
the five made it ever more impossible for me to raise my eyes.
Shame forbade my leaving the place I had taken, so I sat
there despairingly counting and recounting the checks on the
tablecloth. Great was my relief when the waiter brought me
my beer in a thick and heavy glass. At length I could move,
and as I drank I could look at my companions furtively. Yes,
I was the centre of all their eyes; and their expression, though
not one of positive hatred, betrayed immeasurable estrangement. They knew me for an interloper into their dull world.
With the instinct of their class they felt that I was in search
of something which did not belong to my own surroundings.
Not from love, not from longing, not from simple pleasure in
waltzes or in beer, not in search of the placid enjoyments of
the day of rest, could I have come to this resort. They felt that
I must have been impelled by some desire beyond the range
of their understanding, and they mistrusted me, as the youngster had mistrusted my offer to pay for his ride on the roundabout, as the thousand nameless frequenters of this place of
merry-making mistrusted my unfamiliar appearance, manners,
and mode of speech. Yet I felt sure that if I could only happen upon a cordial, straightforward, and genuinely human
way of opening up a conversation, the father or the mother
would answer me, the daughters would giggle approvingly,
and I should be able to take the boy with me to one of the
shooting galleries, or to enjoy whatever sport might best please
him. In five or ten minutes I should be delivered from myself, should be breathing the frank atmosphere of familiar
converse, should be accepted as a desirable acquaintance—but
the words I wanted were undiscoverable; I was stifled by false
shame; and I sat among these simple folk wearing a hang-
dog expression as if I were a criminal, tormented by the sense

that my unwelcome presence was spoiling the last hour of
their Sunday. In this formidable silence I atoned for all the
years of careless arrogance in which without a glance I had
passed thousands of such tables, millions upon millions of my
brother human beings, concerned only with success in my
own smart circle. I perceived that the way leading to unrestrained converse with them in this hour of my need had been
walled up from my side.

Thus I, who had hitherto been a free man, sat humbly with
bowed head, counting and recounting the checks on the cloth,
until the waiter came that way again. I settled up, left most
of my beer, and uttered a civil farewell. The response was
friendly, but not unmixed with astonishment. I knew, without looking, that, directly my back was turned, directly the
foreign body had been removed, the round of cheerful talk
would be resumed.

Again I threw myself into the maelstrom of the crowd—
more eagerly this time and more despairingly. The press had
become less dense under the black canopy of the trees, nor
was there so great a throng where the roundabout cast its
glare; but in the darker parts of the square, along the edges,
there seemed to be as many people as ever. The deep roar of
the pleasure-seekers had broken up into a number of distinct
smaller sounds, though these were fused into one from time
to time when the music raged furiously as if in an attempt to
summon back the seceders. New elements were conspicuous
in the crowd. The children, with their air-balloons, paper
windmills, and streamers, had been taken home, and the
family parties had disappeared. Some of those who remained
were uproariously drunk; vagabonds on the prowl were conspicuous in the side alleys; during the hour in which I had
been glued to the table in the beer-garden, this remarkable
world had changed considerably for the worse. But the stimulating aroma of rascality and danger was more congenial to

me than the atmosphere of working-class respectability had
been. The instinct that had awakened in me was in tune with
the like tensions of those I was now contemplating. I seemed
to see myself reflected in the slouching demeanour of these
questionable shapes, these outcasts of society. Like myself,
they were in search of some vivid adventure, some swift excitement. I positively envied the ragged prowlers, envied them
for their lack of restraint. For there I stood leaning against
one of the pillars of the roundabout, longing to break the
spell of silence, to free myself from the torment of loneliness,
and yet incapable of movement or speech. I stood and stared
across the square, across the brilliantly lighted open space,
into the darkness on the other side, expectantly scrutinizing
everyone who drew near. But none would meet my gaze.
All looked at me with chill indifference. No one wanted me,
no one would set me free.

How can I attempt to describe or explain what must sound
like lunacy? Here was I, a man of education, rich and independent, at home in the best society of the capital—and that
night I stood for a whole hour beside one of the pillars of a
giddy-go-round, listening to twenty, forty, a hundred repetitions of the same waltz, the same polka, and watching the
revolutions of the same idiotic horses of carved and painted
wood—while an obdurate defiance, a determination to await
the magic turn of fate, kept me rooted to the spot. I know that
my conduct was absurd, but my torment during that hour
was an expiation. And what I was expiating was not my theft,
but the dull vacancy of my life prior to that afternoon. I had
sworn to myself that I would not leave the spot until a sign
had been vouchsafed that fate had set me free.

As the hour passed, the merry-making gradually came to an
end. In one booth after another the lamps were extinguished,
so that the darkness seemed to advance like a flood. The island
of light where I was standing grew ever more isolated. In

alarm I glanced at my watch. Another quarter of an hour and
the garish wooden horses would cease to turn, the red and
green lamps dangling from their foreheads would be switched
off, and the blaring orchestrion would be silenced. Then I
should be in the dark, alone in the murmuring night, outcast
and forlorn. More and more uneasily I looked across the
darkling square, traversed now only at intervals by a couple
hastening homewards or by one or two reeling roisterers. But
opposite me in the deep shadow there lurked a restless and
stimulating life. When a man passed by, I could hear, emerging from this darkness, a whispered invitation. If, in answer,
the passer-by turned his head, a woman's voice would speak
more distinctly, and sometimes a woman's laugh was borne
to me on the breeze. Little by little these dwellers in the darkness, growing bolder, began to invade the lighted square, but
vanished instantly if the spiked helmet of a policeman loomed
anywhere within sight. Directly the constable had passed on
his round, the prowling shadows returned, and now, when
they ventured farther into the light, I could make out plainly
enough the ultimate scum that remained from the current of
busy human life. They were prostitutes of the lowest class,
those who have no homes to which they can take their customers, those who sell themselves for a trifle in any dark corner,
harried by the police, harried by hunger, and harried by their
own bullies, continually hunted and continually on the prowl
for prey. Like hungry hounds they nosed their way across the
lighted square towards anything masculine, towards any late
straggler who might be tempted to satiate his lust for a crown
or two. The money would buy a hot drink and a morsel of
food at a coffee-stall, and would help to keep the life in them
until its flicker should be extinguished in hospital or jail.

Here was the very scum, the last spume, of the sensual flood
of this Sunday crowd. With immeasurable horror I watched
these wolfish forms slinking out of the gloom. But even in

my horror there was an elemental pleasure, for in this tarnished mirror I could see vestiges of my own forgotten past. Here was a morass through which I had myself made my way in earlier years, and its phosphorescent marsh-lights were glowing anew in my senses. I recalled the days of adolescence, when my eye would rest on such figures as these with a mixture of alarm and eagerness; and I recalled the hour when I had first followed such a woman up a damp and creaky stair. Suddenly, as if illumined by a lightning-flash, I saw in sharp relief every detail of that forgotten hour: the insipid oleograph over the woman's bed, the mascot she wore round her neck; and I remembered the ardour of yore, tinged with loathing and also with the pride of budding manhood. With a clarity of vision that was new to me I realized why sympathy with these outcasts was stirring within me. The instinct that had roused me to my crime of the afternoon made me feel my kinship with these hungry marauders. The pocket-book with the stolen money in it seemed to burn my breast where I carried it. I felt that across there in the darkness were human creatures, breathing and speaking, who wanted something of others, perhaps of me—of me who only waited to give himself, who was filled with a yearning for his fellows. At length I understood what drives men to such women. Seldom, indeed, are they driven merely by the urge of the senses. The main motive is dread of solitude, of the terrible feeling of aloofness which severs us one from another, and which I for the first time had fully realized that day. I recalled when I had last experienced it, though more dully. It had been in England, in Manchester, one of those towns hard as iron, roaring under grey skies with the noise of an underground railway, but where the visitor is apt to experience the chill of utter loneliness. I had passed three weeks there, staying with relatives, spending my evenings in bar-rooms, music-halls, and like places, always in search of the warmth of human com-

panionship. One evening, I encountered such a woman, whose
gutter English I could scarcely understand. Almost unawares,
I found myself with her. I drank laughter from a strange
mouth. A body was close to me, warm and soft. The cold,
black town had vanished; the gloomy, thunderous abode of
solitude was no longer there. In their stead was a fellow-creature, an unknown woman, who waited for all comers, and
could bring deliverance. I breathed freely once more, I discerned the brightness of life even in this iron cage. How
precious to the lonely, to those who are prisoned within themselves, is this knowledge that after all they can find relief, that
there is something to which they can cling, though it be something worn and besmirched. This is what I had forgotten during that hour of unspeakable loneliness. I had forgotten that
out there in the darkness there were still those ready to give
the uttermost in exchange for a trifling coin—which is assuredly too small a return for that which they bestow with
their eternal readiness to give the great gift of human companionship.

The orchestrion of the roundabout by which I was standing
began once more. This was the last turn; the last time the circling light would flash out into the dark before the Sunday
passed into the drab weekdays. But there were very few riders;
the tired woman at the receipt of custom was counting up the
day's takings, and the odd man was standing by with a hook
ready to pull down the noisy shutters directly the round was
finished. I stood leaning against the post, looking across the
empty square—empty except for the prowling figures I have
described. Like me, they were expectant; and yet between
them and me was a barrier of estrangement I could not cross.
Now one of them must have noticed me, for she sidled past
me, and from beneath my lowered eyelids I took in every
detail of her appearance. She was a small woman, crippled by
rickets, hatless, wearing a tawdry outfit, and down-at-heel

dancing shoes, the whole probably bought at an old-clothes shop, and since then much worsened by the rough usage incidental to her trade. She stopped close at hand, and looked at me with a wheedling expression, and a smile of invitation that showed her bad teeth. I could hardly breathe. I feigned not to see her, and yet could not tear away my eyes. As if hypnotized, I realized that a human being was coveting me, was wooing me, that at length with a word or a gesture I could put an end to my hateful loneliness, to my tormenting sense of being an outcast. But I could not say the word or make the sign; I was as wooden as the post beside which I was standing. Nevertheless, while the tune of the roundabout dragged wearily to its close, even my impotence was suffused with pleasure because of the near presence of this woman who wooed me. I closed my eyes for a moment to enjoy the magnetic lure of invitation from a fellow-creature.

The merry-go-round stopped turning, and therewith the waltz wheezed out into silence. I opened my eyes to perceive that the woman had begun to move away. Obviously she was tired of soliciting a wooden image. I was alarmed, and turned cold of a sudden. Why had I let her go, the one human being that had made advances to me on this amazing night? Behind me the lights were switched off, and the steel rollers were clattering down into their sockets. The revels were over.

Suddenly—how shall I describe the ferment within me? Suddenly I was overwhelmed with the longing that this bedraggled and rickety little prostitute would turn her head that I might speak to her. Not that I was too proud to follow her (my pride had been stamped into the dust, and had been replaced by feelings quite new to me); I was too irresolute. I stood there yearning that this poor little wretch would turn once more and favour me with her look of invitation.

And, she turned. Almost mechanically, she glanced over her shoulder. The release of tension must have been plainly manifest in my eyes, for she stopped to watch me. Then, turning half round, she beckoned with a movement of the head, beckoned me towards the darker side of the square. At length the hideous spell that had held me rigid was lifted. I was again able to move, and I nodded assent.

The invisible treaty had been signed. In the faint light she walked across the square, looking back from time to time to see if I was following her. And I followed. I was drawn along in her wake. She slackened her pace in an alley between the booths, and there I overtook her.

For a few seconds she looked me up and down with suspicion. Something about me made her doubtful—my timidity, and the contrast between my appearance and the place in which she found me. But after this brief hesitation, she pointed along the alley, which towards the end was black as pitch, saying:

"Let's go down there. It's quite dark behind the circus."

I could not answer. The horrible commonness of this encounter struck me dumb. I should have liked to buy myself off with a crown or two and a word of excuse, but my will had no power over my actions. I felt as one feels on a toboggan, sweeping round a curve leading to a precipitous descent, when a sense of fear is pleasantly fused with the exhilaration of speed, so that, instead of trying to hold back, one surrenders to the delight of the plunge. Thus I could not hold back, and perhaps no longer even wished to do so. When she pressed up against me, I took her involuntarily by the arm. It was very thin—not a woman's arm, but that of an undersized child—and when I felt it through her flimsy sleeve, I was overwhelmed with pity for this poor little fragment of downtrodden humanity which the night had tossed into my path.

We crossed the dimly lighted roadway and entered a little wood where the tree-tops brooded over an evil-smelling darkness. I noticed that she half turned to look back as we entered, and that she did the same thing a few paces farther on. Even though I seemed paralysed as I slipped into this sordid adventure, my senses were keenly awake. With a lucidity which nothing could escape, I perceived that a shadow was following us along the edge of the path, and I could hear a stealthy footstep. The situation was clear to me in a flash. I was to be lured into an out-of-the-way spot, where the girl and her bully would have me at their mercy. With the marvellous insight which comes in moments betwixt life and death, I weighed up the chances. There was still time to get away. We were close to the main road, for I could hear the sound of a tram-car. A cry or a whistle would bring help. Thus I turned over in my mind all the possibilities of flight or rescue.

Strangely enough, however, the danger of my position inflamed my ardour instead of cooling it. Today I find it difficult to account for the absurdity of my behaviour. Even as I moved onward, I knew that I was needlessly putting my head into a noose; but the anticipation thrilled me. Something repulsive awaited me, perhaps deadly peril. Loathsome was the thought of the base issues in which I was becoming involved. But in my then mood of intoxication, even the menace of death exercised a sinister lure. What drove me forwards? Was I ashamed to show the white feather, or was I simply weak? I think, rather, that the ruling passion was a desire to taste the very dregs of life, a longing to stake my whole existence upon one cast. That was why, though fully aware of the risks I was running, I went on into the wood arm-in-arm with the wench who had no physical attractions, and who regarded me only as a pigeon for her and her companion to pluck. I must play out the play which had begun with my crime on the race-course, must play it to the end, even if the fall of the curtain should be death.

After a few more paces, she stopped and looked back yet again. Then she glanced at me expectantly, and said:

"Well, how much are you going to give me?"

Ah, yes, I had forgotten that aspect of the matter. But her question did not sober me. Far from it. I was so glad to be able to give riotously. Searching my pockets, I poured into her extended hand all the silver I had with me and two or three crumpled notes. Now there happened something so remarkable that it warms my heart when I think of it. Perhaps the girl was amazed at my largesse; perhaps, in my spendthrift gesture, there was something quite new to her. Anyhow, she stepped back a pace, and through the thick, evil-smelling obscurity I could feel that her eyes were fixed on mine with astonished inquiry. At length I could enjoy what I had been craving for all the evening. Someone was concerned with me as an individual; for the first time I had become really alive to someone in this new world. The fact that it was an outcast among outcasts, a derelict who hawked her poor worn body in the darkness and never even saw the buyer's face—that this was the creature who now looked questioningly at me and was trying to understand what sort of human being I might be—served only to intensify my strange exaltation. She drew closer to me, no longer in professional fulfilment of the task for which she had been paid, but animated, I believe, by an unconscious sense of gratitude, by a feminine desire for a caressive contact. Once more I took her by the emaciated arm; I felt the touch of her frail twisted body; and I pictured to myself what her life had been and was. I thought of the foul lodging in some slum, where from early morning till noon she had to snatch what sleep she could amid a noisy rabble of children. I pictured the souteneur who would knock her about; the drunken wretches who would be her usual clients; her life in the lock hospital; the workhouse infirmary in which she would end her days. Touched with infinite compassion, I stooped, and, to her amazement, kissed her.

At this moment there was a rustling behind me, and a

fallen branch snapped. There was a guffaw; then a man spoke.

"Caught you in the act! Thought I should!"

Before I saw them, I knew who they were. I had not forgotten that I was being spied upon, and all the time I had been expecting this intervention. A figure became visible to me, followed by a second; two savage-looking louts. There were more chuckles, and then:

"At your dirty tricks here in public. A gentleman, too, if you please! But we'll make him squeal."

I stood unmoved. My temples throbbed, but I was quite free from anxiety, and merely waited to see what would happen. Now I was indeed in the depths. At last would come the climax towards which I had been drifting.

The girl had started away from me, but not to join the men. She stood between us, and apparently the part assigned to her was not altogether congenial. The louts were obviously discomfited by my indifference. They looked at one another in perplexity, wondering why I did not betray any anxiety, or beg to be let off. At last one of them cried in a menacing tone:

"Aha! he's got nothing to say."

The other stepped up to me, and spoke imperatively:

"You must come with us to the station."

Still I made no answer. Then the man near me touched me on the shoulder, and gave me a little push.

"Step it," he said.

I did as I was bid, making no attempt to resist. Of course I was well aware that these fellows must be much more afraid of the police than I was, and that I could ransom myself for a few crowns; but I wanted to savour all the horrible humours of the situation. Slowly and mechanically I moved in the direction they indicated.

But this patient acceptance of the position, this willingness to return to the light, confounded my tormentors.

"Hist! Hist!"—they exchanged signals, and then began to speak with forced loudness.

"Better let the beggar go," said one of the two, a pock-marked shrimp of a man.

The other assumed a tone of stricter morality:

"No, no, that won't do. If he were a poor devil of our sort, without a morsel to line his belly with, they'd lock him up fast enough. We can't let our fine gentleman go scot free."

Through the words and the tone breathed an awkward invitation that I should begin bargaining. The criminal in me understood the criminal in them. I knew that they wanted to cow me, and that they themselves were cowed by my ready compliance. There was a dumb contest between myself and the two. How glorious it was! In imminent danger, in this filthy grove, dogged by a couple of bullies and a whore, I felt for the second time within twelve hours the magical charm of hazard—but this time the stake was higher, the stake was life itself. I surrendered wholly to the strange sport, awaiting the cast of the dice.

"Ah, there's a copper," said one of the men. "Our fine gentleman will have a jolly time of it. They won't give him less than a week in quod."

This was intended to alarm me, but I could hear that the speaker was far from sure of himself. I walked on confidently towards the lamp, where in actual fact I could see the gleaming spike of a policeman's helmet. Twenty paces, and we should reach him. The men behind me had nothing more to say. They were already lagging, and in a moment, I was sure, they would vanish into the darkness. They would slip back into their own world, embittered by their failure, and would perhaps wreak their anger upon the unhappy drab. The game was finished, and once more that day I was a winner. Just before reaching the bright circle of light cast on the ground by the street lamp, I turned, and for the first time looked

into the faces of the two bullies. Their eyes betrayed both vexation and shame. They stood there cowed, ready for instant
flight. Their power was at an end; the tables were turned, and
they had good cause to be afraid of me.

At this instant, however, I was overcome by a feeling of
immense sympathy, of brotherly sympathy for these two fellows. After all, what had they wanted of me, the two hungry
loafers? What had they wanted of me, the overfed parasite?
Two or three paltry crowns! They might have throttled me
there in the gloomy wood, might have robbed me and murdered me. Yet they had merely tried, in clumsy fashion, to
frighten me into handing over some of my loose silver. How
could I dare, I who had been a thief from sheer caprice, who
had become a criminal because I wanted a thrill, how could
I dare to torment the poor devils? In my turn, I was ashamed
because I had played with their fears. Now, at the last moment, when I had escaped from their toils, I would soothe
the disappointment which was so obvious in their hollow
eyes.

With an abrupt change of front, I went up to one of them,
and simulated anxiety as I said:

"Why do you want to hand me over to the police? What
do you expect to get out of it? Perhaps I shall be put in
prison for a few days, perhaps not. Will you be any the
better off? Why should you wish to do me harm?"

They stared at me in hopeless perplexity. Anything else
they might have been prepared for, a denunciation, a threat,
before which they would have cringed like dogs; but they
did not know what to make of my yielding at the eleventh
hour. At length one of them answered, not menacingly, but
as if in self-exculpation:

"Justice must take its course. We are only doing our duty."

Plainly this was a stock phrase, conned for such occasions.
But this time there was no spirit in it. Neither of them ven-

tured to look at me. They waited. I knew what they were waiting for. They wanted me to beg for mercy, and then to offer them money.

I can recall the whole scene perfectly, and can remember every detail of my own feelings. I know, therefore, that malice prompted me to keep them on tenterhooks, in order that I might enjoy their discomfiture the more. But I constrained my will, for I knew that it behoved me to set their anxieties at rest. I began, therefore, to play a little comedy of terror, imploring them not to denounce me. I saw how embarrassed were these inexperienced blackmailers, and I felt that I must break down the barrier of silence between us.

At length I came to the words in expectation of which their mouths had been watering.

"I will give you . . . I will give you a hundred crowns."

All three of them were startled, and looked at one another in amazement. They had never expected such a sum at this stage, when they had given the game up for lost. But after a while the pock-marked man with the shifty eyes braced his courage a little. He made two unsuccessful attempts to break the spell. At last, and shamefacedly, he managed to get out the words:

"Make it two hundred, Guv'nor."

"Drop it, can't you!" the girl suddenly broke in. "You can be jolly glad if he gives you anything at all. He hardly touched me. It's really a bit too thick."

She was furious, and my heart sang within me. Someone sympathized with me, interceded for me. Kindness rose out of the depths; there was an obscure craving for justice in this blackmailer's hussy. It was like a cordial to me. I could not play with them any longer, could not torment them in their fear and their shame.

"All right," I said, "two hundred crowns."

They made no answer. I took out my note-case. I opened it

slowly and ostentatiously. It would have been easy for any one of them to snatch it and be off. But they looked timidly away. Between them and me there was a secret bond; no longer a struggle for mastery, but an understanding, mutual confidence, a human relationship. I detached two notes from the stolen bundle, and handed them to the nearest of the bullies.

"Thank you, Sir," he said in spite of himself, and turned to go.

It was plain that he felt how absurd it was to thank me for a blackmailer's gains. He was ashamed of himself for doing so, and I was sorry for him in his shame. I did not want him to feel shame before me, for I was a man of his own kidney; I was a thief just as much as he; I, too, was a coward and a weakling. His humiliation distressed me, and I wanted to restore his self-respect. I refused, therefore, to accept his thanks.

"It is my place to thank you," I replied, marvelling at my tone of genuine conviction. "If you had given me in charge I should have been ruined. I should have had to blow my brains out, and you would not have been any the richer. This is the best way out of the difficulty. Well, I shall take that turning to the right, and no doubt you'll be going in the opposite direction. Good night!"

There was a moment's hesitation. Then one of the men said good-night, then the other, and last of all the girl, who had kept back in the shadows. These parting words were charged with a genuine sentiment of goodwill. Their voices showed me that they had in some sort taken a fancy to me, and that they would never forget the episode. It would recur to their minds on a day to come in penitentiary or hospital. Something had gone from me into them, and would live on in them; I had given them something. The joy of this giving was the most poignant feeling I had ever experienced.

I walked on alone towards the gate leading out of the Prater. My sense of oppression had been wholly lifted. The trees whispered to me, and I loved them. The stars shone down on me, and I rejoiced in their luminous greeting. Voices raised in song were audible in the distance; they were singing for me. Everything was mine, now that I had broken the shell in which I had been confined. The joy of giving, the joy of prodigality, united me with the world-all. "How easy," I thought, "to give joy and win joy! We need merely raise the sluices, and then from man to man the living current flows, thundering from the heights into the depths and foaming from the depths upward into the infinite."

When I reached the exit from the Prater, I caught sight of an old woman sitting near the cab-stand—a hawker, wearily bent over her petty wares. She had some dusty cakes on her stall, and a little fruit. No doubt she had been there since morning to earn a few pence. "Why should you not enjoy yourself as well as I?" I thought, so I chose a cake and handed her a note. She started to fumble for the change, but I waved it away. She trembled with delight and astonishment, and began to pour out expressions of gratitude. Disregarding these, I went up to the horse which stood drooping between the shafts of her itinerant stall and offered him the cake. He nuzzled me in friendly fashion, as if he too would like to say thank you. Thereupon I was filled with the longing to dispense more pleasure, to learn more fully how easy it is to kill cares and diffuse cheerfulness with the aid of a few silver coins or some printed pieces of coloured paper. Why were there no beggars about? Where were the children who would like to have the air-balloons which that morose, white-haired old fellow was limping home with? He had a huge bundle of them tied to strings, and had obviously had a poor day's custom. I accosted him:

"Give me those balloons."

"Penny each," he said dubiously, for he could not believe that a well-dressed idler would want to buy his coloured air-balloons at midnight.

"I'll take the lot," I said, and gave him a ten-crown note.

He positively staggered in his amazement, and then held out the cord to which the whole bundle was fastened. I felt the pull of it on my fingers. The balloons were longing for freedom, longing to fly skyward. Why should they not do what they wanted? I loosed the cord, and they rose like great tinted moons. People ran up laughing from all directions; pairs of lovers turned up out of the darkness; the cabmen cracked their whips, and called to one another as they pointed to the air-balloons sailing over the tree-tops and the roofs. Everyone made merry over my prank.

Why had I never known how easy it is and how enjoyable to give others pleasure? Once more the notes in my wallet began to burn me, they plucked at my fingers like the cord that had held the balloons; they, too, wanted to fly away into the unknown. I took them all out, not only the ones I had stolen from Lajos, but all the others I had with me, for I no longer recognized any difference between them, no longer felt that some of them were stained with crime. There they were, ready for anyone who wanted them. I went across to a street-sweeper who was listlessly cleaning up the deserted street. He fancied I was going to ask him the way, and looked at me surlily. Laughing, I offered him a twenty-crown note. He stared uncomprehendingly, but at length took the note, and waited to know what I wanted of him.

"Buy whatever you like with it," I said, and went on my way.

I peered in all directions, looking for someone who might ask a gift of me. Since no one did so, I had to make the offers. A prostitute accosted me, and I gave her a note. I handed two to a lamplighter. One I threw in at the area window of a bakery. Thus I made my progress, leaving a trail of surprise, gratitude, and delight.

At last I began to throw the notes here, there, and everywhere—in the street, on the steps of a church. I smiled to think how the old apple-woman who had a stall there would find the hundred crowns in the morning and would praise God for the windfall. Some poor student, or maidservant, or workman would pick up the notes with the same feeling of wonder and delight that animated me while scattering them abroad.

When I had got rid of the last of them, I felt incredibly lighthearted, almost as if I could fly, and I enjoyed a sense of freedom such as I had never before known. Towards the street, the sky, the houses, I had a new feeling of kinship. Never, up till now, even in the most ardent moments of my existence, had I felt the reality of all these things so strongly —that they were alive and I was alive, and that the life in them and in me was the same life, the great and mighty life that can never be overfilled with happiness—the life that only one who loves and one who gives can understand.

I had one last moment of uneasiness. It was when I had turned the latchkey in my door and I glimpsed the dark entry to my own rooms. Suddenly there came over me a rush of anxiety lest this should be a re-entry into my earlier life, now that I was going back into the familiar dwelling, was about to get into the familiar bed, to resume associations with all the things from which, that night, I had been able to break away. The one thing needful was that I should not again become the man I had been; that I should no longer be the gentleman of yesterday, the slave of good form, who was unfeeling, and lived apart from the world. Better to plunge into the abysses of crime and horror, so long as I could be truly alive! I was tired out, and yet I dreaded sleep, for I was afraid that during sleep the fervour, the sense of new life,

would vanish. I dreaded lest the whole experience should
prove as fugitive as a dream.

But I woke next morning in a cheerful mood, to find that
the current of new feeling was still vigorous. Four months
have passed since then, and there has been no return of the
old stagnation. The amazing elation of that day, when I left
all the traditional paths of my world to launch forth into the
unknown, plunging into the abysses of life, giddy with speed,
and intoxicated with delight—this climax of ardour is, indeed,
over. Yet in all my hours since then I have never ceased to feel
renewed pleasure in life. I know that I have been reborn,
with other senses, responsive to other stimuli, and animated
with a clearer consciousness. I cannot venture to judge whether
I am a better man, but I know that I am a happier one. Life
had grown cold and unmeaning; but now it has acquired a
meaning, one for which I can find no other name than the
very word "Life." I have thrown off artificial restraints, for
the rules and conventions of the society in which I was brought
up have ceased to bind me. I am no longer ashamed either
before others or before myself. Such words as honour, crime,
and vice have grown hollow-sounding, and I find it distaste-
ful to use them. My vital impetus comes from the power
which I first recognized on that wonderful night. I do not
know whither it is driving me: perchance towards a new
abyss, towards what others call vice or crime; perchance towards something sublime. I neither know nor care to know.
For I believe that he only is truly alive who does not seek
to probe the mystery of the future.

Of one thing I am sure, that I have never loved life more
keenly; and I know that whoever is indifferent to any of the
forms and modes of life commits a crime (the only crime there
is!). Since I have begun to understand myself, I understand enormously better all that goes on around me. The
covetous glances of someone gazing in at a shop window can

move me profoundly; the gambols of a dog can fill me with
enthusiasm. I am interested in everything; nothing is indifferent to me. In the newspaper, which I used barely to glance
at, I now read a hundred items with zest. Books which used
to bore me now make a strong appeal. The strangest thing is
that I can talk to my fellow human beings about other matters than those which form the substance of what, in good society, is termed "conversation." My manservant, who has been
with me for seven years, interests me, and I often have a
talk with him. The porter of the flats, whom I used to pass
unheeding as if he had been one of the door-posts, told me
the other day about the death of his little girl, and the recital
moved me more than I have ever been moved by one of
Shakespeare's tragedies. It would seem, too, though in outward semblance I still live the old life of respectable boredom, that the change in me must be obvious to others. People
greet me far more cordially than of old; three times last week
a strange dog came and fawned on me in the street. My
friends look at me with affectionate pleasure, as one looks at
a person who is convalescent from illness, and tell me that I
have grown younger.

Have I grown younger? All I know is that I have only just
begun to live. Oh, I know, too, of the everyday illusion. I
know how apt people are to think that all their past has been
error and preparation. Doubtless it is arrogant to take a cold
pen into my warm, living hand, and to write upon the dry
paper that at length I am really alive. But even if it be an
illusion, it is the first illusion that has made me happy, the
first that has warmed my blood and unlocked my senses. If I
sketch here the miracle of my awakening, I do it for myself
alone, though I know it all better than words can describe. I
have not spoken of the matter to any of my friends: they
never knew how dead I had become; they will never guess
how my life has blossomed afresh. Nor am I perturbed by

the thought that death's hand may suddenly be laid upon this living life of mine, and that these lines may be read by other eyes. Those who have never known the magic of such an hour as I have described, will understand just as little as I could have understood six months ago how the fugitive and almost inconsequent happenings of one afternoon and evening could so have touched my life to flame. The thought of such a reader does not shame me, for he will not understand what I have written. But one who understands will not judge, and will have no pride. Before him I shall not be ashamed. Whoever has found himself can never again lose anything in this world. He who has grasped the human in himself understands all mankind.

Fear

Irene came down the stairs leading from her lover's flat.
Once again, as so many times before, she was overwhelmed by an unwarrantable fear. Her eyes flickered, her
knees felt like putty, and she had to lean heavily upon the
banister to save herself from falling. How well she knew the
feeling! Almost on every occasion she had ventured to visit
her lover, these fits of unreasonable fear had submerged her
on leaving. Yet the way thither was far more thickly strewn
with dangers. It was ridiculous of her to feel like this after the
tryst. If she had felt nervous beforehand, that would have been
understandable, for she came to the rendezvous in a taxi
which she left waiting at the corner of the street while she
scuttled along furtively to her beloved's dwelling and scurried up to his flat. What anxiety she experienced then was
soon forgotten in the imperishable hours spent with her dear.
But when arrived the moment for going home—then—oh,
then—a strange horror, a sense of guilt, a kind of madness

invaded her, and the street seemed to cock its eye at her and ask why she was so troubled. The last few minutes spent in his company were poisoned with the premonition of this uneasiness. As she took her leave, quivering with impatience to be gone, she could scarcely heed his parting words and would fend off his farewell endearments, eager to get away and be back again in the comfortable life of middle-class respectability she was used to. He would comfort her and speak enheartening phrases which in her excitement she failed to hear for suspense lest someone should meet her as she rejoined the cab. Was anybody coming upstairs or going down? She listened from behind the shelter of her lover's door. But fear lay in ambush on the next landing, ready to pounce upon her, and seized her so roughly that by the time she reached the hall she was panting for breath.

Today, she stood for a while drinking in the cooler air rising from below in the darkened staircase. A door banged. Instinctively, she drew her hat down on to her forehead and lowered her veil while she made for the exit. Like a diver preparing for the plunge, she tucked in her chin and dashed towards the half-open entry. As she was crossing the threshold, she collided with another female, uttered a crestfallen, "Beg your pardon," and tried to slink by. But the female spread out two long arms and barred Irene's passage. A harsh voice issued from the creature, and mocking, despiteful words:

"So I've caught you at last, my fine lady. Just what I expected! Not satisfied with your husband, your wealth, and all the rest of it, but must come stealing a poor girl's lover and . . ."

"You are mistaken," muttered Irene, endeavouring to get by. Whereupon the female thrust her bulky form into the doorway, thus blocking it as a cork blocks a bottle-neck, and continued haranguing.

"No, no," she cried shrilly, "I'm not mistaken. I know you.

I know you have just this minute come from Edward's rooms.
He's my very own and particular friend, see? Now I've caught
you, now I know why he can spare so little time for me lately.
It's you, you mean baggage . . ."

"For heaven's sake," interrupted Irene in a toneless voice,
"don't scream like that."

She stepped back into the hall, while the female stared at
her with scornful eyes. Irene's tell-tale fear, her utter helpless-
ness, seemed to do her aggressor good, for the woman looked
her victim up and down with a taunting and satisfied smile
wrinkling the corners of her mouth. Modifying her voice, she
reflected aloud:

"That's what she looks like, this noble dame, this married
lady, who comes filching other people's men. Veiled, of course;
veiled so she can't be recognized, and can go on playing the
respectable lady in high society. . . ."

"What do you want?" asked Irene. "I have not the pleasure of your acquaintance, and I really must be going. . . ."

"Going? Naturally you must be going—back to your worthy
spouse, eh? Back to a cosy room, hot bath, and be dressed
by your maid so as to be ready to receive your high and
mighty guests. But you don't care tuppence if a person like
me dies of hunger . . . you'll steal the last, the very last treasure I own. . . ."

Irene dug her hand into her bag and pulled out nearly all
the notes it contained. Thrusting the wad into the woman's
hand, she said huskily:

"There, there . . . take these . . . and now let me pass. I
shall never come here again . . . I promise. . . ."

The female accepted the money, twisting her face into a
malignant grin.

"Dirty bitch," was all she said as she made way for Irene.

The latter wilted under the words, and precipitated herself down the street much as a suicide might hurl herself

from a tower. Faces like tattered masks rushed by her while she made all speed to rejoin the taxi waiting round the corner. Her body felt leaden. She crumpled up on the springy seat, her mind a blank, her lips rigid. The driver, surprised at not receiving any orders, at length turned his head and asked: "Where to, Ma'am?" Irene looked blankly at him for a moment. Then, making a supreme effort, she managed to say:

"To the station."

Suddenly the thought of that female pursuing her flashed through her mind, and she added:

"Quick! Quick! Drive as quickly as you can."

During the drive she came to realize how profoundly the meeting had agitated her. Her hands were stiff and cold; they looked like dead things hanging from her wrists; then a shiver ran down her back, and she shook all over. There was a choking sensation in her throat, a bitter taste in her mouth, clammy perspiration on her brow; she felt sickened. She wanted to scream or to strike out with her fists in order to rid herself of the horrible memory. But it stuck like a fish-hook in her brain. Oh, that dreadful face, distorted and jeering, the commonness, the vulgarity of it, the onion-laden breath so frequent among working-class women, that shapeless mouth which had spoken the coarse words, and the reddened hands raised threateningly. . . . Nauseated and miserable, she jolted up and down while the taximan pressed the accelerator. She was about to ask him to drive a trifle slower when she remembered having given most of her cash to the blackmailer. Had she enough wherewith to pay? Yes, thank goodness! But her available money would not suffice to take her so far as the station. She called to the driver to pull up, and astonished him by springing out and dismissing him. She would have to walk home. The neighbourhood where the man had deposited her was unknown to her, and the shops and passers-by with their rough speech distressed her unspeakably. Her knees

still trembled with her recent panic, so that she found it difficult to walk. Still, she had to get home somehow. Summoning
her flagging energies to the rescue, she crept along from street
to street, walking slowly and heavily as if she were wading
through snow. At last she reached her house, and was about
to rush up the steps when she remembered that undue haste
would arouse suspicion.

In the hall, the maid relieved her of her coat. From upstairs
came the sound of her boy's voice at play with his little sister.
The things that surrounded her were her own, they conveyed
a sense of security, and gave her back the mask of self-
possession she so urgently needed. She smoothed the troubled
look from brow and eyes with the tips of her fingers, assumed
an innocent air, and went into the dining-room where the
table was set for the evening meal. Here she found her husband reading his paper.

"You are late, my darling, very late," he said with a note of
tender reproach in his voice. Then he got up and kissed her
affectionately on the cheek.

This produced in her a renewed feeling of guilt, which she
found it difficult to hide. They took their places, and the
man, from behind his paper, asked casually:

"What kept you so long?"

"I . . . I was having a chat . . . with Emily . . . and she
had some shopping to do . . . so I went with her."

What an ass not to have prepared a sensible story! Irene
was furious with herself for telling so clumsy a lie. Usually she
had concocted a plausible tale beforehand; but today fear had
made her forget. . . . Suppose he . . .

"What's up, Irene, my dear?" her husband inquired. "You
seem quite flurried; and why are you dining in your hat?"

Her hand darted up to the incriminating headgear. Caught
again, she thought, as she went to her room to make herself
more presentable. How restless her eyes looked in the mirror.

She must get hold of yourself. A few minutes sufficed, and then she rejoined her husband.

The maid served them their meal, and thenceforward the evening ran its usual course. Perhaps the couple were a little more chary of words, and a little less companionable than ordinary; when they did exchange a few remarks, these came hesitatingly. Irene's thoughts went wool-gathering, and if she managed to think consecutively at all she invariably retraced her way to that dreadful encounter. Then she would raise her eyes and look around at the familiar objects with which her home was furnished. Such contemplation brought solace to mind and heart. The things were associated with pleasant memories, she felt tender and loving towards them, and peace returned to her soul. The clock broke the silence with its leisurely ticking, and this rhythmical sound acted like a sedative to her jangled nerves, calming her, and bringing her fevered pulse-beats back to the normal.

Next morning, after her husband had gone to his office and the children had been sent for a walk, Irene found a moment of leisure, the first since that disastrous meeting. She rallied, and was at length able to throw off the incubus of fear which had weighed so heavily upon her. She recalled that her veil was a specially thick one, and that the woman could not possibly have discerned any features behind its opacity. Easy, therefore, to take the necessary precautions. Never again would she visit her lover in his own quarters. Thus might she be safeguarded from a repetition of yesterday's adventure. As for that "female," it was unlikely she had followed the taxi, or dogged Irene's wanderings as far as the house-door. She had nothing to fear for the nonce. But even suppose the creature had found some means of discovering Irene's identity and address, there remained other methods of defence. Now that

Irene was no longer under the immediate pressure of fear, she
could think her course of action out clearly. Nothing easier
than flatly to give the lie to every accusation, and if matters
came to the worst she would denounce the woman as a blackmailer. It must be remembered that Irene was the wife of one
of the ablest of barristers, and through long years of associa-
tion had come to know a few points of the law. From what
she had picked up during her husband's talks with his colleagues at the bar, she had learned that any form of blackmail was dealt with stringently.

The first thing to do was to write the briefest note possible
to her lover saying that she would be unable to see him for
several days. Her pride was mortified by the discovery that
her predecessor in Karl Brustmann's affections was of such
common clay. Now, as she wrote, she deliberately chose words
which would convey the impression—wounding to a sensitive heart—that she had entered into the relationship cold-
bloodedly and as the outcome of a whim. Such was the fact!

She had met the young man, a pianist by profession, at an
evening party; and, hardly realizing what was happening, had
become his mistress. There had been nothing specially attractive about him, she had felt no passion for him, and there
existed no particular spiritual sympathy between the pair to
account for the liaison. Irene had given herself to him without any sensuous desire on her part, but, rather, because she
was too indolent to oppose his will. Besides, she had been
vaguely curious to discover what the youth's love-making
would be like. Her marriage was a happy one, and she did
not require a lover to gratify her intellectual, moral, or bodily
needs. These things her husband fulfilled amply. In addition
she had two charming children, and led a comfortable and
protected life. But an existence which is rendered too easy
is often as hard to bear contentedly as one that is positively

unhappy. Satiety is as difficult to stomach as hunger, and it was precisely this utter security which rendered Irene eager for an adventure.

When, therefore, the young pianist made it obvious that he coveted her as a woman and wooed her in that spirit, this was a pleasant and exciting relief to the banal flattery and the respectful attitude of her habitual male entourage. She had not been so strongly moved since she was a girl. The most alluring attribute the musician possessed was a veil of melancholy which overcast his countenance as he sat playing the piano amid a circle of well-fed and self-satisfied society men and women. In despite of her better inspiration, Irene felt compelled to step beyond the frontiers of her customary feelings and to study this drooping aspect more closely. Something vehement and unusual in the words she chose to express her appreciation of the artist's performance caused him to look up from the keyboard and gaze at the speaker. Already in that first glance Irene felt a grip at her heart. She was alarmed, and yet she revelled in her fear. They exchanged a few words, meaningless in themselves, but charged with inner significance for the two human beings who spoke. Her interest and curiosity were so strongly aroused that she looked forward to a further meeting when Brustmann gave his next recital. Thereafter, they saw one another frequently, and certainly not by chance. Her vanity was deliciously tickled when, a few weeks later, he proposed that she should be the first to hear a composition he had recently been at work on. A genuine, an acknowledged master and artist was asking her to act as judge of his creation. This seemed almost too good to be true. She agreed to meet him at his rooms. Maybe on either side they had arranged the tryst with the best intentions, but it nevertheless ended in kisses and in her yielding to his desire. On coming to her senses, Irene had been amazed at such a sudden and unforeseen denouement. She had never meant to break her marriage vows. She felt guilty, and yet she was proud of having consciously—as she believed—overstepped the code of smug respectability which encompassed her. Her wickedness appalled her; nevertheless she came to experience a certain pride in her exploit. But even this strange excitement was ephemeral. Instinctively she felt antagonistic to her lover, and especially to what was novel in him, to the attribute which had enthralled her at the outset. He was a man who put a formidable amount of passion into his pianoforte playing, and in his love-life he was no less impulsive. This excessive and masterful procedure disquieted her, and she involuntarily compared such unrestraint with the reverential approaches of her husband, who was shy and considerate even after a good many years of married life.

Still, since she had once been unfaithful to her legal spouse, it was easier and easier to continue seeking her lover's ardours. These encounters did not add to her happiness, nor was she in any way disillusioned. She expected no better, being activated merely by a sense of duty towards her paramour, and by a certain lassitude which inhibited her from changing what soon became a habit. After a month or so of intimacy, the young man fitted neatly into the general pattern of her existence like part of a mosaic—just as did the weekly visit to her parents-in-law, or any other social obligation. She relinquished nothing of her orderly life to this new love of hers; it became a mere addition to the familiar routine. What pleasure Karl added to her experiences was no more than might have been provided by a third child or by an automobile. Very soon the adventure was no more exhilarating to her than the permitted pleasures of connubial bliss.

At the first hint of danger, Irene recognized the scant value of such a relationship. Fate had, so far, dealt kindly with her. From earliest childhood she had been cosseted and spoiled by her parents, whose circumstances were so easy that the girl

could have anything her heart desired. Thus mollycoddled, she
had become soft, and the faintest zephyr heralding a possible
storm ruffled the fair pool of her equanimity. She felt no inclination to sacrifice a jot of her personal comfort to a
lover. . . .

That same afternoon she got an answer from young Karl.
It was an excited and overwrought epistle, wherein he pleaded
and reproached. This disturbed her again, and she was no
longer quite so sure that she would put an end to the liaison,
since the man's plain-spoken passion flattered her vanity and
she was fascinated by his ecstatic despair. Brustmann besought
her to grant him at least one last interview so that he might
learn wherein he had been remiss, if he had unwittingly of-
fended her. This suggested a fresh amusement to Irene. She
might keep him dangling, uncertain as to her feelings, and
thus render herself more precious to him. With such a notion
in mind, she gave him an appointment at a tea-room where, as
a girl, she had once met a certain actor she had had a fleeting
pash for. How paltry that youthful enthusiasm appeared to
her in retrospect, after she had been married for several years
and had acquired a lover in addition to her legitimate spouse.
"Strange," she mused, "if romance is once more to enter my
life." Irene felt almost happy, now that she had stumbled
upon "that creature," for it was ages since she had experienced
anything like so strong an emotion. Her all-too-placid nerves
were agreeably stimulated, and she felt decidedly refreshed.

She was careful to put on a dark gown for the present meeting, and a different hat, in order that, should occasion demand, the "creature" might be puzzled as to her identity.
Further, Irene took up a veil wherewith to mask her features,
but as she was about to arrange it a momentary defiance led
her to thrust it back into the drawer. Why should she, a re-

spectable and respected woman, not venture forth openly into the streets? At bottom she had nothing to fear.

And yet fear clutched at her heart as she stepped forth from the safety of her home. She shivered, like a swimmer who has tested the water with a toe and found it exceeding chill. This passed, and was followed by a glow. The adventure was a joyful one after all, and her step was elastic, her bearing gallant. Irene's only regret was that the tea-room was so near to her dwelling. Once under way, she could have walked far to the accompaniment of the magnetic cadence of her own footfalls. Still, there was no time to linger; the hour for the meeting had struck, and she knew that her lover would be awaiting her. He was seated in a retired corner, restlessly eyeing the door, and sprang to his feet the moment she entered. His excitement was pleasurable to Irene, and at the same time a trifle irritating, for she had to warn him to moderate his voice and the tumult of words which gushed from his lips. Without telling him in plain terms the reasons for her decision to cease seeing him, she hinted at this, that, and the other cause, and only succeeded in making him more ardent than ever. She remained adamant so far as young Karl's wishes were concerned, not even holding out any hope, for she recognized that her sudden and apparently groundless refusal merely served to enhance the artist's desire. She took leave of him after half an hour of fevered argument, refused him a chance of showing the slightest tenderness, vouchsafed no promise as to future meetings, and betook herself home with a glow at her heart she had not enjoyed since her girlhood. It seemed as though a tiny flame glimmered deep down in her being, and that it needed but a puff to convert it into an all-consuming fire. She treasured every appreciative look that was cast in her direction as she marched homeward; never before had she been aware of men's admiration to the

same extent. So moved was she, that at last she felt impelled
to stop in front of a flower-shop and study her face in the
mirror. There she contemplated with immense satisfaction the
reflection of her own beauty, framed in a garland of red roses
and dew-sprayed violets. Not since girlhood days had she felt
so light-hearted, so sensuously happy; not in the early months
of her marriage, not even when in the arms of her lover, had
her body quivered with such dancing delight, such buoyancy,
such irrepressible joyance. It was insufferable, she thought, to
have to waste this sweet intoxication, and revert to a humdrum existence. Thereupon she discovered that she was tired,
and trailed home as best she might. At the front door she stood
still for a moment trying to recapture the aroma of her late
adventure. She threw back her shoulders and breathed deeply.

A tug at her sleeve brought her to earth with a rush. Irene
turned on her heel.

"What . . . what on earth do you want, bothering me again
like this?" she asked petulantly, struck with a sudden chill
as she recognized the hateful figure of her persecutor.

Hardly had she uttered the words when she bit her lip in
dismay. She had betrayed herself irremediably. Had she not
determined to cut the creature if any further molestation occurred? Now it was too late. She had completely given herself away, and the female could dun to all eternity.

"I've been waiting for you close on an hour, Frau Wagner. . . ."

So the blackmailer had discovered Irene's name and address!
But how? All was lost!

"Yes, close on an hour, Frau Wagner," repeated the woman
with a menace and a reproach in her voice.

"What do you want?"

"You know very well, Frau Wagner. You know as well as
I do why I've come."

"But I've not seen him since . . . I told you I wasn't going to see him again . . . never . . ."

"No use telling a pack of lies. I followed you to the tea-room. You see, I'm out of work, and had nothing better to do. Got the chuck because, so the boss said, business was bad. It's nice to have a bit of time to spare for a walk, just as if I was a fine lady."

She spoke with such icy malice that Irene's heart froze. The woman's brazen vulgarity left her defenceless and an easy prey. Again that sense of unutterable fear submerged her. Suppose the creature spoke loud enough for the servants to hear? Suppose Herr Wagner should pass by? Hastily pulling out her purse—a pretty bauble made of silver links—she emptied the contents into the coarse hand. But the hand, instead of closing over the money, remained outstretched like the claw of a rapacious bird.

"Best give me the purse as well so's I don't lose the cash," came from the mocking mouth, accompanied by a gust of hoarse laughter.

Irene stared her tormentress squarely in the face. Physically and mentally she felt nauseated. Oh, to be rid of the past as quickly as possible! Turning aside so as not to have to look again into those jeering eyes, Irene thrust the costly purse into the woman's reddened paw, slammed the door, and fled up the stairs.

Herr Wagner had not come home yet. She had time for a rest, and flung herself on to her bed. There she lay motionless, as if felled by an axe. But directly she heard her husband's voice in the hall, she sprang up, and went automatically into the dining-room. All the life had been taken out of her.

Dame Care henceforward became an inmate of Irene's home; she sat day after day by Irene's side, and followed the

young woman from room to room. As one empty hour succeeded another, Irene had more than enough time to recapitulate the details of each meeting. How could "that person" have
discovered her name and address? Certain it was that, since
the first attempts at blackmail had proved so successful, others
would follow. For years upon years this burden of misery
would weigh upon her shoulders. She saw no end to it. Besides, though she had a fortune in her own right and her
husband was well endowed with this world's goods, how
would she be able to raise the large sum necessary to be quit
of the blackmailer unless she took Herr Wagner into her
confidence? Again—so much she had learned from the law-
suits her husband had been connected with—such persons,
even when paid what they claimed, were not to be trusted to
make no further attempts to procure additional hush-money.
You might possibly find peace for a month or so, but then
the wretched business would begin anew. And if you made
up your mind to denounce the ill-omened bird of prey, shame
and discredit would descend upon yourself and your whole
household. Thus the satisfaction of bringing the blackmailer
to book would be trifling compared with the smashing up of
home and self.

What was going to happen? Irene cogitated this question
from morning till night. She fancied that one day a letter
would come addressed to her husband, that after reading it his
brows would pucker and his face turn ashen, that he might
seize her by the arm, question her. . . . Yes, but what then?
What would he do? Her imagination refused to work any
longer. Fear, a horrible and irrational fear, overmastered her.
She simply did not know, and her every conjecture exploded
like a pricked bubble. Her meditations brought her to a realization of how very slight was her knowledge of her husband's character, of how little she could guess the way in
which he would react to circumstances. Her parents and his

had arranged the marriage, and she had entered into the union without putting up the slightest opposition. After eight years of matrimony, she found no reason to regret the choice. They had been leisurely, happy years; she had given birth to two children, had created a comfortable home, and had enjoyed innumerable hours of physical companionship with her husband. Yet now that she tried to divine what his attitude might be to certain issues, she found herself at a loss. For the first time she began to analyse her husband's disposition, attempted to fathom the main aspects of his character, to recall little incidents which might elucidate him. The deeper she delved, the more did fear oppress her. . . .

He sat reading, his face brightly illuminated by the electric lamp. It seemed to her that she was looking at a stranger. His massive and noble brow reflected the energy of his mental activity; his mouth was perhaps too firm, and bespoke an excess of severity and a lack of the power to yield. Manly features, full of strength, in which she was surprised to discover beauty. Irene would have liked to look into his eyes, but they were cast downward upon the book he was reading. She felt sure they would have revealed more than the whole of the rest of his person. They must hide the real secret of his character. She gazed, wonderingly, at his profile. Would he dismiss her backsliding with a caution? Or would he condemn her? . . . The man was a stranger; the clean-cut profile alarmed her; and yet it was a beautiful profile, as she recognized for the first time in all these years. . . . It was a pleasure merely to look at him, a pleasure which filled her with pride. . . . He suddenly lifted his eyes, and Irene shrank back into the dark so that the ardent question in her own gaze might not betray her.

For three days she did not leave the house. The servants began to wonder at this sudden change in her habits. Her chil-

dren, too, and especially the boy, noticed that Mummy never
went out now, and asked her why. The governess talked the
thing over with anyone who was willing to listen. Irene did
her best to appear natural and cheerful, as if nothing unusual
was taking place. She even tried to occupy herself in house-
wifely tasks, but merely succeeded in hindering, and in arousing suspicion. Instead of staying quietly in one room reading
or sewing, fear made her restless, so that she had to keep perpetually on the go. She started and flushed every time the telephone burred or the front-door bell sounded. Her quiet existence was thus disrupted; and she contemplated the future
with anguish, seeing no way out of her wretchedness. The
three days of confinement to the house dragged so wearily that
they seemed immensely longer than the eight years of her
married life.

Then, on the third evening, she remembered that a long-
standing engagement fell due. She recalled the fact too late
to be able, civilly, to put the thing off. Besides, if she were
not to founder completely, she must make an effort to break
down the wall of dread that was rising around her. Human
companionships, a few hours' respite from brooding, from this
suicidal solitude of fear—these she felt were essential to her
sanity. Furthermore, the best concealment was surely among
friends, in another house than her own.

A pang griped her heart as she crossed the threshold to
go into the street. Was the person spying out the land? She
linked her hand in her husband's arm, closed her eyes, stepped
briskly over the pavement, and sank back in the waiting automobile. As the car glided swiftly along, she was able at length
to throw off her terrors, and on arrival at her friend's house
she began to feel safe, protected from harm. For a couple of
hours she could be her natural self, just the care-free, happy
young woman of yore, but with the superimposed delight of
a prisoner released from jail. No persecution could reach her

here, hatred would not pursue her within these walls; she was among people who loved her, who respected her, people who were well dressed and bejewelled, men and women who dwelt for ever in the rosy atmosphere of enjoyment, who danced light-heartedly through life and who carried Irene, too, along on the current of gaiety and laughter. She was more than content, for, as she made her entry leaning on her husband's arm, she knew, from the looks of admiration cast upon her by her fellow-guests, that she was beautiful. Her consciousness of this fresh loveliness of hers put an added glow to her charms.

Strains of music came from a neighbouring room, and the sound penetrated deep beneath her burning flesh. People were beginning to dance; and, almost before she was aware, Irene found herself swept into the mass of whirling couples. Every atom of heaviness disappeared from her limbs, her body was nothing but rhythm and ardent movement. When the band stopped, the silence weighed upon her spirits; but no sooner had it struck up afresh, than the cooling waters of oblivion enveloped her once more, and the ache at her heart was cured as her partner carried her forward among the swaying multitude. She had never been more than a mediocre dancer, too careful as to her steps, too circumspect, too restrained; but in the joyful flood of her newly won freedom, all shackles were broken, and she danced as though inspired. Her blood responded to the arm which encircled her, to the hands which touched her, to the words whispered in her ear, to the gay laughter, to the music. Her body was so lusty with joy that her gown actually felt too tight, and she would gladly have thrown aside every shred of vesture in order, naked as God made her, to relish the full tide of her present intoxication.

"Irene, what's up, my dear?"

She swung round, her eyes beaming, her gait slightly unsteady, to encounter the reproving eye of her husband. Had she let herself go too insanely? Had she betrayed herself?

"I don't understand . . . Fritz," she stammered, once more a prey to fear.

His steely glance bored into her, so that she could have cried aloud in her pain.

"You are not yourself," he muttered, after a long pause.

There was a note of amazement in his voice, but she had not the courage to ask what he meant to imply. He turned away without another word, and a shudder passed over her as she contemplated those massive shoulders, and the neck above. "Like a murderer," flew through her mind. She was no longer mistress of herself. Her own husband—how horrible—was dangerous and strong. . . .

Music again. Mechanically, she accepted the partner who offered himself. Now she felt leaden-footed, and the cheerful melody could no longer lift her as on wings. Every step was torture to her soul. She begged to be excused. As she slipped from the man's enfolding arm, she glanced over her shoulder, and lo, there stood her husband, as if waiting for her to join him, and still with that challenge in his eyes. What did he want? Had he guessed? She drew the folds of her dress about her, to shield her bosom from his gaze. His obstinate silence was more than she could bear.

"Shall we go?" she inquired anxiously.

"Yes."

His voice was harsh and unfriendly. He went before, while she followed meekly in his wake. Again she became conscious of those menacing shoulders, that stubborn neck. Someone helped her into her furs, but she shivered as she and her husband drove home in unrelieved silence. Danger threatened on all sides—of that she felt sure.

That same night Irene had a most depressing dream. Strange music filled the air, a big room brilliantly lighted, she went in, there were many people and many colours, a young man approached her, his features seemed familiar and yet she found it difficult to place him, he put his arm round her, they danced together. She felt happy, the music made her so light-footed that she seemed to flit over the polished floor like a bird. Thus they were wafted along through many halls lighted with golden chandeliers that swung so high as to appear like constellations in the sky. Her smiling visage was reflected back to her from a hundred mirrors, and was then reflected again into the infinite. The dance grew increasingly animated, the music more ardent. She became aware that the young man was pressing closer and closer to her, that his hand sought her naked arm, that she herself sighed with pleasure at his touch, and that, as she searched his eyes, she recognized him—the actor she had worshipped at a distance when she was a little girl. She was about to utter his name, when he closed her lips with a burning kiss. Thus enlaced they floated from room to room, as thistledown is borne upon the wind. The walls streamed by, and, so far as she knew, the ceilings no longer existed. Time had ceased to count; she felt inexpressibly buoyant, her limbs no longer earthbound. Then someone tapped her on the shoulder. She paused, the band paused, the lights went out, the dark walls closed in upon her, all the dancers vanished. "Give him back to me, you thief!" cried the female she dreaded, closing ice-cold fingers round her wrist. Irene mustered her faculties to the combat. The two women wrestled together, but "that person" was stronger, and plucked the pearl necklace from her neck and half her pretty gown from her body so that arms and breasts were exposed. Then the room filled with people flocking from every point of the compass, people who stared at her derisively while the woman screamed: "She stole him from me, adulteress, whore!" Irene knew not where to hide, where to look, for the throng clustered round her, curious, trying to touch her naked flesh. She looked in every direction for aid,

and became aware of her husband standing in the shadowy
doorway. He kept motionless. His right hand was hidden behind his back. With a cry of alarm, she fled from room to
room pursued by the motley crowd. As she ran, her dress fell
away from her, and there remained no more than a few rags
which she clutched at to veil her nudity. She burst open a
door, dashed down a flight of stairs. Now she was saved. But
no! At the bottom stood that awful woman in her rough
woollen dress and with her coarse, red hands. Springing to
one side, Irene ran like a hare with the other close at her
heels. The chase went on down endless streets, while the
lamps leaned forward to grin. Irene heard the clatter of the
woman's cheap shoes behind, and yet at every corner she met
with the creature's leering face. The female spectre lurked behind every house, always pursuing and always in advance,
multiplying herself incessantly, springing on to her victim,
grappling with her, until the hunted Irene felt her knees giving way. At last she reached her house, leapt to the door, and
wrenched it open. There stood Fritz, a knife in hand, his
piercing eyes upon her. "Where have you been?" he asked
dully. "Nowhere," she heard herself saying, when a shrill
laugh interposed, and a common voice said: "I saw her! I saw
her!" Fritz raised the knife to strike. "Help," cried Irene.
"Help!"

She sat up in bed and blinked her eyes. There was her husband staring at her uneasily. He had turned on the light. So
she was at home, and all this had been a dream. But why was
Fritz sitting on the edge of her bed and looking at her as
though she were a sick woman? Who had switched on the
light? Why did he sit motionless and dumb? Fear transfixed
her. She glanced down at his hand. There was no knife in it.
Slowly the mists of sleep rose from her brain. A dream, nothing but a dream in which she had called aloud for aid and

had awakened him. But why was he gazing at her so intently?

She tried to laugh.

"What's up? Why this serious mien? I've only had a night-mare."

"You cried in your sleep. I heard you from the next room."

"What could I have said? How much does he know?" Thus ran her thoughts. Irene dared not look him straight in the eyes. But he was unwontedly quiet in demeanour, and merely continued to gaze down at her without a smile.

"What's the matter with you, Irene? Something's wrong, I feel sure. You've not been yourself these three or four days past. Seems as if you had a touch of fever, you're so excitable, so unstable, and calling as you just did for help in your sleep. . . ."

Again she endeavoured to laugh the matter off.

"No," he continued. "You must not hide anything from me. Got anything on your mind? Someone bothering you? The whole household has noticed the change in you. Trust me, Irene, my dear."

He slid nearer to her, and she felt his fingers caressing her bare arm, while his eyes were aflame with a strange light. She longed to cling to his strong body, to make a clean breast of her troubles, now, at this very moment, when he knew that she was suffering.

But the electric lamp shone down so unsympathetically, illuminating her face so vividly, that shame overwhelmed her.

"Don't worry, Fritz," she said, again trying to force a laugh. A shiver ran the length of her body. "I'm just a trifle overwrought. It'll pass."

The hand which had been ready for an embrace withdrew abruptly. His face was ashen. His brow clouded with gloomy thoughts. Slowly, he rose to his feet.

"I don't know why, but these last few days I've felt, somehow, that you wanted to tell me . . . A matter that concerns you and me . . . just you and me. We are quite alone now, Irene . . ."

She lay motionless, hypnotized by his steady stare. How lovely, she thought, to speak two little words, and all would be well between them. "Forgive me." He would not question further. But the electric light shone down on her so pitilessly . . . In the dark, she felt she could have made full confession. The crude light sapped her strength.

"So you have nothing, absolutely nothing to tell me?"

His voice was muted and tender. The temptation to confide her troubles to him was great. Only there was that soul-destroying light. . . .

She shrugged, saying:

"I don't know what you're driving at," and the spurious cheerfulness of the laugh she achieved struck her as terrible. "Because my sleep is a little disturbed you fancy I've a secret. What nonsense! Perhaps you even suspect me of having a lover."

Irene herself was aghast at the false ring of the words, and she turned her eyes away.

"All right. Sleep well," he said curtly. His voice had lost its tenderness, and was sharp, as if charged with a threat.

He switched off the light. Irene saw his white silhouette in the doorway; he vanished noiselessly, like a ghost, and when he closed the door it seemed to her that someone was screwing her into a coffin. The world was dead, her body hollow, save for the furious beating of her heart. Pain, pain—pain, pain—throbbed with every pulse.

As she sat at luncheon with her husband and children next day—the youngsters had just been pacified after a violent quarrel—the parlourmaid brought in a letter.

"It's for you, Ma'am," said Lizzie, "and the man's waiting for an answer."

Irene tore open the envelope, and her cheeks blanched as she read the brief message: "Please give bearer one hundred crowns." Neither date nor signature; and the note was written in an assumed handwriting, that was patent.

Frau Wagner hastened to her room to fetch the money. But she had mislaid the key to her cash-box. She rummaged one drawer after another till she found it. With trembling fingers she folded the bank-notes, placed them in an envelope, and herself handed the package to the messenger. All these actions were done as if she were in a hypnotic trance; there was never a moment's hesitation between one movement and the next. Barely two minutes had elapsed since she had left her seat at the dining-table.

Irene slipped back into her place. The family stared at her in stony silence. She was about to turn off the awkward situation with a joke, when, glancing down, she beheld with horror the note, open for all who wished to read, lying beside her plate. Her fingers closed on it stealthily, and she hid it away in her pocket. Then her eyes met those of her husband fixed upon her with a piercing, reproachful, tortured expression such as she had never seen in his face before. She felt as if a rapier had pricked her heart. How could she parry such a thrust? He had glared at her last night at the party with just the same piercing look; it was the identical look, too, which had hung like a sword over her sleep. She tried vainly to think of something plausible to say. Then, a long-forgotten memory stole into her mind. Fritz had once told her that he had acted as counsel for the defence in a case where the public prosecutor had a special way of dealing with recalcitrant witnesses. He made as if he were very short-sighted, and buried his nose in the legal documents lying before him on the table. Then, as the decisive question was put, he would suddenly raise his eyes and fix the offender with a dagger-like stare which so alarmed the culprit that all the carefully elaborated pack of lies was scattered to the four winds of heaven. Was Fritz trying the same dodge on her? She was the more aghast because she knew how keen an interest he took in the psychological aspect of his profession—an interest far beyond the ordinary. Tracking down a crime, finding out its motives and the method of its execution, were as absorbing to him as is the hazard of the dice to a gambler, the pursuit of Eros to the habitual seducer. When he was at this game of psychological sleuth-hound, the entire man glowed like a brazier. He remained in a high state of nervous tension, unable to eat or drink, roused from his sleep at night by the pressure of some hitherto unsolved riddle. Smoking inordinately during the days preceding the trial, he would be chary of words, reserving himself for the great hour ahead when he would have to stand at the bar and fulfil the part assigned him for prosecution or defence. She had once been present at a civil trial where he acted on behalf of the plaintiff. She could never be induced to go into court again, so horrified was she by the passionate, well-nigh evil fervour of his eloquence and the cruel glint in his eyes. Now, it was she herself, his wife, who had to suffer the scrutiny of those piercing eyes.

These memories flashed back in a second of time, and they killed the words which rose to her lips. Irene sat silent, and her confusion grew in proportion as she realized how dangerous such a silence was for her. Happily, the meal soon came to an end. The children ran shouting into the day-nursery, and made so much noise that the governess had to call them to order. Herr Wagner, likewise, rose, and went into his study without looking round.

She was alone. Drawing the fateful note from her pocket, Irene read it again: "Please give bearer one hundred crowns."

Rage overcame her; she crumpled the paper into a tight ball
and hurled it into the waste-paper basket. Then a thought
came to her. She bent down and picked up the incriminating
document, went to the stove, and dropped the paper into the
flames. The loathsome thing curled and wriggled as the greedy
fire licked it up. Relieved from this immediate menace, Irene
prepared in her turn to leave the room.

But her intention was frustrated, for at that moment she
heard footsteps approaching down the passage. Her husband
stood at the door. Her face was flushed by the heat from the
stove, and now she blushed deeper at being caught. The trap
of the stove was still open, and she made a clumsy endeavour
to hide the fact by standing in front of it. Fritz struck a
match in order to light his cigar, and, as the little flame
lighted up his face by fits and starts, Irene thought that his
nostrils were quivering. This, she knew, meant that he was
angry. Nevertheless, he looked at her calmly enough as he
said:

"I came back to tell you that you are not bound to give me
your private letters to read. You are perfectly free to have
secrets apart from me if you wish."

Irene remained tongue-tied, and dared not raise her eyes.
He waited a second or two, then he blew the cigar smoke
through his lips with violence, and slowly left the room.

Frau Wagner did not wish to think any more. She wanted
to be left in peace, and to fill her life with senseless occupations. The house had become unbearable. She longed to go
out, to be with friends; otherwise, she knew she would go mad
with fear. Surely the hundred crowns would keep her tormentress quiet for a few days? A walk might do her good. Besides, there was some necessary shopping which would relieve her from the close observation of her household—for
she recognized clearly that they were all of them puzzled by

her eccentric behaviour. She had adopted a very peculiar way of leaving the house. Standing for a moment upon the threshold, she closed her eyes and plunged into the current of the street like a diver from the springboard. Once she felt the hard stones beneath her feet she would let herself drift in the warm tide of humanity, and then walk as quickly as was seemly for a lady who did not wish to make herself conspicuous. Today she kept her eyes lowered, lest they meet again that terrible look. . . . If she was being followed, she refused to be made aware of the fact. Yet she was haunted by the idea, and her heart nearly stood still every time someone jostled against her. Each sound was a martyrdom; each footfall behind her was like a knell; each shadow across the path a bad omen. She never felt safe unless in a friend's house, or driving in a taxi.

A gentleman raised his hat to her. On looking up she was relieved to find a friend of the family, an amiable, garrulous greybeard, whom as a rule she avoided because he entertained her interminably on the subject of a host of minor ailments from which he suffered. This afternoon Irene would have been glad of his company, but unfortunately she had allowed him to go on his way before realizing how useful a redoubt he would have been against another attack on the part of the blackmailer. Half turning to call her old acquaintance to her side, she became aware of a figure hastening towards her. Instinctively, without lingering to see who it might be, she dashed blindly forward again. But she knew now that she was being followed. Her shoulders cowered as she thought of the hand that would soon be laid upon them. The person was gaining on her. How escape? Her knees trembled, so that it was hard to keep going. Closer and closer drew the pursuer. Now a voice, soft yet determined, sounded in her ear. "Irene!" But this was not the voice she dreaded.

She stopped and turned about so suddenly that Karl Brustmann nearly fell over her. His face was white with emotion,
but as she gazed at him disconcertedly he blushed with mortification. He stretched forth his hand, and, since she did not
shake it in greeting, he allowed the poor thing to drop to his
side again. She had so little expected to meet him, that it
was a good two seconds before she realized that she was staring him out of countenance. During all these days, since fear
had become her constant companion, she had not given her
lover a thought. Now, when confronted by his pale and questioning face, with its expression of vacant perplexity, her fury
rose up like a torrent within her. At first her lips trembled too
violently for her to utter a syllable, and the volcanic force of
her excitement was writ so plainly upon her that the young
man crumpled up.

"Irene, what's the matter?" he stammered. She made an impatient gesture, and he added humbly: "Have I done anything I shouldn't?"

She looked at him with an anger she was at no trouble to
conceal.

"Done anything!" she cried mockingly. "Oh, no, you've
not done anything—except nice, sweet, agreeable things."

Karl stood open-mouthed with amazement.

"But, Irene . . . Irene . . ."

"Better not make a scene in public," she said in a domineer-
ing tone. "I don't want any of your play-acting. Your ex-
quisite friend is probably spying upon us as usual, and when
we separate she'll be after me again. . . ."

"Whom are you talking about?"

She would have liked to smack his silly, pasty face. Never
had she hated anyone so fiercely as this snivelling little cur.

"But, Irene . . . Irene," he stuttered, feeling more and more
dismayed. "What have I done? You suddenly made up your

mind never to see me again . . . I've been waiting for you day and night. . . . All today I've been waiting outside your house in the hope of a few minutes' talk. . . ."

"You have been waiting? You too." Her anger made her unreasonable. If she could only give him a good slap in the face, what a relief such reckless violence would be. But she kept a grip on herself, merely looking her disgust, and meditating whether or not to tell him exactly what she thought of him. Early training won the day. She turned away abruptly; and, without looking round, was swallowed up in the press of people. Karl stood with outstretched hand, horrified, not knowing what next to do, until the current of humanity swept him along like a leaf that has fluttered down into the river and is carried unresistingly towards the sea.

Irene's hopes of being left in peace for a while were shattered when next day she received another peremptory demand for funds. Her fear was whipped up anew. This time it was for two hundred crowns—which she handed over without protest. These increased claims were horrible in the extreme for, though her private circumstances were ample enough, she knew very well that disbursements on such a scale could not pass unnoticed. Tomorrow she might be asked to pay out four hundred crowns. The amount would increase by degrees to a thousand, and so on till she could pay no more. Then would come a series of anonymous letters; then—the inevitable disaster. What she was now buying was time, a breathing-space full of fear and strain. No longer could she read or even sew. At times she felt so ill that she had to sit down, for her head swam and an indefinable lassitude made her limp and listless. Yet for all this sense of fatigue, she was unable to sleep. Meanwhile she had to appear gay, to make her cheerfulness seem natural. Who can tell the amount of heroic effort that was put into the endeavour to behave as usual?

One only, among all the individuals who surrounded her, seemed to grasp the tragedy of what was going on in Irene's soul—and he knew, because he kept perpetually on the watch. The consciousness, the absolute conviction of this watchfulness, made her redouble her precautions, and she kept a wary eye on her husband's movements. By day and by night they spied upon one another, unremittingly, remorselessly. Fritz had changed considerably since the struggle began. His inquisitorial behaviour of the beginning had given place to the gentleness and consideration of the early years of their marriage. He treated her as though she were an invalid, profiting by every opportunity to encourage her to open her heart to him. Irene was acutely aware of her husband's kindness; and, for very shame, she became increasingly reluctant to confide her troubles to his tender mercy.

On one occasion Fritz spoke to her unambiguously. Irene had been for a walk, and on returning home had heard loud voices issuing from the nursery, her husband's, strong and energetic, the governess's, shrilly reprobatory, to an accompaniment of childish snivelling and sobbing. Instantly, she was alarmed. After a first horrified convulsion, lest a letter might have been delivered during her absence, Irene pulled herself together and went upstairs. The commotion was no more than a child's squabble over a rocking-horse Aunt Suzie had brought a few days ago. It had been given to Rudi, and Helen felt aggrieved that so fine a gift had fallen to her brother. Since he would not even share it with her, she had revenged herself by breaking it and had hidden the pieces in a cupboard. On being accused, she stoutly maintained her innocence, and as a last resort the governess had called in Father to act as judge. A proper trial was being held when Irene entered the room. The child denied having had anything to do with the crime, the governess acted as witness, Rudi as plaintiff. At length Helen could hold her own no longer, and broke down in a tumult of sobs and tears.

Irene had eyes only for her husband. It seemed to her that he was not sitting in judgment upon the child but upon herself. Might she not as early as tomorrow have to stand before him, the guilty party, trembling like her baby daughter and with the self-same catch in her voice? So long as Helen stuck to her lie, Father had frowned and spoken severely; but no sooner did she begin to acknowledge her wrong-doing than his manner softened. He argued the matter out with her gently, showed the child how unkind it had been to spoil her brother's pretty plaything. As Helen began to understand how naughty she had been, she broke into fresh tears, and howled out the truth.

Irene rushed to her little daughter's side, but the child pushed her mother away. Fritz, too, reproached her for such premature sympathy, for he was not inclined to let the culprit off without punishment. The two children had been invited to a party on the morrow and they had been looking forward to the treat for weeks. Well, Helen would have to stay at home. This was a blow, indeed; and when she had heard her sentence she set up a despairing wail. Rudi jumped round the room in triumph, which was short-lived, for his father said that gloating over another's unhappiness was an ungentlemanly thing to do, and to teach the lad better manners Herr Wagner told his son that neither he nor his sister would go to the party. It was a very crestfallen pair that finally withdrew, comforted only by the thought of their common misery.

Husband and wife were alone, and it was borne in upon Irene that now, if ever, she could confide her troubles, taking her daughter's misconduct as an excuse for opening the discussion. She would put in a plea for the little girl, and if

he took the suggestion kindly she would know whether to
venture upon an explanation of her own troubles.

"I say, Fritz, are you serious about not allowing the poor
darlings to go tomorrow? They'll both be awfully cut up,
especially Helen. She did not do anything so terrible after
all. Why are you set on punishing her? Don't you think you
are being a trifle over-severe? Aren't you sorry for her?"

He looked at her steadily.

"Sorry for her? Yes, I was; but now she no longer needs
sympathy. Her heart is lighter for the punishment, though
of course she's grieved to miss the party. Yesterday she was
to be pitied because all the time we were hunting for the
broken scraps of rocking-horse and were wondering who
could be the culprit she was aching with suspense, knowing
that sooner or later all would be discovered. Fear is much
worse to bear than punishment, because the latter is something tangible. There is nothing more trying than to be in
a state of tension. The sentence I pronounced on my girlie
snapped the strain, and she immediately felt relieved. Don't
be misled by the child's tears. They've been there all the
time, repressed within; now she can cry to her heart's content; there's nothing to hide. Tears hurt horribly so long
as they are pent up. . . ."

Was he speaking about his wife or his daughter? Irene
glanced up speculatively, but he did not seem to notice, continuing:

"Take my word for it, things work out like that. So much
at least I have learned from being a man of law who has
taken part in numberless trials. The prisoner under examination is always wretched so long as there is anything to hide;
fear of discovery, the appalling need to keep up the lie, are
sufficient to undermine the courage of the hardiest offender.
I have seen men squirm as if they were having a tooth out
when question after question came nearer to extracting the

inevitable acknowledgment. Sometimes the word sticks in the throat, it is about to be pronounced. Then an inner devil, part defiance and part fear, drags it back again. The struggle begins anew. A judge frequently suffers more than the victim while the fight lasts. Yet the offender looks upon him as the enemy, he who in reality is trying his best to help. As for myself, since I am usually working in their defence, I ought to encourage them to stick to their lies through thick and thin. Well, I cannot invariably do my duty in this way, for I know that their agony will cease only when sentence has been pronounced and they have no more to hide. I have never been able to understand how people can enter upon a course of action which they know to be dangerous, and then lack courage to admit their fault. That a mere word, a word acknowledging one's guilt, should cause such senseless fear, appears to me more pitiable than the initial crime."

"Is it your opinion, Fritz, that fear is the main cause of concealment? Might not shame play a part? Shame at having to explain, at having, so to speak, to undress beneath the public gaze. . . ."

He looked up perplexed and astonished. She had not been wont to take an active share in their discussions. The word she had chosen fascinated him.

"Shame? Shame is only another form of fear. I admit it is a higher and better form, that it is not due to anxiety on account of punishment but, rather . . . Yes, yes, I understand . . ."

He had got up, and was striding about the room in unusual excitement. Something had touched him on the raw. Suddenly he stopped in front of her, and spoke less sententiously, for he was profoundly moved.

"Agreed! Shame may have a role to play when one has to make an admission before strangers, before the masses who lap up scandal from the sensational press as a cat laps up

milk. But I can't see the need for feeling ashamed to acknowledge a fault to a person one is fond of."

"And suppose," Irene had to turn her head aside for she
could not bear the gleam of his eyes, and she was aware
that her voice trembled, "suppose . . . the feeling of shame
is greater precisely in relation to the person one loves?"

He stood motionless, as if under a spell.

"You mean . . . you mean then"—and as he stammered the
words his tone became caressing and low-pitched—"you mean
. . . that Helen would have found it easier to admit her
naughty prank to, let us say, Fräulein Marie, than . . . ?"

"I'm sure of it. She was headstrong and recalcitrant because your opinion is of more importance to her than anyone else's, because . . . she loves you better than anyone else,
because . . ."

Irene faltered, and again her husband stopped in his march
to and fro and confronted her.

"Maybe you're right . . . I'm sure you are right . . .
Strange that I should never have thought of such an explanation. But you are right, and I would not have you believe I
am incapable of forgiveness. No, I could not bear for you,
Irene, to imagine I cannot be lenient on occasion. . . ."

She reddened under his gaze. Was it by chance that he
spoke thus, or did he intend . . . did he mean to imply . . . ?
Irene stood irresolute.

"The sentence is quashed," said he gaily. "Helen is free,
and I'm going this minute to tell her the glad tidings. Does
that please you, dear? Or have you some other wish? Better
make the most of my generous mood . . . I'm happy to have
been saved from perpetrating an injustice. One feels so relieved, Irene, always so relieved when . . ."

She fancied she could guess what he was hinting at, and,
unconsciously, stepped up closer to him. The releasing word
trembled on her lips. He, too, came nearer as if he would

himself lift the burden that was crushing her. She met his
eyes, in which she read a great longing that she should own
up—and her resolution collapsed. Her hands dropped listlessly to her sides, and she turned away. "Impossible," she
thought, "I can't do it, I shall never be able to confess, my
lips refuse to speak the words that would bring peace to my
soul." In her heart of hearts all she wished was for a speedy
disclosure of the whole torturing business.

And her wish seemed likely to be granted even sooner
than she could have hoped. The mischief had been going
on for a fortnight, and Irene felt that she was at the end of
her tether. Four days had elapsed since she had heard anything of the creature, and fear was now so bone of her bone
that every ring of the door-bell made her start. She kept perpetually on the alert for a missive from the blackmailer. Her
impatience grew to become a yearning, for with every payment she knew that she had bought peace for at least one
evening, peace to romp with her children, peace to go for a
stroll.

Again the bell sounded through the house, and Irene flew
downstairs to answer the door herself. A stranger stood before her, a lady in fashionable furs and a smart hat. . . . No,
not a stranger, for under the brim Irene recognized the hated
visage. . . .

"Glad to see you, Frau Wagner, for I have something important to talk to you about," and without waiting to be
asked, the woman pushed past into the hall and slid her red
parasol into the stand.

She behaved as though the place were her own, absolutely
sure of herself, and evidently delighted at having intruded
into so stately a mansion. Once more, without being asked,
she made her way to a little reception-room on the right,
whose door stood ajar.

"In here? Yes?" she asked mockingly.

Irene, still speechless with fear, would have hindered this uninvited guest from advancing farther, but the woman, with a wave of the hand, said cajolingly:

"There, there; we'll soon have done our little business. If you find it unpleasant we'll speed it up."

Frau Wagner, without another word, followed the person into the room and shut the door. "Brazen-faced hussy," thought Irene, "to dare to push herself into my house. Never occurred to me she'd be so bold." She seemed to be living through a nightmare.

"Very pretty, I'm sure," said the intruder gazing round her as she took a seat. "Lovely and comfy this easy-chair. And, my! what a lot of pictures. Now I realize how miserably furnished we are. Oh, yes, Frau Wagner, it's all wonderfully pretty and cosy."

The impertinence of the woman, the way she made herself at home in another's house, she, a common criminal, broke down Irene's controls. Her long-dammed-up fury burst in a flood.

"You're nothing but a blackmailer," she cried. "What do you want? How dare you force your way into my house? But I'm not going to allow you to torture me any longer. I've made up my mind to . . ."

"Not so loud, please, your servants might overhear. Of course it's nothing to me. I'm not denying that what you say is true, and if I go to jail, oh, well, it can't be much worse than the life I am leading now. But Frau Wagner needs to be more cautious. Better be quite sure the door is shut if you mean to make a scene. Only let me tell you this—accuse me and berate me as much as you please, it won't make the slightest impression on me."

Anger had given Irene a momentary spurt of energy, but now her courage oozed away in face of the woman's imperturbability. Like a child waiting to be told what its next lesson is to be, she stood in her own reception-room, submissive and expectant.

"Very well, Frau Wagner, I'd better go straight to the point. As you know, things are not going so mighty strong with me just at present. I'm long overdue with the rent, and the landlord's starting to make a fuss. There are other debts hanging over my head. It's time I got a move on, and put my affairs in order. So here I am, come to you for help. I want four hundred crowns."

"I simply cannot manage such a sum. The truth is that I have not so much left. You've already had three hundred from me from my monthly allowance. Where do you expect me to get the money from?"

"You'll find a way, never fear. A wealthy lady like you can always get money when she needs it. But she's got to make up her mind she's jolly well going to get it. Give the matter a little thought, Frau Wagner. You'll find ways and means . . ."

"But I tell you I have no such sum left. I'd give it to you if I had it. Believe me, I have not got that much. The most I can manage at the moment is a hundred . . ."

"I've already explained that I need four hundred to put things straight," answered the woman, ignoring Irene's offer as beneath notice.

"I have not got it," cried Irene in despair, fearing lest at any moment her husband might return and catch the woman under his roof. "I give you my word, I have not got such a sum. . . ."

"Best make haste and find it."

"I cannot."

The person looked Irene up and down as though setting a price on her.

"What about that ring? Only got to pawn it, and you'll

have more than enough. Of course, I'm not in the know about
such things and what they're worth, never having had any
jewellery of my own. But I'm pretty sure they'd let you have
four hundred crowns for it."

"My ring," exclaimed Irene, horrified by the suggestion, for
it was her engagement ring, the only one of all her rings she
never put away. The stone was one of the purest water, and
was exquisitely set.

"Why not? I'll give you the pawn-ticket, and you can
redeem it when you please. You'll get it back. I shan't keep
it, you may be sure. What would a poor creature like me do
with so costly a trinket?"

"Why are you persecuting me? Why are you tormenting
me? Oh, I cannot stand it any more. Try to grasp that fact
I'm through. Can't you show a little mercy?"

"No one never had any mercy on me. They just let me rot
with hunger. Why should I be moved to pity so rich a lady
as yourself?"

Irene was about to answer, when she heard a latchkey
pushed into the front door. Her husband, back from the
office! Hardly knowing what she did, Irene wrenched the
ring from her finger, and handed it over.

"Don't be frightened. I'm off," said the woman, made
keenly aware by the look of fear in Irene's eyes, and the
strained expression of her whole physiognomy, that the heavy
tread in the hall was doubtless that of her victim's husband.

She opened the door, bowed her head deferentially to the
master of the house who glanced at her so casually that she
might never have existed, and disappeared into the street.

No sooner had the door closed upon her retreating figure
than, with a final lash to her flagging energies, Irene lamely
informed her husband that "the lady came to make inquiries
about something." The danger was over for the moment.
Herr Wagner seemed hardly to notice his wife's words; he

went quietly into the dining-room, and sat down to luncheon.

Where the ring had been on her finger, Irene felt there was now a circlet of flame, and that everybody would notice the absence of her beautiful gem. No matter where she tried to conceal her hand, she knew that Fritz's eyes were upon it. With faculties whetted to avert discovery, she set conversation flowing, she asked him question after question, joked with the children—to find in the end that she was breathless with excitement, that the talk petered out, that a distressful silence brooded over the little company. Another effort, a fresh endeavour to bring cheerfulness to the family board! She teased the two youngsters—but they refused to laugh; she tried to make them quarrel—but they remained on the best of terms. Evidently her gaiety must be producing a false note, must be sounding forced, otherwise how explain such antagonism? The more she was determined to make them laugh, the more coldly were her sallies received. In the end she became silent from very weariness.

Her table companions were silent likewise. The only noise to disturb the perfect quiet was the rattle of knives and forks on plates.

"Where's your ring?" asked Herr Wagner suddenly.

The inevitable question had come. One last effort must be made, one last lie be told. "Well, here goes," said Irene to herself, while aloud she answered:

"I've taken it to be cleaned and overhauled." The lie encouraged her to add: "It will be ready in a day or two, when I am to fetch it."

Thus she was committed to producing the ring the day after tomorrow at latest. Some means would have to be found to redeem the pledge. A sense of relief, both mental and physical, pervaded her. She felt almost happy, for now she knew precisely the term of her incertitude. The decisive

hour was at hand. Spiritual strength grew up within her—
the strength to continue living, or the strength to die.

Knowledge of the near approach of this decisive hour in
her destiny brought with it an unexpected clarity of vision.
The nervous excitability which had so distraught her was
replaced by orderly deliberation; her fear, by an unwonted
quietude of mind; and this inner power and tranquillity enabled her to contemplate her life with the eye of a seer and
to balance up its intrinsic worth. She weighed her existence,
and found that it could even now become of value if, in the
light of what she had recently gone through, she could raise
it to fresh and higher planes, if she could give it new foundations, stable and strong, and based upon truth. To continue
to live as a divorced woman, as an adulteress, besmirched by
scandal—no, of that she did not feel capable, she was too
tired. Too tired, likewise, was she to keep up the perilous
jugglery of recent weeks. No longer had she the strength
to endure. Husband, children, governess, domestics—all were
suspicious and uneasy; she herself was suspect to herself.
Flight was out of the question; for, no matter where she hid,
her persecutor would track her down. The sole thing that
might have helped her, confession of her fault, was now impossible. One road only lay open to her, but along that road
no traveller returns.

On the following day, Irene burned every incriminatory
letter, put minor things in order, and avoided seeing the
children—or anything for which she had a tender affection.
She needed to keep all that was sweet and attractive in life
at a distance so that she might not be lured from her purpose. Having set things to rights, she went out and walked
the streets, hoping to run up against her tormentress. She
wandered about with no positive end in view and with no

sense of exaltation. Her spirit was weary; the fight had gone
out of her. For two hours she walked, more from a sense
of duty than from pleasure or necessity. The person she had
hoped to meet was nowhere to be seen. But Irene was past
suffering; she remained wholly indifferent to this disappointment. She wellnigh hoped now that the woman would not
be abroad to accost her. The faces she looked at seemed dead,
far away, for ever lost, and did not concern her.

Panic seized her for a moment when she imagined she
caught her husband's eye across the street. But the form she
dreaded was at that instant hidden behind a delivery van,
and she comforted herself with the thought that it could not
have been Fritz, seeing that he was invariably busied in the
law-court at this hour. She lost all sense of time during her
interminable peregrination, and came in late for luncheon.
Her husband, too, was late. He returned a few minutes
after and seemed perturbed.

Counting the hours till nightfall, Irene was alarmed to
find how many there were before her. To her surprise, she
found that it needed only a very few minutes to bid farewell,
and that things lost all their value once a person had realized
that they could not be taken on the everlasting journey. A
feeling of sleepiness overtook her. Mechanically, she set out,
walking, walking, without a thought in her head, blind to
her surroundings. While crossing a street, she was within
an inch of being run over; but, though the driver swore
vehemently, Irene passed on, unruffled by the narrowly missed
disaster. That would have been an easy way out, necessitating
no effort on her part. It was restful not to have to think any
more, but merely to float along like a cork, barely conscious
of the approaching end.

Irene glanced up to see whereabouts she was, and was
horrified to find that, in her aimless wanderings, she had
come quite near to the house where her lover dwelt. Could

it be a sign? Perhaps he would help her. At least he would
know the address of the blackmailer. Relief made her tremble
with joyful anticipation. Why had she not thought of this
earlier? Her body instantly responded to her mood: her limbs
became less leaden, hope flooded her gloom, clarity permeated
her thoughts. She would insist upon his accompanying her
to that creature's rooms, and then she could make an end of
everything once and for all. Karl would demand that the
woman cease blackmailing; maybe a substantial sum would
suffice to induce her to leave the town. . . . Irene felt re-
morseful for having treated the young man so harshly. . . .
But he would help her; she had no doubt of that. Strange that
so easy a way out should have occurred to her only now, at
the last minute. . . . Here was salvation.

She hurried up the stairs, and pressed the button of the
electric bell. No one came to open. And yet she was aware
of tip-toeing down the passage. Again she sounded the bell.
Again dead silence—save for that same faint rustle behind
doors. . . . Her patience gave out. This was a matter of
life and death. She kept her finger on the knob, and the bell
rang and rang and rang. . . .

At length the door-latch slid back and a small crack opened.
She whispered eagerly:

"It's me. It's only me."

Karl opened the door wide.

"You . . . you, Frau Wagner? I was . . . I hardly . . . I
had not expected a visit from you . . . Please excuse my
rig," he added, awkwardly enough, for he was in his shirt-
sleeves and had discarded collar and tie.

"I must have a word with you at once. It's vital. You'll have
to help me," she said breathlessly. "Oh, please let me come in.
I shan't keep you more than a minute."

"But . . . but . . . I'm busy . . . I can't exactly . . ."

"Nonsense. You simply must give me a hearing. After all,

it's your fault. It's your duty to help me. You must; you have to get me back my ring. Or, at least you can give me the address . . . She follows me about wherever I go . . . and now when I want her, I cannot find her. You've got to—do you hear—you've got to help me . . ."

He stared at her, speechless with amazement.

"Ah, I see," continued Irene, "you pretend not to know whom I mean. Well, it's the lady-love you had before I came on the scene. She caught me as I was coming away, and ever since that day she has been torturing me, blackmailing me— so that now I am determined to put an end to everything. I'm sick of life. But I must have my ring back . . . at latest this evening. . . . Please help me. Give me her address. . . ."

"But . . ."

"Are you going to do what I ask, or are you not?"

"But I honestly do not know to whom you refer. I've never had any dealings with a blackmailer. . . ."

"You don't know her? She just invented the whole thing, did she? Yet she knows my name and address. Perhaps I am mistaken, too, in thinking she is a blackmailer? All a dream, eh?"

She laughed fiercely. Karl felt wretched. Irene's eyes were so bright, that for a moment he feared for her reason. He looked at her anxiously.

"Try to be calm, Frau Wagner. I am sure that you are making a mistake. It is difficult to understand why . . . No, really, I do not know any such woman. . . . Since I've been here—and you know it's not long—I have had only two . . . Please believe me . . . There's a mistake . . ."

"Am I to take it that you refuse to help me?"

"No, no! I'll give you any help I can."

"Very well, then. We shall go to her place . . ."

"To whose 'place'?" he asked, and again he feared that he had to do with a lunatic.

"To her place. Are you coming or are you not?"

"Certainly, certainly. Anything to please you . . ."

"So that's that. You realize, I suppose, that it's a question of life and death so far as I myself am concerned?"

Karl was hard put to it not to laugh. Then, very courteously, he said:

"I am extremely sorry, Frau Wagner, but for the time being I am otherwise engaged. . . . A music lesson . . . It is difficult to . . ."

"That puts the finishing touch! You give your piano lesson in your shirt-sleeves? Ugh, you're a liar. . . ."

Irene was suddenly seized with an inspiration. She pushed by him, and entered his flat.

"I guess she's here all the time, and you are both playing the same game. You are probably sharing the proceeds—a blackmailer by proxy. But I'm determined to get to the bottom of this. I am no longer frightened . . ."

Karl tried to hold her back, but Irene slipped from his grasp and made for his bedroom.

A figure withdrew hastily at her approach. Evidently an eavesdropper! Irene looked at the woman whose dress was in disorder—but this was not the woman she sought.

"Sorry," she said, withdrawing as quickly as possible. "Awfully sorry . . . I'll explain everything—tomorrow. As a matter of fact—I don't understand—it's beyond me . . ."

She spoke to Karl as though he were a stranger. No one could have guessed from her manner that at one time these two had been lovers. Her brain was in a whirl. Someone must be lying. But she was too exhausted, too tired to think, too tired even to look round. She closed her eyes and descended the stairs, feeling like a condemned criminal.

The street was dark. Was the person waiting over the way? Might not salvation be lurking just round the corner? Ought

she not to fold her hands in prayer to a neglected god? If
only things could be postponed for a month or two . . .
Then she would be far away, in the country. The blackmailer
would leave her in peace there among the meadows, the
vineyards . . . Irene cast a furtive look up and down the
street. Someone seemed to be lurking in a doorway over the
road. . . . But the figure disappeared as she approached. For
a moment she thought she recognized her husband. How
awful if she were to meet him now, in her present plight. . . .
She stopped, and peered into the recess. The figure was swallowed up in the shadows. Irene walked on with a queer feeling in her back. All the while she felt that someone was
pursuing her, yet when she turned, there was not a soul to
be seen.

A drug-store. Irene went in, and handed a prescription over
the counter. She became acutely aware of the weighing
machine, the labels, the bottles full of medicaments with their
Latin names inscribed on each. The clock hanging from the
wall ticked persistently, the whole place reeked of the sickly
scent of pharmaceutical products. She remembered how as
a child she had begged her mother to allow her to go and
fetch any medicine that had been prescribed, because she
loved the strange perfume of the apothecary's shop and the
lovely coloured globes in the windows. This memory reminded her that she had not bid her mother farewell—a
most disturbing thought, for the old lady would be terribly distressed by what was about to happen. However,
the dispenser was pouring the liquid into a blue bottle . . .
death, in a little phial . . . the deadly liquid flowing through
the veins . . . Irene felt cold all over. She gazed, fascinated,
at the man's fingers pushing in the cork, then pasting on the
coloured label indicating that the bottle held poison, then
the neat wrapping stuck down at the ends with red sealing

wax. Her limbs were paralysed at the gruesome thought
of . . .

"Two crowns, please," said the dispenser.

Irene started as if waking from a dream. She stared round
her, sought the money in her bag, mechanically counted
the coins.

Then someone jerked her arm, and she heard the sound
of money thrown on the counter. A hand was thrust forward
to seize the bottle.

She turned, and stared the intruder in the face. Her husband stood before her with tightly pressed lips. His cheeks
were livid, and beads of perspiration glistened upon his forehead.

A feeling of faintness made her sway, and she leaned
against the counter to steady herself. Suddenly it occurred to
her that his had been the shadowy form in the doorway. He
had been following her.

"Come," he said curtly.

She was amazed to find how docile she was, obeying without demur. Hardly realizing what she was about, she automatically dropped into his stride. Neither looked at the other.
He still held the bottle in his hand. Once he stopped to wipe
the sweat from his brow. She stopped likewise, not knowing
that she did so. Still she did not venture to look up at him.
They did not speak, the noise of the street ebbing and flowing around them.

He stepped aside so that she might pass into the house
before him. But she missed his protection at once, and began
to totter. He slipped an arm about her. At the contact, she
shrank and hastily made her way indoors. She reached her
room; he followed. The walls and furnishings were barely
discernible in the darkness. No word had as yet passed their
lips. Fritz tore the wrapping from the bottle, and poured the

contents away. Then he threw the empty bottle into a corner. Irene shivered at the noise caused by breaking glass.

And still they kept silence. At length he stepped up to her, close, and closer, so that she was intensely aware of his heavy breathing. She waited patiently for the storm to burst, and she quailed under the fierce grip of his hand on her arm. But even now he kept silent, and abruptly she recognized that, far from being the hard task-master she dreaded, he was gentle and kind.

"Irene, how much longer are we going to torture one another?"

The pent-up unhappiness of recent weeks broke forth in convulsive sobs; she was shaken so powerfully that she tottered and would have fallen had he not supported her.

"Irene, Irene," he said comfortingly.

He repeated her name over and over again, each time in a gentler and more endearing tone, as if to calm her spiritual turmoil by an excess of tenderness. For all answer, Irene sobbed and sobbed, a prey to wave after wave of agony. Fritz carried her to the divan, and tucked her up cosily amid cushions and under a warm rug. But the sobbing did not cease. Her body was quivering, and a cold shiver ran up and down her.

He held her hands in his, kissed her throat, her gown. The tears streamed down her cheeks, her temples beat furiously. Fritz was becoming anxious. Kneeling beside the couch, he brought his face close to hers and whispered:

"Irene, my darling, why are you crying now? Everything is finished and done with. Don't worry any more. She'll never come again. . . ."

Her body was convulsed anew, and he held her in a tight embrace. Such despair made him uneasy. He felt almost as though he were a murderer. Again he kissed her, and yet again, murmuring incoherently:

"No, dear, never again. She'll never come again, I prom- ise. How could I guess you'd be so frightened? I only meant to remind you of your duty as wife and mother, only wanted to call you home, away from him, back to us who love you. What choice had I, when the affair came to my ears? I could not speak to you personally about such a thing. I always thought you'd come back to us of your own accord. And since you did not, I engaged the poor mortal to force matters by giving you a fright. She's an unhappy wretch, a decayed actress, and it was hard to persuade her to do what I required of her. I see now that I was wrong to force your hand. But, Irene, my dear, I did so want to get you back to us. And all the time I have thrown out hint after hint—and very obvious ones—that I was ready and eager to overlook everything. Only, you failed to understand. Believe me, I had no inten- tion to drive you to such extremities. I, too, have suffered agonies, watching you, step by step. . . . It is for the chil- dren's sake, perhaps more than anything, that I wanted you back. Now all is over. Now all will be well."

His voice floated towards her as if from an infinite dis- tance, and she hardly took in what he said. Her mind was in a tumult; she was past feeling. And yet she was dimly aware of kisses and endearments, and of tears wetting her cheeks. From within came a sensation of clamouring bells. Then she knew no more. As she came to, she was conscious of someone undressing her. She opened her eyes, and saw her husband leaning over her with an anxious and kindly expression. Then, again, darkness enfolded her, but this time it was the healing unconsciousness of sleep.

She did not awake until it was broad day. A sense of light came from within her likewise, a feeling of serenity, as of fine weather after storm. She tried to remember what had happened, but her mind was befogged. As in a dream, she

floated weightless through space, and in order to come down
on to earth she felt herself all over.

What was this? The ring was on her finger. . . . Immediately she was fully awake. Half-understood words abruptly
became clear, became real, acquired a sequence. The whole
business was elucidated as in a flash: her husband's question-
ings, her lover's amazement. Clouds rolled aside, and she saw
the net in which she had allowed herself to be caught. Bitterness and shame overwhelmed her; she trembled; she was sorry
to be awake again. How restful had been that dreamless, care-
free sleep.

Children's voices came from the nursery. The youngsters
were getting up amid frolic and laughter, like birds greeting
the dawn. That was Rudi's voice. She had never noticed
before that it resembled his father's. Her lips parted in a smile.
She closed her eyes, the better to enjoy everything that made
her life worth living and filled her days with happiness. A
little pain still lurked in her heart. But that was no more
than the smart of a wound in the process of healing. Soon,
she knew, it would be healed for ever.

The Fowler Snared

Last summer I spent a month at Cadenabbia—one of those little places on Lake Como, where white villas are so prettily bowered amid dark trees. The town is quiet enough even during the spring season, when the narrow strand is thronged with visitors from Bellaggio and Menaggio; but in these hot weeks of August it was an aromatic and sunny solitude. The hotel was almost empty. The few stragglers that remained looked at one another quizzically each morning, surprised to see anyone else staying on in so forsaken a spot. For my part, I was especially astonished by the persistence of an elderly gentleman, carefully dressed and of cultivated demeanour, who might have been a cross between an English statesman and a Parisian man-about-town. Why, I wondered, did he not go away to some seaside resort? He spent his days meditatively watching the smoke that rose from his cigarette, and occasionally fluttering the pages of a book. There came a couple of rainy days, and in these we struck up acquaint-

203

ance. He made such cordial advances that the difference between our ages was soon bridged over, and we became quite intimate. Born in Livonia, educated in France and England, he had never had either a fixed occupation or a fixed place of abode. A homeless wanderer, he was, as it were, a pirate or viking—a rover who took his toll of beauty from every place where he chanced to set his foot. An amateur of all the arts, he disdained to practise any. They had given him a thousand happy hours, and he had never given them a moment's creative fire. His life was one of those that seem utterly superfluous, for with his last breath the accumulated store of his experiences would be scattered without finding an heir.

I hinted as much one evening, when we sat in front of the hotel after dinner, watching the darkness steal across the lake.

"Perhaps you are right," he said with a smile. "I have no interest in memories. Experience is experienced once for all; then it is over and done with. The fancies of fiction, too—do they not fade after a time, do they not perish in twenty, fifty, or a hundred years? But I will tell you an incident which might be worked up into a good story. Let us take a stroll. I can talk better when I am on the move."

We walked along the lovely road bordering the lake, beneath the cypresses and chestnut trees. The water, ruffled by the night breeze, gleamed through the foliage.

"Let me begin with a confession. I was in Cadenabbia last year, in August, and staying at the same hotel. No doubt that will surprise you, for I remember having told you that I make a point of avoiding these repetitions. But you will understand why I have broken my rule as soon as you have heard my story.

"Of course the place was just as deserted as it is now. The man from Milan was here, that fellow who spends the whole day fishing, to throw his catch back into the lake when eve-

ning comes, in order to angle for the same fish next morning.
There were two Englishmen, whose existence was so tranquil,
so vegetative, that one hardly knew they were there. Besides
these, there was a handsome stripling, and with him a charming though rather pale girl. I have my doubts whether she
was his wife—they seemed much too fond of one another for
that.

"Last of all, there was a German family, typical North
Germans. A lean, elderly woman, a faded blonde, all elbows
and gawkiness; she had piercing blue eyes, and her peevish
mouth looked like a slit cut by a knife. The other woman
was unmistakably her sister, for she had the same traits,
though somewhat softened. The two were always together,
silently bent over their needlework, into which they seemed
to be stitching all the vacancy of their minds—the pitiless
Grey Sisters of a world of tedium and restraints. With them
was a girl, sixteen or seventeen years old, the daughter of one
or the other. In her, the harshness of the family features was
softened, for the delicate contours of budding womanhood
were beginning to show themselves. All the same she was
distinctly plain, being too lean and still immature. Moreover,
she was unbecomingly dressed, and yet there was something
wistful about her appearance.

"Her eyes were large, and full of subdued fire; but she
was so bashful that she could not look anyone in the face.
Like the mother and the aunt, she always had some needlework with her, though she was not as industrious as they;
from time to time the movements of her hands would grow
sluggish, her fingers would doze, and she would sit motionless, gazing dreamily across the lake. I don't know what it
was that I found so attractive in her aspect on these occasions. Was it no more than the commonplace but inevitable
impression aroused by the sight of a withered mother beside
a daughter in the fresh bloom of youth, the shadow behind

the substance; the thought that in every cheek there lurks a
fold; in every laugh, weariness; in every dream, disillusion-
ment? Was it the ardent but aimless yearning that was so
plainly manifest in her expression, the yearning of those
wonderful hours in a girl's life when her eyes look covetously
forth into the universe because she has not yet found the one
thing to which in due time she will cling—to rot there as
algæ cling to and rot on a floating log? Whatever the cause,
I found it pathetic to watch her, to note the loving way in
which she would caress a dog or a cat, and the restlessness
with which she would begin one task after another only
to abandon it. Touching, too, was the eagerness with which
she would scan the shabby books in the hotel library, or turn
the well-thumbed pages of a volume or two of verse she
had brought with her, would muse over the poems of Goethe
or Baumbach."

He broke off for a moment, to say:

"What are you laughing at?"

I apologized.

"You must admit that the juxtaposition of Goethe and
Baumbach is rather quaint."

"Quaint? Perhaps it is. But it's not so funny after all.
A girl at that age doesn't care whether the poetry she reads
is good or bad, whether the verses ring true or false. The
metrical lines are only the vessels in which there can be conveyed something to quench thirst; and the quality of the
wine matters nothing, for she is already drunken before she
puts her lips to the cup.

"That's how it was with this girl. She was brim-full of
longing. It peeped forth from her eyes, made her fingers wander tremulously over the table, gave to her whole demeanour
an awkward and yet attractive appearance of mingled timidity and impulsiveness. She was in a fever to talk, to give expression to the teeming life within her; but there was no

one to talk to. She was quite alone as she sat there between
those two chill and circumspect elders, whose needles were
plied so busily on either side of her. I was full of compassion
for her, but I could not make any advances. What interest
has such a girl in a man of my age? Besides, I detest opening up acquaintance with a family circle, and have a particular dislike to these philistine women of a certain age.

"A strange fancy seized me. 'Here,' I thought to myself, 'is
a girl fresh from school, unfledged and inexperienced, doubtless paying her first visit to Italy. All Germans read Shakespeare, and thanks to Shakespeare (who never set foot in
Italy!) this land will be to her the land of romance and love—
of Romeos, secret adventures, fans dropped as signals, flashing daggers, masks, duennas, and billets-doux. Beyond question she must be dreaming of such things; and what limits
are there to a girl's dreams, those streamlets of white cloud
floating aimlessly in the blue, and flashing red and gold when
evening falls? Nothing will seem to her improbable or impossible.' I made up my mind to find her a lover.

"That evening I wrote a long letter, a tender epistle, yet
full of humility and respect. It was in German, but I managed to impart an exotic flavour to the phrasing. There was
no signature. The writer asked nothing and offered nothing.
It was the sort of love-letter you will find in a novel—not
too long—and characterized, if I may use the term, by a reserved extravagance. Knowing that, driven by the urge of her
inner restlessness, she was always the first to enter the break-
fast-room, I rolled this letter inside her table-napkin.

"Next morning, I took up a post of observation in the
garden. Watching her through the window, I marked her
incredulous surprise. She was more than surprised, she was
startled; her pale cheeks were tinted with a sudden flush,
which spread down the neck. She looked round in alarm;
her hands twitched; furtively, she hid the missive. Through-

out breakfast she was restless, and could hardly eat a morsel, for her one desire was to get away into an unfrequented alley where she could pore over the mysterious letter.—Did you speak?"

I had made an involuntary movement, and had to account for it.

"You were taking a big risk. Did you not foresee that she might make inquiries, might ask the waiter how the letter found its way into her table-napkin? Or that she might show it to her mother?"

"Of course I thought of such possibilities. But if you had seen the girl, had noted how she was scared if anyone spoke loudly, you would have had no anxiety at all. There are some young women who are so shamefaced that a man can take with them any liberties he pleases. They will endure the uttermost because they cannot bear to complain about such a thing.

"I was delighted to watch the success of my device. She came back from her walk in the garden, and my own temples throbbed at sight of her. She was a new girl, with a more sprightly gait. She did not know what to do with herself; her cheeks were burning once more, and she was adorably awkward in her embarrassment. So it went on throughout the day. She glanced at one window after another as if hoping to find there the clue to the enigma, and looked searchingly at every passer-by. Once her eyes met mine, and I averted my gaze, being careful not to betray myself by the flicker of an eyelid. But in that fugitive instant I became aware that a volcano of passionate inquiry was raging within her; I was, indeed, almost alarmed at the realization, for I remembered what I had learned long years before, that no pleasure is more seductive and more dangerous than that which comes to a man when he is the first to awaken such a spark in a girl's eyes.

"I watched her as she sat with idle fingers between the two stitching elders, and I saw how from time to time her hand moved towards a particular part of her dress where I was sure the letter lay hid. The fascination of the sport grew. That evening I wrote a second letter, and continued to write to her night after night. It became more and more engrossing to instil into these letters the sentiments of a young man in love, to depict the waxing of an imaginary passion. No doubt one who sets snares for game has similar sensations; the deer-stalker must enjoy them to the full. Almost terrified at my own success, I was half in mind to discontinue the amusement; but the temptation to persevere in what had been so well begun was too much for me.

"By now she seemed to dance as she walked; her features showed a hectic beauty. All her nights must have been devoted to expectation of the morning letter, for there were black rings beneath her eyes. She began to pay more attention to her appearance, and wore flowers in her hair. She touched everything more tenderly, and looked ever more questioningly at the things upon which her glance lighted, for I had interwoven into the letters numerous indications that the writer was near at hand, was an Ariel who filled the air with music, watched all she did, but deliberately remained invisible. So marked was the increase of cheerfulness, that even the dull old women noticed it, for they watched her springing gait with kindly inquisitiveness, noted the bloom on her cheeks, and exchanged meaning smiles with one another. Her voice became richer, more resonant, more confident; often it seemed as if she were on the point of bursting out into triumphant song, as if— But you're amused once more!"

"No, no, please go on with your story. I was only thinking how extraordinarily well you tell it. You have a real talent, and no novelist could better this recital."

"You seem to be hinting that I have the mannerisms of your German novelists, that I am lyrically diffuse, stilted, sentimental, tedious. I will try to be more concise. The marionette danced, and I pulled the strings skilfully. To avert suspicion from myself (for I sometimes felt her eyes rest on me dubiously), I had implied in the letters that the writer was not actually staying at Cadenabbia but at one of the neighbouring resorts, and that he came over here every day by boat. Thenceforward, whenever the bell rang to indicate the approach of the steamer, she would make some excuse for eluding maternal supervision, and from a corner of the pier would breathlessly watch the arrivals.

"One day—the afternoon was overcast, and I had nothing better to do than to watch her—a strange thing happened. Among the passengers was a handsome young fellow, rather overdressed, after the Italian manner. As he surveyed the landing stage, he encountered the young girl's glance of eager inquiry. A smile involuntarily played round her lips, and her cheeks flamed. The young man started; his attention was riveted. Naturally enough, in answer to so ardent a look, full of so much unexpressed meaning, he smiled, and moved towards her. She took to flight; stopped for a moment, in the conviction that this was the long-expected lover; hurried on again, and then glanced back over her shoulder. The old interplay between desire and dread, yearning and shame, in which tender weakness always proves the stronger! Obviously encouraged, in spite of his surprise, the young man hastened after her. He had almost caught up with her, and I was feeling in my alarm that the edifice I had been building was about to be shattered, when the two elderly women came down the path. Like a frightened bird, the girl flew to seek their protection. The young man discreetly withdrew, but he and the girl exchanged another ardent glance before he turned away. I had had a warning to finish the game, but still the lure

overpowered me, and I decided to enlist chance in my service. That evening I wrote her a letter that was longer than
ever, in terms that could not fail to confirm her suspicion.
To have two puppets to play with made the amusement twice
as great.

"Next morning I was alarmed to note signs of disorder.
The charming restlessness had been replaced by an incomprehensible misery. Her eyes were tear-stained, and her silence
was like the silence which preludes a fit of weeping. I had
expected signs of joyous certainty, but her whole aspect was
one of despair. I grew sick at heart. For the first time an
intrusive force was at work; my marionette would not dance
when I pulled the string. I racked my brains vainly in the
attempt to discover what was amiss. Vexed and anxious at
the turn things had taken, and determined to avoid the unconscious accusation of her looks, I went out for the whole
day. When I returned, the matter was cleared up. Their
table was not laid; the family had left. She had had to go
away without saying a word to her lover. She could not dare
to tell her mother and her aunt all that another day, another
hour, might mean to her. They had snatched her out of this
sweet dream to some pitiful little provincial town. I had
never thought of such an end to my amusement. There still
rises before my eyes the accusation of that last look of hers,
instinct with anger, torment, and hopelessness. I still think
of all the suffering I brought into her young life, to cloud
it perhaps for many years to come."

He had finished. But now it was quite dark, and the moon
was shining fitfully through the clouds. We walked for some
distance before my companion broke the silence.

"There is my story. Would it not be a good theme for a
writer of fiction?"

"Perhaps. I shall certainly treasure it amid much more
that you have told me. But one could hardly make a story

of it, for it is merely a prelude. When people cross one another's paths like this without having their destinies inter-
twined, what more is there than a prelude? A story needs
an ending."

"I see what you mean. You want to know what happened
to the girl, her return home, the tragedy of her everyday
life . . ."

"No, I was not thinking of that. I have no further interest
in the girl. Young girls are never interesting, however remarkable they may fancy themselves, for all their experiences
are negative, and are therefore too much alike. The girl of
your prelude will in due time marry some worthy citizen,
and this affair will be to her nothing more than an ardent
memory. I was not thinking of the girl."

"You surprise me. I don't know what can stir your interest
in the young man. These glances, these sparks struck from
flint, are such as everyone knows in his youth. Most of us
hardly notice them at the time, and the rest forget them as
soon as the spark is cold. Not until we grow old do we
realize that these flashes are perhaps the noblest and deepest
of all that happens to us, the most precious privilege of
youth."

"I was not thinking of the young man either."

"What then?"

"I should like to tell the end of the older man's story, the
letter writer. I doubt if any man, even though well on in
years, can write ardent letters and feign love in such a way
without paying for it. I should try to show how the sport
grew to earnest, and how the man who thought he was playing a game found that he had become a pawn in his own
game. Let us suppose that the growing beauty of the girl,
which he imagines he is contemplating dispassionately, charms
him and holds him in thrall. Just when everything slips out
of his hands, he feels a wild longing for the game—and the

toy. It would delight me to depict that change in the love impulse which must make an ageing man's passion very like that of an immature youth, because both are aware of their own inadequacy. He should suffer from love's uneasiness and from the weariness of hope deferred. I should make him vacillate, follow up the girl to see her once more, but at the last moment lack courage to present himself in her sight. He should come back to the place where he had begun his sport, hoping to find her there again, wooing fortune's favour only to find fortune pitiless. That is the sort of end I should give the story, and it would be . . ."

"False, utterly false!"

I was startled. The voice at my ear was harsh and yet tremulous; it broke in upon my words like a threat. Never before had I seen my acquaintance moved by strong emotion. Instantly I realized that, in my thoughtless groping, I had laid my finger on a very sore spot. In his excitement he had come to a standstill, and when I turned to look at him the sight of his white hair was a distress to me.

I tried, rather lamely, to modify the significance of what I had said. But he turned this attempt aside. By now he had regained his composure, and he began to speak once more in a voice that was deep and tranquil, but tinged with sadness:

"Perhaps, after all, you are right. That would certainly be an interesting way of ending the story. 'L'amour coûte cher aux vieillards.' The phrase is Balzac's if I mistake not. I think it is the title of one of the most touching of his stories. Plenty more could be written under the same caption. But the old fellows, those who know most about it, would rather talk of their successes than of their failures. They think the failures will exhibit them in a ludicrous light, although these failures are but the inevitable swing of time's pendulum. Do you think it was merely by chance that the missing chapters of

Casanova's Memoirs are those relating to the days when the adventurer was growing old, when the fowler was in danger of being caught in his own snare? Maybe his heart was too sore to write about it."

My friend offered me his hand. The thrill had quite passed out of his voice.

"Good night," he said. "I see it is dangerous to tell a young man tales on a summer evening. Foolish fancies, needless dreams, are so readily aroused at such times. Good night!"

He walked away into the darkness with a step which, though still elastic, was nevertheless a little slackened by age. It was already late. But the fatigue I might have felt this sultry night was kept at bay by the stir of the blood that comes when something strange has happened, or when sympathetic understanding makes one for an instant relive another's experiences. I wandered along the quiet and lonely road as far as the Villa Carlotta, where the marble stairs lead down to the lake, and seated myself on the cool steps. The night was wonderfully beautiful. The lights of Bellaggio, which before had seemed close at hand, like fireflies flickering amid the leaves, now looked very far away across the water. The silent lake resembled a black jewel with sparkling edges. Like white hands, the rippling waves were playing up and down the lowest steps. The vault of heaven, radiant with stars, was infinite in its expanse. From time to time came a meteor, like one of these stars loosened from the firmament and plunging athwart the night sky; downwards into the dark, into the valleys, on to the hills, or into the distant water, driven by a blind force as our lives are driven into the abysses of unknown destinies.

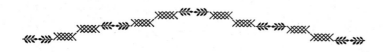

The Governess

The two girls were alone in their room. The light had been extinguished, and all was dark except for a faint shimmer from the two beds. They were both breathing so quietly that they might have been supposed to be asleep.

"I say," came a gentle, hesitating whisper from one of the beds. The twelve-year-old girl was speaking.

"What is it?" asked her sister, who was a year older.

"I'm so glad you're still awake. I've something to tell you."

There was no answer in words, only a rustle from the other bed. The elder girl had sat up, and was waiting, her eyes asparkle in the dim light.

"Look here, this is what I want to tell you. But, first of all, have you noticed anything funny about Miss Mann lately?"

"Yes," said the other after a moment's silence. "There is something, but I hardly know what. She's not so strict as she used to be. For two days I haven't done my exercises, and she never scolded me about it. I don't know what's

215

happened, but she doesn't seem to bother about us any more. She sits all by herself, and doesn't join in our games as she used to."

"I think she's unhappy, and tries not to show it. She never plays the piano now."

There was a pause, and then the elder girl spoke once more:

"You said you had something to tell me."

"Yes, but you must keep it to yourself. You mustn't breathe a word about it to Mother, or to your friend, Lottie."

"Of course I won't," answered the other indignantly. "Do get on!"

"Well, after we'd come up to bed, it suddenly struck me that I'd never said good-night to Miss Mann. I didn't bother to put on my shoes again, and I tiptoed across to her room, meaning to give her a surprise. So I opened her door quietly, and for a moment I thought she wasn't there. The light was on, but I couldn't see her. Then suddenly—I was quite startled—I heard someone crying, and I saw that she was lying dressed on her bed, her head buried in the pillows. She was sobbing so dreadfully that it made me feel all queer, but she never noticed me. Then I crept out and shut the door as softly as I could. I stood outside there for a moment, for I could hardly walk, and through the door I could still hear her sobbing. Then I came back."

Neither of them spoke for a moment. Then the elder said with a sigh:

"Poor Miss Mann!" and there was another pause.

"I wonder what on earth she was crying about," resumed the younger girl. "She hasn't been in any row lately, for Mother hasn't been nagging at her as she always used to, and I'm sure we've not been troublesome. What can there be to make her cry?"

"I think I can guess," said the elder.

"Well, out with it!"

The answer was delayed, but at length it came:

"I believe she's in love."

"In love?" The younger girl started up. "In love? Who with?"

"Haven't you noticed?"

"You can't mean Otto?"

"Of course I do! And he's in love with her. All the three years he's been living with us he never came for a walk with us until two or three months ago. But now he doesn't miss a day. He hardly noticed either of us until Miss Mann came. Now he's always fussing round. Every time we go out, we seem to run across him, either in the Park or in the Gardens or somewhere—wherever Miss Mann takes us. Surely you've noticed?"

"Yes, of course I've noticed," answered the younger. "But I just thought . . ."

She did not finish her sentence.

"Oh, I didn't want to make too much of it either. But after a time I was sure that he was only using us as an excuse."

There was a long silence, while the girls were thinking things over. The younger was the first to resume the conversation.

"But if so, why should she cry? He's very fond of her. I've always thought it must be so jolly to be in love."

"So have I," said the elder dreamily. "I can't make it out."

Once more came the words, in a drowsy voice:

"Poor Miss Mann!"

So their talk ended for that night.

They did not allude to the matter again in the morning, but each knew that the other's thoughts were full of it. Not that they looked meaningly at one another, but in spite of themselves they would exchange glances when their eyes had rested on the governess. At meals they contemplated their cousin Otto aloofly, as if he had been a stranger. They did not speak to him, but scrutinized him furtively, trying to discover if he had a secret understanding with Miss Mann. They had no heart in their amusements, for they could think of nothing but this urgent enigma. In the evening, with an assumption of indifference, one of them asked the other:

"Did you notice anything more today?"

"No," said the sister, laconically.

They were really afraid to discuss the subject. Thus matters continued for several days. The two girls were silently taking notes, uneasy in mind and yet feeling that they were on the verge of discovering a wonderful secret.

At length, it was at supper, the younger girl noticed that the governess made an almost imperceptible sign to Otto, and that he nodded in answer. Trembling with excitement, she gave her sister a gentle kick under cover of the table. The elder looked inquiringly at the younger, who responded with a meaning glance. Both were on tenterhooks for the rest of the meal. After supper the governess said to the girls:

"Go to the schoolroom and find something to do. My head is aching, and I must lie down for half an hour."

The instant they were alone, the younger burst out with:

"You'll see, Otto will go into her room!"

"Of course," said the other, "that's why she sent us in here."

"We must listen outside the door."

"But suppose someone should come. . . ."

"Who?"

"Mother."

"That would be awful," exclaimed the younger in alarm.

"Look here, I'll listen, and you must keep cavy in the passage."

The little one pouted.

"But then you won't tell me everything."

"No fear!"

"Honour bright?"

"Honour bright! You must cough if you hear anyone coming."

They waited in the passage, their hearts throbbing with excitement. What was going to happen? They heard a footstep, and stole into the dark schoolroom. Yes, it was Otto. He went into Miss Mann's room and closed the door. The elder girl shot to her post, and listened at the keyhole, hardly daring to breathe. The younger looked enviously. Burning with curiosity, she too stole up to the door, but her sister pushed her away, and angrily signed to her to keep watch at the other end of the passage. Thus they waited for several minutes, which to the younger girl seemed an eternity. She was in a fever of impatience, and fidgeted as if she had been standing on hot coals. She could hardly restrain her tears because her sister was hearing everything. At length a noise startled her, and she coughed. Both the girls fled into the schoolroom, and a moment passed before they had breath enough to speak. Then the younger said eagerly:

"Now then, tell me all about it."

The elder looked perplexed, and said, as if talking to herself:

"I don't understand."

"What?"

"It's so extraordinary."

"What? What?" said the other furiously.

The elder made an effort:

"It was extraordinary, quite different from what I expected. I think when he went into the room he must have wanted to put his arms round her or to kiss her, for she said: 'Not now, I've something serious to tell you.' I couldn't see anything, for the key was in the way, but I could hear all right.

'What's up?' asked Otto, in a tone I've never heard him use before. You know how he generally speaks, quite loud and cheekily, but now I am sure he was frightened. She must have noticed that he was humbugging, for all she said was: 'I think you know well enough.'—'Not a bit.'—'If so,' she said in ever so sad a tone, 'why have you drawn away from me? For a week you've hardly spoken to me; you avoid me whenever you can; you are never with the girls now; you don't come to meet us in the Park. Have you ceased to care for me all of a sudden? Oh, you know only too well why you are drawing back like this.' There was no answer for a moment. Then he said: 'Surely you realize how near it is to my examination. I have no time for anything but my work. How can I help that?' She began to cry, and while sobbing, she said to him gently: 'Otto, do speak the truth. What have I done that you should treat me like this? I have not made any claim on you, but we must talk things out frankly. Your expression shows me plainly that you know all about . . .'"

The girl began to shake, and could not finish her sentence. The listener pressed closer, and asked:

"All about what?"

"'All about our baby!'"

"Their baby!" the younger broke in. "A baby! Impossible!"

"That's what she said."

"You can't have heard right."

"But I did. I'm quite sure. And he repeated it: 'Our baby!' After a time she went on: 'What are we to do now?' Then . . ."

"Well?"

"Then you coughed, and I had to bolt for it."

The younger was frightfully perplexed.

"But she can't have a baby. Where can the baby be?"

"I don't understand any more than you."

"Perhaps she's got it at home. Of course, Mother would

not have let her bring it here. That must be why she is so unhappy."

"Oh, rot, she didn't know Otto then!"

They pondered helplessly. Again the younger girl said:

"A baby, it's impossible. How can she have a baby? She's not married, and only married people have children."

"Perhaps she is married."

"Don't be an idiot. She never married Otto, anyhow."

"Well, then?"

They stared at one another.

"Poor Miss Mann," said one of them sorrowfully.

They always seemed to come back to this phrase, which was like a sigh of compassion. But always their curiosity blazed up once more.

"Do you think it's a boy or a girl?"

"How on earth can I tell?"

"What if I were to ask her, tactfully?"

"Oh, shut up!"

"Why shouldn't I? She's so awfully nice to us."

"What's the use. They never tell us that sort of thing. If they are talking about them when we come into the room they immediately dry up, and begin to talk rot to us as if we were still kids—though I'm thirteen. What's the use of asking her, just to be humbugged?"

"But I want to know."

"Well, of course, I should like to know too."

"What bothers me is that Otto pretended not to know anything about it. One must know when one has a baby, just as one knows one has a father and mother."

"Oh, he was only putting it on. He's always kidding!"

"But not about such a thing. It's only when he wants to pull our leg."

They were interrupted by the governess coming in at that moment, and they pretended to be hard at work. But it did not escape them that her eyelids were red, and that her voice betrayed deep emotion. They sat perfectly quiet, regarding her with a new respect. "She has a baby," they kept on thinking; "that is why she is so sorrowful." But upon them, too, sorrow was stealing unawares.

At dinner next day, they learned a startling piece of news. Otto was going away. He had told his uncle that he had to work extra hard just before the examination, and that there were too many interruptions in the house. He was going into lodgings for the next two months.

The girls were bubbling with excitement. They felt sure that their cousin's departure must be connected in some way with the previous day's conversation. Instinct convinced them that this was a coward's flight. When Otto came to say good-bye to them they were deliberately rude, and turned their backs on him. Nevertheless, they watched his farewell to Miss Mann. She shook hands with him calmly, but her lips twitched.

The girls were changed beings these days. They seldom laughed, could not take pleasure in anything, were sad-eyed. They prowled restlessly about, and distrusted their elders, suspecting that an intention to deceive was lurking behind the simplest utterance. Ever on the watch, they glided like shadows, and listened behind doors, eager to break through the net which shut them off from the mystery—or at least to catch through its meshes a glimpse into the world of reality. The faith, the contented blindness of childhood, had vanished. Besides, they were continually expecting some new revelation, and were afraid they might miss it. The atmosphere of deceit around them made them deceitful. Whenever their parents were near, they pretended to be busily engaged in childish occupations. Making common cause against the world of grown-ups, they were drawn more closely together. A caressive impulse would often make them embrace one another when overwhelmed by a sense of their ignorance and impotence; and sometimes they would burst into tears. Without obvious cause, their lives had passed into a critical phase.

Among their manifold troubles, one seemed worse than all the rest. Tacitly, quite independently of one another, they had made up their minds that they would give as little trouble as they could to Miss Mann, now that she was so unhappy. They were extremely diligent, helping one another in their lessons; were always quiet and well behaved; tried to anticipate their teacher's wishes. But the governess never seemed to notice, and that was what hurt them more than anything. She was so different now. When one of the girls spoke to her, she would start as though from slumber, and her gaze seemed to come back to them as if it had been probing vast distances. For hours she would sit musing, and the girls would move on tiptoe lest they should disturb her, for they fancied she was thinking of her absent child. In their own awakening womanhood, they had become fonder than ever of the governess, who was now so gentle towards them. Miss Mann, who had been lively, and at times a trifle overbearing, was more thoughtful and considerate, and the girls felt that all her actions betrayed a secret sorrow. They never actually saw her weeping, but her eyelids were often red. It was plain she wanted to keep her troubles to herself, and they were deeply grieved not to be able to help her.

One day, when the governess had turned away towards the window to wipe her eyes, the younger girl plucked up courage to seize her hand and say:

"Miss Mann, you are so sad. It's not our fault, is it?"

The governess looked tenderly at the child, stroked her hair, and answered:

"No, dear. Of course it is not your fault." She kissed the little maid's forehead.

Thus the girls were continually on the watch, and one of them, coming unexpectedly into the sitting-room, caught a word or two that had not been intended for her ears. Her parents promptly changed the conversation, but the child had heard enough to set her thinking.

"Yes, I have been struck by the same thing," the mother had been saying. "I shall have to speak to her."

At first the little girl had fitted the cap on her own head, and had run to consult her sister:

"What do you think the row can be about?"

But at dinner-time they noticed how their father and mother were scrutinizing the governess, and how they then looked significantly at one another. After dinner, their mother said to Miss Mann:

"Will you come to my room please? I want to speak to you."

The girls were tremulous with excitement. Something was going to happen! By now, eavesdropping had become a matter of course. They no longer felt any shame; their one thought was to discover what was being hidden from them. They were at the door in a flash, directly Miss Mann had entered.

They listened, but all they could hear was a faint murmur of conversation. Were they to learn nothing after all? Then one of the voices was raised. Their mother said angrily:

"Did you suppose we were all blind—that we should never notice your condition? This throws a pretty light upon your conception of your duties as a governess. I shudder to think that I have confided my daughters' education to such hands. No doubt you have neglected them shamefully . . ."

The governess seemed to break in here with a protest, but she spoke softly, so that the girls could not hear.

"Talk, talk! Every wanton finds excuses. A woman such as you gives herself to the first comer without a thought of the consequences. God will provide! It's monstrous that a hussy like you should become a governess. But I suppose you don't flatter yourself that I shall let you stay in the house any longer?"

The listeners shuddered. They could not fully understand, but their mother's tone seemed horrible to them. It was answered only by Miss Mann's sobs. The tears burst from their own eyes. Their mother grew angrier than ever.

"That's all you can do now, cry and snivel! Your tears won't move me. I have no sympathy with such a person as you are. It's no business of mine, what will happen to you. No doubt you know where to turn for help, and that's your affair. All I know is that you shan't stay another day in my house."

Miss Mann's despairing sobs were still the only answer. Never had they heard anyone cry in this fashion. Their feeling was that no one who cried so bitterly could possibly be in the wrong. Their mother waited in silence for a little while, and then said sharply:

"Well, that's all I have to say to you. Pack up your things this afternoon, and come to me for your salary tomorrow morning. You can go now."

The girls fled back into their own room. What could have happened? What was the meaning of this sudden storm? In a glass darkly, they began to have some suspicion of the truth. For the first time, their feeling was one of revolt against their parents.

"Wasn't it horrid of Mother to speak to her like that?" said the elder.

The younger was a little alarmed at such frank criticism, and stammered:

"But . . . but . . . we don't know what she's done."

"Nothing wrong, I'm certain. Miss Mann would never do anything wrong. Mother doesn't know her as well as we do."

"Wasn't it awful, the way she cried? It did make me feel so bad."

"Yes, it was dreadful. But the way Mother shouted at her was sickening, positively sickening!"

The speaker stamped angrily, and tears welled up into her eyes.

At this moment Miss Mann came in, looking utterly worn out.

"Girls, I have a lot to do this afternoon. I know you will be good, if I leave you to yourselves? We'll have the evening together."

She turned, and left the room, without noticing the children's forlorn looks.

"Did you see how red her eyes were? I simply can't understand how Mother could be so unkind to her."

"Poor Miss Mann!"

Again this lament, in a voice broken with tears. Then their Mother came to ask if they would like to go for a walk with her.

"Not today, Mother."

In fact, they were afraid of their mother, and they were angry because she did not tell them that she was sending Miss Mann away. It suited their mood better to be by themselves. They fluttered about the room like caged swallows, crushed by the atmosphere of falsehood and silence. They wondered if they could not go to Miss Mann and ask her what was the matter; tell her they wanted her to stay, that they thought Mother had been horribly unfair. But they were afraid of distressing her. Besides, they were ashamed, for how could they say a word about the matter when all they knew had been learned by eavesdropping? They had to spend the interminable afternoon by themselves, moping, crying from time to time, and turning over in their minds memories of what they had heard through the closed door—their mother's heartless anger and Miss Mann's despairing sobs.

In the evening, the governess came to see them, but only to say good-night. As she left the room, the girls longed to break the silence, but could not utter a word. At the door, as if recalled by their dumb yearning, Miss Mann turned back, her eyes shining with emotion. She embraced both the girls, who instantly burst out crying. Kissing them once more, the governess hurried away.

It was obvious to the children that this was a final leave-taking.

"We shall never see her again," sobbed one.

"I know. She'll be gone when we come back from school tomorrow."

"Perhaps we shall be able to visit her after a time. Then she'll show us the baby."

"Yes, she's always such a dear."

"Poor Miss Mann!"

The sorrowful phrase seemed to hold a foreboding of their own destiny.

"I can't think how we shall get on without her!"

"I shall never be able to stand another governess, after her."

"Nor shall I."

"There'll never be anyone like Miss Mann. Besides . . ."

She did not venture to finish her sentence. An unconscious womanliness had made them feel a sort of veneration for Miss Mann, ever since they had known she had a baby. This was continually in their thoughts, and moved them profoundly.

"I say," said one.

"Yes?"

"I've got an idea. Can't we do something really nice for

Miss Mann before she goes away, something that will show her how fond we are of her, and that we are not like Mother? Will you join in?"

"Rather!"

"You know how much she likes white roses. Let's go out early tomorrow and buy some, before we go to school. We'll put them in her room."

"But when?"

"After school."

"That's no use, she'll be gone then. Look here, I'll steal out quite early, before breakfast, and bring them back here. Then we'll take them to her."

"All right, we must get up early."

They raided their money-boxes. It made them almost cheerful, once more, that they would be able to show Miss Mann how much they loved her.

Early in the morning, roses in hand, they knocked at Miss Mann's door. There was no answer. Thinking the governess must be asleep, they peeped in. The room was empty; the bed had not been slept in. On the table lay two letters. The girls were startled. What had happened?

"I shall go straight to Mother," said the elder girl.

Defiantly, without a trace of fear, she accosted her mother with the words:

"Where's Miss Mann?"

"In her room, I suppose."

"There's no one in her room; she never went to bed. She must have gone away last night. Why didn't you tell us anything about it?"

The mother hardly noticed the challenging tone. Turning pale, she sought her husband, who went into Miss Mann's room.

He stayed there some time, while the girls eyed their mother with gloomy indignation, and she seemed unable to meet their gaze.

Now their father came back, with an open letter in his hand. He, too, was agitated. The parents retired into their own room, and conversed in low tones. This time, the girls were afraid to try and overhear what was said. They had never seen their father look like that before.

When their mother came out, they saw she had been weeping. They wanted to question her, but she said sharply:

"Be off with you to school, you'll be late."

They had to go. For hours they sat in class without attending to a single word. Then they rushed home. There, a dreadful thought seemed to dominate everyone's mind. Even the servants had a strange look. Their mother came to meet them, and began to speak in carefully rehearsed phrases:

"Children, you won't see Miss Mann any more; she is . . ."

The sentence was left unfinished. So furious, so menacing, was the girls' expression that their mother could not lie to them. She turned away, and sought refuge in her own room.

That afternoon, Otto put in an appearance. One of the two letters had been addressed to him, and he had been summoned. He, too, was pale and uneasy. No one spoke to him. Everybody shunned him. Catching sight of the two girls sitting disconsolate in a corner of the room, he went up to them.

"Don't you come near us!" both screamed, regarding him with horror.

He paced up and down for a while, and then vanished. No one spoke to the girls, and they said nothing to one another. They wandered aimlessly from room to room, looking silently into one another's tear-stained faces when their paths crossed. They knew everything now. They knew that they had been cheated; they knew how mean people could be. They did not love their parents any more, did not trust Father or Mother any longer. They were sure they would never trust

anyone again. All the burden of life pressed heavily upon
their frail young shoulders. Their careless, happy childhood
lay behind them; unknown terrors awaited them. The full
significance of what had happened was still beyond their
grasp, but they were wrestling with its dire potentialities.
They were drawn together in their isolation, but it was a
dumb communion, for they could not break the spell of silence. From their elders they were completely cut off. No one
could approach them, for the portals of their souls had been
closed—perhaps for years to come. They were at war with all
around them. For, in one brief day, they had grown up!

Not till late in the evening, when they were alone in their
bedroom, did there reawaken in them the child's awe of solitude, the haunting fear of the dead woman, the terror of dread
possibilities. It was bitterly cold; in the general confusion the
heating apparatus had been forgotten. They both crept into
one bed, and cuddled closely together, for mutual encouragement as well as for warmth. They were still unable to discuss
their trouble. But now, at length, the younger's pent-up emotion found relief in a storm of tears, and the elder, too, sobbed
convulsively. Thus they lay weeping in one another's arms.
They were no longer bewailing the loss of Miss Mann, or
their estrangement from their parents. They were shaken by
the anticipation of what might befall them in this unknown
world into whose realities they had today looked for the first
time. They shrank from the life into which they were growing up; from the life which seemed to them like a forest full
of threatening shapes, a forest they had to cross. But by degrees this sense of anxiety grew visionary; their sobs were less
violent, and came at longer intervals. They breathed quietly,
now, in a rhythmical unison of peace. They slept.

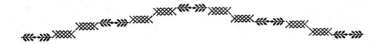

Buchmendel

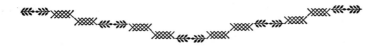

Having just got back to Vienna, after a visit to an out-of-
the-way part of the country, I was walking home from the
station when a heavy shower came on, such a deluge that the
passers-by hastened to take shelter in doorways, and I myself
felt it expedient to get out of the downpour. Luckily there is
a café at almost every street-corner in the metropolis, and I
made for the nearest, though not before my hat was dripping
wet and my shoulders were drenched to the skin. An old-
fashioned suburban place, lacking the attractions (copied from
Germany) of music and a dancing-floor to be found in the
centre of the town; full of small shopkeepers and working folk
who consumed more newspapers than coffee and rolls. Since
it was already late in the evening, the air, which would have
been stuffy anyhow, was thick with tobacco-smoke. Still, the
place was clean and brightly decorated, had new satin-covered
couches, and a shining cash-register, so that it looked thoroughly attractive. In my haste to get out of the rain, I had not

troubled to read its name—but what matter? There I rested, warm and comfortable, though looking rather impatiently through the blue-tinted window panes to see when the shower would be over, and I should be able to get on my way.

Thus I sat unoccupied, and began to succumb to that in-ertia which results from the narcotic atmosphere of the typical Viennese café. Out of this void, I scanned various individuals whose eyes, in the murky room, had a greyish look in the arti-ficial light; I mechanically contemplated the young woman at the counter as, like an automaton, she dealt out sugar and a teaspoon to the waiter for each cup of coffee; with half an eye and a wandering attention I read the uninteresting advertise-ments on the walls—and there was something agreeable about these dull occupations. But suddenly, and in a peculiar fashion, I was aroused from what had become almost a doze. A vague internal movement had begun; much as a toothache sometimes begins, without one's being able to say whether it is on the right side or the left, in the upper jaw or the lower. All I be-came aware of was a numb tension, an obscure sentiment of spiritual unrest. Then, without knowing why, I grew fully conscious. I must have been in this café once before, years ago, and random associations had awakened memories of the walls, the tables, the chairs, the seemingly unfamiliar smoke-laden room.

The more I endeavoured to grasp this lost memory, the more obstinately did it elude me; a sort of jellyfish glistening in the abysses of consciousness, slippery and unseizable. Vainly did I scrutinize every object within the range of vision. Cer-tainly when I had been here before the counter had had neither marble top nor cash-register; the walls had not been panelled with imitation rosewood; these must be recent acqui-sitions. Yet I had indubitably been here, more than twenty years back. Within these four walls, as firmly fixed as a nail driven up to the head in a tree, there clung a part of my ego, long since overgrown. Vainly I explored, not only the room, but my own inner man, to grapple the lost links. Curse it all, I could not plumb the depths!

It will be seen that I was becoming vexed, as one is always out of humour when one's grip slips in this way, and reveals the inadequacy, the imperfections, of one's spiritual powers. Yet I still hoped to recover the clue. A slender thread would suffice, for my memory is of a peculiar type, both good and bad; on the one hand stubbornly untrustworthy, and on the other incredibly dependable. It swallows the most important details, whether in concrete happenings or in faces, and no voluntary exertion will induce it to regurgitate them from the gulf. Yet the most trifling indication—a picture postcard, the address on an envelope, a newspaper cutting—will suffice to hook up what is wanted as an angler who has made a strike and successfully imbedded his hook reels in a lively, struggling, and reluctant fish. Then I can recall the features of a man seen once only, the shape of his mouth and the gap to the left where he had an upper eye-tooth knocked out, the falsetto tone of his laugh, and the twitching of the moustache when he chooses to be merry, the entire change of expression which hilarity effects in him. Not only do these physical traits rise before my mind's eye, but I remember, years afterwards, every word the man said to me, and the tenor of my replies. But if I am to see and feel the past thus vividly, there must be some material link to start the current of associations. My memory will not work satisfactorily on the abstract plane.

I closed my eyes to think more strenuously, in the attempt to forge the hook which would catch my fish. In vain! In vain! There was no hook, or the fish would not bite. So fierce waxed my irritation with the inefficient and mulish thinking apparatus between my temples that I could have struck myself a violent blow on the forehead, much as an irascible man will shake and kick a penny-in-the-slot machine which, when he has inserted his coin, refuses to render him his due.

So exasperated did I become at my failure, that I could no longer sit quiet, but rose to prowl about the room. The instant I moved, the glow of awakening memory began. To the right of the cash-register, I recalled, there must be a doorway leading into a windowless room, where the only light was artificial. Yes, the place actually existed. The decorative scheme was different, but the proportions were unchanged. A square box of a place, behind the bar—the card-room. My nerves thrilled as I contemplated the furniture, for I was on the track, I had found the clue, and soon I should know all. There were two small billiard-tables, looking like silent ponds covered with green scum. In the corners, card-tables, at one of which two bearded men of professorial type were playing chess. Beside the iron stove, close to a door labelled "Telephone," was another small table. In a flash, I had it! That was Mendel's place, Jacob Mendel's. That was where Mendel used to hang out, Buchmendel. I was in the Café Gluck! How could I have forgotten Jacob Mendel. Was it possible that I had not thought about him for ages, a man so peculiar as wellnigh to belong to the Land of Fable, the eighth wonder of the world, famous at the university and among a narrow circle of admirers, magician of book-fanciers, who had been wont to sit there from morning till night, an emblem of bookish lore, the glory of the Café Gluck? Why had I had so much difficulty in hooking my fish? How could I have forgotten Buchmendel?

I allowed my imagination to work. The man's face and form pictured themselves vividly before me. I saw him as he had been in the flesh, seated at the table with its grey marble top, on which books and manuscripts were piled. Motionless he sat, his spectacled eyes fixed upon the printed page. Yet not

altogether motionless, for he had a habit (acquired at school in
the Jewish quarter of the Galician town from which he came)
of rocking his shiny bald pate backwards and forwards and
humming to himself as he read. There he studied catalogues
and tomes, crooning and rocking, as Jewish boys are taught
to do when reading the Talmud. The rabbis believe that, just
as a child is rocked to sleep in its cradle, so are the pious ideas
of the holy text better instilled by this rhythmical and hypno-
tizing movement of head and body. In fact, as if he had been
in a trance, Jacob Mendel saw and heard nothing while thus
occupied. He was oblivious to the click of billiard-balls, the
coming and going of waiters, the ringing of the telephone bell;
he paid no heed when the floor was scrubbed and when the
stove was refilled. Once a red-hot coal fell out of the latter,
and the flooring began to blaze a few inches from Mendel's
feet; the room was full of smoke, and one of the guests ran
for a pail of water to extinguish the fire. But neither the
smoke, the bustle, nor the stench diverted his attention from
the volume before him. He read as others pray, as gamblers
follow the spinning of the roulette board, as drunkards stare
into vacancy; he read with such profound absorption that ever
since I first watched him the reading of ordinary mortals has
seemed a pastime. This Galician second-hand book dealer,
Jacob Mendel, was the first to reveal to me in my youth the
mystery of absolute concentration which characterizes the artist and the scholar, the sage and the imbecile; the first to make
me acquainted with the tragical happiness and unhappiness
of complete absorption.

A senior student introduced me to him. I was studying the
life and doings of a man who is even today too little known,
Mesmer the magnetizer. My researches were bearing scant
fruit, for the books I could lay my hands on conveyed sparse
information, and when I applied to the university librarian

for help he told me, uncivilly, that it was not his business to hunt up references for a freshman. Then my college friend suggested taking me to Mendel.

"He knows everything about books, and will tell you where to find the information you want. The ablest man in Vienna, and an original to boot. The man is a saurian of the book-world, an antediluvian survivor of an extinct species."

We went, therefore, to the Café Gluck, and found Buch-mendel in his usual place, bespectacled, bearded, wearing a rusty black suit, and rocking as I have described. He did not notice our intrusion, but went on reading, looking like a nod-ding mandarin. On a hook behind him hung his ragged black overcoat, the pockets of which bulged with manuscripts, cata-logues, and books. My friend coughed loudly, to attract his attention, but Mendel ignored the sign. At length Schmidt rapped on the table-top, as if knocking at a door, and at this Mendel glanced up, mechanically pushed his spectacles on to his forehead, and from beneath his thick and untidy ashen-grey brows there glared at us two dark, alert little eyes. My friend introduced me, and I explained my quandary, being careful (as Schmidt had advised) to express great annoyance at the librarian's unwillingness to assist me. Mendel leaned back, laughed scornfully, and answered with a strong Galician accent:

"Unwillingness, you think? Incompetence, that's what's the matter with him. He's a jackass. I've known him (for my sins) twenty years at least, and he's learned nothing in the whole of that time. Pocket their wages—that's all such fellows can do. They should be mending the road, instead of sitting over books."

This outburst served to break the ice, and with a friendly wave of the hand the bookworm invited me to sit down at his table. I reiterated my object in consulting him; to get a list of all the early works on animal magnetism, and of contemporary and subsequent books and pamphlets for and against Mesmer. When I had said my say, Mendel closed his left eye for an instant, as if excluding a grain of dust. This was, with him, a sign of concentrated attention. Then, as though reading from an invisible catalogue, he reeled out the names of two or three dozen titles, giving in each case place and date of publication and approximate price. I was amazed, though Schmidt had warned me what to expect. His vanity was tickled by my surprise, for he went on to strum the keyboard of his marvellous memory, and to produce the most astounding bibliographical marginal notes. Did I want to know about sleepwalkers, Perkins's metallic tractors, early experiments in hypnotism, Braid, Gassner, attempts to conjure up the devil, Christian Science, theosophy, Madame Blavatsky? In connexion with each item there was a hailstorm of book-names, dates, and appropriate details. I was beginning to understand that Jacob Mendel was a living lexicon, something like the general catalogue of the British Museum Reading Room, but able to walk about on two legs. I stared dumbfounded at this bibliographical phenomenon, which masqueraded in the sordid and rather unclean domino of a Galician second-hand book dealer, who, after rattling off some eighty titles (with assumed indifference, but really with the satisfaction of one who plays an unexpected trump), proceeded to wipe his spectacles with a handkerchief which might long before have been white.

Hoping to conceal my astonishment, I inquired:

"Which among these works do you think you could get for me without too much trouble?"

"Oh, I'll have a look round," he answered. "Come here tomorrow and I shall certainly have some of them. As for the others, it's only a question of time, and of knowing where to look."

"I'm greatly obliged to you," I said; and, then, wishing to be civil, I put my foot in it, proposing to give him a list of the books I wanted. Schmidt nudged me warningly, but too late. Mendel had already flashed a look at me—such a look, at once triumphant and affronted, scornful and overwhelmingly superior—the royal look with which Macbeth answers Macduff when summoned to yield without a blow. He laughed curtly. His Adam's apple moved excitedly. Obviously he had gulped down a choleric, an insulting epithet.

Indeed he had good reason to be angry. Only a stranger, an ignoramus, could have proposed to give him, Jacob Mendel, a memorandum, as if he had been a bookseller's assistant or an underling in a public library. Not until I knew him better did I fully understand how much my would-be politeness must have galled this aberrant genius—for the man had, and knew himself to have, a titanic memory, wherein, behind a dirty and undistinguished-looking forehead, was indelibly recorded a picture of the title-page of every book that had been printed. No matter whether it had issued from the press yesterday or hundreds of years ago, he knew its place of publication, its author's name, and its price. From his mind, as if from the printed page, he could read off the contents, could reproduce the illustrations; could visualize, not only what he had actually held in his hands, but also what he had glanced at in a bookseller's window; could see it with the same vividness as an artist sees the creations of fancy which he has not yet reproduced upon canvas. When a book was offered for six marks by a Regensburg dealer, he could remember that, two years before, a copy of the same work had changed hands for four crowns at a Viennese auction, and he recalled the name of the purchaser. In a word, Jacob Mendel never forgot a title or a figure; he knew every plant, every infusorian, every star, in the continually revolving and incessantly changing cosmos of the book-universe. In each literary specialty, he knew more than the specialists; he knew the contents of the libraries better than the librarians; he knew the book-lists of most publishers better

than the heads of the firms concerned—though he had nothing
to guide him except the magical powers of his inexplicable but
invariably accurate memory.

True, this memory owed its infallibility to the man's limita-
tions, to his extraordinary power of concentration. Apart from
books, he knew nothing of the world. The phenomena of
existence did not begin to become real for him until they had
been set in type, arranged upon a composing stick, collected
and, so to say, sterilized in a book. Nor did he read books for
their meaning, to extract their spiritual or narrative substance.
What aroused his passionate interest, what fixed his attention,
was the name, the price, the format, the title-page. Though in
the last analysis unproductive and uncreative, this specifically
antiquarian memory of Jacob Mendel, since it was not a
printed book-catalogue but was stamped upon the grey matter
of a mammalian brain, was, in its unique perfection, no less
remarkable a phenomenon than Napoleon's gift for physiognomy, Mezzofanti's talent for languages, Lasker's skill at
chess-openings, Busoni's musical genius. Given a public position as teacher, this man with so marvellous a brain might
have taught thousands and hundreds of thousands of students,
have trained others to become men of great learning and of
incalculable value to those communal treasure-houses we call
libraries. But to him, a man of no account, a Galician Jew, a
book-pedlar whose only training had been received in a Tal-
mudic school, this upper world of culture was a fenced pre-
cinct he could never enter; and his amazing faculties could
only find application at the marble-topped table in the inner
room of the Café Gluck. When, some day, there arises a great
psychologist who shall classify the types of that magical power
we term memory as effectively as Buffon classified the genera
and species of animals, a man competent to give a detailed
description of all the varieties, he will have to find a pigeon-
hole for Jacob Mendel, forgotten master of the lore of book-

prices and book-titles, the ambulatory catalogue alike of incunabula and the modern commonplace.

In the book-trade and among ordinary persons, Jacob Mendel was regarded as nothing more than a second-hand book
dealer in a small way of business. Sunday after Sunday, his
stereotyped advertisement appeared in the "Neue Freie Presse"
and the "Neues Wiener Tagblatt." It ran as follows: "Best
prices paid for old books, Mendel, Obere Alserstrasse." A telephone number followed, really that of the Café Gluck. He
rummaged every available corner for his wares, and once a
week, with the aid of a bearded porter, conveyed fresh booty
to his headquarters and got rid of old stock—for he had no
proper bookshop. Thus he remained a petty trader, and his
business was not lucrative. Students sold him their textbooks,
which year by year passed through his hands from one "gen-
eration" to another; and for a small percentage on the price
he would procure any additional book that was wanted. He
charged little or nothing for advice. Money seemed to have no
standing in his world. No one had ever seen him better dressed
than in the threadbare black coat. For breakfast and supper
he had a glass of milk and a couple of rolls, while at midday
a modest meal was brought him from a neighbouring restaurant. He did not smoke; he did not play cards; one might
almost say he did not live, were it not that his eyes were alive
behind his spectacles, and unceasingly fed his enigmatic brain
with words, titles, names. The brain, like a fertile pasture,
greedily sucked in this abundant irrigation. Human beings
did not interest him, and of all human passions perhaps one
only moved him, the most universal—vanity.

When someone, wearied by a futile hunt in countless other
places, applied to him for information, and was instantly put
on the track, his self-gratification was overwhelming; and it
was unquestionably a delight to him that in Vienna and elsewhere there existed a few dozen persons who respected him

for his knowledge and valued him for the services he could render. In every one of these monstrous aggregates we call towns, there are here and there facets which reflect one and the same universe in miniature—unseen by most, but highly prized by connoisseurs, by brethren of the same craft, by devotees of the same passion. The fans of the book-market knew Jacob Mendel. Just as anyone encountering a difficulty in deciphering a score would apply to Eusebius Mandyczewski of the Musical Society, who would be found wearing a grey skull-cap and seated among multifarious musical MSS., ready, with a friendly smile, to solve the most obstinate crux; and just as, today, anyone in search of information about the Viennese theatrical and cultural life of earlier times will unhesitatingly look up the polyhistor Father Glossy; so, with equal confidence did the bibliophiles of Vienna, when they had a particularly hard nut to crack, make a pilgrimage to the Café Gluck and lay their difficulty before Jacob Mendel.

To me, young and eager for new experiences, it became enthralling to watch such a consultation. Whereas ordinarily, when a would-be seller brought him some ordinary book, he would contemptuously clap the cover to and mutter, "Two crowns"; if shown a rare or unique volume, he would sit up and take notice, lay the treasure upon a clean sheet of paper; and, on one such occasion, he was obviously ashamed of his dirty, ink-stained fingers and mourning finger-nails. Tenderly, cautiously, respectfully, he would turn the pages of the treasure. One would have been as loath to disturb him at such a moment as to break in upon the devotions of a man at prayer; and in very truth there was a flavour of solemn ritual and religious observance about the way in which contemplation, palpation, smelling, and weighing in the hand followed one another in orderly succession. His rounded back waggled while he was thus engaged, he muttered to himself, exclaimed "Ah" now and again to express wonder or admiration, or

"Oh, dear" when a page was missing or another had been
mutilated by the larva of a book-beetle. His weighing of the
tome in his hand was as circumspect as if books were sold by
the ounce, and his snuffling at it as sentimental as a girl's
smelling of a rose. Of course it would have been the height
of bad form for the owner to show impatience during this
ritual of examination.

When it was over, he willingly, nay enthusiastically, ten-
dered all the information at his disposal, not forgetting relevant anecdotes, and dramatized accounts of the prices which
other specimens of the same work had fetched at auctions or
in sales by private treaty. He looked brighter, younger, more
lively at such times, and only one thing could put him seriously out of humour. This was when a novice offered him
money for his expert opinion. Then he would draw back with
an affronted air, looking for all the world like the skilled cus-
todian of a museum gallery to whom an American traveller
has offered a tip—for to Jacob Mendel contact with a rare book
was something sacred, as is contact with a woman to a young
man who has not had the bloom rubbed off. Such moments
were his platonic love-nights. Books exerted a spell on him,
never money. Vainly, therefore, did great collectors (among
them one of the notables of Princeton University) try to recruit
Mendel as librarian or book-buyer. The offer was declined
with thanks. He could not forsake his familiar headquarters
at the Café Gluck. Thirty-three years before, an awkward
youngster with black down sprouting on his chin and black
ringlets hanging over his temples, he had come from Galicia
to Vienna, intending to adopt the calling of rabbi; but ere
long he forsook the worship of the harsh and jealous Jehovah
to devote himself to the more lively and polytheistic cult of
books. Then he happened upon the Café Gluck, by degrees
making it his workshop, headquarters, post-office—his world.
Just as an astronomer, alone in an observatory, watches night

after night through a telescope the myriads of stars, their mysterious movements, their changeful medley, their extinction and their flaming-up anew, so did Jacob Mendel, seated at his table in the Café Gluck, look through his spectacles into the universe of books, a universe that lies above the world of our everyday life, and, like the stellar universe, is full of changing cycles.

It need hardly be said that he was highly esteemed in the Café Gluck, whose fame seemed to us to depend far more upon his unofficial professorship than upon the godfathership of the famous musician, Christoph Willibald Gluck, composer of *Alcestis* and *Iphigenia*. He belonged to the outfit quite as much as did the old cherrywood counter, the two billiard-tables with their cloth stitched in many places, and the copper coffee-urn. His table was guarded as a sanctuary. His numerous clients and customers were expected to take a drink "for the good of the house," so that most of the profit of his far-flung knowledge flowed into the big leathern pouch slung round the waist of Deubler, the waiter. In return for being a centre of attraction, Mendel enjoyed many privileges. The telephone was at his service for nothing. He could have his letters directed to the café, and his parcels were taken in there. The excellent old woman who looked after the toilet brushed his coat, sewed on buttons, and carried a small bundle of underlinen every week to the wash. He was the only guest who could have a meal sent in from the restaurant; and every morning Herr Standhartner, the proprietor of the café, made a point of coming to his table and saying "Good morning!"—though Jacob Mendel, immersed in his books, seldom noticed the greeting. Punctually at half-past seven he arrived, and did not leave till the lights were extinguished. He never spoke to the other guests, never read a newspaper, noticed no changes; and once, when Herr Standhartner civilly asked him whether he did not find the electric light more agreeable to read by

than the malodorous and uncertain kerosene lamps they had
replaced, he stared in astonishment at the new incandescents.
Although the installation had necessitated several days' ham-
mering and bustle, the introduction of the glow-lamps had
escaped his notice. Only through the two round apertures of
the spectacles, only through these two shining and sucking
lenses, did the milliards of black infusorians which were the
letters filter into his brain. Whatever else happened in his vicinity was disregarded as unmeaning noise. He had spent
more than thirty years of his waking life at this table, reading,
comparing, calculating, in a continuous waking dream, interrupted only by intervals of sleep.

A sense of horror overcame me when, looking into the inner
room behind the bar of the Café Gluck, I saw that the marble-
top of the table where Jacob Mendel used to deliver his
oracles was now as bare as a tombstone. Grown older since
those days, I understood how much disappears when such a
man drops out of his place in the world, were it only because,
amid the daily increase in hopeless monotony, the unique
grows continually more precious. Besides, in my callow youth
a profound intuition had made me exceedingly fond of Buchmendel. It was through the observation of him that I had first
become aware of the enigmatic fact that supreme achievement
and outstanding capacity are only rendered possible by mental
concentration, by a sublime monomania that verges on lunacy.
Through the living example of this obscure genius of a second-
hand book dealer, far more than through the flashes of insight
in the works of our poets and other imaginative writers, had
been made plain to me the persistent possibility of a pure life
of the spirit, of complete absorption in an idea, an ecstasy as
absolute as that of an Indian yogi or a medieval monk; and
I had learned that this was possible in an electric-lighted café
and adjoining a telephone box. Yet I had forgotten him, dur-

ing the war years, and through a kindred immersion in my
own work. The sight of the empty table made me ashamed
of myself, and at the same time curious about the man who
used to sit there.

What had become of him? I called the waiter and inquired.

"No, Sir," he answered, "I'm sorry, but I never heard of
Herr Mendel. There is no one of that name among the frequenters of the Café Gluck. Perhaps the head-waiter will
know."

"Herr Mendel?" said the head-waiter dubiously, after a
moment's reflection. "No, Sir, never heard of him. Unless you
mean Herr Mandl, who has a hardware store in the Floriani-
gasse?"

I had a bitter taste in the mouth, the taste of an irrecoverable
past. What is the use of living, when the wind obliterates our
footsteps in the sand directly we have gone by? Thirty years,
perhaps forty, a man had breathed, read, thought, and spoken
within this narrow room; three or four years had elapsed, and
there had arisen a new king over Egypt, which knew not
Joseph. No one in the Café Gluck had ever heard of Jacob
Mendel, of Buchmendel. Somewhat pettishly I asked the head-
waiter whether I could have a word with Herr Standhartner, or with one of the old staff.

"Herr Standhartner, who used to own the place? He sold
it years ago, and has died since. . . . The former head-waiter?
He saved up enough to retire, and lives upon a little property
at Krems. No, Sir, all of the old lot are scattered. All except
one, indeed, Frau Sporschil, who looks after the toilet. She's
been here for ages, worked under the late owner, I know. But
she's not likely to remember your Herr Mendel. Such as she
hardly know one guest from another."

I dissented in thought.

"One does not forget a Jacob Mendel so easily!"

What I said was:

"Still, I should like to have a word with Frau Sporschil, if she has a moment to spare."

The "Toilettenfrau" (known in the Viennese vernacular as the "Schocoladefrau") soon emerged from the basement, white-haired, run to seed, heavy-footed, wiping her chapped hands upon a towel as she came. She had been called away from her task of cleaning up, and was obviously uneasy at being summoned into the strong light of the guest-rooms—for common folk in Vienna, where an authoritative tradition has lingered on after the revolution, always think it must be a police matter when their "superiors" want to question them. She eyed me suspiciously, though humbly. But as soon as I asked her about Jacob Mendel, she braced up, and at the same time her eyes filled with tears.

"Poor Herr Mendel . . . so there's still someone who bears him in mind?"

Old people are commonly much moved by anything which recalls the days of their youth and revives the memory of past companionships. I asked if he was still alive.

"Good Lord, no. Poor Herr Mendel must have died five or six years ago. Indeed, I think it's fully seven since he passed away. Dear, good man that he was; and how long I knew him, more than twenty-five years; he was already sitting every day at his table when I began to work here. It was a shame, it was, the way they let him die."

Growing more and more excited, she asked if I was a relative. No one had ever inquired about him before. Didn't I know what had happened to him?

"No," I replied, "and I want you to be good enough to tell me all about it."

She looked at me timidly, and continued to wipe her damp hands. It was plain to me that she found it embarrassing, with her dirty apron and her tousled white hair, to be standing in the full glare of the café. She kept looking round anxiously, to see if one of the waiters might be listening.

"Let's go into the card-room," I said, "Mendel's old room. You shall tell me your story there."

She nodded appreciatively, thankful that I understood, and led the way to the inner room, a little shambling in her gait. As I followed, I noticed that the waiters and the guests were staring at us as a strangely assorted pair. We sat down opposite one another at the marble-topped table, and there she told me the story of Jacob Mendel's ruin and death. I will give the tale as nearly as may be in her own words, supplemented here and there by what I learned afterwards from other sources.

"Down to the outbreak of war, and after the war had begun, he continued to come here every morning at half-past seven, to sit at this table and study all day just as before. We had the feeling that the fact of a war going on had never entered his mind. Certainly he didn't read the newspapers, and didn't talk to anyone except about books. He paid no attention when (in the early days of the war, before the authorities put a stop to such things) the newspaper-venders ran through the streets shouting, 'Great Battle on the Eastern Front' (or wherever it might be), 'Horrible Slaughter,' and so on; when people gathered in knots to talk things over, he kept himself to himself; he did not know that Fritz, the billiard-marker, who fell in one of the first battles, had vanished from this place; he did not know that Herr Standhartner's son had been taken prisoner by the Russians at Przemysl; never said a word when the bread grew more and more uneatable and when he was given bean-coffee to drink at breakfast and supper instead of hot milk. Once only did he express surprise at the changes, wondering why so few students came to the café. There was nothing in the world that mattered to him except his books.

"Then disaster befell him. At eleven one morning, two po-

licemen came, one in uniform, and the other a plainclothes
man. The latter showed the red rosette under the lapel of his
coat and asked whether there was a man named Jacob Mendel
in the house. They went straight to Herr Mendel's table. The
poor man, in his innocence, supposed they had books to sell, or
wanted some information; but they told him he was under
arrest, and took him away at once. It was a scandal for the
café. All the guests flocked round Herr Mendel, as he stood
between the two police officers, his spectacles pushed up under
his hair, staring from each to the other bewildered. Some ventured a protest, saying there must be a mistake—that Herr
Mendel was a man who wouldn't hurt a fly; but the detective
was furious, and told them to mind their own business. They
took him away, and none of us at the Café Gluck saw him
again for two years. I never found out what they had against
him, but I would take my dying oath that they must have
made a mistake. Herr Mendel could never have done anything wrong. It was a crime to treat an innocent man so
harshly."

The excellent Frau Sporschil was right. Our friend Jacob
Mendel had done nothing wrong. He had merely (as I sub-
sequently learned) done something incredibly stupid, only ex-
plicable to those who knew the man's peculiarities. The military censorship board, whose function it was to supervise cor-
respondence passing into and out of neutral lands, one day
got its clutches upon a postcard written and signed by a certain
Jacob Mendel, properly stamped for transmission abroad. This
postcard was addressed to Monsieur Jean Labourdaire, Li-
braire, Quai de Grenelle, Paris—to an enemy country, therefore. The writer complained that the last eight issues of the
monthly "Bulletin bibliographique de la France" had failed to
reach him, although his annual subscription had been duly
paid in advance. The jack-in-office who read this missive (a
high-school teacher with a bent for the study of the Romance

languages, called up for "war-service" and sent to employ his
talents at the censorship board instead of wasting them in the
trenches) was astonished by its tenor. "Must be a joke," he
thought. He had to examine some two thousand letters and
postcards every week, always on the alert to detect anything
that might savour of espionage, but never yet had he chanced
upon anything so absurd as that an Austrian subject should
unconcernedly drop into one of the imperial and royal letter-
boxes a postcard addressed to someone in an enemy land, regardless of the trifling detail that since August 1914 the Central Powers had been cut off from Russia on one side and
from France on the other by barbed-wire entanglements and
a network of ditches in which men armed with rifles and
bayonets, machine-guns and artillery, were doing their utmost
to exterminate one another like rats. Our schoolmaster en-
rolled in the Landsturm did not treat this first postcard seriously, but pigeon-holed it as a curiosity not worth talking
about to his chief. But a few weeks later there turned up another card, again from Jacob Mendel, this time to John Al-
dridge, Bookseller, Golden Square, London, asking whether
the addressee could send the last few numbers of the "Antiquarian" to an address in Vienna which was clearly stated on
the card.

The censor in the blue uniform began to feel uneasy. Was
his "class" trying to trick the schoolmaster? Were the cards
written in cipher? Possible, anyhow; so the subordinate went
over to the major's desk, clicked his heels together, saluted,
and laid the suspicious documents before "properly constituted
authority." A strange business, certainly. The police were in-
structed by telephone to see if there actually was a Jacob
Mendel at the specified address, and, if so, to bring the fellow
along. Within the hour, Mendel had been arrested, and (still
stupefied by the shock) brought before the major, who showed
him the postcards, and asked him with drill-sergeant rough-

ness whether he acknowledged their authorship. Angered at being spoken to so sharply, and still more annoyed because his perusal of an important catalogue had been interrupted, Mendel answered tartly:

"Of course I wrote the cards. That's my handwriting and signature. Surely one has a right to claim the delivery of a periodical to which one has subscribed?"

The major swung half-round in his swivel-chair and exchanged a meaning glance with the lieutenant seated at the adjoining desk.

"The man must be a double-distilled idiot" was what they mutely conveyed to one another.

Then the chief took counsel within himself whether he should discharge the offender with a caution, or whether he should treat the case more seriously. In all offices, when such doubts arise, the usual practice is, not to spin a coin, but to send in a report. Thus Pilate washes his hands of responsibility. Even if the report does no good, it can do no harm, and is merely one useless manuscript or typescript added to a million others.

In this instance, however, the decision to send in a report did much harm, alas, to an inoffensive man of genius, for it involved asking a series of questions, and the third of them brought suspicious circumstances to light.

"Your full name?"

"Jacob Mendel."

"Occupation?"

"Book-pedlar" (for, as already explained, Mendel had no shop, but only a pedlar's license).

"Place of birth?"

Now came the disaster. Mendel's birthplace was not far from Petrikau. The major raised his eyebrows. Petrikau, or Piotrkov, was across the frontier, in Russian Poland.

"You were born a Russian subject. When did you acquire Austrian nationality? Show me your papers."

Mendel gazed at the officer uncomprehendingly through his spectacles.

"Papers? Identification papers? I have nothing but my hawker's license."

"What's your nationality, then? Was your father Austrian or Russian?"

Undismayed, Mendel answered:

"A Russian, of course."

"What about yourself?"

"Wishing to evade Russian military service, I slipped across the frontier thirty-three years ago, and ever since I have lived in Vienna."

The matter seemed to the major to be growing worse and worse.

"But didn't you take steps to become an Austrian subject?"

"Why should I?" countered Mendel. "I never troubled my head about such things."

"Then you are still a Russian subject?"

Mendel, who was bored by this endless questioning, answered simply:

"Yes, I suppose I am."

The startled and indignant major threw himself back in his chair with such violence that the wood cracked protestingly. So this was what it had come to! In Vienna, the Austrian capital, at the end of 1915, after Tarnow, when the war was in full blast, after the great offensive, a Russian could walk about unmolested, could write letters to France and England, while the police ignored his machinations. And then the fools who wrote in the newspapers wondered why Conrad von Hötzendorf had not advanced in seven-leagued boots to Warsaw, and the general staff was puzzled because every movement of the troops was immediately blabbed to the Russians.

The lieutenant had sprung to his feet and crossed the room to his chief's table. What had been an almost friendly conversation took a new turn, and degenerated into a trial.

"Why didn't you report as an enemy alien directly the war began?"

Mendel, still failing to realize the gravity of his position, answered in his singing Jewish jargon:

"Why should I report? I don't understand."

The major regarded this inquiry as a challenge, and asked threateningly:

"Didn't you read the notices that were posted up everywhere?"

"No."

"Didn't you read the newspapers?"

"No."

The two officers stared at Jacob Mendel (now sweating with uneasiness) as if the moon had fallen from the sky into their office. Then the telephone buzzed, the typewriters clacked, orderlies ran hither and thither, and Mendel was sent under guard to the nearest barracks, where he was to await transfer to a concentration camp. When he was ordered to follow the two soldiers, he was frankly puzzled, but not seriously perturbed. What could the man with the gold-lace collar and the rough voice have against him? In the upper world of books, where Mendel lived and breathed and had his being, there was no warfare, there were no misunderstandings, only an ever-increasing knowledge of words and figures, of book-titles and authors' names. He walked good-humouredly enough downstairs between the soldiers, whose first charge was to take him to the police station. Not until, there, the books were taken out of his overcoat pockets, and the police impounded the portfolio containing a hundred important memoranda and

customers' addresses, did he lose his temper, and begin to resist and strike blows. They had to tie his hands. In the
struggle, his spectacles fell off, and these magical telescopes,
without which he could not see into the wonderworld of
books, were smashed into a thousand pieces. Two days later,
insufficiently clad (for his only wrap was a light summer
cloak), he was sent to the internment camp for Russian ci-
vilians at Komorn.

I have no information as to what Jacob Mendel suffered
during these two years of internment, cut off from his beloved
books, penniless, among roughly nurtured men, few of whom
could read or write, in a huge human dunghill. This must
be left to the imagination of those who can grasp the torments
of a caged eagle. By degrees, however, our world, grown
sober after its fit of drunkenness, has become aware that,
of all the cruelties and wanton abuses of power during the
war, the most needless and therefore the most inexcusable was
this herding together behind barbed-wire fences of thousands
upon thousands of persons who had outgrown the age of
military service, who had made homes for themselves in a
foreign land, and who (believing in the good faith of their
hosts) had refrained from exercising the sacred right of hos-
pitality granted even by the Tunguses and Araucanians—the
right to flee while time permits. This crime against civilization
was committed with the same unthinking hardihood in
France, Germany, and Britain, in every belligerent country
of our crazy Europe.

Probably Jacob Mendel would, like thousands as innocent
as he, have perished in this cattle-pen, have gone stark mad,
have succumbed to dysentery, asthenia, softening of the brain,
had it not been that, before the worst happened, a chance
(typically Austrian) recalled him to the world in which a
spiritual life became again possible. Several times after his
disappearance, letters from distinguished customers were de-

livered for him at the Café Gluck. Count Schönberg, sometime lord-lieutenant of Styria, an enthusiastic collector of
works on heraldry; Siegenfeld, the former dean of the theo-
logical faculty, who was writing a commentary on the works
of St. Augustine; Edler von Pisek, an octogenarian admiral
on the retired list, engaged in writing his memoirs—these
and other persons of note, wanting information from Buchmendel, had repeatedly addressed communications to him at
his familiar haunt, and some of these were duly forwarded to
the concentration camp at Komorn. There they fell into the
hands of the commanding officer, who happened to be a man
of humane disposition, and was astonished to find what
notables were among the correspondents of this dirty little
Russian Jew, who, half-blind now that his spectacles were
broken and he had no money to buy new ones, crouched in
a corner like a mole, grey, eyeless, and dumb. A man who had
such patrons must be a person of importance, whatever he
looked like. The C.O. therefore read the letters to the short-
sighted Mendel, and penned answers for him to sign—answers
which were mainly requests that influence should be exercised
on his behalf. The spell worked, for these correspondents had
the solidarity of collectors. Joining forces and pulling strings
they were able (giving guarantees for the "enemy alien's"
good behaviour) to secure leave for Buchmendel's return to
Vienna in 1917, after more than two years at Komorn—on
the condition that he should report daily to the police. The
proviso mattered little. He was a free man once more, free
to take up his quarters in his old attic, free to handle books
again, free (above all) to return to his table in the Café Gluck.
I can describe the return from the underworld of the camp
in the good Frau Sporschil's own words:

"One day—Jesus, Mary, Joseph; I could hardly believe my
eyes—the door opened (you remember the way he had) little
wider than a crack, and through this opening he sidled, poor

Herr Mendel. He was wearing a tattered and much-darned
military cloak, and his head was covered by what had perhaps
once been a hat thrown away by the owner as past use. No
collar. His face looked like a death's head, so haggard it was,
and his hair was pitifully thin. But he came in as if nothing
had happened, went straight to his table, and took off his
cloak, not briskly as of old, for he panted with the exertion.
Nor had he any books with him. He just sat there without a
word, staring straight in front of him with hollow, expression-
less eyes. Only by degrees, after we had brought him the big
bundle of printed matter which had arrived for him from
Germany, did he begin to read again. But he was never the
same man."

No, he was never the same man, not now the miraculum
mundi, the magical walking book-catalogue. All who saw
him in those days told me the same pitiful story. Something
had gone irrecoverably wrong; he was broken; the blood-red
comet of the war had burst into the remote, calm atmosphere
of his bookish world. His eyes, accustomed for decades to look
at nothing but print, must have seen terrible sights in the wire-
fenced human stockyard, for the eyes that had formerly been
so alert and full of ironical gleams were now almost completely veiled by the inert lids, and looked sleepy and red-
bordered behind the carefully repaired spectacle-frames. Worse
still, a cog must have broken somewhere in the marvellous
machinery of his memory, so that the working of the whole
was impaired; for so delicate is the structure of the brain (a
sort of switchboard made of the most fragile substances, and
as easily jarred as are all instruments of precision) that a
blocked arteriole, a congested bundle of nerve-fibres, a fatigued
group of cells, even a displaced molecule, may put the apparatus out of gear and make harmonious working impossible.
In Mendel's memory, the keyboard of knowledge, the keys
were stiff, or—to use psychological terminology—the associa-

tions were impaired. When, now and again, someone came to
ask for information, Jacob stared blankly at the inquirer,
failing to understand the question, and even forgetting it before he had found the answer. Mendel was no longer Buchmendel, just as the world was no longer the world. He could
not now become wholly absorbed in his reading, did not rock
as of old when he read, but sat bolt upright, his glasses turned
mechanically towards the printed page, but perhaps not reading at all, and only sunk in a reverie. Often, said Frau Sporschil, his head would drop on to his book and he would fall
asleep in the daytime, or he would gaze hour after hour at
the stinking acetylene lamp which (in the days of the coal
famine) had replaced the electric lighting. No, Mendel was
no longer Buchmendel, no longer the eighth wonder of the
world, but a weary, worn-out, though still breathing, useless
bundle of beard and ragged garments, which sat, as futile as
a potato-bogle, where of old the Pythian oracle had sat; no
longer the glory of the Café Gluck, but a shameful scarecrow,
evil-smelling, a parasite.

That was the impression he produced upon the new proprietor, Florian Gurtner from Retz, who (a successful profi-
teer in flour and butter) had cajoled Standhartner into selling
him the Café Gluck for eighty thousand rapidly depreciating
paper crowns. He took everything into his hard peasant grip,
hastily arranged to have the old place redecorated, bought
fine-looking satin-covered seats, installed a marble porch, and
was in negotiation with his next-door neighbour to buy a
place where he could extend the café into a dancing-hall.
Naturally while he was making these embellishments, he was
not best pleased by the parasitic encumbrance of Jacob
Mendel, a filthy old Galician Jew, who had been in trouble
with the authorities during the war, was still to be regarded
as an "enemy alien," and, while occupying a table from morning till night, consumed no more than two cups of coffee and

four or five rolls. Standhartner, indeed, had put in a word for
this guest of long standing, had explained that Mendel was a
person of note, and, in the stock-taking, had handed him over
as having a permanent lien upon the establishment, but as an
asset rather than a liability. Florian Gurtner, however, had
brought into the café, not only new furniture, and an up-to-
date cash register, but also the profit-making and hard temper
of the post-war era, and awaited the first pretext for ejecting
from his smart coffee-house the last troublesome vestige of
suburban shabbiness.

A good excuse was not slow to present itself. Jacob Mendel
was impoverished to the last degree. Such banknotes as had
been left to him had crumbled away to nothing during the
inflation period; his regular clientele had been killed, ruined,
or dispersed. When he tried to resume his early trade of book-
pedlar, calling from door to door to buy and to sell, he found
that he lacked strength to carry books up and down stairs. A
hundred little signs showed him to be a pauper. Seldom, now,
did he have a midday meal sent in from the restaurant, and
he began to run up a score at the Café Gluck for his modest
breakfast and supper. Once his payments were as much as
three weeks overdue. Were it only for this reason, the head-
waiter wanted Gurtner to "give Mendel the sack." But Frau
Sporschil intervened, and stood surety for the debtor. What
was due could be stopped out of her wages!

This staved off disaster for a while, but worse was to come.
For some time the head-waiter had noticed that rolls were
disappearing faster than the tally would account for. Naturally suspicion fell upon Mendel, who was known to be six
months in debt to the tottering old porter whose services he
still needed. The head-waiter, hidden behind the stove, was
able, two days later, to catch Mendel red-handed. The unwelcome guest had stolen from his seat in the card-room, crept
behind the counter in the front room, taken two rolls from

the bread-basket, returned to the card-room, and hungrily
devoured them. When settling-up at the end of the day, he
said he had only had coffee; no rolls. The source of wastage
had been traced, and the waiter reported his discovery to the
proprietor. Herr Gurtner, delighted to have so good an excuse
for getting rid of Mendel, made a scene, openly accused him
of theft, and declared that nothing but the goodness of his
own heart prevented his sending for the police.

"But after this," said Florian, "you'll kindly take yourself
off for good and all. We don't want to see your face again at
the Café Gluck."

Jacob Mendel trembled, but made no reply. Abandoning his
poor belongings, he departed without a word.

"It was ghastly," said Frau Sporschil. "Never shall I forget
the sight. He stood up, his spectacles pushed on to his forehead, and his face white as a sheet. He did not even stop to
put on his cloak, although it was January, and very cold.
You'll remember that severe winter, just after the war. In his
fright, he left the book he was reading open upon the table.
I did not notice it at first, and then, when I wanted to pick
it up and take it after him, he had already stumbled out
through the doorway. I was afraid to follow him into the
street, for Herr Gurtner was standing at the door and shouting at him, so that a crowd had gathered. Yet I felt ashamed
to the depths of my soul. Such a thing would never have
happened under the old master. Herr Standhartner would not
have driven Herr Mendel away for pinching one or two rolls
when he was hungry, but would have let him have as many
as he wanted for nothing, to the end of his days. Since the
war, people seem to have grown heartless. Drive away a man
who had been a guest daily for so many, many years. Shameful! I should not like to have to answer before God for such
cruelty!"

The good woman had grown excited, and, with the passion-

ate garrulousness of old age, she kept on repeating how shameful it was, and that nothing of the sort would have happened
if Herr Standhartner had not sold the business. In the end I
tried to stop the flow by asking her what had happened to
Mendel, and whether she had ever seen him again. These
questions excited her yet more.

"Day after day, when I passed his table, it gave me the
creeps, as you will easily understand. Each time I thought to
myself: 'Where can he have got to, poor Herr Mendel?' Had
I known where he lived, I would have called and taken him
something nice and hot to eat—for where could he get the
money to cook food and warm his room? As far as I knew,
he had no kinsfolk in the wide world. When, after a long
time, I had heard nothing about him, I began to believe that
it must be all up with him, and that I should never see him
again. I had made up my mind to have a mass said for the
peace of his soul, knowing him to be a good man, after twenty-
five years' acquaintance.

"At length one day in February, at half-past seven in the
morning, when I was cleaning the windows, the door opened,
and in came Herr Mendel. Generally, as you know, he sidled
in, looking confused, and not 'quite all there'; but this time,
somehow, it was different. I noticed at once the strange look
in his eyes; they were sparkling, and he rolled them this way
and that, as if to see everything at once; as for his appearance,
he seemed nothing but beard and skin and bone. Instantly it
crossed my mind: 'He's forgotten all that happened last time
he was here; it's his way to go about like a sleepwalker noticing nothing; he doesn't remember about the rolls, and how
shamefully Herr Gurtner ordered him out of the place, half
in mind to set the police on him.' Thank goodness, Herr
Gurtner hadn't come yet, and the head-waiter was drinking
coffee. I ran up to Herr Mendel, meaning to tell him he'd
better make himself scarce, for otherwise that ruffian" [she

looked round timidly to see if we were overheard, and hastily amended her phrase], "Herr Gurtner, I mean, would only have him thrown into the street once more. 'Herr Mendel,' I began. He started, and looked at me. In that very moment (it was dreadful), he must have remembered the whole thing, for he almost collapsed, and began to tremble, not his fingers only, but to shiver and shake from head to foot. Hastily he stepped back into the street, and fell in a heap on the pavement as soon as he was outside the door. We telephoned for the ambulance, and they carried him off to hospital, the nurse who came saying he had high fever directly she touched him. He died that evening. 'Double pneumonia,' the doctor said, and that he never recovered consciousness—could not have been fully conscious when he came to the Café Gluck. As I said, he had entered like a man walking in his sleep. The table where he had sat day after day for thirty-six years drew him back to it like a home."

Frau Sporschil and I went on talking about him for a long time, the two last persons to remember this strange creature, Buchmendel: I to whom in youth the book-pedlar from Galicia had given the first revelation of a life wholly devoted to the things of the spirit; she, the poor old woman who was caretaker of a café-toilet, who had never read a book in her life, and whose only tie with this strangely matched comrade in her subordinate, poverty-stricken world had been that for twenty-five years she had brushed his overcoat and had sewn on buttons for him. We, too, might have been considered strangely assorted, but Frau Sporschil and I got on very well together, linked, as we sat at the forsaken marble-topped table, by our common memories of the shade our talk had conjured up—for joint memories, and above all loving memories, always establish a tie. Suddenly, while in the full stream of talk, she exclaimed:

"Lord Jesus, how forgetful I am. I still have the book he

left on the table the evening Herr Gurtner gave him the key
of the street. I didn't know where to take it. Afterwards,
when no one appeared to claim it, I ventured to keep it as a
souvenir. You don't think it wrong of me, Sir?"

She went to a locker where she stored some of the requisites
for her job, and produced the volume for my inspection. I
found it hard to repress a smile, for I was face to face with
one of life's little ironies. It was the second volume of Hayn's
Bibliotheca Germanorum erotica et curiosa, a compendium of
gallant literature known to every book-collector. "Habent sua
fata libelli!" This scabrous publication, as legacy of the vanished magician, had fallen into toilworn hands which had perhaps never held any other printed work than a prayer-book.
Maybe I was not wholly successful in controlling my mirth,
for the expression of my face seemed to perplex the worthy
soul, and once more she said:

"You don't think it wrong of me to keep it, Sir?"

I shook her cordially by the hand.

"Keep it, and welcome," I said. "I am absolutely sure that
our old friend Mendel would be only too delighted to know
that someone among the many thousand he has provided with
books, cherishes his memory."

Then I took my departure, feeling a trifle ashamed when
I compared myself with this excellent old woman, who, so
simply and so humanely, had fostered the memory of the dead
scholar. For she, uncultured though she was, had at least
preserved a book as a memento; whereas I, a man of education
and a writer, had completely forgotten Buchmendel for years—
I, who at least should have known that one only makes books
in order to keep in touch with one's fellows after one has
ceased to breathe, and thus to defend oneself against the in-
exorable fate of all that lives—transitoriness and oblivion.

Leporella

Crescentia Anna Aloisia Finkenhuber was thirty-nine years of age, and had been born (an illegitimate child) in a mountain hamlet not far from Innsbruck. Under the rubric "Special Peculiarities" in her identity paper as servant-maid was drawn a line signifying "none"; but if the officials who fill in such documents were obliged to enter characterological details, there would certainly have been written here: "Looks like an over-driven, bony, lean mountain nag." Beyond question there was something horse-like in the aspect of the cumbrous lower lip; in the elongated and sharply bounded oval of the brownish visage; in the dull eyes almost denuded of lashes; and, above all, in the coarse hair, plastered on to the forehead with pomade. Her gait, too, was as stiff and reluctant as that of a mule, one of those unhappy beasts which, winter after summer and summer after winter, have to carry loads of wood up and down the same rough and stony or muddy trackway. When freed from the halter of toil,

Crescenz, clasping her bony fingers and sticking out her elbows in ungainly fashion, would usually sit down and fall
into a doze, no more lightened by intelligence than that of
one of the aforesaid mules standing patiently in its stable when
the day's work was done. Everything about her was hard,
wooden, and heavy. Thought, with her, was a slow process. A
new idea made its way into her mind with much difficulty,
as if it had to traverse the meshes of a choked sieve; but,
once she had grasped it, she retained it as a miser clings to a
coin. She never read, not even the newspaper or her prayer-
book. Writing was a great labour to her, and the awkwardly
formed letters in her marketing-book reminded one of her
own clumsy and angular figure, which was utterly lacking
in feminine charm. As hard as her bones, her forehead, her
hips, and her knuckles, was her voice, which, despite the
guttural Tyrolese accent, creaked like the hinges of a rusty
iron gate. Nor was this rustiness surprising, for Crescenz never
uttered a superfluous word. No one had seen her laugh. In
this respect, likewise, she resembled the lower animals; for
more cruel even than the denial of speech to those we term
"dumb beasts" is the denial of laughter, that free and joyful
vent to the emotions.

    Being a bastard, she had been brought up at the charge
of the community, and at the age of twelve had been sent out
to service, at first as maid-of-all-work in a restaurant; but
then, having gained a good character by her indomitable and
almost bestial diligence, as cook-general in a second-rate hotel
on one of the main routes of travel. Rising daily at five,
Crescenz slaved, swept, scrubbed, did the rooms, lighted fires,
cooked, kneaded and baked, washed and ironed, till late at
night. She never asked for a day out; never went into the
street, except to church and back. The kitchen-fire was her
sun, and her only acquaintance with the forest came from

splitting thousands upon thousands of billets every year in order to feed the flames.

Men did not trouble her: maybe because, as previously explained, twenty-five years spent as a robot had rubbed off the very inadequate feminine graces which Mother Nature had bestowed on her; maybe because she so fiercely repelled any amorous advances. Her only pleasure was found in the amassing of money, for she had the magpie hoarding-instincts of the peasant, and dreaded lest, when she grew old, she would once more be forced to accept the unwelcome lot of being dependent upon the community. The bitter bread of public charity would have choked her.

Nothing but the lust for gain had, when she was thirty-seven, allured this dull being from her Tyrolese homeland. The manageress of an employment agency, spending a summer holiday in the Tyrol, was amazed by Crescenz's berserker-rage for work, and told her that in Vienna she could get twice her present earnings.

On the railway journey, Crescenz maintained her usual taciturnity, seated in solemn silence while holding in her lap the wicker basket which contained all her worldly possessions, though her knees ached beneath its weight. Some of her fellow-travellers, friendly and companionable, offered to put it in the rack, but the dour woman snapped a refusal, for, in her peasant mind, cheating and theft were the only associations with the great city to which she was journeying. In Vienna it was some days before she could make her way alone to market, for at first the traffic frightened her almost out of her poor wits. But once she had grown familiar with the four streets she had to traverse, she became independent, and trotted safely to the market and back carrying a basket on her arm. In her new place, she swept, scrubbed, lighted the fires, and did the rooms, just as before. At nine, the customary

hour in Tyrol, she went to bed, and slept like an animal with
her mouth wide open, until she was called in the morning.
No one could tell whether she liked her new situation; perhaps she herself did not know. Her reserve was unbroken.
She acknowledged orders with a monosyllabic "Right"; or,
if in a refractory mood, with a shrug of the shoulders. She
ignored her fellow-servants, being, as a rule, absolutely indifferent to their inclination to tease and to make fun of her.
Once only, when another maid, a cheerful Viennese girl,
persistently mocked her Tyrolese accent, Crescenz lost patience. In a fury she snatched a burning log from the stove,
and, brandishing this dangerous weapon, rushed at her tormentress, who fled shrieking with dismay. Thenceforward no
one ventured to gibe.

Every Sunday morning, dressed in her voluminous skirt
and wearing a Tyrolese head-dress, she went to Mass. Once
only, being given a day off, she tried a walk through Vienna.
She would not take a tram, and her peregrinations in the
bewildering streets brought her, at length, to the Danube.
After staring at the current as if it were a familiar friend, she
turned about and retraced her steps, sedulously avoiding the
busier highways. This first excursion must have been a disappointment, for it was never repeated. She preferred to spend
her free Sundays doing needlework, or sitting idly at a window. Thus her coming to the metropolis wrought no change
in the treadmill of her life, except that at the end of each
month four blue banknotes instead of two were put into her
toilworn, withered, and calloused hands. These notes were
always suspiciously scrutinized. Each was separately folded
and smoothed out, before being stacked with the others and
laid to rest in the yellow box of carved wood which she had
brought with her from the village. This clumsy little treasure-
chest contained the innermost purpose of her life. At night

she always had the key under her pillow. No one in the house
knew where it was kept in the daytime.

Such were the characteristics of this weird human being
(for "human being" we must call her, although the human
attributes were queerly obscured); and perhaps a more normal
woman could not have long endured to stay as a servant in
the remarkable household of young Baron von Ledersheim.
The atmosphere was so quarrelsome that in general the
domestics were quick to give notice. The hysterical scoldings
of their mistress were more than they could bear. The elderly
daughter of an extremely rich manufacturer, she had made
the baron's acquaintance at a health-resort. Though he was
many years younger than herself, and his birth was nothing
to boast of, while he was over head and ears in debt, he was
a handsome fellow, with distinguished manners, and willing
enough to marry money. Things were speedily arranged between the pair, notwithstanding the strenuous opposition of
the lady's parents, who were on the look-out for more solid
advantages than Baron von Ledersheim could offer. Before
the honeymoon was over, Baroness von Ledersheim was to
learn that her father and mother had been right. The young
husband had by no means finished sowing his wild oats,
and was more interested in this form of agriculture than in
the fulfilment of his conjugal duties. Nor had he even made
a clean breast of it as to the amount of his debts.

Good-natured in a way, a pleasant companion like most
libertines, he had no principles, and considered any attempt
to regulate his expenditure to be the outcome of plebeian
prejudices. The husband wanted to remain a dissolute spendthrift, after marriage as before; the wife wanted an orderly
domestic life such as she had been used to in her parental
home at Essen. This bourgeoisdom jarred on his aristocratic
nerves. Since, wealthy though she was, she tried to draw the

purse-strings tight, and refused to finance his pet scheme of building and running a racing-stable, his response to her "meanness" was, as far as husbandly relations went, to ignore his North-German bride, whose dictatorial ways and harsh voice became increasingly offensive to him. As the saying goes, he "shelved" her, without obvious brutality, but in a way which caused her grievous disappointment. When she reproached him, he listened courteously and with apparent sympathy, but as soon as the sermon was over he blew away her exhortations as unconcernedly as the smoke of his cigarette, and continued to follow his own bent. This seeming amiability was more galling than open resistance. Since she was disarmed by his unfailing civility, her suppressed wrath found vent in other directions, and, above all, in railing at the servants, with reason or without. In less than two years, she had changed her domestic staff no less than sixteen times, having once used violence, and had to pay heavy compensation in order to avoid a lawsuit and public scandal.

Crescenz was the only one of the servants who could endure these storms of scolding unmoved, and stood stolidly while they raged, looking like a cab-horse in the rain. She never took sides, was unaffected by the frequent changes in the staff, hardly seemed to notice that her associates in the servants' hall varied continually in name, aspect, and character. For she never passed the time of day with her workmates, was indifferent to the passionate slamming of doors, the frequent interruptions at mealtimes, her mistress's fainting-fits and hysterical outbursts. She went on with her daily marketing expeditions and her work in the kitchen, unconcerned as to anything that happened outside the daily round of toil. Hard and insensitive as a flail, she threshed on as day followed day, and two years of her life in the metropolis passed by without effecting the slightest change in her mentality. As far as externals were concerned, the only difference to be noticed was that the pile of blue banknotes in her cashbox had grown thicker by an inch; and that, when (licking her finger to facilitate the process) she counted them at the second year's end, she found she was very close to the aim of her desire, the magical figure of a thousand.

But chance works with diamond-drills; and fate, cunning of hand, often produces strange modifications even in the rockiest of natures. In Crescenz's case the manifest cause of change was as commonplace as she herself seemed. At the close of a ten-year cycle, the government was taking a new census, and a complicated census-paper had to be filled in every dwelling-house. The baron, who had good reason to know that most of his domestics were unskilled in the use of the pen, decided to tabulate the information himself, and, in due course, Crescenz was summoned to his writing-table. When he asked her full name, age, and birthplace, the first item and the third proved of unexpected interest to the master of the house. A keen sportsman, he had often stayed with an old college-friend who was owner of a Tyrolese shooting; and he had once done a fortnight's mountaineering in pursuit of chamois, accompanied by a guide, Finkenhuber by name, who turned out to have been Crescenz's uncle. Ledersheim had taken a fancy to the man. This fact, and his knowledge of the cook's native village, led to a conversation between master and maid, with the resulting further disclosure that, in the inn where she had formerly worked, the baron had once partaken of an extraordinarily good haunch of venison. Trifling matters, no doubt; but the long arm of coincidence handles such trifles, and to Crescenz, who for the first time encountered in Vienna a person acquainted with her home, they seemed wonderful. Her face flushed with unwonted excitement, she stood in front of the baron, curtsying in ungainly fashion, and highly flattered when he proceeded to crack jokes with her, asking her with an assumed Tyrolese

accent, whether she knew how to yodel—and the like. At
length, entering into the spirit of the game, he spanked her
with peasant familiarity on her hard behind, saying: "Be off
with you, now, my good Cenzi, and let me get on with my
job; but take these two extra crowns with you because you
hail from the Zillertal."

The master had not shown any deep feeling. Nothing, one
might have thought, to stir the old maid to the depths. But
on her dull and unimpressionable nature these few minutes'
talk had the effect of a stone thrown into a stagnant pool,
forming circular waves which moved, slowly widening, to
lap upon the margin of consciousness. Not for years upon
years had the taciturn creature had any sort of personal relations with one of her fellows; and it seemed to her almost
uncanny that the first to show a friendly interest in her, from
among the millions who lived in this wilderness of bricks and
mortar, should be a man who knew her own mountains, and
had actually eaten venison cooked there by her own hands.
Superadded came the clout upon the backside, which, to her
peasant mind was a laconic invitation to the woman in her.
Even though Crescenz did not make so bold as to fancy that
the elegantly dressed and distinguished gentleman actually
coveted her wizened body, still the physical familiarity stirred
her slumbering senses.

Thus, thanks to this encounter, there began in the woman's
inmost being a transformation, obscure at the outset, but
growing continually more definite—and culminating in a new
feeling, akin to that sudden recognition which leads a dog
to single out one from among the innumerable bipeds that
surround it, and to look upon him thenceforward as master,
nay as god. The dog thus transformed follows its master
everywhere, wriggles with delight and wags a friendly tail
when meeting him again after an absence, obeys, fetches, and
carries with slavish subservience. Into the narrow chambers

of Crescenz's mind, which had hitherto been completely filled
with a bare half-dozen of ideas—money, marketing, kitchen-
fire, church, and bed—there had suddenly been thrust a new
element, which demanded accommodation, and roughly el-
bowed the previous occupants aside. With the "havingness"
that makes the peasant so reluctant to surrender anything that
has once been gripped, she interpolated this new element
sedulously into the confused world of her lethargic impulses.
It was a little while, of course, before the change in her habits
became fully manifest, and the initial signs of the transformation were obscure. For instance, she brushed the baron's
clothes and cleaned his shoes with meticulous care, while leaving the baroness's dresses and footgear to the lady's maid to
look after. Then she would often scurry forth into the hall
the instant she heard the baron's latchkey in the lock, eager
to relieve him of hat, coat, and stick. In the kitchen, she
worked harder than ever, and would sometimes laboriously
ask her way to the big market, in search of a haunch of venison. She also began to pay more attention to the niceties of
dress.

A week or two elapsed before this first shoot of her new
feelings showed its leaves plainly above the ground. Several
more weeks were needed until a second shoot pushed up from
the seedling, and assumed a definite tint. The second feeling
was the obvious complement of the first, hatred for the baroness, for the wife who could live with the baron, sleep with
him, speak to him whenever she pleased, but nevertheless did
not revere the master as she herself, Cenzi, did. It may have
been because (having now learned to take notice) she had
been shocked by one of the scenes in which the infuriated
wife "slanged" her husband unmercifully, or it may have
been because she had become aware how painfully the cold
and arrogant manners of the North German mistress contrasted with the geniality of the Viennese master of the house

—in any case Crescenz began, in manifold ways, to show that
she had conceived a spite against the baroness. Brigitta von
Ledersheim had always to ring twice, at least, before Crescenz
would deign to answer the bell; and then the maid came with
irritating slowness and obvious reluctance. Her raised shoulders produced the same impression as the turning back of its
ears by a stubborn and vicious horse, a conviction of insuper-
able antagonism. She said nothing in response to her mistress's
orders, so that the baroness never knew whether she had been
understood and would be obeyed. A repetition produced only
a contemptuous nod, or a "I heard you all right," in her broad
peasant accent. Again, just before a visit to the theatre, when
the mistress was dressing, the key of a drawer containing
some indispensable trinket would have gone astray—to be
discovered in a corner of the room after half an hour's frantic
search. Crescenzi made a point of failing to deliver telephone
messages to the baroness, and when scolded for the omission
would pertly reply "I just forgot." She never looked her
mistress squarely in the face, perhaps from fear lest her loathing should peep out.

Meanwhile these domestic discomforts led to continually
more violent scenes between husband and wife—for there
can be little doubt that the maid's state of mind and uncivil
manners reacted on the mistress to increase the latter's uncon-
trol. Brigitta's nerves had been overstrained by too long a
period of spinsterhood; she had been further embittered by
her husband's neglect and by her failure to hit it off even with
her servants; so that she now grew more and more unbalanced. The bromides and the veronal she took to relieve in-
somnia made matters worse; but no one sympathized with
the poor woman in her nervous crises, or tried to help her
to live more hygienically and to regain self-mastery. A neu-
rologist whom she consulted advised a couple of months' stay
in a sanatorium, and her husband endorsed the proposal with

such injudicious enthusiasm that the baroness at first refused
to consider it. In the end, however, she gave way. She would
take the lady's maid with her, while Crescenz would be left
alone to look after the baron in the roomy flat.

The news that the care of her beloved master was to be
left wholly in her hands had an electrifying effect on
Crescenzi. She seemed to have been given the contents of a
magic phial—a philtre which stirred the lees of her undis-
charged passions and modified her behaviour. Her limbs were
no longer stiff and ungainly; she moved lightly, easily, and
swiftly. When the time came for the baroness's journey,
the maid ran from room to room, packed the trunks without
waiting to be told, shouldered them like a porter, and carried them down to the cab. When, late in the evening, the
baron returned from seeing his wife off at the station, handed
hat and overcoat to the expectant Crescenz, and, with a sigh
of relief, said: "Well, I've got her safely away!"—a remarkable
thing happened. Crescenz, as already explained, resembled
the lower animals, in that she never laughed. But now her
lips were animated by an unfamiliar phenomenon. Her
mouth broadened into a grin so unrestrained that Ledersheim,
to whom the awkward servantmaid's expression of countenance came as a painful surprise, felt ashamed of having been
so open with a menial, and went into his bedroom without
saying another word.

The discomfort lasted for a fleeting moment, and during
the next few days master and maidservant were united in the
enjoyment of a precious sense of quietude and agreeable
ease. The wife's exit from the scene had cleared the atmosphere. Rudolf, freed from the burden of responsibility, and
from the perpetual risk of being called to account for his
movements, came home late next evening, and Crescenz's
silent adoration was a welcome contrast to the loquacious

inquisitiveness with which Brigitta was wont to receive him. Crescenz devoted herself to her work with more than customary zeal, got up earlier than usual, polished the furniture till you could see your face in it, was never satisfied with the brightness of the door-handles, provided exceptionally tasty meals—and, greatly to the baron's surprise, served them on a dinner-set which was supposed to be kept for great occasions. Though as a rule he was blind to such matters, he could not but notice the peculiar and delicate attentions of this strange maidservant, and, being a good-natured fellow at bottom, he expressed his gratification. He praised her culinary skill, and, in a day or two, when his birthday came round and Crescenz had made him a jam tart in which the pastry was decorated with his initials and the family coat-of-arms, he said with a smile: "You are spoiling me, Cenzi. But what the devil shall I do when the mistress comes home again?"

To the inhabitants of other lands, such free-and-easy ways, such want of reserve in the remarks of a master to a servant, may seem incredible, but there was nothing out of the ordinary in them as far as pre-war Austria was concerned. They were, in fact, manifestations of the boundless contempt of the aristocracy for the mob, a contempt in witness whereof the gentry rode with a loose rein. Just as an archduke, stationed in some out-of-the-way Galician town, would send his orderly to the brothel to fetch him a bedfellow, and, having satisfied his desires, would hand the girl over to the underling—regardless of the salacious gossip that would ensue when the cits got wind of the affair—so a man of title who was out shooting would be more inclined to hobnob over luncheon with his loader or his groom, than to be friendly with a university professor or a wealthy man of business. But these ostensibly democratic relationships, easy-going though they seemed, must

not be taken at their face value; the master remained the
master, and knew how to keep his distance once more, the
instant he rose from his meal. Since, however, the minor
gentry were always inclined to ape the manners of the feudal
aristocracy, the baron made no bones about speaking deroga-
torily of his wife to a country wench who was in her service,
assured that she would never give him away, but failing to
realize what a profound impression his words were producing in her simple mind.

All the same, he imposed some vestiges of restraint upon
his tongue and his general behaviour for a few days. Then,
feeling confident that he could trust her, he began, unheeding
dangerous possibilities, to resume bachelor habits. This was
his own house, his wife was away, and he could amuse himself as he pleased. One day towards the close of the first week
he spent as a grass-widower, he rang for Crescenzi, and, as if
the matter were of no moment, told her that that evening
she was to lay a cold supper for two, and to go to bed without
waiting up for his return. He would himself see to everything
when he came in.

"Very good, Sir," answered Crescenz, without the smallest
change of expression to show that she understood what lay
behind. But that she was sharper of wit than she seemed was
plain to the amused Rudolf when, returning towards midnight accompanied by one of the young ladies of the opera,
he found the supper-table decked with flowers; and, on going
into his bedroom, discovered, not only that his own bed had
been made ready as usual, but that the adjoining bed had
been invitingly turned down, and that one of his wife's silk
nightgowns and her slippers were laid out ready for use. The
husband whose marriage vows sat so lightly on his conscience
could not but laugh at the length to which this extraordinary
abigail was prepared to go in her attentions. Thenceforward

she was his acknowledged confederate, and next morning he had no hesitation in ringing for Crescenz to act as lady's maid to his light-of-love.

It was at this juncture that Crescenz was rechristened. The budding diva was understudy for the role of Donna Elvira, and found it congenial to call her lover Don Juan. On her next visit to the flat, she said merrily:

"Don Juan, I wish you'd send for that Leporella of yours."

The name took his fancy, were it only for the reason that it was too grotesquely misapplicable to the withered Tyrolese peasantwoman, and from that time on he always addressed her as Leporella. Crescenz, though startled at first by her new appellation, accepted it as a compliment. She knew nothing of its Don Giovannesque associations, but it was euphonious to her untutored ears, and her vanity was tickled that her master should give her a pet-name. Whenever she heard the impudent call "Leporella!" her thin lips parted in a smile that showed her horse-like teeth; and, obsequiously, she hastened to fulfil the commands of her liege lord.

The name had been lightly chosen, and I have called it misapplicable. Nevertheless, it hit the mark, for "Leporella," like her namesake Leporello, was a sympathetic accomplice. An old maid who had known nothing of love, she took a vicarious pride in her lusty young master's adventures. No matter whether the delight came from knowing that the detested baroness's bed was dishonoured almost every night by some new illicit occupant, or from an imaginary participation in these sensuous pleasures—there could be no question as to its existence. Her bony frame, wasted and wizened by decades of arduous toil until it had been almost completely desexualized, thrilled with bawdy pleasure at sight of a second and then a third fleeting occupant of Baroness von Ledersheim's rightful couch. Her confederateship and the unfamiliar erotic atmosphere were powerful stimulants to her slumbering senses. Crescenz became really and truly Leporella, became, like Leporello in Da Ponte's libretto, vigorous and sprightly. Unaccustomed qualities, stirred up from the depths by this ardent copartnership, came to the surface; petty wiles and artifices, an inclination to spy and eavesdrop. She listened at the door, squinted through the keyhole, buzzed eagerly hither and thither, until her curiosity and alertness transformed what had been little better than an automaton into living flesh and blood. To the astonishment of the neighbours, Crescenz became sociable; she gossiped with the servants, cracked jokes with the postman, began to talk of miscellaneous subjects with the market-women. Then, one evening, when the lights in the attic (where the servants' quarters were) had been extinguished, the maids in the rooms on the opposite side of the court heard a remarkable humming from her window, usually so silent. Clumsily, mezzo voce, she was singing one of those folk-songs which dairymaids sing in Alpine pastures. Monotonously she produced the air, with untrained lips and vocal cords, like a child fingering the keys of a neglected piano—the effect being simultaneously touching and repulsive. Not since early youth had she tried to sing, but now something that came from the darkness of forgotten years seemed to be struggling towards the light.

This extraordinary transformation was least obvious to the man who had brought it about—for who troubles to notice his own shadow? We see, of course, with half an eye, how it dogs our footsteps, or sometimes runs in advance (like a wish of which we are not yet fully aware); but how rarely do we heed its parody of our form, or recognize in it a caricature of our personality. All that Ledersheim noticed in Crescenz was that she seemed ever ready to serve him diligently, silently, and self-sacrificingly. Her mute worship was agreeable to him. From time to time, as if patting a dog, he said a friendly word or two; sometimes he jested with her,

took her good-naturedly by the ear, gave her a banknote or a
theatre ticket—trifles he extracted from his waistcoat-pocket,
but, for her, treasures of inestimable value, which she hoarded
as relics in her cashbox. Gradually it became a habit with
him to think aloud in her presence, and even to entrust her
with difficult commissions; and the more marked these signs
of his confidence, the more slavish became her devotion. She
tried to anticipate his desires; to enter into his being as the
executant of his will; to see with his eyes, hear with his ears;
to enjoy his pleasures and share in his conquests. She beamed
when a new bedfellow accompanied him on his return, and
was visibly disappointed if he came back alone. Her brain
now worked as unceasingly as aforetime her hands had done,
and a new light of understanding sparkled in her eyes. The
overdriven beast of burden had developed into a human
being; though still reserved, tight-up, crafty, and dangerous,
meditative and much occupied, restless and rancorous.

Once, when the baron came home earlier than usual, he
was amazed on entering the hall to hear from behind the door
of the kitchen, where inviolable silence usually prevailed, the
noise of sniggering. The door was half-open, and in the aper-
ture Leporella showed herself, rubbing her hands on her
apron, simultaneously cheeky and embarrassed.

"Beg pardon, Sir, for being so free," she said, with downcast eyes; "but I've got the pastrycook's daughter in there;
she's such a pretty girl, and she'd be main glad to make your
acquaintance."

Ledersheim stared at Crescenz, not knowing whether to
reject these impudent advances forthwith, or whether to grasp
at the skirts of happy chance and accept the impromptu
bawd's offer. In the end, desire stirred within him, and got
the upper hand.

"Let's have a look at the beauty," he replied.

The girl, a fair-haired hussy of sixteen, whom Leporella had limed with flattering tales, emerged from the kitchen, blushing and giggling, and, revolving awkwardly, showed off her charms to the stylish gentleman whom she had often furtively admired from the shop across the way. The baron was pleased with her looks, and invited her to drink tea with him in his room. She glanced towards Crescenz for a pointer, but Crescenz had vanished, and the pastrycook's daughter, thus inveigled into an adventure, inquisitive and excited (for all her blushes and embarrassment), felt she had no option but to accept the invitation. "Will you walk into my parlour?" said the spider to the fly!

But nature makes no leaps. Although, under stress of a warped passion, a measure of spiritual mobility had resulted in this ossified personality, the new but limited thought-processes did not enable Crescenz to look ahead. She remained as unimaginative as the lower animals, whose actions are guided by short-sighted instincts. Concerned only with the longing to serve the master whom she loved with the fidelity of a dog, she completely forgot the absent wife. It came, therefore, like a bolt from the blue when, one morning, the baron, with knitted brows and holding a letter in his hand, entered the kitchen and told her to devote the day to a general house-cleaning, for next afternoon his wife would be back from the sanatorium. Crescenz turned livid at the news, standing open-mouthed, with the horrified aspect of one who has been stabbed. She stared dumbly at her master, until the baron, wishing her to pull herself together, said:

"You don't look best pleased, Cenzi; but there's nothing we can do about the matter!"

At this her rigid countenance began to stir, as though something were at work in the depths. A wave seemed to rise from her inwards, and her pale cheeks flushed dark red. Her throat twitched, and, with immense difficulty she got out the words:

"After all . . . one might . . . one might . . . surely . . ."

She choked, and did not finish the sentence. Her face was contorted with malice, and so sinister was her expression, that it was Ledersheim's turn to be frightened, and he shrank back in alarm. But Crescenz had resumed her work, and was scouring a copper saucepan with a violence that threatened to take the skin off her fingers.

With the return of the mistress, the sense of comfort that had prevailed during her absence was dispelled. Once more began the regime of banging doors and causeless scoldings. Maybe some of the neighbours had sent her anonymous letters to inform her of her husband's "goings-on" during her absence, or maybe the lack of warmth in his welcome had been enough to disclose the state of his feelings; in any case, she seemed worse instead of better for her two months' treatment, since outbursts of weeping alternated with menaces and hysterical scenes. The relations between the couple grew more intolerable day by day. For a few weeks the baron confronted the storm of reproaches, answering evasively and consolingly, with his habitual civility, when she threatened to sue for a divorce or to write to her parents. But this indifferent attitude had an evil effect upon her. She was beginning to believe herself surrounded by secret enemies, and her nervous excitement verged upon persecution mania.

Crescenz had put on her old armour of silence. But now this silence became aggressive and menacing. When her mistress returned, she remained in the kitchen, from which she would not emerge even when summoned to welcome the baroness home. She stood like a figure carved out of wood,

her shoulders raised stubbornly, giving such curt answers to
questions that the impatient mistress soon ceased asking any,
and turned away, while Crescenz glared at her unsuspecting
back with venom and hatred. Her avarice made her feel that
she had been robbed by this return of the mistress of the
house, had been deprived of the joys of companionable service and thrust back to toil in the kitchen, while her pet-name
of Leporella had been stolen from her. For the baron was
careful, in his wife's presence, to avoid showing any marks
of sympathy for Crescenz. Now and again, however, exhausted by the scenes the baroness made, and wanting to draw
a breath of relief, he would steal into the kitchen, plump
down on one of the hard wooden stools, and exclaim with a
groan:

"I can't stand it any longer!"

These moments in which her idolized master sought refuge
in her sympathy were the happiest known to Leporella. She
never dared to answer or to attempt consolation, but remained
dumb, while looking compassionately at her enslaved god.
This soundless sympathy did Ledersheim good for a time.
But as soon as he left the kitchen, his worries came back to
him with a rush, while Crescenz wrung her hands in impotent fury, or tried to work off her rage by a vengeful scouring of pots and pans and a polishing of silver.

At length the sultry atmosphere of the baroness's return
broke in a terrible storm. During one of the scenes, the baron
lost patience, and, abandoning his customary attitude of
courteous indifference (that of a schoolboy who is being
scolded), he flung out of the room, and, before banging the
door so that every window in the flat rattled, he yelled:

"I'm absolutely fed up."

His face blue with wrath, he burst into the kitchen and
shouted to the trembling Crescenz:

"Pack my portmanteau at once and take down my gun-case. I shall go for a week's shooting. The devil himself could not stick it in such a hell as this."

Crescenz looked up at him, her eyes shining with enthusiasm. He was master once more, had asserted himself! With a hoarse laugh she said:

"Quite right, Sir. Time and more to put a stop to this!"

Quivering with zeal, she hastened from room to room and got together all he could possibly want for the expedition. She carried portmanteau and gun-case to the cab. But when he was about to say a word of thanks, he was startled by her aspect. Her pinched lips were parted in the malicious smile which always alarmed him, reminding him as it did of what a beast of prey looks like when about to spring. But she curtsied becomingly, and, as he drove off, whispered with an air that was only impertinent because of the intimacy it implied:

"Have a good time, Sir, while you're away. I'll tend to everything."

Three days later the baron was recalled by a laconic wire: "Essential return home instantly."

The cousin who had sent it met him at the station, and Ernst's face was enough to show Rudolf that something terrible had happened. After a futile attempt to "break the news," he told the baron that Baroness von Ledersheim had been found dead in bed that morning, with the room full of gas from the unlighted gas-heater. Accident was out of the question. The death must have been intentional, for the gas-heater had not been used throughout the summer, and the weather was still warm. Besides, overnight the dead woman had taken a dozen or more tablets of veronal. Furthermore, Crescenz, the cook, who had been alone in the house with her mistress, testified to having heard the latter go into the

dressing-room, presumably in order to turn on the master-tap
of the gas-stove, which for safety was placed there instead
of in the bedroom. In view of these facts, the police surgeon
had certified the death to be suicidal.

The baron's hands trembled. When his cousin mentioned
Crescenz's report, his flesh crept, for a distressing thought
flashed into his mind. But he repressed the tormenting idea,
and silently accompanied Ernst to the flat. The corpse had
already been removed. His relatives, hostile of mien, were
awaiting him in the drawing-room, and their condolences
were icy. As if accusingly, they "felt it their duty" to inform
him that there would be no possibility of hushing up the
scandal, for in the morning the servantmaid had rushed out
on to the public staircase screaming, "The missus has killed
herself!" They had arranged for a quiet funeral, but already
"society folk" were saying ill-natured things. Rudolf listened
confusedly, raised his eyes involuntarily towards the door
leading from sitting-room into bedroom, and then quickly
looked back at the floor. There was that haunting thought
he wanted to think out to its logical conclusion—but this idle
and hostile chatter made connected thinking impossible. For
half an hour his relatives stayed, black-a-vised and reproachful; then, one after another, they bade farewell, leaving Rudolf
alone in the darkening chamber, stricken by the unexpected
blow, with aching head and weary limbs. He still stood, too
listless even to sit down.

Someone knocked at the door.

"Come in!" he cried.

The door behind him opened, and there was a sound of
hesitating, shuffling footsteps—footsteps he recognized. He
was horrified, had a feeling of strangulation in his throat
and of goose-flesh all over his body and limbs. He tried to
turn round, but his muscles would not obey his will. Thus
he remained standing in the middle of the room, tremulous,

silent, hands clenched, while fully aware how contemptible must be the aspect of this guilty silence. Then, still from behind, came in a dry, indifferent, matter-of-fact tone, the words:

"I only come to ask whether the master will dine at home or out."

The baron trembled even more violently, and the icy chill gripped him at the heart. He made three attempts before he could answer:

"Thanks, I want nothing to eat."

The shuffling footsteps receded before he found courage to look round. Then his immobility was broken. He shook like an aspen leaf, but had strength to leap towards the door and turn the key in the lock, resolved to hinder the re-entry of those detestable and ghostly footsteps. Then he flung himself on the sofa, and vainly tried to strangle the loathsome thought which obtruded itself into his reluctant mind. It was an obsession which kept him awake the livelong night, and would not leave him even when day returned, nor when, clad in the customary suit of solemn black, he stood as chief mourner at the head of his deceased wife's coffin.

Directly the funeral was over, the baron fled from the capital. He could not bear the way in which his friends and relatives looked at him. Their sympathy was tinged with an inquisitorial demeanour—or did he only fancy this to be so? Fancied or real, it was insupportable. Even inanimate objects looked at him accusingly. Every piece of furniture in the flat, and especially those in the bedroom (where the sickly-sweet odour of gas lingered), repelled him whenever he entered the place. But the insufferable hag-riding, whether by night or by day, was the imperturbability of his sometime confidante, who went about her business in the empty dwel-

ling as if nothing untoward had happened. Since that moment at the station when his cousin had mentioned her name,
he dreaded contact with her. Whenever he heard her step,
it was difficult for him to control the impulse to run away.
He was nauseated by the thought of her: her harsh voice;
her greasy hair; her dull, bestial pitilessness. Rage overmastered him because he lacked strength to rid himself of
the incubus, to tear the stranglehold of her fingers from his
throat. His only resource was flight. He packed his trunk
secretly, without saying a word to her; and stole away, having scribbled a note to the effect that he was going to stay
with friends in Carinthia.

He did not return till the summer was over, except for one
brief visit necessitated by matters connected with his late
wife's property. Then he stayed at a hotel, to avoid having
to set eyes upon the bird of evil omen at the flat. Crescenz,
who kept herself to herself, never knew that he had been in
Vienna. Unoccupied, gloomy as an owl, she spent her days in
the kitchen, but went twice to Mass (instead of once only,
as previously). The baron's solicitor provided her with funds
and checked her accounts. Of her master she heard not a
word, for he neither wrote to her nor sent a message. During this time of silent waiting, her face grew harsher and
leaner, her movements became wooden as of old. Thus the
months passed for her in a strange condition of rigid apathy.

In the autumn, however, the baron was recalled to the flat
by urgent business. He stood hesitant on the threshold. Many
weeks spent with intimate friends had enabled him to forget
a good deal; but now that he was about to see again in the
flesh the woman who had perhaps been his accomplice, he
was agitated and near to vomiting, as he had been the day
after his wife's death. Step by step, as he mounted the stairs,
it seemed to him that an invisible hand was gripping his

throat. He moved slower and slower, and had to summon
all his forces before he could bring himself to turn his latchkey in the lock.

At the sound, Crescenz rushed out of the kitchen in astonishment. When she saw her master, she turned pale, and then,
as if making an obeisance, stooped to pick up the hand-
valise he had put down in the entry. She forgot to say a word
of welcome, and the baron was equally remiss. No "Good
day" passed his lips. Silently she carried the valise into his
bedroom, and silently he followed. In silence he waited, looking out of the window, till she had left the room. Then he
hurriedly locked the door.

That was their only greeting after his long absence.

Crescenz waited. The baron waited, too, in the hope that
these paroxysms of horror at sight of her would cease to
trouble him. But there was no improvement. Even before he
saw her, when he merely heard her shuffling footsteps in the
passage, he became giddy and had a sensation of nausea. He
could not eat a morsel of the breakfast she prepared for him.
Morning after morning, he slipped from the house as soon as
he was dressed, and did not return till late at night, his object
being to avoid a glimpse of her, and to be out of hearing of
her movements. The few orders he was obliged to give were
given without looking at her. He was choked by the air she
breathed.

Crescenz, for her part, spent her days sitting mumchance
upon her stool in the kitchen. She did not trouble to prepare
food for herself, having no appetite; and she would not
say a word to anyone. She sat, timidly awaiting the master's
whistle, like a whipped cur that recognizes it has done wrong.
How, precisely, she could have been at fault, she was too stupid
to guess. All she knew was that her master, her god, had

turned his face away from her, and that his displeasure was agony.

Three days after the baron's return, the door-bell rang. A grey-haired man, with a quiet demeanour, clean-shaven, carrying a hand-bag, stood on the landing. Crescenz waved him away, but the newcomer explained that he was the valet, that the Herr Baron had ordered him to come at ten, and that Crescenz must announce him. She turned as white as chalk, and stood stock-still for a moment, hand raised and fingers outspread. Then this hand dropped like a winged bird.

"Go and announce yourself," she said snappishly to the astonished valet, turned on her heel, and retreated into the kitchen, slamming the door behind her.

The manservant stayed on. Thenceforward Rudolf had no need to say a word to Crescenz, giving his orders through the instrumentality of this quiet fellow, who was elderly, and accustomed to service in the best families. Crescenz no longer knew what went on in the flat outside the kitchen, the life of the place flowing over her head like deep water over a stone.

This distressing state of affairs lasted a fortnight, and had upon Crescenz the effect of a wasting disease. Her face fell away, and the hair on her temples turned grey. If her movements had before been wooden, now she seemed turned into stone. She sat motionless as an idol, staring vacantly out of the window; but, when she had work to do, she did it in furious, quasi-maniacal outbursts.

When the fortnight was up, the manservant came one morning unsummoned into the master's study, and waited discreetly to indicate that he had a communication to make. Once before he had ventured to complain about the offensive manners of the "Tyrolese baggage," as he disdainfully called her, and had advised her being given notice. On that occasion, however, the baron, feeling sorry for Crescenz, had refused to act on the suggestion. The valet did not dare to press the point. This time, however, the man was more urgent in his representations. When Rudolf said that Crescenz had been a long time in his service, and he saw no adequate ground for dismissing her, the valet, instead of taking no for an answer, looked perplexedly at the baron, reiterated his request, and then, with considerable embarrassment, said:

"Sir, I'm afraid you'll think me a fool, but the fact is . . . I'm afraid of the woman. . . . She's furtive, malicious. . . . The Herr Baron really does not realize how dangerous a person he has as member of his household."

Ledersheim was alarmed in spite of himself. But the information was too vague.

"Anton," he said, "you must speak more plainly, if I'm to do what you want."

"Well, Herr Baron, I really can't say anything definite. What I feel is that Crescenz is like a wild beast, or a beast only half-tamed; and that at any moment she might do me, or you, Sir, a mischief. Yesterday, when I was giving her your orders, she looked at me . . . it was something more than a look . . . she glared at me as if about to spring upon me and fix her teeth in my throat. I'm really afraid, Sir, to eat the food she cooks. She might poison me, or you, Sir, any day. The Herr Baron really doesn't know how dangerous she is. It's not what she says. She says nothing. But I'm positive she's ripe for committing a murder."

Rudolf looked at the accuser in alarm. Had the man heard some gossip? Had he conceived any definite suspicion? Rudolf became aware that his fingers were trembling, and he laid his cigar on the ash-tray, lest this tremor should betray him. But Anton's face was impassive, and conveyed no sign of unuttered knowledge. The baron hesitated. The valet's advice marched with his own wishes. He would like to get rid of Crescenz.

"I don't want to be precipitate," he said. "Perhaps you are right, but wait a little longer. If she is rude to you again, you can give her notice without consulting me, saying, of course, that you do so on my orders."

"Very good, Sir," answered Anton, and the baron went out with a sense of relief—though anything that reminded him of this enigmatical creature poisoned the day for him. The best thing would be, he thought, if Crescenz could be cleared out of the house while he was away—at Christmas, perhaps. The thought of being freed from the incubus did him a lot of good. Christmas would be most suitable. He was going to spend Christmas with friends.

The very next morning, however, immediately after breakfast, when he had seated himself in his study, there came a knock at the door. Unthinkingly he looked up from his newspaper, and called:

"Come in!"

Thereupon, with the hard yet shuffling step he had come to loathe, she entered, the figure that haunted his dreams. He was startled at the change in her. Always ill-favoured, her bony, wasted visage now looked like a death's-head above her black garments. His detestation was tinged with compassion when he noticed how the down-trodden woman stopped short at the edge of the carpet, too humble to advance nearer. To hide his own emotion, he spoke as unconcernedly as possible:

"What is it, Crescenz?"

Yet, for all he could do, his tone, instead of being cordial, was repellent and angry.

Crescenz did not move, but stared gloomily at the carpet. After a long pause, she managed (like one kicking something out of the way) to eject the words:

"Anton . . . Anton says that the Herr Baron gives me notice."

Genuinely distressed, Rudolf von Ledersheim rose to his

feet. He had never intended matters to take so swift a course. Stammeringly he explained that Anton had been too precipitate. Everything could be smoothed over if she could manage to be a little less cross-grained towards the valet. Servants must behave decently to one another; and so on.

Crescenz stood unheeding, her eyes boring into the carpet, her shoulders stubbornly raised, her head hanging disconsolately. She was awaiting a word that did not come. When at last, out of humour at having to assume an apologetic role towards a domestic, he stayed the flow of his eloquence, she still had no answer but a mutinous silence.

After this awkward pause had lasted two or three minutes, she said:

"What I want to know is, whether the master himself told Anton to give me notice."

She flung the words at him, fiercely, morosely. Was there an implied threat? A challenge? Both his cowardice and his sympathy took wings and vanished. Hatred for this woman, which had been accumulating for weeks and months, burst the dams and overflowed. His one desire was to see the last of her. With an abrupt change of tone, he assumed the cutting and circumstantial manner he had learned to use on occasions when he had been an under-secretary of State, and replied:

"Yes, Crescenz, such is the fact. To save trouble, I have put Anton in charge of household affairs. If he has given you notice, you must go. Unless, indeed, you can bring yourself to behave decently to him. Then I might say a word for you, and ask him to overlook your past boorishness. Otherwise, you'll have to leave; and the sooner the better."

If she meant to threaten him, she should get as good as she gave! He would stand no nonsense!

But the look which Crescenz now raised from the carpet had no menace in it. Merely that of a hunted beast, which sees the pack break from the coppice where it is about to take refuge.

"Thank you, Sir," she said in a broken voice. "I'll leave at once. I don't want to be a trouble to you."

Slowly turning, she shuffled out of the room.

That evening when, having returned from the opera, the baron went into his study to look at the letters delivered during the afternoon, he saw on the table an unfamiliar object—an oblong box of peasant workmanship. It was not locked. The contents, carefully arranged, were the trifles Crescenz had received from him: a few postcards sent when he had been away shooting, two theatre tickets, a silver ring. Besides these, there was a pile of banknotes (the savings of a lifetime), and a snapshot, taken in Tyrol twenty years before. In it her eyes, dazzled by the flashlight, had the distressful and whipped-cur expression with which she had received his confirmation of her dismissal.

Much perplexed, the baron rang for Anton to ask why on earth Crescenz had placed her belongings on his study-table. The valet went to call his enemy to account. But Crescenz was not to be found in the kitchen, in her attic bedroom, or anywhere else in the building. Not until next day, when they read a news-item in the paper to the effect that a woman about forty years of age had drowned herself in the Danube, did master and man know what had become of Leporella.

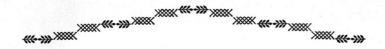

The Runaway

One night during the summer of 1918, a fisherman, in his
boat on Lake Geneva, not far from the little Swiss town
of Villeneuve, caught sight of something unusual on the surface of the water. Drawing nearer to this object he perceived
it to be a raft made of beams roughly tied together, which a
naked man was awkwardly trying to paddle forwards by
means of a plank. The paddler was cold and exhausted, and
the amazed fisherman was touched to pity. He helped the
shivering voyager on board his own boat, wrapped him in
some nets which were the only available covering, and tried
to open up a conversation. But the rescued stranger, cowering
in the bottom of the boat, answered in a tongue of which the
fisherman could not recognize a syllable. Giving up the attempt as a bad job, the latter hauled in the net he had come
to examine, and rowed with steady strokes towards the land.

When the outline of the shore grew plain in the gathering
light of dawn, the naked man began to look more cheerful.

A smile played about the large mouth half hidden in an exuberant and disorderly growth of moustache and beard. Pointing shoreward, he repeatedly exclaimed—half question-ingly and half exultantly—a word which sounded like "Ros-siya." His tone grew ever more confident and more joyful as the boat came nearer to the land. At length the keel grated on the beach. The fisherman's womenfolk, who ran down to help in the landing of the night's catch, dispersed with cries of alarm, like Nausicaa's maidens of old when they caught sight of the naked Ulysses. At the strange tidings of what the fisherman had found in the lake, the other men of the village flocked to the strand, among them the mayor of the little place. This worthy fellow, self-important and full of the dig-nity of office, called to mind all the instructions that had come from headquarters during the four years of the war. Con-vinced that the new-comer must be a deserter from the French shore of the lake, he promptly endeavoured to make a formal inquiry, but was soon baffled by an impenetrable obstacle—they could not understand one another. To all questions the stranger (rigged out by now in an old pair of trousers and a coat found for him by one of the villagers) made no other answer than his own query, "Rossiya? Rossiya?" uttered in imploring but ever more faltering tones. A trifle annoyed at his failure, the mayor strode off towards the court-house, sign-ing imperatively to the refugee to follow. Amid the babble of the youngsters, who had by now assembled, the bare-footed man, his borrowed habiliments flapping loosely about him, did as he was bid, and thus came to the court-house, where he was placed in safe custody. He made no protest; uttered no word; but his face was once more overcast with gloom, and he stooped timidly as if in expectation of a blow.

The news of the fisherman's remarkable haul soon spread to the neighbouring hotels. Well-to-do visitors, delighted to hear of something which would help them to while away an hour, came in great numbers to inspect the wild man. A lady offered him some sweets, but with monkey-like suspicion he refused to touch them. A visitor with a camera took a snapshot. Crowding round the raree-show, they all chattered merrily. At length there arrived upon the scene the manager of one of the largest hotels in the vicinity, a man who had lived in many lands and was a good linguist. He tried the stranger, who was by now bewildered and even frightened, in one tongue after another—German, Italian, English, and finally Russian. At the first word of Russian, the poor fellow started, and instantly plucked up heart. His homely but good-natured countenance was split by a smile reaching from ear to ear. Instantly, and with confident mien, he began to pour out his history. It was long and confused, and was not in all points intelligible to the chance interpreter. But substantially the story ran as follows.

He had fought in Russia. One day he and a thousand others had been packed into railway carriages, and had travelled a vast distance by train. Then they had all embarked on a ship, and had made a yet longer journey, a voyage across seas on which it was so hot that—as he phrased it—his very bones had been grilled. At length they had landed. Another railway journey, and immediately after leaving the train they had been sent to storm a hill. Of this fight he could say little, for at the very outset he had gone down with a bullet in the leg.

To the auditors, taking up the story as interpreted sentence after sentence by the hotel manager, it was at once obvious that this refugee had belonged to one of the Russian divisions sent across Siberia and shipped to France from Vladivostok. Curiosity mingled with compassion, and everyone wanted to know what had induced the man to start on the remarkable journey that had led him to the lake.

With a smile that was frank, and yet not free from cunning, the Russian explained that while in hospital with his wound he had asked where Russia was, and the general direction of his home had been pointed out to him. As soon as he was able to walk, he had deserted, and had guided his homeward course by sun and stars. He had walked by night; and by day, to elude the patrols, he had hidden in haystacks. For food, he had gathered fruit, and had begged a loaf of bread here and there. At length, after ten nights' march, he had reached this lake. Now his tale grew confused. He was a Siberian peasant; his home was close to Lake Baikal; he could make out the other shore of Lake Geneva, and fancied that it must be Russia. He had stolen two beams from a hut, and, lying face downwards on these and using a board as a paddle, he had made his way far across the lake when the fisherman had found him. He finished his story with the eager question:

"Shall I be able to reach home tomorrow?"

The translation of this inquiry provoked an outburst of laughter from those whose first thought was "Poor simpleton!" But their second thought was tinged with sympathy, and everyone contributed a trifle when a collection was made for the timid and almost tearful deserter.

But now a police official of high rank, summoned by telephone from Montreux, put in an appearance, and with no small difficulty drew up a formal report. Not only was the chance-found interpreter often out of his depth, but the Siberian's complete lack of culture imposed a barrier between his mind and that of these westerners. He knew little more of himself than that his name was Boris; he could give no surname. He had lived with his wife and three children fifty versts from the great lake. They were the serfs of Prince Metchersky (he used the word "serfs," although it is more than half a century since serfdom was abolished in Russia).

A discussion concerning his fate now ensued, while, with bowed shoulders and depressed visage, he stood among the disputants. Some considered that he ought to be sent to the

Russian embassy in Berne, but others objected that this could only lead to his being shepherded back to France. The police official explained how difficult it was to decide whether he was to be treated as a deserter, or simply as a foreigner without identification papers. The relieving officer of the district was prompt to explain that this wanderer had certainly no claim to food and lodging at the cost of the local community. A Frenchman excitedly intervened, saying that the case of this wretched absconder was plain enough: let him be put to work, or sent back across the frontier. Two women protested that the poor man was not to blame for his misfortunes; it was a crime to tear people away from their homes, and to convey them into a foreign land. Political quarrels were imminent when an old gentleman, a Dane, suddenly declared his willingness to pay for the stranger's keep throughout the ensuing week; meanwhile the local authorities could discuss matters with the Russian embassy. This unexpected solution put a term to the official perplexities, and made the lay controversialists forget their differences.

While the argument had been waxing hot, the timid eyes of the runaway had been riveted on the lips of the hotel manager, as the only person in the medley who could make his fate known to him. In a dull fashion, he seemed to understand the complications his coming had aroused. Now, when the tumult of voices ceased, he raised his clasped hands beseechingly towards the manager's face, like a woman praying before a holy image. All were touched by the gesture. The manager cordially assured him that he could be quite easy in his mind. He would be allowed to stay here for a time. No one would harm him, and his wants would be supplied in the village hostelry. The Russian wanted to kiss the manager's hand, but the latter would not permit the unfamiliar form of thanksgiving. He took the refugee to the inn where bed and board were to be provided, gave the man reiterated assurances that all was well, and, with a final nod of friendly leave-taking, made his way back to the hotel.

The runaway stared after the manager's retreating form, and his face clouded over once more at the loss of the only person who could understand him. Regardless of those who were watching his strange demeanour with amusement, he followed the manager with his eyes until his friend vanished into the hotel some way up the hill. Now one of the onlookers touched the Russian compassionately on the shoulder, and pointed to the door of the inn. With hanging head the runaway entered his temporary abode. He was shown into the taproom, and seated himself at the table, where the maid, in welcome, served him with a glass of brandy. Here, overcast with gloom, he spent the rest of the morning. The village children were continually peeping at him through the window; they laughed, and they shouted to him from time to time, but he paid no heed. Customers looked at him inquisitively; but all the time he sat with his eyes fixed on the table, shamefaced and shy. When dinner was served, the room was filled with merry talkative people; but the Russian could not understand a word of their conversation. Painfully aware that he was a stranger among strangers, he was practically deaf and dumb amid folk who could all exchange ideas in lively fashion. His hands were so tremulous that he could hardly eat his soup. A tear coursed down over his cheek, and dropped heavily on to the table. He glanced timidly round. The other guests noticed his distress, and a silence fell upon the company. He was overwhelmed with shame; his unkempt head drooped nearer and nearer to the black wooden table.

He stayed in the tap-room till evening. People came and went, but he was no longer aware of them nor they of him. He continued to sit in the shadow of the stove, resting his hands on the table. Everyone had forgotten his presence.

When, in the gloaming, he suddenly rose and went out, no-body marked his going. Like a dumb beast, he walked heavily up the hill to the hotel, and stationed himself humbly, cap in hand, just outside the main door. For a whole hour he stood there without claiming notice from anyone. But at length this strange figure, stiff and black like a tree-trunk rooted in front of the brightly lit entrance to the hotel, attracted the attention of one of the porters, who went to fetch the mana-ger. A flicker of cheerfulness came once more into the Sibe-rian's face at the latter's first words.

"What do you want, Boris?" asked the manager kindly.

"Beg pardon, Sir," said the runaway haltingly. "All I want to know is . . . whether I may go home."

"Yes, Boris, of course you may go home," said the manager with a smile.

"Tomorrow?"

The other grew serious. The word was said so imploringly that the smile vanished.

"No, Boris, not yet. . . . Not till the war is over."

"How soon? When will the war be over?"

"God knows! No man can say."

"Must I wait all that time? Can't I go sooner?"

"No, Boris."

"Is my home so far away?"

"Yes."

"Many days' journey?"

"Many, many days."

"But I can walk there. I'm a strong man. I shan't get tired."

"You can't do that, Boris. There's another frontier to cross before you can get home."

"A frontier?" He looked perplexed. The word had no meaning for him.

Then, with his marvellous persistency he went on:

"I can swim across."

The manager could hardly restrain a smile. But he was grieved at the other's plight, and he said gently:

"No, Boris, you won't be able to do that. A 'frontier' means a foreign country. The people who live there won't let you through."

"But I shan't do them any harm. I've thrown away my rifle. Why should they refuse to allow me to go back to my wife, when I beg them to let me pass for Christ's sake?"

The manager's face became still graver. Bitterness filled his soul.

"No," he said, "they will not let you pass, Boris, not even for Christ's sake. Men no longer hearken to Christ's words."

"But what am I to do, Sir? I cannot stay here. No one understands what I say, and I do not understand anyone."

"You'll learn to understand them in time."

"No, Sir." He shook his head. "I shall never be able to learn. I can only till the ground, nothing more. What can I do here? I want to go home! Show me the way!"

"There isn't any way, Boris."

"But, Sir, they can't forbid my going back to my wife and children! I'm not a soldier any more!"

"Yes, Boris, they can forbid you."

"But the Tsar? Surely he will help me?" This was a sudden thought. The runaway trembled with hope, and mentioned the Tsar with intense veneration.

"There is no Tsar now, Boris. He has been deposed."

"No Tsar now?" He stared vacantly at the manager. The last gleam of hope was extinguished, and the spark faded from his eyes. He said wearily: "So I can't go home?"

"Not yet. You must wait, Boris."

"Will it be long?"

"I don't know."

The face in the darkness grew ever more despondent.

"I have waited so long! How can I wait any longer? Show me the way. I will try."

"There is no way, Boris. They will arrest you at the frontier. Stay here, and we will find you something to do."

"They don't understand me here, and I can't understand them," he faltered. "I can't live here! Help me, Sir!"

"I cannot, Boris."

"Help me, Sir, for Christ's sake! Help me, for otherwise I have no hope."

"I cannot help you, Boris. Men can no longer help one another."

The two stood gazing into each other's eyes. Boris twisted his cap between his fingers.

"Why did they take me away from home? They said I had to fight for Russia and the Tsar. But Russia is a long way off, and the Tsar . . . what did you say they had done to the Tsar?"

"They have deposed him."

"Deposed?" He repeated the word vaguely. "What am I to do, Sir? I must get home. My children are crying for me. I cannot live here. Help me, Sir, please help me!"

"I cannot, Boris."

"Can no one help me?"

"No one, now."

The Russian hung his head still more sadly. Suddenly he spoke in a dull tone:

"Thank you, Sir," and therewith turned on his heel and departed.

Slowly he walked away down the hill. The manager watched him as he went, and wondered why he did not enter the inn, but passed onwards down the steps leading to the lake. With a sigh, the kindhearted interpreter went back to his work in the hotel.

As chance would have it, the very same fisherman who had

rescued the living Siberian from the lake found the drowned man's naked body in the morning. The runaway had carefully folded the borrowed coat and trousers, had laid them on the shore with the borrowed cap, and had marched down into the water, nude as he had come forth from it. Since the foreigner's name was unknown, no memorial but a nameless wooden cross could be erected over his grave.

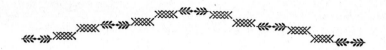

The Invisible Collection

AN EPISODE OF THE INFLATION PERIOD
IN GERMANY

At the first junction beyond Dresden, an elderly gentleman entered our compartment, smiled genially to the company, and gave me a special nod, as if to an old acquaintance. Seeing that I was at a loss, he mentioned his name. Of course I knew him! He was one of the most famous connoisseurs and art-dealers in Berlin. Before the war, I had often purchased autographs and rare books at his place. He took the vacant seat opposite me, and for a while we talked of matters not worth relating. Then, changing the conversation, he explained the object of the journey from which he was returning. It had, he said, been one of the strangest of his experiences in the thirty-seven years he had devoted to the occupation of art-pedlar. Enough introduction. I will let him tell

the story in his own words, without using quote-marks—to
avoid the complication of wheels within wheels.

You know [he said] what has been going on in my trade
since the value of money began to diffuse into the void like
gas. War-profiteers have developed a taste for old masters
(Madonnas and so on), for incunabula, for ancient tapestries.
It is difficult to satisfy their craving; and a man like myself,
who prefers to keep the best for his own use and enjoyment,
is hard put to it not to have his house stripped bare. If I let
them, they would buy the cuff-links from my shirt and the
lamp from my writing-table. Harder and harder to find wares
to sell. I'm afraid the term "wares" may grate upon you in
this connexion, but you must excuse me. I have picked it up
from customers of the new sort. Evil communications . . .
Through use and wont I have come to look upon an invalu-
able book from one of the early Venetian presses much as the
philistine looks upon an overcoat that cost so or so many hundred dollars, and upon a sketch by Guercino as animated by
nothing more worthy of reverence than the transmigrated
soul of a banknote for a few thousand frances.

Impossible to resist the greed of these fellows with money
to burn. As I looked round my place the other night, it seemed
to me that there was so little left of any real value that I might
as well put up the shutters. Here was a fine business which
had come down to me from my father and my grandfather;
but the shop was stocked with rubbish which, before 1914, a
street-trader would have been ashamed to hawk upon a hand-
cart.

In this dilemma, it occurred to me to flutter the pages of
our old ledgers. Perhaps I should be put on the track of former customers who might be willing to resell what they had
bought in prosperous days. True, such a list of sometime pur-
chasers has considerable resemblance to a battlefield laden

with the corpses of the slain; and in fact I soon realized that most of those who had purchased from the firm when the sun was shining were dead or would be in such low water that it was probable they must have sold anything of value among their possessions. However, I came across a bundle of letters from a man who was presumably the oldest yet alive —if he was alive. But he was so old that I had forgotten him, since he had bought nothing after the great explosion in the summer of 1914. Yes, very, very old. The earliest letters were dated more than half a century back, when my grandfather was head of the business. Yet I could not recall having had any personal relationships with him during the thirty-seven years in which I had been an active worker in the establishment.

All indications showed that he must have been one of those antediluvian eccentrics, a few of whom survive in German provincial towns. His writing was copperplate, and every item in his orders was underlined in red ink. Each price was given in words as well as figures, so that there could be no mistake. These peculiarities, and his use of torn-out fly-leaves as writing paper, enclosed in a scratch assortment of envelopes, hinted at the penuriousness of a confirmed backwoodsman. His signature was always followed by his style and title in full: "Forest Ranger and Economic Councillor, Retired; Lieutenant, Retired; Holder of the Iron Cross First Class." Since he was obviously a veteran of the war of 1870–1871, he must by now be close on eighty.

For all his cheese-paring and for all his eccentricities, he had manifested exceptional shrewdness, knowledge, and taste as collector of prints and engravings. A careful study of his orders, which had at first totalled very small sums indeed, disclosed that in the days when a taler could still pay for a pile of lovely German woodcuts, this country bumpkin had got together a collection of etchings and the like outrivalling the widely trumpeted acquisitions of war profiteers. Merely those which, in the course of decades, he had bought from us for trifling sums would be worth a large amount of money today; and I had no reason to suppose that he had failed to pick up similar bargains elsewhere. Was his collection dispersed? I was too familiar with what had been going on in the art trade since the date of his last purchase not to feel confident that such a collection could scarcely have changed hands entire without my getting wind of the event. If he was dead, his treasures had probably remained intact in the hands of his heirs.

The affair seemed so interesting that I set forth next day (yesterday evening) on a journey to one of the most out-of-the-way towns in Saxony. When I left the tiny railway station and strolled along the main street, it seemed to me impossible that anyone inhabiting one of these gimcrack houses, furnished in a way with which you are doubtless familiar, could possibly own a full set of magnificent Rembrandt etchings together with an unprecedented number of Dürer woodcuts and a complete collection of Mantegnas. However, I went to the post-office to inquire, and was astonished to learn that a sometime Forest Ranger and Economic Councillor of the name I mentioned was still living. They told me how to find his house, and I will admit that my heart beat faster than usual as I made my way thither. It was well before noon.

The connoisseur of whom I was in search lived on the second floor of one of those jerry-built houses which were run up in such numbers by speculators during the sixties of the last century. The first floor was occupied by a master tailor. On the second landing to the left was the name-plate of the manager of the local post-office, while the porcelain shield on the right-hand door bore the name of my quarry. I had run him to earth! My ring was promptly answered by a very old, white-haired woman wearing a black lace cap. I handed her

my card and asked whether the master was at home. With
an air of suspicion she glanced at me, at the card, and then
back at my face once more. In this God-forsaken little town a
visit from an inhabitant of the metropolis was a disturbing
event. However, in as friendly a tone as she could muster, she
asked me to be good enough to wait a minute or two in the
hall, and vanished through a doorway. I heard whispering,
and then a loud, hearty, masculine voice: "Herr Rackner from
Berlin, you say, the famous dealer in antiquities? Of course I
shall be delighted to see him." Thereupon the old woman reappeared and invited me to enter.

I took off my overcoat, and followed her. In the middle of
the cheaply furnished room was a man standing up to receive
me. Old but hale, he had a bushy moustache and was wearing
a semi-military frogged smoking-jacket. In the most cordial
way, he held out both hands towards me. But though this
gesture was spontaneous and nowise forced, it was in strange
contrast with the stiffness of his attitude. He did not advance
to meet me, so that I was compelled (I must confess I was a
trifle piqued) to walk right up to him before I could shake.
Then I noticed that his hand, too, did not seek mine, but was
waiting for mine to clasp it. At length I guessed what was
amiss. He was blind.

Ever since I was a child I have been uncomfortable in the
presence of the blind. It embarrasses me, produces in me a
sense of bewilderment and shame to encounter anyone who
is thoroughly alive, and yet has not the full use of his senses.
I feel as if I were taking an unfair advantage, and I was
keenly conscious of this sensation as I glanced into the fixed
and sightless orbs beneath the bristling white eyebrows. The
blind man, however, did not leave me time to dwell upon this
discomfort. He exclaimed, laughing with boisterous delight:

"A red-letter day, indeed! Seems almost a miracle that one
of the big men of Berlin should drop in as you have done.

There's need for us provincials to be careful, you know, when a noted dealer such as yourself is on the war-path. We've a saying in this part of the world: 'Shut your doors and button up your pockets if there are gipsies about!' I can guess why you've taken the trouble to call. Business doesn't thrive, I've gathered. No buyers or very few, so people are looking up their old customers. I'm afraid you'll draw a blank. We pensioners are glad enough to find there's still some dry bread for dinner. I've been a collector in my time, but now I'm out of the game. My buying days are over."

I hastened to tell him he was under a misapprehension, that I had not called with any thought of effecting sales. Happening to be in the neighbourhood I felt loath to miss the chance of paying my respects to a long-standing customer who was at the same time one of the most famous among German collectors. Hardly had the phrase passed my lips when a remarkable change took place in the old man's expression. He stood stiffly in the middle of the room, but his face lighted up and his whole aspect was suffused with pride. He turned in the direction where he fancied his wife to be, and nodded as if to say, "D'you hear that?" Then, turning back to me, he resumed—having dropped the brusque, drill-sergeant tone he had previously used, and speaking in a gentle, nay, almost tender voice:

"How charming of you. . . . I should be sorry, however, if your visit were to result in nothing more than your making the personal acquaintanceship of an old buffer like myself. At any rate I've something worth while for you to see—more worth while than you could find in Berlin, in the Albertina at Vienna, or even in the Louvre (God's curse on Paris!). A man who has been a diligent collector for fifty years, with taste to guide him, gets hold of treasures that are not to be picked up at every street-corner. Lisbeth, give me the key of the cupboard, please."

Now a strange thing happened. His wife, who had been listening with a pleasant smile, was startled. She raised her hands towards me, clasped them imploringly, and shook her head. What these gestures signified was a puzzle to me. Next she went up to her husband and touched his shoulder, saying:

"Franz, dear, you have forgotten to ask our visitor whether he may not have another appointment; and, anyhow, it is almost dinner-time.—I am sorry," she went on, looking to me, "that we have not enough in the house for an unexpected guest. No doubt you will dine at the inn. If you will take a cup of coffee with us afterwards, my daughter Anna Maria will be here, and she is much better acquainted than I am with the contents of the portfolios."

Once more she glanced piteously at me. It was plain that she wanted me to refuse the proposal to examine the collection there and then. Taking my cue, I said that in fact I had a dinner engagement at the Golden Stag, but should be only too delighted to return at three, when there would be plenty of time to examine anything Herr Kronfeld wanted to show me. I was not leaving before six o'clock.

The veteran was as pettish as a child deprived of a favourite toy.

"Of course," he growled, "I know you mandarins from Berlin have extensive claims on your time. Still, I really think you will do well to spare me a few hours. It is not merely two or three prints I want to show you, but the contents of twenty-seven portfolios, one for each master, and all of them full to bursting. However, if you come at three sharp, I dare say we can get through by six."

The wife saw me out. In the entrance hall, before she opened the front door, she whispered:

"Do you mind if Anna Maria comes to see you at the hotel before you return? It will be better for various reasons which I cannot explain just now."

"Of course, of course, a great pleasure. Really, I am dining alone, and your daughter can come along directly you have finished your own meal."

An hour later, when I had removed from the dining-room to the parlour of the Golden Stag, Anna Maria Kronfeld arrived. An old maid, wizened and diffident, plainly dressed, she contemplated me with embarrassment. I did my best to put her at her ease, and expressed my readiness to go back with her at once, if her father was impatient, though it was short of the appointed hour. At this she reddened, grew even more confused, and then stammered a request for a little talk before we set out.

"Please sit down," I answered. "I am entirely at your service."

She found it difficult to begin. Her hands and her lips trembled. At length:

"My mother sent me. We have to ask a favour of you. Directly you get back, Father will want to show you his collection; and the collection . . . the collection. Well, there's very little of it left."

She panted, almost sobbed, and went on breathlessly:

"I must be frank. . . . You know what troublous times we are passing through, and I am sure you will understand. Soon after the war broke out, my father became completely blind. His sight had already been failing. Agitation, perhaps, contributed. Though he was over seventy, he wanted to go to the front, remembering the fight in which he had taken part so long ago. Naturally there was no use for his services. Then, when the advance of our armies was checked, he took the matter very much to heart, and the doctor thought that may have precipitated the oncoming of blindness. In other respects, as you will have noticed, he is vigorous. Down to 1914 he could take long walks, and go out shooting. Since the failure of his eyes, his only pleasure is in his collection. He looks at it every day. 'Looks at it,' I say, though he sees nothing. Each afternoon he has the portfolios on the table, and fingers the prints one by one, in the order which many years have rendered so familiar. Nothing else interests him. He makes me read reports of auctions; and the higher the prices, the more enthusiastic does he become.

"There's the dreadful feature of the situation. Father knows nothing about the inflation; that we are ruined; that his monthly pension would not provide us with a day's food. Then we have others to support. My sister's husband was killed at Verdun, and there are four children. These money troubles have been kept from him. We cut down expenses as much as we can, but it is impossible to make ends meet. We began to sell things, trinkets and so on, without interfering with his beloved collection. There was very little to sell, since Father had always spent whatever he could scrape together upon woodcuts, copperplate engravings, and the like. The collector's mania! Well, at length it was a question whether we were to touch the collection or to let him starve. We didn't ask permission. What would have been the use? He hasn't the ghost of a notion how hard food is to come by, at any price; has never heard that Germany was defeated and surrendered Alsace-Lorraine. We don't read him items of that sort from the newspapers!

"The first piece we sold was a very valuable one, a Rembrandt etching, and the dealer paid us a long price, a good many thousand marks. We thought it would last us for years. But you know how money was melting away in 1922 and 1923. After we had provided for our immediate needs, we put the rest in a bank. In two months it was gone! We had to sell another engraving, and then another. That was during the worst days of inflation, and each time the dealer delayed settlement until the price was not worth a tenth or a hundredth of what he had promised to pay. We tried auction-rooms, and were cheated there too, though the bids were raised by millions. The million- or milliard-mark notes were waste-paper by the time we got them. The collection was scattered to provide daily bread, and little of that.

"That was why Mother was so much alarmed when you turned up today. Directly the portfolios are opened, our pious fraud will be disclosed. He knows each item by touch. You see, every print we disposed of was immediately replaced by a sheet of blank cartridge-paper of the same size and thickness, so that he would notice no difference when he handled it. Feeling them one by one, and counting them, he derives almost as much pleasure as if he could actually see them. He never tries to show them to anyone here, where there is no connoisseur, no one worthy to look at them; but he loves each of them so ardently that I think his heart would break if he knew they had been dispersed. The last time he asked someone to look at them, it was the curator of the copper-plate engravings in Dresden, who died years ago.

"I beseech you"—her voice broke—"not to shatter his illusion, not to undermine his faith, that the treasures he will describe to you are there for the seeing. He would not survive the knowledge of their loss. Perhaps we have wronged him; yet what could we do? One must live. Orphaned children are more valuable than old prints. Besides, it has been life and happiness to him to spend three hours every afternoon going through his imaginary collection, and talking to each specimen as if it were a friend. Today may be the most enthralling experience since his sight failed. How he has longed for the chance of exhibiting his treasures to an expert! If you will lend yourself to the deception . . ."

In my cold recital, I cannot convey to you how poignant was this appeal. I have seen many a sordid transaction in my business career; have had to look on supinely while persons ruined by inflation have been diddled out of cherished heirlooms which they were compelled to sacrifice for a crust. But my heart has not been utterly calloused, and this tale touched me to the quick. I need hardly tell you that I promised to play up.

We went to her house together. On the way I was grieved (though not surprised) to learn for what preposterously small amounts these ignorant though kind-hearted women had parted with prints many of which were extremely valuable and some of them unique. This confirmed my resolve to give all the help in my power. As we mounted the stairs we heard a jovial shout: "Come in! Come in!" With the keen hearing of the blind, he had recognized the footsteps for which he had been eagerly waiting.

"Franz usually takes a siesta after dinner, but excitement kept him awake today," said the old woman with a smile as she let us in. A glance at her daughter showed her that all was well. The stack of portfolios was on the table. The blind collector seized me by the arm and thrust me into a chair which was placed ready for me.

"Let's begin at once. There's a lot to see, and time presses. The first portfolio contains Dürers. Nearly a full set, and you'll think each cut finer than the others. Magnificent specimens. Judge for yourself."

He opened the portfolio as he spoke, saying:

"We start with the Apocalypse series, of course."

Then, tenderly, delicately (as one handles fragile and precious objects), he picked up the first of the blank sheets of cartridge-paper and held it admiringly before my sighted eyes and his blind ones. So enthusiastic was his gaze that it was difficult to believe he could not see. Though I knew it to be fancy, I found it difficult to doubt that there was a glow of recognition in the wrinkled visage.

"Have you ever come across a finer print? How sharp the impression. Every detail crystal-clear. I compared mine with the one at Dresden; a good one, no doubt, but 'fuzzy' in contrast with the specimen you are looking at. Then I have the whole pedigree."

He turned the sheet over and pointed at the back so convincingly that involuntarily I leaned forward to read the nonexistent inscriptions.

"The stamp of the Nagler collection, followed by those of Remy and Esdaille. My famous predecessors never thought that their treasure would come to roost in this little room."

I shuddered as the unsuspecting enthusiast extolled the blank sheet of paper; my flesh crept when he placed a fingernail on the exact spot where the alleged imprints had been made by long-dead collectors. It was as ghostly as if the disembodied spirits of the men he named had risen from the tomb. My tongue clave to the roof of my mouth—until once more I caught sight of the distraught countenances of Kronfeld's wife and daughter. Then I pulled myself together and resumed my role. With forced heartiness, I exclaimed:

"Certainly you are right. This specimen is peerless."

He swelled with triumph.

"But that's nothing," he went on. "Look at these two, the *Melancholia,* and the illuminated print of the *Passion.* The latter, beyond question, has no equal. The freshness of the tints! Your colleagues in Berlin and the custodians of the public galleries would turn green with envy at the sight."

I will not bore you with details. Thus it went on, a pæan, for more than two hours, as he ransacked portfolio after portfolio. An eerie business to watch the handling of these two or three hundred blanks, to chime in at appropriate moments with praise of merits which for the blind collector were so eminently real that again and again (this was my salvation) his faith kindled my own.

Once only did disaster loom. He was "showing" me a first proof of Rembrandt's *Antiope,* which must have been of inestimable value and which had doubtless been sold for a song. Again he dilated on the sharpness of the print, but as he passed his fingers lightly over it the sensitive tips missed some familiar indentation. His face clouded, his mouth trembled, and he said:

"Surely, surely it's the *Antiope?* No one touches the woodcuts and etchings but myself. How can it have got misplaced?"

"Of course it's the *Antiope,* Herr Kronfeld," I said, hastening to take the "print" from his hand and to expatiate upon various details which my own remembrance enabled me to conjure up upon the blank surface.

His bewilderment faded. The more I praised, the more gratified he became, until at last he said exultantly to the two women:

"Here's a man who knows what's what! You have been inclined to grumble at my 'squandering' money upon the collection. It's true that for half a century and more I denied myself beer, wine, tobacco, travelling, visits to the theatre, books, devoting all I could spare to these purchases you have despised. Well, Herr Rackner confirms my judgment. When I am dead and gone, you'll be richer than anyone in the town, as wealthy as the wealthiest folk in Dresden, and you'll have good reason for congratulating yourself on my 'craze.' But so long as I'm alive, the collection must be kept together. After I've been boxed and buried, this expert or another will help you to sell. You'll have to, since my pension dies with me."

As he spoke, his fingers caressed the despoiled portfolios. It was horrible and touching. Not for years, not since 1914, had I witnessed an expression of such unmitigated happiness on the face of a German. His wife and daughter watched him with tear-dimmed eyes, yet ecstatically, like those women of old who—affrighted and rapturous—found the stone rolled away and the sepulchre empty in the garden outside the wall of Jerusalem. But the man could not have enough of my appreciation. He went on from portfolio to portfolio, from "print" to "print," drinking in my words, until, outwearied, I was glad when the lying blanks were replaced in their cases and room was made to serve coffee on the table.

My host, far from being tired, looked rejuvenated. He had story after story to tell concerning the way he had chanced upon his multifarious treasures, wanting, in this connexion, to take out each relevant piece once more. He grew peevish when I insisted, when his wife and daughter insisted, that I should miss my train if he delayed me any longer. . . .

In the end he was reconciled to my going, and we said good-bye. His voice mellowed; he took both my hands in his and fondled them with the tactile appreciation of the blind.

"Your visit has given me immense pleasure," he said with a quaver in his voice. "What a joy to have been able at long last to show my collection to one competent to appreciate it. I can do something to prove my gratitude, to make your visit to a blind old man worth while. A codicil to my will shall stipulate that your firm, whose probity everyone knows, will be entrusted with the auctioning of my collection."

He laid a hand lovingly upon the pile of worthless portfolios.

"Promise me they shall have a handsome catalogue. I could ask no better monument."

I glanced at the two women, who were exercising the utmost control, fearful lest the sound of their trembling should reach his keen ears. I promised the impossible, and he pressed my hand in response.

Wife and daughter accompanied me to the door. They did not venture to speak, but tears were flowing down their cheeks. I myself was in little better case. An art-dealer, I had come in search of bargains. Instead, as events turned out, I had been a sort of angel of good-luck, lying like a trooper in order to assist in a fraud which kept an old man happy. Ashamed of lying, I was glad that I had lied. At any rate I had aroused an ecstasy which seems foreign to this period of sorrow and gloom.

As I stepped forth into the street, I heard a window open, and my name called. Though the old fellow could not see me, he knew in which direction I should walk, and his sightless eyes were turned thither. He leaned out so far that his anxious relatives put their arms round him lest he should fall. Waving a handkerchief, he shouted:

"A pleasant journey to you, Herr Rackner."

His voice rang like a boy's. Never shall I forget that cheerful face, which contrasted so grimly with the careworn aspect of the passers-by in the street. The illusion I had helped to sustain made life good for him. Was it not Goethe who said:
"Collectors are happy creatures"?

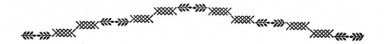

Impromptu Study of a Handicraft

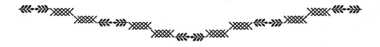

A glorious April morning in 1931! After a drenching shower, the air was sweet, cool, moist, resplendent in the renewed sunshine. Incarnate springtime, fluid ozone; and, even in the centre of Paris, even in the Boulevard Sébastopol, I inhaled the aromas of meadows and the seashore. This miracle was the outcome of one of those capricious cloud-bursts in which a belated spring delights to herald its coming. An hour before, on the way westward towards the capital, our express had thundered into a black storm which hung low over the horizon. At Épernay, when the advertisement hoard-ings of the great city were already beginning to thicken in the outraged fields, and when the elderly Englishwoman seated in the opposite corner was packing away her goods and chattels in an attaché-case, the huge raindrops had splashed down from the heavy cloud which had been racing over our train along the Marne valley ever since we had first encountered it at Vitry-le-François. A pale flash of lightning had given the

319

signal, instantly followed by the drumming note of the rain
with which the express was bombarded as if by machine-gun
fire. The windows rattled protestingly under the hail; and the
locomotive, capitulating before the assault, lowered its grey
streamer to touch the earth. Nothing to be seen, nothing to
be heard, but hail and rain upon steel and glass; and, like a
whipped beast, the train sped onward as if hoping to outrun
the storm.

But the violence of the elements was spent by the time we
reached the Gare de l'Est. As the passengers engaged porters,
the boulevard was glistening in the sunshine beneath the dis-
persing rain-cloud, the house-fronts shone like polished metal,
and great rifts of azure showed in the sky. Bathed and refreshed like Venus Anadyomene rising from the waves, the
town, in its golden nudity, emerged from the cloak of rain
in which it had been enwrapped. To right and to left, from
the hundreds of places in which they had sought shelter,
people thronged back on to the pavements, laughing merrily
as they resumed their course; the suspended wheel-traffic
rolled on its noisy way; everyone obviously rejoicing in the
restored sunshine. Even the sickly-looking trees of the boulevard, growing out of hard asphalt instead of soft earth, in-
vigorated by the douche, seemed glad to stretch their be-
blossomed fingers upward into the blue, and did their best
to fill the air with perfume. Wonderful to relate, for a few
minutes after the shower they were successful. In the very
heart of Paris, in the Boulevard Sébastopol, one could actually
enjoy the aroma of horse-chestnut flowers.

As if this had not been enough to fill me with delight
on so lovely an April morning, I was further in luck; for,
arriving early, I had no appointment to bother me until late
afternoon. Not one among the five and a half million of
Parisian bipeds knew of my coming or was expecting me, so
I was divinely free to follow my own bent. I could saunter

up and down the boulevards; read the newspapers; sit in a
café; look into the shop-windows; go book-hunting along the
Seine; telephone to my friends; or, simply, enjoy the fresh
April air. Having no ties, I could do any one of these things,
or a thousand others. Fortune favouring me, however, or the
promptings of instinct, I chose the best course of all, which
was to do nothing definite. I made no plan, sought no goal,
but wandered aimlessly through the streets, slowly along the
sidewalks, but quickening my steps when I came to a crossing.
At length chance brought me into the big boulevards, and I
was fairly tired by the time I reached the terrace of a café at
the corner of the Boulevard des Italiens and the Rue Drouot.

"Well, here I am once more," I thought, leaning back in a
comfortable chair, while I lighted a cigar; "and here are you,
Paris, the same old Paris. It must be fully two years since we
friends last met. Now, we're going to have a good look at one
another again. Go ahead, Paris! Show me what new tricks you
have learned since I was last here. Begin right away. Unroll
your incomparable sound-film, *Les Boulevards de Paris,* that
masterpiece of light and colour and movement with its hundreds of thousands of unpaid supers; and make music for
me, the inimitable clattering music of your streets. Be lavish;
smarten up; show what you can do; turn on your huge orchestrion with its marvellous harmonies and discords, its reckless automobiles, its shouting hawkers, its glaring posters, its
hooters, its flashing shop-fronts, its hurrying foot-passengers.
Here I sit, more receptive than ever in my life, with leisure
and longing to look and listen till my eyes are dazzled and my
head spins. On, on, more and more riotously, giving vent to
perpetually new cries, shouts, and hootings, unwearyingly, for
all my senses are open to impressions; and I, tiny foreign in-
sect that I am, alive and breathing, am ready to suck my fill
of blood out of your titanic body. On, on, as ready to give
yourself to me as I am ready to give myself up to the enjoy-

ment of you, unknowable city whose witchery is everlastingly reborn."

For (a third wonder of a most wonderful morning) an effervescence in my blood had already shown me that this was to be one of my absorbingly interesting days such as are apt, in me, to follow a journey or a wakeful night. On such days I am, as it were, doubled or manifolded; my one restricted life does not suffice me, and a sense of inward tension makes me want to slough my skin as the imago bursts the pupa-case. Every pore is astretch; every nerve-ending develops into a grappling-iron; my sight and hearing grow unusually keen, to the accompaniment of an almost sinister lucidity of mind. I have a sense of a peculiarly intimate contact between myself and the objects in my environment, a contact like that of an electric switch which is working satisfactorily, and I am animated by a painful eagerness to multiply these contacts wherever possible. Whatever my eyes light upon has an eerie aspect. I can spend hours watching a navvy breaking up the surface of an asphalted street with a mechanical drill, and so intimate is my sympathy with his toil that my shoulders ache as I look on. Or I can stand for hours in front of a window, letting my imagination run riot concerning the destinies of the fellow-creatures who live in the room to which it admits the daylight; I can follow some casual passer-by for miles, magnetically drawn in his wake by idle curiosity; and, though I am aware all the time that an independent observer would regard my conduct as incomprehensible and foolish, my attention is more intoxicatingly riveted than it would be by a skilfully staged play or by the adventures described in an engrossing book. It may well be that this excessive sensitiveness, this pseudo-clairvoyance, is induced by the sudden change of locality, is the outcome of variations in barometric pressure and of the resulting chemical modifications in the blood—but I have never tried to discover the scientific explanation. Whatever the reason, when the state I am now describing takes possession of me, my ordinary life seems like a dream, and the memories of commonplace days grow jejune and void. It is only in this abnormal condition that I am fully myself, and wholly conscious of the amazing multiplicity of life.

In this receptive mood, ready for what chance would bring, I sat on the bank of the human stream, awaiting I knew not what. But my waiting was tinged by the tremulous expectation of the angler who is on the watch for a nibble. My zest was full of the conviction, the inviolable certainty, that something would happen to gratify my curiosity. For a while, however, nothing occurred; and in half an hour my eyes were wearied by the passing throng, so that I could no longer see anything distinctly. The people walking along the boulevard became featureless, a mere confused mass of faintly tinted ovals with anxious, yearning, or masterful faces beneath hats, caps, or képis—a tedious swill of dirty human water which grew greyer and duller the more my gaze was fatigued. I was tired out, as by the flickering of a badly produced and badly screened film, and was on the point of leaving my seat and resuming my peregrinations. Then at length, at length, I discovered Him.

What first drew my attention to this stranger was the trifling fact that he was continually re-entering my field of vision. The thousands upon thousands of others who had appeared during the last half-hour had vanished once for all, as if drawn by invisible threads. Hardly had I caught sight of a profile, a shadow, a sketch, when it was swept away by the current, never to reappear. But this man returned again and again to the same spot. That was why I noticed him. Just as, on the seashore, the waves will, with incredible obstinacy, wash up the same ragged piece of seaweed ever and again, only to lick it back once more with their wet tongues, before depositing it on the beach anew, so did this one figure emerge and re-

emerge repeatedly from the whirlpool at the same spot on its
marge, and with the same humble and submissive mien.

Except for the way in which he kept bobbing up like a cork,
he was not much to look at—a wizened, hungry fellow, whose
lean body was wrapped in a light canary-coloured overcoat
which had certainly not been cut to his measure, for his hands
were lost in the long sleeves. Enormously too large for him,
this yellow garment (of a bygone fashion) matched ill with
a visage almost as pointed as that of a shrew-mouse, and with
his thin lips, disfigured by a blond toothbrush moustache and
the stubble of a beard. There was something ridiculous, too,
about his movements, for this yellow wraith moved hither
and thither upon painfully thin shanks, turning up furtively
now from the right and now from the left side of the human
vortex. At each emergence, he looked as timid as a hare coming out of an oat-field, snuffing the air anxiously, bowing his
head subserviently, and then vanishing again in the throng.

The second point that struck me about the shabbily dressed
creature (who reminded me, by some quaint trick of associa-
tion, of one of the petty officials in Gogol's play *The Inspector-
General*) was that he must be extremely shortsighted or very
awkward, for repeatedly I saw other pedestrians hurrying
along with some more definite aim collide with and narrowly
escape overturning this piece of human flotsam. He did not
seem to take offence at such mishaps, but humbly drew aside,
vanished, re-emerged—at length (perhaps) for the tenth or
twelfth time during the half-hour I had been sitting in front
of the café.

Well, this interested me. Nay, rather, I was annoyed with
myself because, on one of my inquisitive and observant days,
I could not guess what the fellow was about. The more I
cudgelled my brains, the more vexatious became my ungrati-
fied curiosity. "What the devil are you at?" I thought. "Why
are you waiting, and continually bobbing up at the same cor-

ner? You're not a beggar, certainly, for the professional mendi-
cant does not choose a pitch where everyone is in a hurry,
without an instant to feel in his pocket for a coin. Nor are
you a workman, for a workman with a job to do has not so
much time to waste. You can't be waiting for a girl, for the
oldest and ugliest of women would never make a date with
such a pitiful scarecrow as you are. What's your little game?
Are you one of the rascals who style themselves 'guides,' but
whose real business it is to peddle smutty photographs, and
offer to show clodhoppers on the razzle-dazzle in Paris all
the wonders of Sodom and Gomorrah? No, that theory doesn't
fit either, for I have not seen you accost a soul. Indeed, your
main object seems to be to avoid notice or conversation. What
on earth are you looking for in my cabbage-patch?" I watched
him more and more keenly, for in five minutes it had become
a really urgent matter for me to discover what this canary-
coated prowler was doing in the boulevard. Then the solution
dawned on me. The man was a detective!

Yes, he was a plainclothes police officer. This was made clear
to me by a detail—by the obliquely directed but lightning
glance with which he scanned the faces of all whom he
passed. During the first year of their training, the police have
to learn the trick of seeing essentials in a moment, without
attracting attention. Not so easy, thus in an instant to register
fully how the person under observation is dressed, to study
the features and compare them with the memory of those of
"wanted" criminals. But, I repeat, the scrutiny must be ef-
fected without arousing suspicion in the mind of the person
scrutinized. Now, the man I was myself surreptitiously ob-
serving had learned his trade. With seeming indifference he
made his way through the press, allowing people to jostle him
as they pleased, but, from between his half-opened lids, taking
a snapshot of each of them. No one noticed his trick of observation; and I myself should never have noticed it on any

other than one of my specially observant days, when I was persistently on the watch.

My plainclothes man must certainly be a past master of his art, for he was so successful in imitating, not merely the garb, but also the gait of a tramp, thus hiding his dread occupation. As a rule one can recognize a plainclothes policeman a hundred paces away by the peculiarities of the drilled man's walk, and the self-important air which makes him look like a sergeant in mufti. His spine is unbending; he lacks the obsequious manner usual in those who have been daunted by years of poverty and hardship. The present specimen, however, had reached perfection in his role of tatterdemalion and broken-down loafer. What fine touches that the canary-coloured overcoat and the brown bowler worn rakishly to one side should have, still clinging to them, vestiges of the elegance of a former owner, while the frayed-out trouser-legs and the threadbare collar of the coat showing above the wrap indicated extreme poverty. A skilled psychologist, the man must have noticed how destitution, like a famished rat, begins by gnawing at the edges of garments. In admirable keeping with this melancholy rig-out were the wasted features, the thin stubble of beard and moustache (probably stuck on with spirit gum), the tousled locks which would have convinced every unprejudiced observer that the poor wretch must have passed the previous night upon a bench or upon a plank-bed in the lock-up. Superadded was a hacking cough, a continual pulling of the thin wrap together as if to ward off the chill of the spring breeze, and a weary, leaden walk—so that the whole picture was an impersonation of advanced pulmonary consumption.

Let me frankly admit that I plumed myself upon my discovery. I delighted at being thus able undetected to watch a watcher, to detect a detective—although in another part of my mind I was furious that on so splendid a morning, when the sun of God's April shone on the world in so friendly a fashion, a disguised and salaried officer of the State should be trying to hunt down some unhappy wight in the hope of dragging his quarry off to jail. Interest, however, overcame scruples, and I continued to watch the man's every movement with almost unalloyed delight.

Until, of a sudden, pleasure in my discovery was dashed as promptly as the chilling of one's sense of genial warmth when a cloud hides the sun. I had become aware that there was something wrong with my diagnosis, something inharmonious in my supposition. I was uncertain once more. Could the man really be a detective? The more closely I now examined the strange figure, the stronger grew my conviction that the signs of abject poverty were too genuine to be merely assumed by a police-spy. That filthy shirt-collar! No one who had anything else to wear could have brought himself to put such a thing round his neck. Then the shoes, if the articles in question really deserved the name. The right one was laced, not with proper laces, but with coarse string; the left one had a sole so loose that it clattered like a croaking frog at each step the wearer took. Who would fabricate such footgear even for the most important of masquerades? No longer could I entertain the notion that this slouching ambulatory scarecrow could be any sort of police-agent. But if not, what was he? Why this ceaseless coming and going; why these furtive glances at all and sundry? Anger gripped me because I could not unriddle his riddle. An impulse moved me to take him by the shoulder and say: "Fellow, what are you doing? What is your business here?"

Another flash of inspiration, and this time I felt my diagnosis was unchallengeable. I had hit the bull's-eye. Of course the man was not a detective! How could I have made so idiotic a mistake? He was (if the phrase can pass muster) the precise opposite of a police-agent. He was a criminal, a pickpocket; a veritable, highly trained, professional pickpocket, prowling up and down the boulevard on the hunt for note-cases, watches, vanity bags, and other "unconsidered trifles" that might be snapped up. He followed the trade of Autolycus. This was made plain to me by the way he pushed into the thickest parts of the throng. His apparent clumsiness, his frequent collisions with passers-by—collisions which gave him a chance of practising his craft—were explained. The position grew steadily clearer. Now, at length, I was able to grasp why he had chosen his pitch in front of the café at the street-corner, for the place was exceptionally crowded thanks to an adjoining shopkeeper's device. The goods exposed for sale were nothing out of the ordinary: cocoanuts, Turkish delight, and various highly coloured caramels. The proprietor, however, had had the happy thought, not only of giving his shop-window an oriental and pseudo-tropical aspect by filling it with palms and by hanging up some exotic landscapes, but of supplementing this southland exuberance by having three monkeys in a huge cage which occupied the upper part of the space behind the plate glass. These beasts were unceasingly engaged in their habitual grimaces and often unseemly contortions.

The plan worked, for there was always a dense crowd in front of the window—a crowd consisting mainly of women, whose outcries of delight and admiration showed that it was a pleasure to them to see the ways of their men-folk parodied in the antics of these naked and tailed quadrumana.

Now, whenever there was a suitable medley of open-mouthed starers gathered in front of this window, my canary-coated friend insinuated himself into the mass. Although so far as I am aware, apart from certain rather old-world belle-tristic accounts such as are to be found, for instance, in *The Winter's Tale* and *Oliver Twist,* the art and craft of pick-pocketing remains to be described, I knew enough of it to remember that the Artful Dodger needs a crowd just as much as herrings need to be in a shoal during the spawning season—

for it is only when people are closely jammed together that the pickpocket's victim fails to notice the hand which is making free with his wallet or his watch. Furthermore, the desired coup is hard to carry out unless the person who is to be robbed has his or her attention diverted by something which dulls the unconscious watchfulness wherewith (in a thievish world) everyone guards his possessions. A street fire is well known to be a thieves' harvest ground. Here the place of the fire was taken by the monkeys, with their farcical gestures. The gibbering, posturing, grimacing little nudities were the unwitting accomplices of my new friend, the pickpocket.

I hope the reader will forgive me when I admit that I was filled with enthusiasm by my discovery. This was my first sight of a pickpocket, and novelties are always interesting. No, let me be scrupulously accurate. It was my second. In London, during my student days, wishing to better my knowledge of the English colloquial, I used often to attend police-court proceedings. There, on one occasion, I saw a carroty-haired and pimply-faced young fellow brought into the dock by two stalwart policemen. On the table lay a purse. Witnesses gave sworn evidence. The magistrate said a few words and the red-haired youth vanished—sentenced (if I rightly understood) to six months' imprisonment.

That was the first pickpocket I ever saw, but there was a notable difference from the present occasion. I had not then really seen a pickpocket, but only a man in custody and under trial, concerning whom two witnesses testified to his guilt. I had not seen the nefarious deed, but merely its juristic reconstruction. I had seen a man accused, then a man condemned, not a thief in the act of plying his trade. Therefore I had not seen a thief. For a thief is only a thief when he is thieving, and not at some later date when he is called upon to answer for his offence; even as a poet is only a poet in the act of creation, and not when (maybe several years afterwards) he

recites his poem over the wireless. An artist is only an artist
when practising his art, and no one is a doer except when
engaged in the deed. There was now, perhaps, to be vouchsafed me the sight of such a magical moment. I was to see a
pickpocket at work; to see him in his most characteristic semblance, when actually stealing, when manifesting his quintes-
sential reality—one of those rare instants which are as seldom
disclosed to public gaze as procreation and birth. The possibility thrilled me.

I need hardly say that I was determined to make the most
of my opportunity. I must not miss any detail of the prelimi-
naries, and still less the supreme moment of action. I was
resolved to unravel the whole mystery of this handicraft. My
seat at the café was not a satisfactory post of observation, so I
quitted it forthwith, wanting a point of vantage from which,
unhindered, I could keep watch upon the activities of the
newly discovered master-craftsman. This outlook was obtain-
able from beside a kiosk plastered with multicoloured placards
to advertise the plays then running in Paris. I stood as if
reading these notices, whereas in truth I was closely following
every movement of my light-fingered friend. Thus I stood
sentinel for more than an hour, while the nimble devil plied
his difficult and dangerous trade—watched with keener interest and closer attention than I can remember to have ever
felt at a first-night performance in the theatre or at the pro-
duction of the most widely trumpeted of films. For concentrated reality excels and outbids the most consummate art.
Vive la réalité!

The time from eleven till twelve thus spent in the boulevard
passed with lightning speed, simply because it was full of enthralling tensions, of countless decisions and incidents. I could
spend hours upon the description of the happenings of this
one hour, whose incessant perils made so tremendous a claim
upon my nervous energy. Never before had I come near to

understanding how complicated, how formidable, how horribly tensing an art is pocket-picking in the open street during broad daylight. Hitherto I had merely thought that the pickpocket must indeed be bold, and must have a sleight of hand akin to that of a conjurer.

I have already mentioned *Oliver Twist*. There Dickens describes how, in Fagin's den, the old rascal trained his apprentices to steal handkerchiefs. There was a lay figure wearing a coat with a handkerchief in the pocket. To the front of the pocket a bell was attached, and what the novice had to learn was how to withdraw the handkerchief so delicately that the bell did not ring. But it now became plain to me that Dickens had laid too much stress upon prestidigitation. Probably he had never watched, as I was now able to watch, a pickpocket at work, and had therefore never realized that a thief who is plying his trade in broad daylight needs to excel in many things besides sleight of hand. The pickpocket must be well equipped with the mental faculties of presence of mind and self-control, must be a cool and quick thinker, and must (above all) be extremely courageous. Twenty minutes' observation sufficed to show me that a thief must have the unerring decision of the operative surgeon. When a wounded heart is being sutured, a second's delay may be fatal. For such an operation, however, the patient is anæsthetized, cannot move, cannot resist; but the pickpocket has to "operate" like lightning upon a person in full possession of his senses—and the region where the pocketbook is carried is always hypersensitive.

Now, while the pickpocket is operating with all possible speed, in the tensest and most exciting moment of action, his face must be calm, indifferent, almost bored. He must on no account betray excitement; must not, like the man of violence, the assassin, allow his eyes to flash when comes the supreme moment of the knife-thrust. The thief, while advancing his

hand to seize his booty, must look civil and friendly, prepared, if he jostles his victim, to say "Sorry" in an ordinary
tone of polite apology. Nor does it suffice that he should be
alert and adroit at the time of action. Beforehand it has been
incumbent upon him to use his intelligence and to exhibit
his knowledge of human nature, to manifest both physiologi-
cal and psychological expertise in deciding whether his chosen
subject is a suitable one. Only the unobservant, the unsus-
picious, are likely persons; and, among these, only those who
have not buttoned up the overcoat, who are not walking too
fast, and can therefore be approached inconspicuously. As my
hour of close observation taught me, among a hundred, among
five hundred foot-passengers, there will not be more than one
or two worth considering from the pickpocket's outlook. Only
on these rare exceptions will the intelligent thief venture to
ply his trade; and, even then, the attempt will probably fail
because such innumerable chances must collaborate to render
success possible. How much experience, watchfulness, and
self-command are requisite will be made plain by the consideration that the pickpocket, while paying the keenest attention
to the task upon which he is engaged, must at the same time
be constantly on the alert to see that he is not being spied
upon. A constable or a sleuth may be watching from round
any one of half a dozen corners. Apart from these professional
thief-takers, the streets are full of persons, many of whom
(like myself on the present occasion) have nothing better to
do than to gratify curiosity about other folks' business. Then
the shop-fronts are full of mirrors in which his doings may
be reflected, so that those whose backs are turned to him may
be watching him unbeknownst. Mirrors apart, the shop-
windows are a perpetual danger, for customers and assistants
may have an eye on him through the plate-glass. The strain
is terrific, the danger overwhelming, for a blunder may cost
the performer three or four years of life; a tremor of the

fingers, or too sharp a pull, may make arrest inevitable.

Pocket-picking in daylight on a boulevard is work for a titan, demanding courage of the highest order. Since that April morning I always feel that injustice has been done when a newspaper dismisses the pickpocket with two or three lines as one of the most insignificant of evil-doers. To steal a watch or a purse under such conditions needs as much boldness and intelligence as a balloon flight into the stratosphere, which will be recorded in scare headlines the world over; needs more reflective ingenuity than many a triumph in technical skill, more nerve than is requisite for most military or political enterprises. Were the world accustomed to judge achievements, not by final results, but by the amount of nervous energy expended in order to bring them about, it would (moral indignation notwithstanding) be less arrogantly inclined to make light of these street marauders. Of all the handicrafts, respectable or otherwise, practised on our planet, the one I am now considering is one of the most difficult, most dangerous, and in its fullest development, most closely akin to a fine art. My experience, my observations, on that April day in Paris have convinced me of this once for all.

Not only experience, not only observation, but in a sense participation as well. Only during the first few minutes was I able to study my canary-coated friend with the calm objectivity of a scientific observer. Passionate contemplation always evokes sympathy. By degrees, therefore, without conscious wish or deliberate intention, I began to identify myself with the thief, to get inside his skin, to join in the movements of his hands. From being a spectator I had, in the mental sphere, become an accomplice. To my surprise, after about a quarter of an hour I found myself scrutinizing the passers-by in order to decide whether they were likely subjects. Were their coats open or buttoned up; did they look absent-minded or wide-awake; was their appearance such as to suggest the possession of a fat wad of notes which would be worthy of my new friend's skill? Soon, indeed, it grew plain to me that I had ceased to be neutral in the struggle which was afoot, but earnestly wished him to bring off a successful coup. I had forcibly to restrain the impulse to help him in his work! Well-nigh irresistible was the longing, when he seemed to be missing a favourable chance, to nod an indication: "There's your man, that fat fellow with the big bunch of flowers tucked under his arm."

Once, when the thief had again pushed into the throng, and, unexpectedly, a policeman came round the corner, my knees shook as if I myself were about to be taken into custody. I seemed to feel a heavy hand on his, nay on my shoulder. But then (thanks be!) the pickpocket slipped out of the press without having tried to steal, and was ignored by the minion of the law. All this was most exciting, but not yet exciting enough, for the more I identified myself with the thief the more impatient did I grow because he had not yet made a strike. His unending hesitations aroused my anger. "Why the devil don't you pluck up heart and get to work? Try that chance, or that. Do something, anyhow, to show you know your trade!"

Luckily my friend, who neither knew nor guessed my interest in his doings, was not disturbed by my impatience. For this is the perennial difference between the accomplished artist and the amateur, that the artist knows full well how many futile efforts must precede the great success, being trained to await patiently the coming of the last, the decisive possibility. Just as the poet ignores a thousand alluring impressions that pass through his mind (impressions at which only a dilettante would prematurely grasp), in order to reserve his energies for the elaboration of the happy thought when it comes—so did this wizened creature let slip a hundred chances which seemed so promising to me, the tyro. He tried hither and thither, and had certainly handled the outside of a hundred pockets. But he had not found a hazard to his liking, and so, with indefatigable patience and with an air of assumed indifference, he continued to tread the thirty paces up to the shop-window and back again, scrutinizing every possibility and weighing the chances of gain against dangers which to me were invisible. His tranquil, unflurried persistence filled me with admiration despite my impatience, and seemed to provide a guarantee of ultimate success, to strengthen my conviction that he would carry on until he had achieved his end. For my part, I was equally determined not to desist from my study of him until he had made his coup, even if it meant my staying at my post till midnight.

Noon had come, the hour when the streets of Paris are flooded, when from the lesser ways and the alleys, from staircases and courtyards, streamlets of human beings pour into the great rivers—the boulevards. From factories and workshops, from offices and schools and shops, workmen and sempstresses and shop-assistants (the women are called "midinettes" because of their sudden emergence at this hour) came into the open; the workmen in white or blue overalls, the midinettes with little bunches of violets in their hair, petty officials clad in shiny frock-coats and each carrying the inevitable leather portfolio, porters, machinists of one sort and another—the countless types of those who do the unseen work of the great city. For long hours they had been pent in stuffy rooms; now they could stretch their limbs, loosen their tongues, and breathe fresh air. They buzzed about; chattered merrily; lighted cigarettes and inhaled the smoke; thronged the cafés, the bars, and the creameries; enlivening the street for an hour. When that hour of freedom was up, they would have to return to confined spaces, and, behind closed windows, resume labour with the needle, at the bench, at the lathe, become again for the rest of the day tailors, cobblers, or what not.

Knowing this, muscles and sinews made the most of the
hour's freedom; knowing this, minds relaxed while the opportunity was given; knowing this, they all sought light and
cheerfulness, novelty and entertainment. It was only to be
expected that the shop where the monkeys were on show
would profit by the need for distraction. Denser than ever
became the crowd in front of the attractive window. The
midinettes were in the front rows, twittering like birds; behind them stood workmen and loafers, uttering salacious
witticisms; and the closer the throng, the more swiftly and
vigorously did the man in the canary-coloured overcoat push
his way through it, reminding me of a lively little goldfish
swimming in a bowl.

"Now or never will he make his venture," I thought; and
as this passed through my mind, I became dissatisfied with the
point of observation at which I had been stationed so long. I
must get closer to the field of operations, must be near enough
to see exactly how the trick was done. Not so easy to fulfil my
wishes in this respect! The man was slippery as an eel, and
could insinuate himself through the narrowest chinks in the
crowd. A moment before, he had been standing close to me;
now he was at the shop-window, in touch with the glass, so
that in the twinkling of an eye he must have traversed five or
six rows of the agglomerated onlookers.

More slowly than he, and more cautiously, I followed him,
keeping my eyes fixed on him, lest (in his elusive manner) he
should have vanished to right or to left before I could get
to him beside the window. I had no cause to be anxious, since
for once in a way he was standing perfectly still. "There must
be a reason for the change," said I to myself, and hastened to
scan his nearest neighbours among the bystanders. One of them
was an extremely stout woman, obviously impoverished. With
her right hand she was holding the hand of an anæmic-looking
girl of about eleven years of age; in her left hand she carried

an oil-cloth marketing-bag from which projected a couple of long cylindrical rolls of the typical French pattern. No doubt they were for the family dinner. Hatless, and dressed in a check cotton gown of rough and cheap material, this worthy woman of the people was enthralled by the monkeys. Her corpulent body was so violently shaken with laughter that the rolls in her bag rattled to and fro. This loud and unrestrained mirth became a rival attraction to the monkeys, and many of those who stood round her were looking at her as more of a raree-show than the four-handed beasts. She was enjoying herself with the frank delight, with the splendid thankfulness, of those whose limited means provide them with few opportunities for enjoyment; and to the poor there is something exceptionally fascinating about a free show, which comes like a gift from the gods. Nor did she desire a selfish gratification. Continually she leaned towards her daughter, saying, in a broad meridional accent, "Rrregarrde doonc, Maargueriite," to make sure that the pale girl (who was shy in so big a crowd) was not missing any of the fun. A magnificent creature, this woman, a healthy and blooming fruit of the French people, she reminded me of the Greek goddess Gæa, the personification of the earth. I could have flung my arms round her to show my sympathy with her candid merriment. But suddenly I grew uneasy. I noticed that the sleeve of the canary-coloured overcoat was continually drawing nearer to the good woman's marketing-bag, which hung carelessly open—with the carelessness characteristic of the poor.

"Good God," I thought, "surely he's not going to grab this good-natured and cheerful woman's slenderly lined purse out of her marketing-bag!" I was revolted at the notion. Hitherto my attitude towards the pickpocket had been that of "a good sport." As previously explained, I had identified myself with him; had hoped, had wished, that in the end he might get a fine haul for so much trouble. Now, when for the first time

I contemplated, not merely the attempt to steal, but the person who was to be robbed, when I looked at this charmingly simple, unsuspecting woman, happy and cheerful, though she probably had to gain her livelihood by scrubbing floors for a few sous an hour, anger seized me. "Hands off, you rascal!" I should have liked to shout. "Choose someone else to play your pranks on, and leave that poor woman alone!" I moved smartly forward, to get between the thief and the threatened marketing-bag. But as I did so, the fellow turned round and thrust past me with a "Pardon, Monsieur" uttered in thin and humble tones which I now heard clearly for the first time. In an instant, canary-coat was outside the crowd. Something (I know not what) gave me the impression that my intervention had come too late, that he had already made his coup.

Well, if so, I would not let him out of my sight. Roughly (a man on whose toes I trod, cursed me heartily) I shouldered my way after him, and was in time to see the canary-coloured overcoat vanish into a narrow side-street. I quickened my pace, and when I caught sight of him once more, I could scarcely trust my eyes. The little man whom I had been watching so closely for more than an hour had suddenly changed in aspect. Whereas hitherto his gait had been tottering and unsteady, like that of a much preoccupied weakling, he was now hurrying like a weasel close to the wall, resembling a clerk who has missed his train and must race along on foot if he is not to be late at the office and risk getting the sack. Instead of, as before, looking repeatedly to right and to left, he kept his lowered head steady as he hastened on his way. My conviction was strengthened. That was the gait of a thief after the act, gait number two, by which the criminal gets away from the scene of his crime as swiftly and inconspicuously as possible. There could be no doubt. The rogue had nipped the poor woman's purse out of her marketing-bag.

In my anger, I was on the point of raising a hue and cry,

of shouting "Stop thief!" But courage failed me. After all, I
had not seen the theft take place, I had nothing but surmise
to guide me. More than this, one must have overweening self-
confidence to be ready to collar a fellow-mortal and give him
in charge; to assume God's prerogative of executing justice.
I have never had self-confidence of that kind. I know too well
how fallible is our "justice," and how presumptuous are those
who endeavour, in this age of confusion and frustration, to
buttress the temple of justice with the straws of particular
instances.

While thus deliberating, and keeping my quarry in sight,
I was myself overtaken by a fresh surprise. After he had
traversed a couple of more streets, this extraordinary man
assumed a new gait. He no longer hastened, and no longer
walked with hanging head, but drew himself up and sauntered
with the independent air of any other citizen. He was outside
the danger-zone; there was no pursuit; he no longer had any
reason to expect trouble. He could take his ease. From being
a pickpocket on active service, he had become an ordinary
civilian, one of the five million inhabitants of Paris who, puff-
ing a cigarette, unconcernedly walk the boulevards. With a
devastating air of innocence, striding easily and comfortably,
he crossed the Chaussée d'Antin, and for the first time I had
the impression that, like a genuine "flaneur," he was sizing
up the looks or the approachability of every woman he encountered.

"Whither away, now, man of perpetual surprises?" We
were in the little square that fronts the church of La Trinité,
where the trees were already budding with fresh green.
"Whither away? Ah, I understand! You want to rest for a
few minutes on one of the benches. Naturally enough, for
your morning's work must have tired you out." No, the man
of incessant surprises did not sit down upon a bench, but confidently steered his course towards (the reader will excuse

me?) a small, dowdy building intended for the satisfaction of
one of the most private of human needs. Entering a compartment, he closed the door behind him.

Laughter shook me. All artists, thieves not excepted, share
a common humanity. Besides, everyone knows that fear makes
the bowels uneasy (the fact is mentioned in many a frank description of a battlefield), and canary-coat had been like a soldier under fire. But once again I was to learn that the farces
of reality are more preposterous than the wildest inventions of
fancy. Reality does not hesitate to confront the extraordinary
with the ludicrous, and, maliciously, to juxtapose the unusual
with the universally human. While I waited upon a bench
(what else could I do?) that commanded a view of the exit,
I opined that this master-craftsman was only acting in accordance with the strict logic of his profession. It does not readily
occur to anyone but an initiate (it had not yet occurred to
me) that the professional thief who has picked a pocket has
immediate need of a quiet place where he can examine his
haul and rid himself of incriminating "exhibits" (to use a legal
term). Yet in a great city, where a million eyes are always
on the watch, it is hard at short notice to find four walls
within which absolute privacy can be secured. Those accustomed to reading the reports of criminal trials must know
how many persons are continually on hand to observe the most
trifling incidents, and persons who seem to be equipped with
formidably tenacious memories.

Tear up a letter and scatter the fragments in the gutter. A
dozen passers-by will have noticed you; and, likely as not,
some inquisitive youngster with nothing better to do will
amuse himself by picking up the torn scraps and piecing them
together. Examine the contents of your pocketbook in the
entrance-hall of a building. Next morning, when there have
been posted notices referring to the theft of such an article, a
woman you never caught sight of but who was watching you

out of the corner of her eye will report the matter to the police
and give a full description of your personal appearance. Go
to a restaurant for luncheon, and the waiter (whom you have
never seen before, and who is for you indistinguishable from
thousands of his fellows) will make a mental note of your
dress, your shoes, your hat, the colour of your hair, and
whether your nails are cut round or pointed. From every
window, from every shop, from behind every curtain, every
flower-jar, a pair of eyes keep you under observation. You
think you are walking unnoticed through the streets, but you
are pried upon by thousands of unsuspected witnesses, and
your daily life is enmeshed by a daily renewed net of curiosity. It was a fine idea of my master-craftsman, to buy absolute privacy for a few minutes at the cost of five sous. He
would have ample time in which to remove the contents of
the stolen purse, and a safe place in which to dispose of the
incriminating article and anything suspect in the way of papers
or the like. He would be under cover while counting the
spoils. Even I, who had been dogging his footsteps, and was
waiting outside in a mood of mingled cheerfulness and disappointment, should be unable to learn how much he had
garnered.

Such, at least, was my expectation, but matters turned out
otherwise. The instant he emerged from the public convenience, I knew, even as if I had myself counted the contents of
the fat woman's purse, that he had not made a lucky strike.
From his weary expression of countenance, his hang-dog air,
the leaden movements of his feet, it was plain to me that the
results of his morning's work had been meagre. In the stolen
hand-bag there had perhaps been a powder-puff, a cracked
mirror, a door-key, a handkerchief, a pencil, and, at most, two
or three dirty ten-franc notes—a trifling reward for many
hours of toil and peril; however much it may have meant to
the unhappy charwoman, who now doubtless in Belleville, or

some such out-of-the-way quarter, her eyes brimming over
with tears, was for the tenth time telling her neighbours of
her misadventure, for the tenth time railing at the rascally
thief, for the tenth time showing the plundered marketing-
bag. The thief was as poor as she, and it was obvious at the
first glance that his plunder did not suffice for his needs. I
was soon to have plain demonstration of the fact. The fragment of human misery to which he had now shrunken, having wearily walked a hundred yards farther, stopped in front
of a bootmaker's shop and appraised the wares exposed for
sale. Which was the cheapest pair he could get to replace the
ruins which scantily covered his feet? He wanted new shoes
far more urgently than did the hundreds of thousands whose
sound leather or rubber soles were at this moment noisily or
silently trampling the Parisian pavements; new shoes were indispensable if he was to go on plying his trade. But his eager
and despairing·eyes disclosed the fact that he had not "earned"
enough that morning to pay as much as fifty-four francs,
which was about the lowest price marked on the shining
wares in the bootmaker's window. With a despairing shrug of
the shoulders, canary-coat resumed his walk.

Whither now? Would he go on with the hunt? Was he
about to risk his liberty once more for so trifling a chance of
gain? "No, poor wretch, better take a rest first." As if he had
divined my thoughts, had been made telepathically aware of
my wishes, he turned into a narrow alley, stopped in front
of a cheap restaurant, and studied the prices on the bill of
fare before venturing inside. I need hardly say that I followed
him, being determined to unravel the mystery of this man
whose proceedings I had studied with tense interest and throbbing pulses for two hours. Buying a newspaper behind which
to entrench myself, and tilting my hat forward over my eyes,
I seated myself at a table not too near. My precautions were
superfluous. The pickpocket was too tired and hungry to be

interested in anyone but himself. He stared blankly at the
white paper which covered the table in lieu of a cloth, and
remained inert until the waiter brought some bread. Then his
lean hands eagerly seized a piece, and he began to eat like a
famished wolf. Plainly he was underfed, had had nothing to
eat since early in the morning, or maybe since yesterday. My
sympathy with him became keener than ever when the waiter
brought him the drink he had ordered—a glass of milk. Shade
of François Villon. A Parisian thief who drank milk!

It is trifles such as this which, like a spark falling upon
tinder, can throw a flame of light into the abysses of a mind.
At this moment, when I saw the pickpocket (a man who
would be officially classed as a criminal) drinking the most
innocent, the most childish of beverages, when I saw him
gulping down soft, white milk—in some inscrutable way he
ceased for me to be a thief. He was but one more of "les
misérables," one more of the numberless poor and hunted
and ailing and pitiable inhabitants of this blighted planet; and
I felt bound to him by ties far more fundamental than those
of curiosity. In all the manifestations of our universal humanity—nudity, cold, sleep, fatigue—in every supreme need of our
mortal flesh, a term is put to the artificial distinctions that
lead us to class people as good or bad, as reputable or dis-
reputable, as honest or dishonest. These artificialities fall away,
and nothing remains but the unhappy animal which suffers
hunger and thirst, which needs sleep and rest, even as do you
and I and others.

I was spellbound as I watched him sipping his milk to the
last drop, devouring his bread to the last crumb; and yet at
the same time I was ashamed to spy upon him, the hunted
creature who had been the objective of my curiosity as he
pursued his toilsome path while I did nothing to help him
even by the bestowal of a few coins. I was seized with intense
longing to go up to him, speak to him, offer him a trifle. I

racked my brains for a method of approach, for a pretext, so
that I could give him money. Yet we are strangely com-
pounded! We are so abominably tactful when the moment
calls for decisive action; so cowardly that we cannot boldly
push our way through the thin film of air that separates us
from a fellow human being in bitter need. All the same,
everyone knows how hard it is to help a man who does not
ask for help, for in his not-asking is the last of his possessions—
his pride. Only to professional beggars does asking come
easily, so that it is easy to help them—and we ought to be
thankful to them for not depriving us of the possibility. But
the man I was now considering had his peculiar pride. Rather
than beg, he would risk his life and liberty; and we are not
entitled to despise him because theft seemed preferable to him
to the asking of alms.

Would he not be terribly alarmed, unspeakably mortified,
if I made him an ill-advised offer of help? Besides, he looked
so tired, that it would have been inconsiderate to disturb him.
To rest more thoroughly, he had pushed his chair against the
wall, so that this could support his head while the chair-back
sustained his body. His grey eyelids were closed, and he
seemed to have dozed off. His pallor alarmed me, looking
like the reflection of a whitewashed prison-cell. Then the hole
in his sleeve, flaunting itself at every movement of the arm,
showed that he had no wife or mistress to look after him with
a woman's loving-kindness. I pictured his life in some attic
room, the rusty iron bedstead in an unheated apartment, a
chipped and cracked washhand basin, a tiny trunk as his sole
private possession in this room which was let "furnished,"
and which was perpetually tenanted by fear—by dread of the
heavy footfall of a policeman on the stone staircase and of a
menacing knock at the door. These images coursed through
my mind during the two or three minutes in which he was

resting his gaunt body in the chair and his grizzled head against the wall.

But the waiter was already clearing the table with an authoritative rattle of plates, knives, and forks. So thrifty a guest must not be encouraged to linger. I paid my own shot forthwith, and went out into the street, where I had not long to wait before canary-coat reappeared without heeding me. As I followed him, he seemed sunk in thought, and what impelled me in his wake was no longer (as it had been in the morning) a love of sport and a lively curiosity, no longer delight in the study of an unfamiliar handicraft, but an oppressive anxiety, which grew almost unbearable when I saw that he was making his way back to the big boulevards.

"Good Lord," I thought, "surely you are not going to be such a fool as to return to your pitch in front of the shop with the monkeys on show? That woman will have complained to the police as soon as she discovered her loss, and officers will be waiting for the chance of arresting you. Apart from this danger, you will do well to give over work today. I conjure you to make no fresh attempt, for you are certainly not in form. You are exhausted, and any sort of artistic job done by a careworn man will be done badly. What you need is rest. Go home to bed. Above all, try no fresh hazard today."

It is hard to account for the firmness of my conviction that at the first attempt he would be apprehended; that, tired as he was, he would infallibly make a mess of things. But, for some reason or other, my anxiety grew as we approached the boulevards. "Whatever you do, keep away from the monkeyshow!" The words were on my lips and my hand was outstretched to seize him by the arm, when he seemed to me on the point of crossing the street to the place where he had robbed the fat woman. But, as if he had again understood my wishes, he turned abruptly into the Rue Drouot, and marched up to a house as confidently as if he lived there. I knew the house. It was the Hôtel Drouot, the most famous auction-room in Paris.

For the umteenth time I was amazed by the behaviour of this inexplicable man. Even as I was endeavouring to understand him, so there must be something within him which marched with my secret desires. Of the hundreds of thousands of houses in Paris, I had planned that morning to visit this one in particular, for it is a place where I have spent many stimulating, informative, and amusing hours. Livelier than a museum and often containing more valuable treasures, continually diversified and yet ever the same, this unostentatious Hôtel Drouot is a place I love as one of the sights of Paris, as a locality which epitomizes the life of the French metropolis. What in an ordinary dwelling-house is assembled into an organic whole, is here to be seen disarticulated, as in a butcher's shop we have the detached fragments of that which, a day or two before, was walking the earth, a living and integral beast. Here the link between the sacred and the profane, the rarest and the commonest, is supplied by the most humdrum of all humdrum things in the world. Everything exposed to view in the Hôtel Drouot is there in order to be turned into money. Beds and crucifixes, hats and carpets, clocks and wash basins, statues by Houdon and sets of boot-brushes, Persian miniatures and pinchbeck cigarette-cases, worn bicycles and first editions of the works of Paul Valéry, Vandyck portraits and hideous oleographs, Beethoven sonatas and broken stoves, the necessary and the superfluous, gimcracks and precious curios, large and small, genuine and spurious, old and new—all are huddled together for conversion into coin of the realm. The sublime and the beautiful are flung into this retort beside the base and the ugly; into this retort which sucks into its maw and then regurgitates all the valuables of the giant town. In this pitiless crucible where everything is inexorably smelted, in this titanic market-place for the commerce between human vanities and human needs, in this grotesque mixing mill, one feels with peculiar intensity the confusing multiplicity of the world.

Where can one who keeps his eyes open and his wits alert better learn archæology, bibliophily, and the history of art? Where can he better study numismatics, and where (not least) can he better study human nature? For as multifarious as the things which come here simply to change owners, and only for a brief space are freed from the tyranny of being mere "belongings"—are the races and the classes which throng the sale-rooms, eager for bargains, or their eyes flashing with the strange lust of the collector. Great dealers wearing fur-lined overcoats and carefully brushed bowler hats sit cheek by jowl with the small fry of unwashed bric-à-brac traders from the "rive gauche" who have come in the hope of replenishing their shops cheaply. Among them, too, are the middlemen, the hyenas of the battlefield, agents and brokers, who snap up an article that is going cheap, or, when they see that a famous collector has fallen in love with some exclusive rarity, nod and wink to one another as they run up the price against him.

Even librarians whose own skins have dried to parchment find their way hither, and, looking like sleepy tapirs, examine incunabula through their thick spectacles. Fashionably dressed ladies, wearing costly pearls and robes as polychrome as a peacock's tail, sit in front places, having sent their servants to keep these for them. In a corner, as still as cranes and as impassive, stand the connoisseurs, the freemasonry of experienced collectors. Filling in the interstices among these various types are members of the common herd—persons attracted into the Hôtel Drouot, not by business enterprise, connoisseurship, or the love of art, but by mere curiosity, or by something simpler still, by a wish to linger for a while in a well-warmed room where they have to pay naught for firing, or by an itch to hear the big figures for which things are sold.

The various motives which have brought this heterogeneous crowd into the Hôtel Drouot are betrayed by an amazing variety of physiognomies. One type, however, I had never seen or dreamed of seeing here, namely, that of the pickpocket. Yet when I saw my friend, guided by a sure instinct, worm his way among the potential buyers and lookers-on, I did not need to have it explained to me that perhaps in all Paris no better place could be found for the practice of the high mystery of his craft. Here must be an ideal hunting-ground for such as he. The necessary elements were admirably combined: an almost unbearable press of people; distraction of their thoughts by expectation, and by the excitement of watching the rival bids; thirdly, except for a race-course or a railway station (both of them favourite haunts of pickpockets!), an auction-room is almost the only place in the world where the rule of cash payment is rigidly enforced—and the payments are often large ones, so that almost every coat is likely to hide a bulging note-case. Here if anywhere there must be ample opportunities for one of the light-fingered gentry. For my friend, it now occurred to me, this morning's venture had been no more than practice "to keep his hand in," but this was the region in which he would execute his master-stroke.

Nevertheless, I wanted to pluck him back by the sleeve as he unconcernedly mounted the stairs to the first floor. "Damn it all, man, don't you see that glaring notice, which seems to shout in three languages?

BEWARE OF PICKPOCKETS!
ATTENTION AUX PICKPOCKETS!
ACHTUNG VOR TASCHENDIEBEN!

Are you blind, you idiot? They're on the look-out for your sort here. Probably there are at least a dozen detectives in the room. Besides, take it from me, this is not one of your fortunate days."

Calmly looking at the poster, and this time (it would appear) uninfluenced by a brain-wave from me, his would-be protector, canary-coat made his way, as I said, to the first floor. His preference for this field of operations was easy to understand. On the ground floor, second-hand furniture was sold, cupboards, chests-of-drawers, and articles of that sort. The old-furniture dealers who wanted to buy such things were in a small way of business, and would be cautious individuals, likely (peasant-fashion) to have their cash stowed away in a belt buckled safely round the waist. It was on the first floor, where pictures, curios, books, autographs, jewellery, and other costly articles were sold, that there would be buyers carrying thick wads of notes in accessible positions.

I found it hard to keep close behind my friend, for he moved quickly from room to room, as if to sample the chances which each offered, diligently reading the notices that were posted up, as a gourmet studies a menu. At length he decided upon Room No. 7, where "La célèbre collection de porcelaine chinoise et japonaise de Mme la Comtesse Yves de G." was being auctioned. Unquestionably there must be valuable articles in this collection, for the sale-room was full to overflowing, a knot of people blocked the doorway, and the table where the auction was proceeding was at first inaccessible, even invisible, to newcomers like ourselves. A dense wall composed of twenty or thirty rows of human beings cut us off from our goal. All that we could see from the passage, craning over the heads of the throng, was the auctioneer as he sat at his high desk, hammer in hand—the white hammer with which he directed the auction as an orchestral conductor directs a musical performance, the auction in which long pauses led up ever and again, prestissimo, to a thrilling climax.

In ordinary life, presumably, a minor employee, living in Menilmontant or one of the other outlying districts, occupying a couple of rooms, gas-heated and with pelargoniums in window-boxes as their sole decorative touch—here he was a man of might and the notable of the occasion. Wearing a smart morning-coat, his hair shining with pomade, surrounded by well-to-do buyers, he was obviously swelling with pride at being able, for hours in succession, to transmute the most precious articles into hard cash by "knocking them down" with the symbol of his authority, the white hammer. With the veneer of amiability one sees on the face of a juggler who keeps a number of balls tossing simultaneously in the air, he graciously caught the bids as they came to him from the right and left, and from the front: "six hundred," "six hundred and five," "six hundred and ten"; flinging back the same syllables, more clearly articulated, more sonorously uttered, across the heads of the crowd.

When the game slackened for a moment, he radiated encouragement, and would say alluringly: "No one on the right? No one on the left?" with surprise indicated by his raised eyebrows as well as by the tone of his voice, while he toyed with his ivory hammer as if about to knock down the lot to the last bidder; or insinuated with a smile: "Surely, Ladies and Gentlemen, we've not reached the top price yet? This splendid article is worth more than six hundred and ten francs." From time to time he would greet some acquaintance who had just entered, or would look inquiringly at possible bidders. As he introduced a new lot with the phrase, "Now we come to lot number thirty-three," or what not, he would speak impressively; and when the bidding rose to his satisfaction there would be a corresponding mellifluousness in his rich tenor voice. Plainly it was gratifying to him that for several hours three or four hundred persons should hang upon the words that fell from his lips and should watch so closely the movements of the hammer in his hand. The illusion that he played the decisive role (whereas in truth he was but the sport of the chance bids) intoxicated him with self-satisfaction.

With his vocal gymnastics he reminded me of a peacock showing off its tail; but for me, with my remembrance of what I
had witnessed in the morning, he was on the same footing
as the monkeys in the shop-window whose antics had monopo-
lized the attention of the crowd and given my pickpocket an
opportunity.

For the time being, my worthy friend could derive no advantage from this unconscious complicity on the auctioneer's
part, for we were jammed in the doorway, and there seemed
no possibility of our being able to wedge ourselves through
the ·dense mass and reach the auction-table. Once more, however, I was to learn that I was only a prentice hand in this
interesting craft. My comrade, the accomplished technician,
knew from long experience that at the fall of the hammer
(the auctioneer had at that very instant jubilantly exclaimed,
"Gone for 7260 francs") the tension in the wall would slacken.
Heads were lowered, the dealers noted the price in the catalogue, one or two persons who had had enough of it would
depart, gaps formed like leads in an icefield. The pickpocket
promptly seized his opportunity. With a bold thrust, he had
traversed three or four rows on his way towards the table;
and I, who had sworn not to leave the incautious fellow to
his own devices, was left stranded by myself on the outskirts.

I, too, tried to advance, but the auctioneer was already announcing a new lot, the leads had closed, I was caught in the
throng and was helpless. Intolerable was the pressure of strangers' bodies to the right, to the left, in front, and behind; so
close to me that, when a neighbour coughed, my own frame
was shaken. The air, too, was foul, dust-laden, fetid, and
stinking of sweat (as always when people are engaged in the
hunt for money). Myself dripping with perspiration, I wanted
to unbutton my overcoat and to feel whether my pocketbook
was in its place. Stubbornly, meanwhile, I pressed forward,
slowly gaining a row or two, but in vain, for canary-coat had

vanished. Yet he must be somewhere in the room, where I alone knew of his dangerous presence; only I, whose nerves quivered with anxiety lest he should come to harm, for I had an obsession that this was his unlucky day. From moment to moment I was expecting to hear the cry "Stop thief!" to see him standing there caught in the act, gripped by his two coat-sleeves, and held firm while someone ran for the police. It remains a puzzle to me why I was so sure that misfortune awaited him that very day; perhaps the signs of it had been written on his face.

But nothing of the sort happened. No one shouted "Au voleur!" Instead of a clamour, there came a sudden silence, as if the two or three hundred persons in the auction-room were holding their breath; and they were all looking with redoubled attention at the auctioneer, who had moved back a step or two, so that the light from the central pendant shone more strongly on his face. Soon I grasped the reason. The most important article in the catalogue was about to be put up for sale—a huge vase sent three hundred years ago with a special delegation by the Emperor of China to the King of France. With many other art-treasures it had been "lifted" from the court during the revolution, and, after numerous vicissitudes, had found a new home in the Countess Yves's collection. With extreme and significant care, four uniformed porters lifted the enormous piece of pottery—it was blue-veined upon a whitish ground—on to the table. The auctioneer, having solemnly cleared his throat, announced that there was a reserve price and that no bid under one hundred and thirty thousand francs would be considered. One hundred and thirty thousand francs! Reverential silence received the figure consecrated by so many noughts. No one ventured to bid, to stir a foot, or to utter a syllable; the audience was a solid block of mute wonder. At length a small, white-haired man to the left of the table raised his head and muttered, "One hundred and thirty-five thousand," to which, from another quarter, came a quick response of "One hundred and forty thousand." Thereupon the bidding grew brisk. The representative of a wealthy American auctioneering firm did not utter his bids, but was content to raise his finger, this sufficing, each time, to put up the price by five thousand francs. From the other end of the table the private secretary of a famous collector (whose name was whispered all over the room) answered in words. Soon the auction became a duel between the pair who, though opposite one another, sedulously refrained from looking one another in the face. They confined their attention to the auctioneer, who eagerly glanced from one to the other in acceptance of their bids. At length, when the collector's secretary had said, "Two hundred and sixty thousand," and the auctioneer turned towards the American, the latter no longer raised his finger, and the 260,000 was left hanging in the air like a frozen tone. Amid increasing excitement, the auctioneer repeated four times, "Going for two hundred and sixty thousand." Then he waited awhile, hoping for an additional rise, before saying: "No further bid?" Silence. Again, "No further bid?" It sounded almost like a cry of despair. The silence began to vibrate, like a string that does not yet vibrate amply enough to produce a sound. The auctioneer raised his hammer, and three hundred hearts almost ceased to beat. "Going for two hundred and sixty thousand," this time thrice reiterated. All held their breath in suspense. The ivory hammer was raised still higher. "Going," said the auctioneer. No answer. "Going!" No answer. "Going for two hundred and sixty thousand!" No answer. Down came the hammer with a click, to the accompaniment of a definitive "Gone!" It was over.

Two hundred and sixty thousand francs! The rigid wall of the audience broke up into a number of mobile, living faces. There was a general stir, movement, breathing, clearing of throats. Like a single body, the densely packed mass resolved

itself into an excited wave of units, animated by a common
movement, and delivering a thrust.

To me, too, came this thrust, delivered by a stranger's elbow
on my chest. Simultaneously someone murmured to me, "Pardon, Monsieur!" I started. That voice! Yes, it was he. By a
lucky chance, the breaking wave had washed him up close
beside me. For the first time since I had lost him, he was
beside me. Now I could continue to watch him, and could
protect him. Of course I avoided looking him squarely in the
face. Furtively, I glanced at his hands, the tools of his trade,
but they had disappeared! The sleeves of his overcoat hung
down on either side, and, as if he had been cold, he had withdrawn his hands within them. If, now, he should move to
pick a pocket, the victim would be aware only of the chance
contact of an innocent piece of clothing, for the dangerous
fingers were as safely hidden away as the claws in a cat's paw.
"An excellent plan!" I thought; but on whom was he about
to ply his trade? Looking cautiously to his right, I saw a lean
individual carefully buttoned up, in front of whom stood a
solid-looking gentleman with a broad and seemingly impreg-
nable back. I was dubious as to the possibility of an effective
onslaught being made in either of these quarters. Then of a
sudden, when I felt a gentle touch on my own knee, a shudder
ran through me at the thought that I was to be the victim.

"Are you going to be fool enough to try to rob the one man
in the room who knows all about you and your little ways?
Am I, as a last and bewildering lesson in your handicraft, to
learn it through its being practised on my own person?" It
really did seem as if the unlucky creature had singled me out,
me who knew him through and through, me whose sympathies were enlisted in his favour. Yes, I could no longer
doubt, for the pickpocket's elbow was gently pressing my
side; inch by inch the long sleeve that hid his skilful hand
was moving forward, ready, at the first liberating movement

in the crowd, to shoot like a snake's tongue between my coat and my waistcoat.

True, I had ample time to defend myself. I need merely turn my back upon him, or button up my coat. But I lacked the strength to do either, for my whole body was hypnotized by excitement and expectation. My muscles and my nerves seemed frozen as I waited in this condition of senseless agitation. Quickly I tried to reckon up how much money I had in my note-case, and, while thus engaged (since every part of the body—be it tooth, or finger, or toe—grows sensitive the instant one begins to think about it), I became aware of the gentle pressure of the note-case against my chest. It was still there, then; and, thus forewarned and forearmed, I could tranquilly await the onslaught. The strange thing was, however, that I could not tell whether I wanted it to come or not. My feelings were in a whirl—I was bipolar. For his own sake, I wished the fool to leave me alone; on the other hand, I was waiting with the same sensation of tensed anticipation as when one is in the dentist's chair and the drill approaches a sensitive spot. But canary-coat, as if wishing to punish me for my inquisitiveness, showed no sign of hurry, keeping so close to me that I felt the warmth of his body. Inch by inch he softly drew nearer, and, while my sense of touch was almost entirely engrossed by these contacts, with another of my sense-organs I was attending to what passed at the auction-table: "Three thousand seven hundred and fifty. Any further bid? Thank you, three thousand seven hundred and sixty, in two places. Three thousand seven hundred and seventy, eighty, ninety. Any further bid? Four thousand. Four thousand. Four thousand. Going at four thousand. Going, going, gone"—and down came the hammer.

Once more there was the sudden easing of the packed throng, the wave movement that always followed the fall of the hammer, and the consequent release of tension. At this instant I again had a feeling that the wave was breaking against my own chest. Nothing very definite, it was as light as the movement of a snake, a gliding sense of bodily contact, so swift and tenuous that I should never have been aware of it had I not been alert with anticipation, and especially alert at the threatened spot. Only as if a chance gust had ruffled my overcoat, or as if a swallow had brushed me with its wing, and . . .

And what now happened took me by surprise. My own hand leaped up and firmly gripped the slim fingers that had insinuated themselves beneath my coat. I had not planned this rough and brutish action of self-defence. It was a reflex which startled me, the outcome of a defensive purpose which existed as a "purpose" only in the automatic realm of the instinctive life. With the upshot that, to my amazement and horror, my hand now grasped another by the wrist, a cold, trembling wrist. Indubitably my movement, so quickly and successfully executed, was not the outcome of conscious design. It was unwilled.

This second transcends my powers of description. I was rigid with alarm at thus holding in a forcible clasp one of the limbs of a stranger. He, likewise, was paralysed by terror. Just as I lacked the strength and the presence of mind that were needed for letting go his wrist, so did he lack the courage and the presence of mind to snatch his hand away. "Four hundred and fifty; four hundred and sixty; four hundred and seventy," came from the direction of the table in the auctioneer's tenor voice, while I retained my hold of the thief's shuddering hand. "Four hundred and eighty; four hundred and ninety," continued the voice; and all the time no one noticed what was going on between the thief and myself; no one suspected that a struggle (not so much physical as mental) was going on between two persons in the room, and that this struggle was fraught with destiny. "Five hundred, and ten, and twenty, and thirty, and forty, and fifty"—the figures droned on. The whole thing had lasted perhaps ten or twenty seconds when I was able to draw breath once more. I released my grip. The stranger's hand was withdrawn, and vanished within the canary-coloured sleeve.

"And sixty, and seventy, and eighty, and ninety, six hundred, six hundred and ten," said the auctioneer; and we two, the would-be thief and the man he had tried to rob, still stood side by side, accomplices in the mysterious deed, both paralysed by the same experience. I still felt the warmth of his body as it pressed against mine; and when, with the release of tension, my knees began to tremble, I fancied I could feel a responsive tremor in the knee which touched mine. "Six hundred and twenty, and thirty, and forty, and fifty, and sixty, and seventy," intoned the tenor voice, for the lot had not yet been knocked down; and we still stood side by side, as if chained together by a cold ring of horror. At length I found the energy to turn my head and scrutinize him. At the same instant he looked at me. As our eyes met, I read in his the entreaty: "Please, please, don't give me in charge!" I read in them the terror of an oppressed spirit. The primal anxiety of hunted beasts streamed from his contracted pupils, and his stubble beard quivered under stress of alarm. The terrified eyes mainly attracted my attention, but the whole visage betrayed such panic as I have never seen in a human being before or since. I was intolerably ashamed that a fellow-mortal should look at me with so slavish an expression, as if I held in my hands the power of life and death. His anxiety humiliated me, and in embarrassment I turned my face aside.

But he had understood. He knew what he wanted to know, that I should not denounce him or hand him over to the police, and the knowledge gave him back his strength. With a jerk, he drew away from me, and it was plain that his one desire was to be quit of me for ever. No longer did I feel his tremulous knee touching mine, nor the warmth of his adjacent body. Once more master of his craft, he made one of his sinuous movements and wriggled like an eel through the crowd.

At the moment when I ceased to feel the warmth of his body, it came to me with a pang of conscience that I must not let him leave me thus. I owed him compensation for the terror he had just experienced because of me; and I was in his debt for the lessons in his handicraft which, unconsciously, he had given me this day. He was certainly entitled to a substantial fee. Hastily I pressed after him through the exit. But the poor devil saw my movement and misunderstood my intention. He fancied that I had changed my mind, and had determined to hand him over to the police. Before I could get out of the auction-room he had almost disappeared among those who thronged the corridor. He was making for the street with all possible speed. For a moment I saw the yellow sheen of his overcoat before he vanished. My impromptu lesson was over.

Rachel Arraigns God

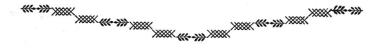

A LEGEND

Once again had the froward and fickle folk of Jerusalem forgotten the Covenant, once again had they offered up sacrifices to brazen idols. Nor were they satisfied with this impiety; for even in God's Temple, which Solomon His servant had built, they set up an image of Baal, and the gutters ran red with the blood of the victims.

When God saw how they mocked him in the heart of the sanctuary, his wrath found vent. He stretched forth His hand, and His voice made the skies tremble. His patience was exhausted; He would shower destruction upon the sinful city and scatter its inhabitants like chaff. His thunders resounded, announcing this resolve from one end of the world to the other.

Now that the Almighty had given utterance to His anger, the earth quaked with terror. The windows of heaven were opened, as they had been in the days of Father Noah, the fountains of the great deep were broken up, and the high hills

359

tottered. The birds of the air dropped to earth, and even the angels were affrighted by the fury of the Lord.

Far beneath, in the doomed town, men, though they heard the thunder of God's voice, were deaf to the meaning of His words. They knew not that they had been sentenced to destruction. Yet full well they were aware that the foundations of the world were crumbling; that at high noon it had grown dark as midnight; that a hurricane was raging which broke the stems of the mighty cedars like straws. Fearful lest the roofs should fall in upon their heads, they fled from their houses into the open, to be even more panic-stricken by the force of the blast, the driving of the rain, the sulphurous reek of the murky air. Vainly did they rend their garments and put ashes on their heads, vainly did they abase themselves and implore God's forgiveness. The fury of the elements was unabated, the darkness unrelieved.

So fierce had been the thunder of God's wrath that it aroused even the dead from the slumbers in which, as is decreed, they lie awaiting the Last Trump. Believing that this dread summons had sounded, they rose and winged their way heavenward, to find, after they had traversed the fearful storm, that the Last Judgment was not yet. Nevertheless, the souls of the fathers and forefathers gathered in a circle round the Throne, to beseech that the doom might be averted from their children and from the pinnacles of the Holy City. Abraham, Isaac, and Jacob led the prayer. But their voices were drowned by the Voice of the Lord, repeating that too long had He endured the stubbornness of His creatures. Ungrateful though these were, the shattering of the Temple would teach the wicked who could not be taught by love.

Since the ancestors of the Chosen People were thus struck dumb, there now petitioned those who in life had been the mouthpieces of God's Holy Word, the prophets Moses, Samuel, Elijah, and Elisha—men with tongues of fire and burning hearts. But the Lord would not hearken, and the tempest of His anger blew their words back into their faces. Brighter than before flashed the lightnings that were to consume the Temple and raze it to the ground.

The prophets and sages, too, lost courage. Their souls quivered like grass in the tempest; they were as dead leaves trodden under foot. No man among them dared to breathe another syllable. But the soul of a woman spake, that of Rachel, the arch-mother of Israel, who in her tomb at Ramah had likewise heard God's proclamation, and had come weeping for her children, refusing to be comforted. Drawing strength from love, she ventured to take up her parable before Him whose face she could not see—for none but the angels can look upon God's countenance until the Judgment Day. Kneeling, she raised her hands and said her word:

"My heart is like water within me, Almighty, thus to address Thee, but Thou madest this heart so timid; and Thou gavest me lips wherewith, though fearfully, to utter my prayer. The bitter need of my children enables me. Thou didst not gift me with either wisdom or cunning, nor know I how to allay Thine anger. But as for Thee, Thou knowest what I would say, for every word forms itself in Thy mind before it is spoken by human lips, and every human action is foreseen by Thee. Nevertheless, I pray Thee to hear me for those poor sinners' sake."

Having thus spoken, Rachel bowed her head. God saw her humility, and noted the tears that coursed down her cheeks. He restrained His wrath, and was silent, to hear her pleading.

Now when God listens in heaven, space is emptied and time stands still. The wind ceased howling, the thunder roared no longer, creeping and crawling things stayed from creeping and crawling, the birds of the air folded their pinions, no one ventured even to draw breath. The movement of the hours was arrested, and the cherubim were motionless as statues.

Even the sun and the moon and the stars rested from their circling, and the rivers from their flow.

Far beneath, the inhabitants of the doomed city knew naught of Rachel's pleading in their behalf, or that the Almighty was hearkening to her prayer. For mortals cannot perceive what passes in heaven. All they were aware of was that the storm had abated. But when, taking heart of grace, they looked skyward, it was to see the black clouds hanging over them like the pall that covers a coffin. In the unrelieved darkness they were still terrified, all the more because the quietude continued to envelop them as a shroud enwraps a corpse.

But Rachel, glad that God was paying heed to her supplication, plucked up courage, raised her head, and continued:

"Lord, as Thou knowest, I dwelt in Haran, the land of the people of the east, where I kept my father Laban's sheep. Came a morning when we maidens drove the sheep to the water, but lacked strength to roll the stone from the well's mouth. Then a youth appeared, a stranger, well-made, who sprang forward to help us, and rolled away the stone so easily that we were astonished at his strength. Jacob was his name, and he was the son of my father's sister Rebekah. When he told us who he was, I led him to my father Laban's house. Within an hour of the meeting by the well, our hearts yearned for one another. At night, I could not sleep for longing—nor am I ashamed to say this, seeing that, if passion flames up in us like the ardours of the Burning Bush, it is through Thy will, Lord, that such things happen. Through Thy will doth it come to pass that a woman craves for a man's embraces, that youth and maiden are magically drawn together. Because these things are so, we did not try to quench the flames, but on that first day of our meeting Jacob and I exchanged vows of betrothal.

"As Thou knowest, Lord, my father Laban was a hard

man; hard as the stony ground he ploughed, hard as the horns of the oxen whose necks he bent beneath the yoke. When Jacob asked me of him in marriage, he had it in mind first of all to discover whether this suitor, his nephew, was a man of his own kind, a strenuous worker and endowed with iron patience. Laban demanded of Jacob seven years' service as the price of my hand. My soul trembled, and Jacob's cheeks paled, for to both of us, young and impatient, seven years seemed an infinity of waiting. For Thee, Lord, seven years are but a moment, the flicker of an eyelash, since time is nothing to the Eternal. But for us mortals (deign to remember it, Lord God) seven years is a tenth of our life. Short is the allotted span, and scarcely have our eyes opened to see Thy holy light, when they are closed in the darkness of death. Like a freshet in springtime races the current of human existence, and a wave that has passed can never return. Seven long years were we to be sundered, though living in close companionship; kept apart, while our lips thirsted for one another's kisses. Nevertheless, Jacob complied with his uncle's wishes, and I obeyed my father's behest. We resolved upon seven years of waiting, of obedience and patience—because we loved one another.

"Yet Thou hast made patience difficult to Thy creatures, having given them hot passions, and instilled into them a brooding anxiety because of the shortness of their lives. We know that our autumn follows close upon our springtime, that the season of our summer is brief. That is why we snatch at fleeting hours of joy, and are eager to make the most of evanescent pleasures. How can we be expected to wait without repining, we who grow older day by day? Of course we burn, since, by Thy decree, time perpetually consumes us. Can we fail to be in a hurry, since we know that Death unceasingly dogs our footsteps? Yet we mastered our impulses, while each day of waiting was as long as a thousand. In the end, when the seven years were accomplished, they seemed, as we looked back on them, to have been no more than a single day. Thus, Lord, did I wait for Jacob, and thus did Jacob love me.

"When the seventh year of waiting had drawn to a close, I went joyfully to Laban, my father, and asked him to prepare the wedding tent. But Laban, my father, looked coldly on my joy. His brows were clouded, and for a space his mouth was sealed. At length he broke silence, and commanded me to summon Leah, my sister.

"Leah, as Thou knowest, Lord, was two years mine elder, and hard-favoured. Hence no man coveted her, whereat she was sorely grieved. Yet I loved her fondly, because of her affliction and her gentleness. When, however, my father bade me summon Leah, it entered my mind in a flash that he had planned to beguile me and Jacob. I therefore hid close to the tent, that I might overhear their conversation. My father spake as follows:

" 'Leah, my nephew Jacob has served me faithfully seven years, in order to win Rachel as his wife. Yet for thy sake I will not do this thing, since it must not be so done in our country, to give the younger before the firstborn. In the beginning, the Almighty commanded us to be fruitful and multiply, that we might people His world and raise up many to praise His holy name. He did not desire the soil to lie fallow, or that a woman should bear no children. No ewe and no heifer feeds on my pastures without bringing forth after their kind. Can it be expected of me that I should allow the womb of my elder daughter to remain closed? Make ready, then, Leah. Don the bridal veil, and Jacob (unknowing) shall wed thee in Rachel's stead.' Thus spake my father to Leah, who listened in a timid silence.

"But I, eavesdropping, was filled with anger against Laban, my father, and against Leah, my sister. Forgive me, Lord, for

being so undaughterly, so unsisterly; but bethink Thee how
Jacob and I had been waiting for one another seven years,
and now, after all his service, my sister was to be imposed
upon him whose life was dearer to me than my own. I mutinied against my father, even as Thy children is Jerusalem have
mutinied against Thee—for thus hast Thou made us, O Lord,
that we grow stiff-necked when we deem that we are un-
justly treated. Secretly I talked with Jacob, and disclosed my
father's plan. That this scheme might be frustrated, I told
him of a sign by which he might know me. 'When thou art
wedded,' I declared, 'thy bride shall kiss thee thrice on the
forehead before she enters the tent.' Jacob understood, and
approved the sign.

"That evening, Laban had Leah veiled for the bridal. Also
he had her face skilfully made up, lest Jacob should recognize
her before he had gone in unto her. He had me barred in
the granary, fearing lest one of the servants might warn me
of what was afoot. Like an owl, I sat there in the gloom, and
as the hours wore on towards nightfall, I ate my heart out
with rage and pain. Not, Lord, as Thou knowest, that I bore
a grudge against my sister because she was to be possessed by
Jacob—but I was wroth that my beloved was to be tricked
out of what he had slaved seven years to secure. I bit my
wrists, when the cymbals clashed merrily, and my passions
gnawed at my vitals as lions tear at their kill.

"Thus prisoned and forgotten I spent the weary hours,
consumed with bitterness, until, when the darkness without was as impenetrable as the darkness of my soul, the bolts
were drawn back, the door was gently opened, and Leah entered. Yes, Leah, my sister, had stolen away to visit me, before
the bridal. I knew her footsteps, but I turned from her in enmity, for my heart was hardened against her. Leah stroked
my hair, and, when I looked up, I could see, by the light of
the lamp she carried, that her face was overcast. Thereupon,

Lord, as I frankly acknowledge, a malicious pleasure stirred
within me. It did me good to know that she was uneasy, that
Leah (too) was suffering on her wedding day. But she, poor
innocent, did not suspect my feelings. Had we not drawn
suck from the same breasts, and had we not always loved one
another? Confidently, she put her arms around me, saying,
with pallid lips:

"'What will be the upshot, Rachel, my sister? I am sore
at heart because of this scheme of our father's. He is taking
your lover from you and giving Jacob to me; grievous is the
thought of tricking him thus. How can I dare to substitute
myself for you? My legs will refuse to carry me; and my
heart is full of fear, for assuredly, Rachel, he will detect the
fraud. How shamefaced I shall be, if thereupon he drives me
forth from his tent! Down to the second and third genera-
tion, children will make mock of me, saying: "That is Leah,
ugly Leah! Don't you know her story? She was thrust upon
a husband, who wouldn't have her when he found out the
trick, and drove her away like a mangy cur." What am I to
do, Rachel, dear? Shall I take the venture, or shall I defy
our father (whose hand is heavy)? How can I prevent Jacob
discovering the fraud too soon, so that shame will be brought
upon my innocent head? Help me, Sister, help me, I implore
you, in the name of the All-Merciful!'

"Lord, I was still exceeding wroth; and, much though I
loved my sister, the evil within me still made her anxiety sweet
to me. Since, however, she had called upon Thy holy name,
the holiest of Thy names, since she had implored me in the
name of the All-Merciful, the might of Thy compassion, the
power of Thy goodness, flowed through my veins like wine,
and entered like a blaze of light into my darkened soul. For
this is one of Thy everlasting miracles, O Lord, that the barriers which separate each of us from others are broken down
the instant we become sympathetically aware of the suffering

of our neighbour and share the pain within our neighbour's tortured breast. My sister's anxiety permeated me, so that, instead of thinking of my private sorrow, I felt her bitter need. Sharing her distress, I, Thy foolish handmaid (mark this, Lord, I pray Thee), had compassion upon her in the hour when she stood before me in tears, even as now, in this hour, I stand before Thee in tears. I had compassion upon her, because she had appealed to me for pity, even as now I appeal to Thee. In my own despite, I taught her how to deceive Jacob, betraying to her the sign I had pledged myself to give him. 'Kiss him thrice on the brow,' said I, 'before thou enterest his tent.' Thus, for love of Thee, the All-Merciful, did I gain the victory over my jealousy, and play the traitor to the man I loved.

"When I had told this secret to Leah, she could no longer contain herself, but prostrated herself before me, fondling my hands and kissing the hem of my raiment; for thus hast Thou fashioned Thy creatures, that always they are filled with humility and gratitude when they discern in another a trace of Thine own goodness. We embraced, making one another's cheeks salt with our mingled tears. Leah was comforted, and prepared to depart. But as she arose, once more her face became shadowed with sorrow, and again her lips blanched.

" 'I thank thee, Sister, for thy loving-kindness,' she said, 'and shall do as thou biddest. But what if the sign fail to convince him? Yet more counsel do I need, Rachel. What shall I do if he address me by thy name? Can I remain stubbornly silent, a bride to whom the bridegroom speaketh? Yet the instant I open my mouth, he will know that it is Leah whom he is taking to wife, and not Rachel. I cannot answer him in thy voice! Help me yet further, Sister, shrewd as thou art; help me in the name of the All-Merciful!'

"Again, Lord, when she thus appealed to me in the holiest of Thy names; again that intoxicating fire flowed through

me, so that once more my heart melted, and ruthlessly I trod
my own wishes under foot. I was ready for the supreme sacrifice, and answered:

"'Be comforted, Leah. Here, too, I can find a way. For the
sake of the All-Merciful I will see to it that Jacob shall not
recognize thee as Leah until after he has known thee, believing thee to be Rachel. This is my plan. I shall slip into Jacob's
tent, and shall there crouch in the darkness beside the nuptial
couch. Should he speak to thee, I shall answer him. Then he
will have no suspicion, but will embrace thee, and will fer-
tilize thy body with his seed. This will I do for thee, Leah,
because of the love we have borne one another since we were
little children together, and for love of the All-Merciful, that
He may have compassion on my children and my children's
children, whenever they may call upon Him by the holiest of
His names.'

"Lord, thereupon Leah embraced me and kissed me on the
lips. Another woman, a woman renewed, was she who rose
from her knees. Freed from care, she went forth, to offer herself to Jacob, her face hidden behind the deceitful veil. As for
me, I drank my cup to the dregs, hiding myself beside the
couch on which my lover was to enter into my sister. Soon
the cymbals clashed once more, as the musicians attended the
wedded pair, who in a minute stood at the entry to the tent.
But before Jacob raised the veil to give his bride a blessing,
he paused in expectation of the sign I had promised. Then
Leah kissed him thrice on the forehead. Jacob, satisfied with
the token, clasped his bride lovingly, lifted her in his arms,
and carried her to the bed behind which I cowered. Even
now, however, as Leah had foreseen, before the final embrace,
he asked: 'Is it truly Rachel whom I hold in my arms?' Then,
Lord (Thou, the All-Knower, knowest how hard it was for
me to utter the words!), I whispered: 'Yes, it is I, Jacob, my
husband.' He, recognizing my voice, he, who had waited

seven years to possess me, thereupon made Leah my sister his own, with all the vigour of a young man in his prime. Lord, Thou whose vision pierces the darkness as a scythe cuts grass, Thou sawest my plight when I crouched there within touch of them, while passionately he possessed Leah believing himself to be entering into me, who so ardently longed for his embraces. Omnipresent Lord, recall, I pray Thee, that memorable night when I spent seven hours of agony, hearing the transports that should have been mine and were denied me. Seven hours, seven æons, did I lie beside that couch, holding my breath, wrestling against my longing to cry out, even as Jacob, later, wrestled with Thy angel until the breaking of the day. Longer, far longer, seemed to me these seven night hours than Jacob's seven years of waiting. Never could I have endured it, this night of forbearance, had I not (in the silence of my soul) called repeatedly upon Thy holy name, and strengthened my resolve with the thought of Thine infinite patience.

"This, Lord, was my deed, the only one upon which I plume myself among all that I did during my earthly pilgrimage, for then I rivalled my Creator in forbearance and compassion. I doubt if ever Thou hast laid so heavy a burden upon a woman as upon me in the anguish of that night. Yet I endured to the uttermost; and at length, when the cocks crew, I rose up wearily while the pair on the bed were in a profound slumber. Hastily I fled to my father's house, for soon the fraud would be disclosed, and my teeth chattered as I thought of Jacob's fury. Alas, my forebodings were justified. Scarcely was I safely ensconced at my father's, when the shouts of the husband whom we had beguiled rent the air of morning like the bellowing of an enraged bull. Armed with an axe, he rushed hither and thither in search of Laban, my father, who was paralysed with terror at sight of his infuriated son-in-law, and sank upon the ground, calling upon Thy holy name. Once again, Lord, this appeal to Thee revived my flagging courage, inspired me with determination, so that I flung myself between Jacob and Laban, to turn my lover's wrath towards myself, and save my unhappy father. Jacob saw red, and directly his eyes lighted upon me who had helped to deceive him, he struck me in the face with his fist, and I fell. Thou knowest, Lord, that I bore this chastisement without repining, being aware that the greatness of his love accounted for the greatness of his wrath. Had he slain me—and, indeed, he raised the axe to smite me—I should have appeared uncomplainingly before Thy Throne.

"But as soon as he saw me stretched at his feet, bruised and bleeding, pity overcame him. The axe dropped from his nerveless hands. Leaning over me, he tenderly kissed the blood from my lips. For my sake, he forgave my father Laban, and did not drive Leah from his tent. A week later, my father gave me to him as second wife. Jacob opened my womb, and I bare him children, which I nourished upon the milk of my breasts and upon the words of Thy Covenant, children which I bade call upon Thee in their need, with the mystery of Thy ineffable name. Today, Lord, Almighty and All-Merciful, in my own uttermost need, I call upon Thee to do what Jacob did, to drop the axe of Thine anger and to dispel the clouds of Thy wrath. Because Rachel was pitiful to Leah, her sister, wilt not Thou be pitiful to Rachel's children and children's children; wilt not Thou be patient, even as I was patient, and spare the Holy City? Have mercy on them, Lord; have mercy on Jerusalem."

Rachel's voice echoed through the vaults of heaven. Her strength was spent, and she sank back upon her knees, exhausted, while her hair fell in a black flood over her trembling body. Thus did Rachel await God's answer.

But God did not answer. He was silent. And in heaven, upon earth, in the circling spheres between, there is nothing

more dreadful than God's silence. When God is silent, the
movement of time ceases; light is merged into darkness, day
into night; and throughout all the worlds of the habitable universe there prevails only the chaos of the days before creation.
The movable moves no longer, the flow of the rivers is stayed,
the flowers do not bloom, even the tides cannot ebb and flow
without the power of God's word. No mortal ear can bear
God's silence, no mortal heart can continue beating in this
awesome void, wherein nothing is but God, and even He, the
life of lives, is alive no longer when He is silent.

Rachel, for all her patience, could not endure the endless
silence with which God answered her proclamation of infinite
need. Once more she lifted her eyes towards the Invisible,
once more she lifted her motherly hands, and anger struck
words of fire from her lips.

"Hast Thou not heard me, Omnipresent? Hast Thou not
understood me, Omniscient? Must Thy handmaid speak yet
more plainly to thrust her meaning home? Learn, then (hard
of hearing though Thou art), that I was jealous because Jacob
had bestowed on my sister what was meant for me, just as
Thou art jealous because my children have sacrificed to other
gods than Thee. But I, a weak woman, mastered my jealousy,
grew pitiful for sake of Thee, whom I have called the All-
Merciful. I had pity on Leah, and Jacob had pity on me. Take
note of this, Almighty! All of us, poor mortals though we be,
control the evil passion of envy. But Thou, Almighty, Creator
of the universe, alpha and omega, the beginning and the end,
Thou who hast an ocean where we have only droplets—Thou
canst not show compassion. Well do I know that my children
are a stiff-necked brood, that again and ever again they revolt against the yoke. But since Thou art God, and Lord of
Plenty, shall not Thy forbearance match their stubbornness,
and shall not Thy forgiveness march with their transgressions?
For this must not be, God; this must not be, that before Thine

own angels Thou shouldest be put to shame, so that the angels will say: 'Once upon earth there was a woman, a frail mortal, Rachel by name, who held her anger in check. But He, God Almighty, Lord and Master of the universe, was the slave of His own wrath.' No, God, that must not be, for unless Thy mercy is infinite, Thou Thyself art not infinite—which means that Thou art not God! Thou art not the God whom I made for myself out of my tears, and whose voice called to me through my sister's tears. Thou Thyself art a 'strange god,' a god of wrath, punishment, and vengeance; and I, Rachel, I, who loved only the Loving God and served only the All-Merciful—I reject Thee before Thine own angels. They and Thy prophets may abase themselves. But I, Rachel, the mother, will not abase me. I stand erect and defy Thee. God, I arraign Thee, before Thou executest Thy will upon my children. Thy word, God, conflicts with Thine own nature, and Thy wrathful mouth gives the lie to the promptings of Thine own heart. Judge, God, betwixt Thyself and Thy word. If Thou art, in very truth, the wrathful and jealous God Thou proclaimest Thyself to be, then will I fling myself down into the darkness to join my children and share their doom. I do not wish to contemplate the visage of an angry God, and I loathe the thought of a jealous one. But if Thou art a merciful God, the God I have loved, and by the guidance of whose teachings I tried to walk, then show Thyself to me in that light; be clement, spare my children, have mercy upon Jerusalem."

When Rachel had uttered this message of defiance, again her strength was spent. She awaited the answer of the Most High, her eyelids closed like those of the dead.

The forefathers and the prophets drew away, in terror of the lightnings which must, they felt assured, blast the impious spirit of her who had arraigned God. Timidly they gazed upward at the Throne. But there was no sign vouchsafed.

The angels, affrighted by the angry aspect of God's visage,

hid their heads under their wings. Then (peeping forth) they
looked aghast at the woman who had denied the omnipotence
of the Lord—and perceived that a light shone on Rachel's forehead. It was as if this radiance emanated from within, and
the tears on her motherly cheeks sparkled red like dew-drops
in the glow of dawn. What was happening? The angels understood. God was showing Rachel the glory of His loving
countenance. They became aware that the Almighty loved this
repudiator of His word for the very reason that she was
froward and impatient, loved her more than He loved the
sages and the prophets, the pious who so servilely complied
with His word. Mastering their terror, the angels confidently
raised their eyes, to behold that a splendid and luminous calm
once more enveloped God's majesty, and that the consoling
azure of His smile filled the infinite spaces of heaven. Thereupon the cherubim winked anew their joyful flight, the rustle
of their pinions making music in the skies. The sheen upon
God's face grew so bright that the firmament glowed with an
intensity no mortal eyes could endure. Now the angels sang
together, the dead who had arisen from their tombs joined
in the chorus of praise, and mingled therein were the innumerable voices of those whom the Almighty had not yet
called to live upon earth.

But they who now dwelt thereon, mortals far beneath, ignoring (as ever) the happenings in heaven, knew naught of
what was going on overhead. Clad in their shrouds, they
bowed their faces sadly towards the darkened earth. Then
to one and another of them came the sound of a stirring, like
the rustle of a March wind. Looking upward they were astonished. The dense clouds had been riven in sunder, and
across the interspace spread an arch, sevenfold in colour,
a rainbow, which was made by the light from God's countenance shining upon Mother Rachel's tears.

It is not by shunning action that we can be really freed from action,
Never can we be freed from all activity, even for a moment.
—*Bhagavatgita,* Third Song.

What is action? What is inaction?—These questions have long puzzled the
   sages.
For we must pay heed to action, must pay heed to forbidden action.
Must pay heed likewise to inaction.—The nature of action is unfathomable.
—*Bhagavatgita,* Fourth Song.

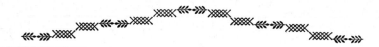

Virata

or The Eyes of the Undying Brother

A LEGEND

This is the Story of Virata who was honoured by his Fellow-Countrymen with the four Names of Virtue. Yet there is no word of him in the Chronicles of the Conquerors or in the Books of the Sages, and his Memory has passed from the Minds of Men.

In the days before the sublime Buddha lived on earth to fill his servants with the light of his knowledge, there dwelt in the land of the Birwagher as subject of a king in Rajputana a noble and upright man named Virata. He was known also as the Flashing of the Sword, for he was a great warrior, bold before all others; and he was a great hunter, whose arrow never missed its mark, whose lance never swerved, and whose trusty sword-arm had the strength of a thunderbolt. His countenance was serene, and his eyes did not quail before any man's glance. He never clenched his fist in anger, nor raised his voice in wrath. Himself a loyal servant of the king, his own slaves served him with veneration, for he was deemed pre-eminent in justice among all who lived in the Land of the Five Rivers. The pious bowed low when they passed before his dwelling, and the children who caught sight of him smiled to see his starry eyes.

But one day misfortune overtook the king his master. The viceroy over half the kingdom, who was brother of the monarch's wife, lusted to make himself ruler of the whole, and by secret gifts had enticed the best warriors of the realm to espouse his cause. He had induced the priests to bring him under cover of darkness the herons of the lake, the sacred herons which for thousands of years had been the insignia of royalty among the Birwagher. He marshalled his elephants in the field, summoned to his army the malcontents from the hills, and marched against the capital.

From morning till evening, by the king's orders, the copper cymbals were beaten and the ivory horns were sounded. At night, fires were lighted upon the towers, and fish-scales were cast into the flames, which flared yellow in the starlight as an alarm signal. Few answered the summons, for the news of the theft of the sacred herons had been bruited abroad, and the leaders' hearts were faint within them. The commander-in-chief and the head of the elephant corps, who had been the most trusted among the king's warriors, had gone over to the enemy. Vainly did the forsaken monarch look around him seeking friends. Alas, he had been a harsh master, ever ready to punish, and strict in the exaction of feudal dues. None of the tried and trusted chiefs were now in attendance at the palace, where only a helpless rabble of slaves and underlings was to be seen.

In this extremity, the king's thoughts turned to Virata, from whom a pledge of loyal service had come the instant the horns had been sounded. He entered his ebony litter, and was borne to the dwelling of his faithful subject. Virata prostrated himself when the king stepped forth from the litter. But the king's mien was that of a petitioner as he besought Virata to take command of the army and lead it against the enemy. Virata made obeisance, and said:

"I will do it, Lord, and will not return to the shelter of this roof until the flames of revolt shall have been stamped out beneath the feet of thy servants."

Thereupon he assembled his sons, his kinsmen, and his slaves, and, going forth with them to join the loyal remnant, he marshalled his forces for the campaign. They made their way through the jungle and came at eventide to the river on whose opposite shore the enemy was drawn up in countless numbers. Confident in their strength, the rebels were felling trees to build a bridge, by which they hoped to cross next morning, and drown the land in blood. But Virata, when hunting the tiger, had discovered a ford above the place of the bridge-building. At dead of night he led his men across the stream, and took the enemy by surprise. With flaming torches, the loyalists scared the elephants and buffaloes in the hostile camp, so that the beasts stampeded, and spread disorder among the sleeping horde. Virata was the first to reach the tent of the would-be usurper; and ere the inmates were fully awake, he put two of them to the sword, and then a third who was reaching out for his own weapon. With a fourth and a fifth he strove man to man in the darkness, cutting down one by a blow on the head, and piercing the other through the unarmoured breast. As soon as they all lay motionless,

shade beside shade, Virata stationed himself at the entry of
the tent, to defend it against any who might seek to carry off
the white herons, the sacred emblem of royalty. But none came
to attempt the deed, for the foe were in flight, hard pressed by
the jubilant and victorious loyalists. Soon the din of the chase
grew faint in the distance. Virata seated himself tranquilly in
front of the tent, sword in hand, to await the return of his
fellow-soldiers.

Ere long, God's day dawned behind the forest. The palm
trees were golden red in the early sunlight, and were mirrored like torches in the river. The sun showed all bloody,
a fiery wound in the east. Virata arose, laid aside his raiment, and walked to the stream, hands uplifted. Having
bowed in prayer before the glowing eye of God, he went
down into the waters for the prescribed ablutions, and cleansed
the blood from his hands. Now, in the white light of morning, he returned to the bank, wrapped himself in his garment,
and, serene of countenance, made his way back to the tent to
contemplate the deeds of the night. The dead lay there with
eyes staring and faces contorted with terror. The usurper's
head was cloven; and the traitor who had been commander-
in-chief in the land of the Birwagher who perished from a
sword-thrust in the breast. Closing their eyes, Virata moved
on to look at those whom he had killed as they slumbered.
These lay half-wrapped in their mats. Two of them were
strangers to him, slaves of the traitor, men from the south
with woolly hair and black faces. But when he looked upon
the last of the dead men, Virata's eyes grew dim, for he saw
before him the face of his elder brother Belangur, the Prince
of the Mountains, who had come to the aid of the usurper, and
whom Virata had struck down all unwitting. Trembling he
stooped to feel for the heart-beat of the misguided man. The
heart was stilled forever; the dead man's eyes encountered his
with a glassy stare—dark eyes which seemed to pierce his

very soul. Hardly able to breathe, Virata sat down among the
dead, feeling as if he himself were one of them, and turning
away his eyes from the accusing gaze of his mother's firstborn.

Soon, shouts were heard without. Glad at heart, enriched
with plunder, and with wild and gleeful cries like those of
birds of prey, the returning soldiers came to the tent. Finding the would-be usurper slain amid his adherents, and learning that the sacred herons were safe, they leapt and danced,
kissed the garment of the unheeding Virata, and acclaimed
him the Flashing of the Sword. As more came back of them
and more, they loaded carts with their booty. So deep sank
the wheels beneath the burden that they had to scourge the
buffaloes with thorns, and the boats were in danger of sinking. A messenger forded the stream, and hastened to bear
tidings to the king; but the others tarried beside the spoil,
and rejoiced over the victory.

Virata, meanwhile, sat silent, as if in a dream. Once only
did he uplift his voice, when the soldiers were about to strip
the dead. Thereupon, rising to his feet, he commanded that
funeral pyres should be built, in order that the slain might
be burned and their souls go forth cleansed to the transmigration. The underlings were amazed that he should deal thus
tenderly with conspirators, who should have been torn limb
from limb by the jackals, and whose bones should have been
left to bleach in the sun: nevertheless, they did as they were
bidden. When the pyres had been built, Virata himself kindled them, and cast spices and sandalwood into the flames.
Then, turning away his face, he stood in silence until the
blazing platforms fell in and the glowing ashes sank to the
ground.

Meanwhile the slaves had finished the bridge whose building had been vauntingly begun the day before by the servitors
of the usurper. The first to cross it were the warriors, crowned

with flowers of the plantain; then came the slaves; then the nobles on horseback. Virata sent most of the warriors in advance, for their shouts and songs were discordant with his mood. Halting in the middle of the bridge, he gazed for a long time to right and to left over the flowing waters, while the soldiers who had crossed in front of him and those who had still to cross and who, by their commander's orders, were keeping well to the rear, marvelled as they looked at him. They saw him raise his sword, as if to threaten heaven, but when he lowered his arm, his fingers loosed their grip, and the weapon sank into the river. From either bank, naked boys jumped into the water, supposing that the sword had been accidentally dropped, and hoping to recover it by diving; but Virata forbade the attempt, and strode forward, sad of mien, between the wondering servitors. No word passed his lips during the long homeward march.

The jasper gates and pinnacled towers of Birwagha were still far distant when a white dust-cloud was seen advancing, heralded by runners and riders who had outstripped the dust. They halted at sight of the army and spread carpets athwart the road as a sign of the advent of the king, the sole of whose foot must never press the common clay from the day of his birth to that hour when the flames of the funeral pyre would enwrap his illustrious corpse. Now the monarch came in sight, borne by the lord of the elephants, and surrounded by youths. Obedient to the ankus, the great beast kneeled, and the king stepped down upon the carpet. Virata wished to prostrate himself before his master, but the king hastened to embrace him—an honour that had never yet been paid to an inferior. Virata had the herons brought, and when they flapped their white wings there was such a clamour of rejoicing that the chargers reared and the mahouts were hard put to it to control the elephants. At sight of these emblems of victory, the king embraced Virata once more, and beck-

oned an attendant, who was carrying the sword of the primal
hero of the Rajputs. For seven times seven hundred years,
this weapon had been preserved in the treasuries of the kings.
The hilt glittered with jewels, and on the blade was inscribed
in golden characters a mystic assurance of victory, in the
ancient writing which none but sages and the priests of the
great temple could now decipher. The king offered this sword
of swords to Virata as a token of gratitude, and to show that
henceforward Virata was to be the chief of his warriors and
the leader of his armies.

But Virata made a deep obeisance, saying:

"May I ask a grace from the most gracious and a favour
from the most generous of monarchs?"

Looking down on the petitioner's bowed head, the king
answered:

"Your request is granted, even before you raise your eyes
to meet mine. You have but to ask, and the half of my kingdom is yours."

Thereupon Virata said:

"Grant then, O King, that this sword may be taken back
to your treasury, for I have vowed in my heart never again
to wield a sword, now that I have slain my brother, the only
fruit besides myself which my mother bore in her womb,
and whom my mother dandled together with me."

The king looked at him in amazement. Then he replied:

"In that case, be the commander of my armies, though
without a sword, that I may know my realm to be safe from
its enemies, for never has a hero led an army more wisely
against overwhelming odds. Take my sash as a token of
power, and my charger likewise, that all may know you as
chief among my warriors."

But Virata prostrated himself once more, and rejoined:

"The Invisible One has sent me a sign, and my heart has
understood. I have slain my brother, and this has taught me

that everyone who slays another human being kills his brother. I cannot lead the armies in war, for the sword is the embodiment of force, and force is the enemy of right. Whosoever participates in the sin of slaying, is himself a slayer. It is not my wish to inspire dread in others, and I would rather eat the bread of a beggar than deny the sign which has been vouchsafed to me. Short is our life amid the unending flux of things, and I would fain live out my days without further wrongdoing."

For a space, the king's brow was dark, and there was the silence of terror where before there had been tumult, for never yet had it happened since the days of fathers and forefathers that a nobleman had renounced war or that a prince had refused to accept his king's gift. But at length the monarch looked upon the sacred herons which Virata had wrested from the insurgents. At sight of these emblems of victory, his face cleared, and he said:

"I have always known you to be brave in conflict with my enemies, and to excel as a just man among the servants of my kingdom. If I must indeed do without your aid in war, I cannot dispense with your services in another field. Since, yourself a just man, you know and can appraise wrongdoing, you shall be the chief among my judges, and shall pass sentence from the threshold of my palace, so that truth may prevail within my walls and right be maintained throughout the land."

Virata prostrated himself before the king, who commanded him to mount the royal elephant. Side by side they entered the sixty-towered town, amid acclamations which thundered like the surges of a stormy sea.

Henceforward, from dawn to sunset, at the summit of the rose-coloured stairway in the shade of the palace, Virata delivered justice in the name of the king. His decisions were like those of a balance whose pointer trembles long before it sways this way or that. His clear eyes searched deeply into the soul of the accused, and his questions burrowed into the profundities of the offence as a badger burrows in the underground darkness. His sentences were rigorous, but were never delivered on the day of the hearing. He always allowed the cool span of night to intervene before passing judgment. During the long hours ere the sun rose, the members of his household could hear his footsteps as he paced the roof of the house while pondering the rights and wrongs of the matter. Before passing sentence, he laved his hands and his brow, that his decision might be free from the heat of passion. Always, too, after passing sentence, he would ask the culprit whether there was any reason to complain of the justice of the decision. Rarely was any objection raised. Silently the offender would kiss the step of the judgment seat, and with bowed head would accept the punishment as if it had been God's decree.

Never did Virata pass sentence of death, even for the most heinous of crimes, resisting all solicitations that he should do so. He dreaded to stain his hands with blood. The basin of the ancient fountain of the Rajputs, over whose margin the headsman would make the criminals lean before he delivered the death-blow, and whose stones had been blackened with blood, were washed white by the rains during the years of Virata's justiceship. Yet there was no increase of evil throughout the land. He confined ill-doers in the prison hewn out of the rock, or sent them to the mountains where they had to quarry stones for the walls of the gardens, or to the rice mills on the river bank where they turned the wheels side by side with the elephants. But he reverenced life, and men reverenced him, for never was any decision of his shown to be wrong, never was he weary of searching out the truth, and never did his words betray anger. From the remotest parts of the country, the peasants would come in buffalo carts bringing their disputes for his settlement; the priests obeyed his admonitions, and the king hearkened to his counsel. His fame grew as the young bamboo grows, and folk forgot they had once named him the Flashing of the Sword. Now, throughout Rajputana, he was known as the Wellspring of Justice.

In the sixth of the years of Virata's judgeship it came to pass that certain plaintiffs brought a youth of the tribe of the Kazars, the wild men who dwelt beyond the rocky hills and served other gods. His feet were bloodstained, for they had compelled him to make long marches during many days. His mighty arms were strongly bound, lest he should use them to do the harm that his fierce and sullen eyes threatened. Bringing him to the seat of judgment, they forced their prisoner to his knees before Virata, and then, prostrating themselves, they lifted up their hands as a sign that they were petitioners.

The judge looked questioningly at the strangers, saying:

"Who are ye, brothers, that come to me from afar, and who is this man whom ye bring to me thus fettered?"

The eldest of the company made obeisance, and answered:

"We are herdsmen, Lord, living peacefully in the eastern land. He whom we bring you is the most evil of an evil stock, a wretch who has slain more men than he has fingers on his hands. A dweller in our village, whose daughter he had asked in marriage, refused, because the men of his tribe have impious customs, being dog-eaters and cow-killers; instead, the father gave her for wife to a merchant in the lowlands. In his wrath, thereupon, this fellow drove off many of our cattle; one night he killed the father of the girl, and her three brothers; and whenever anyone of that household went to herd cattle in the foothills, this man slew him. Eleven from our village had he thus done to death, when at length we assembled our forces and hunted him like a wild beast until we had made him prisoner. Now, most just among judges, we have brought him to you that you may rid the land of the evildoer."

Virata, raising his head, looked at the bound man.

"Is it true, what they say of you?"

"Who are you? Are you the king?"

"I am Virata, servant of the king and servant of justice, that I may atone for my own wrongdoings and sift the true from the false."

The accused was silent for a space, and then gave Virata a piercing look.

"How, on your distant judgment seat, can you know what is true, and what is false, seeing that all your knowledge comes from what people tell you?"

"Give your rejoinder to their accusation, that from the two I may learn the truth."

The prisoner raised his eyebrows contemptuously.

"I shall not dispute with them. How can you know what I did, inasmuch as I myself do not know what my hands do when anger seizes me? I did justice on him who sold a woman for money, and I did justice on his children and his servants. Let these men bring a charge against me if they will. I despise them, and I despise your judgment."

A storm of anger burst forth from the accusers when they heard the prisoner express his scorn of the just judge. The apparitor raised his cudgel for a blow. Virata signed to them to restrain their anger, and resumed his questions. Each time the accusers returned to the charge, the judge asked the prisoner to reply. But the latter clenched his teeth in an angry grin, and spoke only once more, saying:

"How can you learn the truth from the words of others?"

The noon-day sun was directly overhead when Virata had finished his examination. Rising to his feet, he said, as was

his custom, that he would return home and would deliver
sentence on the following day. The accusers raised their hands
in protest.

"Lord," said they, "we have journeyed seven days to see
the light of your countenance, and it will take us another
seven days to return to our homes. How can we wait till the
morrow when our cattle are athirst and our land needs the
plough? We beseech you to deliver judgment forthwith."

Thereupon Virata seated himself once more and was
plunged for a while deep in thought. His brow was furrowed
like that of one who bears a heavy burden upon his head,
for never before had he been constrained to pass sentence
upon any who did not sue for pardon or upon one who remained defiant. His meditation lasted a long time, and the
shadows grew as the hours passed. Then he went to the fountain, and, having laved his forehead and his hands in the cool
water that his words might be free from the heat of passion,
he returned to the judgment seat and said:

"May the decision I shall deliver be a just one. A deadly
sin lies upon this offender, who has hunted eleven living souls
from their warm human bodies into the world of transmigration. For a year the life of man ripens unseen in the mother's
womb, and for this reason, for each one of those whom he has
slain the guilty man must remain hidden for a year in the
darkness of the earth. And because by his deed the blood has
been drained from eleven human bodies, eleven times every
year he shall be given one hundred lashes, that he may pay in
accordance with the number of his victims. But his life shall
not be taken from him, for life is the gift of the gods, and
man must not lay his hand on divine things. May this judgment be just, this judgment which I have uttered in pursu-
ance of no man's orders, but only for the sake of the great
retribution."

When he had spoken, the plaintiffs kissed the step of his seat in token of respect. But the prisoner met his inquiring glance with a gloomy silence. Virata said:

"I exhorted you to speak, that you might give me reasons for passing a light sentence, and that you might help me against your accusers, but your lips were sealed. Should there be any error in my judgment, you must not charge me with it before the Eternal; you must lay it to the account of your own silence. I would fain have been merciful to you."

The prisoner answered:

"I seek no mercy from you. What mercy can you give to compare with the life that you take from me in the drawing of a breath?"

"I am not taking your life."

"Nay, but you are taking my life, and are taking it more cruelly than do the chiefs of my tribe whom these lowlanders term savages. Why do you not kill me? I killed, man to man; but you bury me like a corpse in the darkness of the earth, to rot as the years pass; and you do it because your craven heart fears to shed blood, and because your bowels are weak as water. Your law is caprice, and your sentence is a martyrdom. Slay me, for I have slain."

"I have given you a just measure of punishment . . ."

"A just measure? But what, O Judge, is the measure by which you measure? Who has scourged you, that you may know what scourging is? How is it that you can tick off the years upon your fingers, as if a year passed in the light of day were the same thing as a year prisoned in the darkness of the earth? Have you dwelt in prison, that you may know how many springs you are taking from my days? You are an ignorant man and no just one, for he only who feels the blow knows what a blow is, not he who delivers it; and none but the sufferer can measure suffering. In your pride you pre-

sume to punish the offender, and are yourself the most grievous of all offenders, for when I took life it was in anger, in
the thraldom of my passion, whereas you rob me of my life
in cold blood and mete me a measure which your hand has
not weighed and whose burden you have never borne. Step
down from the seat of judgment ere you fall headlong! Woe
unto him who measures haphazard, and woe to the ignorant
man who fancies he knows what justice is. Step down from
the judgment seat, O ignorant Judge, nor continue to pass
sentence on living men with the death of your word!"

Pale with wrath was the prisoner as he flung forth these in-
vectives, and once more the angry onlookers were about to
fall upon him. Again Virata stayed them, and, turning his
face from the prisoner, he said gently:

"It is not in my power to quash the sentence that I have
spoken here. My hope is that the doom is just."

Virata moved to depart, while they seized the prisoner, who
struggled in his bonds. But, halting after a few steps, the
judge turned back towards the condemned man, only to
encounter his resolute and angry eyes. With a shudder it was
borne in upon Virata that these eyes were exactly like those
of his dead brother, the brother he had slain with his own
hand, and whom he had found lying dead in the tent of the
would-be usurper . . .

That evening, Virata spake no word to anyone. The stranger's look had pierced his soul like an arrow of fire. The folk
of his household heard him hour after hour as, the livelong
night, he strode sleepless to and fro on the roof of his house,
until day dawned red behind the palms.

At sunrise, Virata performed his ablutions in the sacred
pool of the temple. Turning eastward, he prayed, and then,
having returned to the house, he donned a ceremonial robe of
yellow silk. He greeted the members of his household, who

were amazed at his formality but did not venture to question him, and went alone to the king's palace, where he had leave of entry at any time of the day or night. Bowing before the king, Virata touched the hem of the monarch's garment in token of petition.

The king looked at him cordially, saying:

"Your wish has touched my vesture. It is granted before it is spoken."

Virata continued to stand with bowed head.

"You have made me the chief among your judges. For six years I have passed judgment in your name, and know not whether I have judged justly. Grant me a month of rest and quiet that I may find the road to truth; and permit me, in this matter, to keep my own counsel from you and all others. I wish to do a deed free from injustice and to live without sin."

The king was astonished.

"Poor will be my realm in justice from this moon to the next. Nevertheless, I will not ask you what path you wish to follow. May it lead you to the truth."

Kissing the foot of the throne as a sign of his gratitude, and having made a final obeisance, Virata left the presence.

He entered his house and summoned his wife and children.

"For a month you will see me no more. Bid me farewell, and ask no questions. Go to your rooms and shut yourselves in there that none of you may watch whither I go when I leave the house. Make no inquiries for me until the month has passed."

Silently, they did as was commanded.

Virata clad himself in dark attire, prayed before the divine image, and wrote a long letter upon palm leaves which he

rolled into a missive. At nightfall he left the silent house and
went to the great rock where the mines were and the prisons.
He knocked until the sleeping jailer rose from his mat to ask
who was without.

"I am Virata, the chief of the judges. I have come to see
the prisoner who was brought here yesterday."

"His cell is in the depths, Lord, in the lowest darkness of
the prison. Shall I lead you thither?"

"I know the place. Give me the key, and return to your
slumbers. Tomorrow you will find the key outside your door.
Let no one know that you have seen me tonight."

The jailer fetched the key and also a torch. At a sign from
Virata he withdrew, and threw himself on his mat. Virata
opened the bronze door which closed the archway of the
rocky vault, and descended into the depths of the prison.
A century earlier the kings of Rajputana had begun to con-
fine prisoners within this rock. Day by day each of the cap-
tives had to quarry deeper into the cold stone, fashioning
new cells for the inmates of the morrow.

Virata took a final glance at the quadrant of sky with its
sparkling stars visible through the rocky arch. Then he closed
the door, and the damp darkness rose to enwrap him, the darkness through which the unsteady light of his torch leaped
like a beast of prey. He could still hear the rustling of the
trees and the shrill clatter of the monkeys. At the bottom of
the first flight of steps, the rustling sound came from a great
distance. Lower still, the silence was as profound as if he
had been in the depths of the sea, motionless and cold. From
the stones there breathed nothing but dampness, without any
aroma of the fresh earth, and the farther he descended the
more harshly did his footsteps echo amid the silence.

The cell of the prisoned hill-man was five flights from the
surface, deeper beneath the earth than the height of the tall-
est palm tree. Virata entered and held his torch aloft over the

dark mass which hardly stirred for a while. Then a chain rattled.

Bending over the prostrate figure, Virata said:

"Do you know me?"

"I know you. You are he whom they made master of my fate, and you have trodden it under your foot."

"I am no master. I am servant of the king and of justice. It is to serve justice that I have come."

The prisoner looked at the judge with a fixed and gloomy stare:

"What do you want of me?"

After a long silence, Virata answered:

"I hurt you with the words of my judgment, and you have likewise hurt me with your words. I do not know if my decision was just; but there was truth in what you said, for no one ought to measure with a measure he does not know. I have been ignorant, and would gladly learn. I have sent hundreds into this abode of darkness; much have I done to many persons, without knowing what I did. Now I wish to find out, now I desire to learn, that I may grow just, and may encounter the day of transmigration free from all taint of sin."

The prisoner remained motionless, so that nothing was heard beyond a faint clanking of his chains. Virata continued:

"I wish to know what it is that I have doomed you to suffer; I wish to feel the bite of the scourge upon my own body, and to experience in my own soul what imprisonment means. For a month I shall take your place, that I may be taught how much I have exacted by way of atonement. Then I shall once again deliver sentence in the place of judgment, aware at length of the weight of my decisions. Meanwhile, you will go free. I shall give you the key by which you can open the door leading into the world of light, and shall accord you a month of liberty, provided only that you promise to return. Then from the darkness of these depths, light will enter my mind."

The prisoner stood as if carven out of stone. The clanking of his chains was no longer audible.

"Swear to me by the pitiless Goddess of Vengeance, who spares no one, that you will keep silence throughout this month, and I will give you the key and my own clothing. The key you must leave outside the porter's lodge, and then you can go free. But you remain bound by your oath that as soon as the month has sped you will take this missive to the king, in order that I may be delivered from prison, and once more judge righteously. Do you swear by the most high gods to fulfil this my bidding?"

"I swear," came the answer in tremulous tones as if from the depths of the earth.

Virata unloosed the chain and stripped off his own garment.

"Wear this," he said, "and give me your clothing. Muffle your face, that the jailer may take you for me. Now clip my hair and beard, that I also may remain unknown."

Tremblingly and reluctantly, under the compelling glance of Virata, the prisoner did as he was told. Then, for a long time, he was silent. At length, throwing himself on the ground, he cried passionately:

"Lord, I cannot endure that you should suffer in my stead. I killed. My hand is red with blood. The doom was just."

"Neither you nor I can appraise the justice of that doom, but soon the light will break in upon my mind. Go forth, as you have sworn, and when the moon is again full present my letter to the king that he may set me free. When the time is ripe I shall know what are the deeds I am doing, and my decisions thenceforward will be free from injustice. Go forth."

The prisoner knelt and kissed the ground. The closing door clanged in the darkness. Once again, through a loophole, a ray from the torch flickered across the walls, and then the night engulfed the hours.

Next morning, Virata, whom no one recognized, was publicly scourged. At the first stroke of the scourge upon his bared back, he uttered a cry; but thenceforward was silent, with clenched teeth. At the seventieth stroke, his senses grew dim, and he was carried away like a dead beast.

When he recovered consciousness he was lying in his cell, and it seemed to him as if he were stretched upon a bed of glowing charcoal. But his brow was cool, and he breathed the odour of wild herbs. Half-opening his eyes he saw that the jailer's wife was beside him, gently bathing his forehead. As he looked at her more attentively he perceived that the star of compassion shone down upon him in her glance. Amid his bodily torments he realized that the meaning of sorrow dwelt in the grace of kindliness. He smiled up at her and forgot his pain.

Next day he was able to rise to his feet and to grope his way round the cell. At each step a new world seemed to fashion itself beneath his feet. On the third day his wounds were easier and strength was returning to body and mind. Henceforward he sat without moving, and noted the passage of time only by the falling of the water-drops from the rocky roof. The great silence was subdivided into many little spaces, which were pieced together to form day and night as out of thousands of days our life grows to manhood and old age. None came to speak with him, and the darkness entered into his very soul. Yet within, the manifold springs of memory were opened. Flowing gently, they filled a quiet pool of contemplation wherein his whole life was mirrored. What he had experienced bit by bit, coalesced now into a unity. Never had his mind been so limpid as during this motionless insight into a reflected world.

Day by day Virata's vision grew clearer; things shaped themselves in the darkness, displaying their forms to his gaze. In like manner everything grew clearer to the eye of inward vision. The gentle delight of contemplation, spreading unsolicited beyond the illusive appearances of memory, played amid the forms of changing thought as the prisoner's hand played with the irregularities in the walls of his rocky cell. Withdrawn from self, and in the darkness and solitude unaware of the intimacies of his own nature, he grew ever more conscious of the might of the multiform divinity, and was able to wander freely amid these constructions of the imagination, in perfect independence, liberated from servitude to the will, dead in life and living in death. All the anxieties of the passing hour were dissipated in the serene joy of deliverance from the body. It seemed to him as if hour by hour he was sinking deeper into the darkness, down towards the stony and black roots of the earth, but as if he were none the less pregnant with a new germinal life. Perhaps it was the life of a worm, blindly burrowing in the clods; or perhaps that of a plant, striving upwards with its stem; or perhaps only that of a rock, cool, quiet, and blissfully unconscious of its own being.

For eighteen nights Virata enjoyed the divine mystery of devout contemplation, detached from his individual will and freed from the goading of life. What he had undertaken as atonement seemed to him blessedness, and he was already beginning to feel that sin and retribution were no more than dream images as contrasted with the eternal wakefulness of knowledge. But during the nineteenth night he was startled out of sleep by the prick of an earthly thought, boring into his brain like a red-hot needle. His body was shaken with terror, and his fingers trembled as leaves tremble in the wind.

The terrifying thought was that the prisoner might be faith-less and foresworn, might forget him, might leave him to spend a thousand and yet a thousand and yet another thou-sand days in prison, until the flesh dropped from his bones and his tongue grew stiff from perpetual silence. The will-to-live sprang up like a panther in his body, tearing at the wrap-pings in which it was enclosed. The current of time resumed its flow in his soul, and therewith came fears and hopes, and all the turmoil of earthly existence. No longer could he con-centrate upon the thought of the multiform and everlasting deity. He could think only of himself. His eyes craved for the daylight; his limbs, recoiling from the hard stone, longed for wide expanses, for the power to leap and to run. His mind was filled with thoughts of his wife and his sons, of his house and his possessions, of the ardent allurements of the world, which must be enjoyed with full awareness and must be felt with the waking warmth of the blood.

From now onwards, time, which had hitherto lain silent at his feet like the black waters of a quiet pool passively mir-roring events, was magnified in his thoughts, and took on the movement of a stream against which he had unceasingly to struggle. His longing was that it should overpower him, should carry him away like a floating tree to the predestined moment of liberation. But the flow was directed against him; panting for breath he swam desperately up-stream hour after hour. He felt as if the interval between the falling of the water-drops from the roof was being indefinitely prolonged. He could not lie patiently in his lair. The thought that the hill-man would forget him and that he would be doomed to rot in this crypt of silence, made him prowl round and round his narrow cell like a beast in a cage. The stillness choked him; he volleyed words of abuse and complaint at the walls; he cursed himself and the gods and the king. With bleeding fingers he tore at the obdurate rock, and ran with lowered head against the door until he fell insensible. On recovering consciousness, he would spring to his feet once more, only to repeat the ceaseless round.

During these days from the eighteenth of his confinement until the moon was full, Virata lived through æons of horror. He loathed food and drink, for his body was racked with anxiety. Thought had become impossible, though with his lips he continued to count the drops of water as they fell, that he might punctuate the interminable time from one day to another. Meanwhile, though he did not know it, the hair on his throbbing temples turned grey.

But on the thirtieth day there was a noise without, followed by silence. Then came the sound of footsteps on the stair; the door was flung open, a light broke in, and the king stood before the man entombed in darkness. With a loving embrace the monarch greeted him and said:

"I have learned of your deed, which is greater than any recorded in the chronicles of our fathers. It will shine like a star above the dead levels of our life. Come forth that the fire of God may light you with its glow, and that the happy people may behold a righteous man."

Virata shaded his eyes with his hand, for the unaccustomed glare was painful. He rose to his feet unsteadily, like a drunkard, and the servants had to support him. Before going to the door he said:

"O King, you have called me a righteous man, but now I know full well that he who passes judgment on another does injustice and grievous wrong. In these depths there still languish human beings who are here by my decision. Now, for the first time, do I know what they suffer. Now at length I know that the law of retaliation is itself unjust. Set the prisoners free, and tell the people to be gone, for their acclamations fill me with shame."

The king gave a sign, and his servitors dispersed the throng. Once again all was quiet. Then the king said:

"Until now your seat of justice has been at the summit of the stairway leading to my palace. But through your knowledge of suffering you have become wiser than any judge has ever been before you, and henceforward you shall sit beside me that I may hearken to your words and may myself drink in wisdom from your justice."

Virata embraced the king's knee in token of petition.

"Discharge me from my office. No longer can I give true decisions, now that I realize that no one can judge another. Punishment is in God's hands, not in man's, for whoever interferes with the working of destiny commits a crime. I wish to live out my life free from sin."

"So be it," answered the king. "Instead of the chief of my judges, you shall be my chief counsellor, deciding for me the issues of peace and war, and advising me in matters of taxation, that all my undertakings may be guided by your wisdom."

Again Virata clasped the king's knee.

"Do not give me power, O King, for power urges to action; and what action can be just, or what action can fail to counteract that which has been decreed by fate? If I counsel war, I am sowing the seeds of death. What I say, grows into actions; and every act of mine has a significance which I cannot foresee. He only can be just and righteous, who refrains from all activities, and who lives alone. Never have I been nearer wisdom, and never have I been freer from sin than here in solitude, exchanging words with no man. Let me live tranquilly in my own dwelling, doing no other service than that of making sacrifice to the gods, that thus I may remain free from sin."

"I am loath to relinquish your services," replied the king,

"but who can venture to argue with a sage, or to constrain
the will of a righteous man? Live as you think best. It will
be an honour to my kingdom that within its bounds there
should be one living without sin."

They parted at the gate of the prison. Virata walked homeward alone, drinking in the fragrance of the sunlit air. Never
before had he felt so light of heart as now when freed from
all service. Behind him sounded the soft tread of naked feet,
and when he turned he saw the condemned man whose punishment he had taken upon himself. The hill-man kissed the
ground where the sometime judge had trodden, made a timid
obeisance, and vanished. Virata smiled for the first time since
he had looked upon the staring eyes of his dead brother, and
he entered the house glad at heart.

After returning home, Virata lived through a time that was
full of happiness. His awakening was a prayer of thanksgiving that he could look upon the light of heaven instead of
upon darkness, that he could see the colours and inhale the
aroma of the lovely earth, and that he could listen to the
sweet music with which the morning is alive. Each day he
accepted as a new and splendid gift the wonder of breath and
the charm of free movement. With pious affection he would
pass his hands over his own body, over the soft frame of his
wife, and over the sturdy limbs of his sons, rapturously aware
of the imminence of the multiform God in one and all of
them. His soul was winged with gentle pride that he never
had occasion to pass beyond the boundaries of his own life
to interfere with a stranger's destiny, that he never made a
hostile onslaught upon any of the numberless embodiments
of the invisible God. From morn till eve he read the books of
wisdom and practised the different varieties of devotion: the
silence of meditation; loving absorption into the spirit; ben-
efaction to the poor; and sacrificial prayer. He had grown

cheerful. His speech was gracious even to the humblest of his servants, and all the members of his household were more devoted to him than ever they had been before. He brought help to the needy and consolation to the unfortunate. The prayers of the multitude hovered over his sleep, and no longer did men call him as of old the Flashing of the Sword or the Wellspring of Justice, for now he had become the Field of Good Counsel. Not only did his neighbours ask his advice. Though he was no longer a judge in the land, strangers sought him out from afar that he might settle their disputes, and complied unhesitatingly with his words. Virata rejoiced thereat, feeling that counsel was better than command, and mediation better than judgment. It seemed to him that his life was blameless, now that he no longer held forcible sway over anyone's destiny and could none the less adjust the fates of many. Thus he delighted in this high noon of his life.

Three years passed by, and yet another three, and the speeding of them all was like that of one bright day. Gentler and ever gentler grew the disposition of Virata. When a quarrel was brought to him for adjustment, he found it hard to understand why there was so much bickering upon earth, and why men pressed hard on one another with the petty jealousies of ownership when the expanses of life were open to them and the sweet aroma of existence. He envied none and none envied him. His house stood, an island of peace in the level sea of life, untouched by the torrents of passion or by the stream of sensual appetite.

One evening, in the sixth year of this period of calm, Virata had already retired to bed when he heard harsh cries and the thud of blows. He sprang from his couch and saw that his sons were chastising one of the slaves. They had forced the man to his knees, and were lashing him with a leathern thong until the blood gushed forth. The eyes of the victim stared Virata in the face, and once again he seemed to see

the eyes of the brother he had slain. Hastening forth, he
arrested the arm of the son wielding the whip and asked
what was afoot.

From a medley of answers he gathered that this slave,
whose duty it was to draw water from the rocky spring and
bring it to the house in wooden buckets, had on several occasions during the noontide heat, pleading exhaustion, arrived
too late with his burden. Each time, he had been punished;
and yesterday, after a severer chastisement than usual, he had
absconded. Virata's sons had pursued him on horseback, and
had not overtaken him until he had crossed the river. They
had tied him with a rope to the saddle of one of the horses,
so that, half-dragged and half-running, he had reached home
with lacerated feet. Now they were giving him an exemplary
punishment, for his own good and for that of the other slaves,
who looked on trembling. This was the explanation of the
scene which their father had interrupted. Virata glanced down
at the slave. His eyes were widely opened like those of an animal awaiting its death-blow from the slaughterman, and
behind their dark stare Virata sensed the horror that he had
himself once lived through.

"Loose the man," he said to his sons. "The transgression is
atoned."

The slave kissed the dust in front of the master's feet. For
the first time the sons parted from their father in dudgeon.
Virata returned to his room. Unwittingly he began to lave
forehead and hands. At the touch of the cold water he suddenly grew aware of what he was doing, and realized that for
the first time since leaving the rocky prison-house he had become a judge and had interfered in another's destiny. For
the first time, too, during these six years, sleep forsook his pillow. As he lay awake in the darkness, he saw in fancy the
terrified eyes of the slave (or were they the eyes of his own
slain brother?); and he saw the angry eyes of his sons; and

again and again he asked himself whether his children had
not wreaked an injustice upon this servant. On account of a
trifling neglect of duty, blood had moistened the sandy precincts of his house. For a petty act of omission, the lash had
been laid upon living flesh, and this wrongdoing seared him
more deeply than had the strokes of the scourge which aforetime had tortured his own back like scorpions. True, the chastisement he had witnessed that evening had befallen, not a
nobleman, but a slave, whose body by the king's law belonged
to the master from the very day of birth. But was the king's
law right in the eyes of the multiform God? Could it be right
in the eyes of God that the body of one human being should
pass into the absolute power of another; and could that other
be held guiltless before God if he injured or destroyed the life
of the slave?

Virata rose from his bed and kindled a light, that he might
seek instruction in the books of the sages. He found, indeed,
distinctions between man and man established in the ordering
of the castes and the estates; but nowhere amid the manifestations of the multiform being was there warrant for any
difference in fulfilling the demands of love. More and more
eagerly did he drink in wisdom, for never had his soul been
more tensely alive to a problem. But now the flame leaped
for a moment in the socket of the torch, and then the light
went out.

As darkness fell between him and the walls, Virata became strangely aware that the enclosed space his eyes were
blindly searching was no longer that of his familiar room, but
that of his erstwhile dungeon, where, awestricken, he had
acquired the certainty that freedom is the most intimate right
of human beings, and that no one is entitled to prison another, be it for a lifelong term or only for a single year. Yet
he, Virata, had prisoned this slave within the invisible confines of his own will. He had chained this slave to the chances

of his own decisions, so that the underling could no longer take a single footstep in freedom. Clearness came to him as he sat and pondered, feeling how thought was enlarging his comprehension, until from some invisible altitude the light entered into him. Now he became aware that he had still been blameworthy in this, that he had allowed his fellows to be subject to his will, and to be named his slaves in accordance with a law which was but a fragile human construction and not one of the eternal decrees of the multiform God. He bowed himself in prayer:

"I thank thee, O God of a thousand shapes, for that thou sendest me messengers from all thy shapes, to hunt me out of my sins and draw me ever nearer to thee upon the invisible path of thy will. Grant me power to recognize them in the ever-accusing eyes of the undying brother, who encounters me everywhere, who sees with my vision, and whose sufferings I suffer, that I may purify my life and may breathe without sin."

Virata's countenance was again cheerful. Clear-eyed he went forth into the night, to enjoy the white greeting of the stars, and to inhale the breath of the breeze that freshens before dawn. Passing through the garden, he went down to the river. When the sun appeared in the east, he plunged into the sacred stream, and then returned homewards to join the members of his household, who were assembled for morning prayer.

He greeted them with a kindly smile, signed to the women to withdraw, and then said to his sons:

"You know that for years I have had but one care, to be a just and righteous man, and to live my life on earth without sin. Yesterday blood flowed upon the ground within the precincts of my dwelling, the blood of a living man, and I wish to be innocent of this blood and to atone for the wrong that has been done under the shadow of my roof. The slave

here the earth had never yet been broken by the plough.
At dawn he reached a place where the lightning had struck
ancient mango tree, and where the consequent fire had
de a clearing in the jungle. The stream flowed softly past
spot in a wide curve, and numerous birds were drinking
rlessly from its waters. Thus the river offered a clear
spect in front, while the trees gave shade behind. Scattered
r the ground was wood which had been split off by the
tning blast, together with fragments of the undergrowth.
ata contemplated this lonely clearing in the jungle, and re-
ed to built a hut there. He would devote the rest of his
to meditation, far from his fellows and free from sin.
took him five days to build his hut, for his hands were un-
stomed to labour. Even when it was finished, his days
e full of toil. He had to seek fruit for food. Hard work was
ded to keep back the jungle, which continually tended to
roach. A palisade had to be built as a protection from the
gry tigers, prowling in the jungle at night. But no noise
uman beings intruded into his life or disturbed his seren-
The days flowed peacefully like the waters of the river,
gently renewed from an unfailing spring.
he birds found nothing to alarm them in the quiet doings
he newcomer, and ere long they built their nests on the
of his hut. He strewed seeds from the great flowers, and
ut fruits for their repast. Growing more friendly by de-
s, they would fly down from the palm trees at his call.
played with them, and they were not afraid to let him
lle them. In the forest, one day, he found a young mon-
lying on the ground with a broken leg and crying like
ld. Picking the creature up, he brought it to his hut, and
ed it as soon as it was better. The monkey was docile,
ively imitated him, and served him faithfully. Thus he
surrounded by gentle living creatures, but he never forgot
n the animal, no less than in the human kind, force and

who was punished unduly for a trifling fault shall be free
from this hour, free to go whither he lists, so that at the Last
Judgment he may not bear testimony against you and me."

His sons remained silent, and Virata felt that their silence
was hostile.

"You make no answer. I do not wish to act against your
will without hearing what you have to say."

"You propose to bestow freedom upon an offender, to reward him instead of punishing him," said the eldest. "We
have many servants in the house, so one will not be missed.
But a deed works beyond its own confines, and is no more
than a link in a chain. If you set this man free, how can you
keep the others in bondage should they also wish to depart?"

"Should they wish to depart from out my life, I must let
them go. I will not fashion anyone's destiny, for whosoever
fashions another's destiny is a wrongdoer."

"You are loosening the sanctions of the law," the second
son broke in. "These slaves are our own, as our land is our
own, and the trees that grow thereon, and the fruit of the
trees. Inasmuch as they serve you, they are bound to you, and
you are bound to them. That which you are touching is part
of a traditional ordinance which dates back many thousands
of years. The slave is not lord of his own life, but servant of
his master."

"We have but one right from God, and it is the right to
live, which is breathed into all of us with the divine breath.
You did well to exhort me, for I was still in blindness when
I thought I was cleansing myself of sin. All these years I have
been taking away the lives of others. Now at length I see
clearly, and I know that a righteous man may not turn men
into beasts. I shall free them all, that I may free myself of
sin towards them."

The brows of his sons grew dark with defiance. The eldest
returned a stubborn answer:

"Who will irrigate our fields to keep the rice from withering? Who will drive forth the cattle? Are we to become serving men because of your whims? You yourself have never done a hand's turn of work throughout your life, nor have you ever troubled because that life was sustained by the labour of others. Nevertheless, there was others' sweat in the plaited straw on which you were lying, and a slave had to fan you while you slept. Now, of a sudden, you would dismiss them all, that none may labour except your sons, the men of your own blood. Would you have us unyoke the oxen and pull the ploughs ourselves, that the beasts may be free from the goad? Into these dumb beasts, likewise, the multiform God has breathed the breath of life. Touch not that which is ordained, for it also comes from God. Earth yields her fruits unwillingly, yields them only at the spell of force. The law of the world is force, and we cannot evade it."

"But I will evade it, for might is seldom right, and I wish to live out my life in righteousness."

"Might underlies all possession, be it the ownership of man or of beast or of the patient earth. Where you are master, you must be conqueror as well; he who owns is bound to the destiny of men."

"But I will loose myself from everything which binds me to sin. I command you, therefore, to set the slaves free, and yourselves to do the labour that is needful."

The sons' eyes flashed, and they could hardly control their anger. The eldest answered:

"You told us that you wished to constrain no man's will. You would not give orders to your slaves lest thereby you should fall into sin; but you command us to do this and that, and meddle with our lives. In which respect are you doing right before God and man?"

Long time Virata was silent. When he raised his eyes he

saw the flame of greed in theirs, an
within him. He said gently:

"You have taught me a lesson. It is
you in any way. Take the house an
Divide them among you as you thin
have part or lot in these things, or in
them. You have said sooth: He who
their liberty; but, worst of all, he ensl
ever wishes to live without sin must
ership of a house and from the mana
He must not be fed by others' labou
wherewithal to drink because others
his need. The joys of carnal intercou
inertia of satiety must be far from
alone, lives with God; only the a
nought but poverty knows God to
to be near the Invisible One than
for I desire to live without sin. Tal
among you peacefully."

Virata turned and left them. Hi
isfied greed was sweet to them in t
were ashamed.

At nightfall Virata made ready f
a begging bowl, an axe for work,
and palm leaves, inscribed with
Kilting his raiment above the kne
without taking leave of wife, chi
household. Afoot all night, he ca
he had once flung his sword in th
ening, made his way through the
along the farther bank, where th

evil slumber. He saw how the alligators would bite one another and hunt one another in their wrath, how the birds would snatch fish from the river, and how the snakes would encircle and crush the birds. The dreadful enchainment of destruction with which the hostile goddess of destruction had fettered the world became manifest to him as a law whose truth knowledge was forced to admit. Still, it was good to be merely an observer of these struggles, to be blameless amid the enlarging circle of destruction and of liberation.

For a year and many months he had not seen a human face. And then it happened one day that a hunter following the spoor of an elephant, came to the place where the beast had drunk on the opposite bank. A marvellous sight met his gaze. In the yellow glimmer of evening, a white-bearded man was seated in front of a little hut; birds were perching on his head; a monkey at his feet was breaking nuts for him with a stone. But the man was looking up at the tree tops where the multicoloured parrots were sporting, and when he beckoned to them they fluttered down in a golden cloud and alighted on his hands. The hunter fancied that he was looking at the saint of whom it is written: "The beasts will talk to him with the voice of man, and the flowers grow under his footsteps; he can pluck the stars with his lips, and can blow away the moon with his breath." Forgetting his guest, the elephant-hunter hastened to the city to relate what he had beheld.

The very next day quidnuncs arrived to glimpse the wonder from the other side of the stream. More, and ever more, flocked to contemplate the marvel, until at length there arrived one who recognized Virata. Spreading far and wide, the tidings at length reached the king, who had grievously missed his loyal servant. The monarch ordered a boat to be made ready with four times seven rowers. Lustily they plied the oars up stream until the vessel reached the site of Virata's hut. A carpet was spread for the king, who landed and approached the sage. For eighteen months, now, Virata had not listened to human speech. He greeted his guest timidly and with diffident mien, forgot the obeisance due from a subject to a ruler, and said simply:

"A blessing on your coming, O King."

The king embraced him.

"For years I have marked your progress towards perfection, and I have come to look upon the rare miracle of righteousness, that I myself may learn how a righteous man lives."

Virata bowed.

"All my knowledge is but this, that I have unlearned how to live with men, in order that I may remain free from all sin. The solitary can teach none but himself. I do not know if what I am doing is wisdom; I do not know if what I am feeling is happiness. I have no counsel to give and nothing to teach. The wisdom of the solitary is different from the wisdom of the world; the law of contemplation is another law than the law of action."

"But merely to see how a righteous man lives is to learn something," answered the king. "Since I have looked upon your face, I am filled with innocent joy. I ask nothing more.

"Can I fulfil any wish of yours in my kingdom, or carry any tidings to your own folk?"

"Nothing is mine any more, Lord King—or everything on this earth is mine. I have forgotten that I ever had a house among other houses, or children among other children. He who is homeless has the world for home; he who has cut loose from the ties of life has all life for his portion; he who is innocent has peace. My only wish is that my life on earth may be free from sin."

"Farewell, then, and think of me in your devotions."

"I think of God, and thus I think of you and of all on this earth, who are part of him and who breathe with his breath."

The king's boat passed away down the stream, and many

months were to go by before the recluse was again to hear the
voice of man.

Once more Virata's fame took wings unto itself and flew
like a white falcon over the land. To the remotest villages
and to the huts by the seashore came the news of the sage who
had left house and lands that he might live the life of devout
contemplation, and it was now that he was given the fourth
name of virtue, becoming known as the Star of Solitude. In
the temples, the priests extolled his renunciation; the king
spoke of it to his servants; and when any judge uttered his
decision, he added, "May my words be as just as those of
Virata, who now lives wholly for God and knows all wisdom."

It often happened, and more frequently as the years sped
by, that a man who came to realize the unrighteousness of
his actions and to feel the vanity of his life, would leave
house and home, give away his possessions, and wander off
into the jungle, to build a hut like Virata and devote himself
to God's service. Example is the strongest bond on earth;
every deed arouses in others the will to righteousness, the will
that now wakens from dreams and turns to vigorous action.
Those who were thus wakened grew aware of the futility of
their lives. They saw the blood that stained their hands and
the sin that flecked their souls. They rose up and went forth
to solitude, satisfied with enough for the barest needs of the
body, plunged in perpetual meditation. If they chanced to
encounter one another on their walks abroad to gather fruit,
they uttered no word of greeting lest they should form new
bonds thereby, but they smiled cordially at one another, and
their souls exchanged greetings of peace. The common folk
spoke of this forest as the Abode of the Pious. No hunter
ranged its paths, fearing to defile the sanctuary by slaughter.

One morning, when Virata was walking in the jungle, he found an anchorite stretched motionless on the ground. Stooping to lift the fallen man, he perceived that the body was lifeless. Virata closed the eyes of the dead, murmured a prayer, and endeavoured to carry the corpse out of the thicket, intending to build a funeral pyre that the body of this brother might pass duly purified into the transmigration. But his meagre diet of fruits had weakened him, and the burden was beyond his strength. In search of help, he crossed the river by the ford and made his way to the nearest village.

When the villagers saw the sublime figure of him they had named the Star of Solitude, they came in all humility desiring to know his will, and, on being informed, they hastened to make ready for the task. Whithersoever Virata went, the women prostrated themselves before him. The children remained standing, and regarded his silent progress with astonishment. The men came out of their houses to kiss the raiment of their august visitor and to invoke the blessing of the saint. Virata passed through this gentle wave of humanity with a smile of contentment, feeling how pure and ardent was his love for his fellows now that he was no longer bound to them by any tie.

But when he reached the last of the humble cottages, having everywhere cordially returned the kindly salutations of those who accosted him, he saw that in this hut a woman was seated, and that her eyes as she looked at him were full of hatred. He shrank back in horror, for it seemed to him that he had again encountered the eyes which for so long he had forgotten, the rigid, accusing eyes of his slain brother. During these years of solitude, his spirit had grown unused to enmity, and he tried to persuade himself that he had mistaken the meaning of the stare. But when he looked again, the eyes were still gazing forth upon him with the same fixed malevolence. When, having recovered his self-command, he stepped forward towards the cottage, the woman withdrew into the passage, but from its dark recesses her eyes continued to glare at him with the ferocity of the burning eyes of a tiger in the jungle.

Virata plucked up heart, saying to himself:

"How can I have injured this woman whom I have never seen? Why should her hatred stir against me? There must be some mistake, and I will search out the error."

Moving forward, he knocked at the door. There was no sound in answer to his knock, and yet he could feel the malevolent proximity of the stranger woman. Patiently he knocked once more, waited awhile, and knocked again like a beggar. At length, with hesitating step, the woman came to the door, and her face as she looked at him was still dark and hostile.

"What more do you want of me?" she fiercely inquired.

He saw that she had to grip the door posts to steady herself, so shaken was she by anger.

Nevertheless, when Virata glanced at her face his heart grew light, for he was sure that he had never seen her before. She was young, and he was far on the road through life; their paths had never crossed, and he could never have done her an injury.

"I wished to give you the greeting of peace, stranger woman," answered Virata; "and I wished to ask you why you look at me so fiercely. Am I your enemy? Have I done you any harm?"

"What harm have you done me?" She smiled maliciously. "What harm have you done me? A trifle only, a mere trifle. My house was full, and you have made it empty; you have robbed me of my beloved; you have changed my life to death. Go, that I may see you no more, or I shall be unable to contain my wrath."

Virata looked at her again. So frenzied were her eyes that

it seemed to him she must be beside herself. He turned to depart, saying only:

"I am not the person you suppose. I live far from the haunts of men, and have no part in anyone's destiny. You mistake me for another."

But she screamed after him in her hatred:

"Full well do I know you, as all know you! You are Virata, whom they call the Star of Solitude, whom they extol with the four names of virtue. But I will not extol you. My mouth will cry aloud against you until my plaint reaches the last judge of the living. Come, since you have asked me; come and see what you have done."

Grasping the sleeve of the amazed Virata, she dragged him into the house and opened the door leading into a dark low-ceilinged chamber. She drew him towards the corner where a motionless form was lying upon a mat. Virata stooped over the form, and then drew back shuddering, for a boy lay there dead, a boy whose eyes stared up at him like the accusing eyes of the undying brother. Close beside him stood the woman racked with pain, and she moaned:

"He was the third, the last fruit of my womb; and you have murdered him as well as the others, you whom they call saint, and servant of the gods."

When Virata wished to open his mouth in protest, she broke out once more:

"Look at this loom, look at the empty stool. Here sat Paratika, my husband, day after day, weaving white linen, for there was no more skilful weaver in the land. People came from afar to give him orders, and his work was our life. Our days were joyful, for Paratika was a kindly man, and ever industrious. He shunned bad company and kept away from the loafers in the street. By him I bore three children, and we reared them in the hope that they would become men

like their father, kindly and upright. Then came a hunter—
would to God he had never set foot in the village—from
whom Paratika learned of one who had left house and possessions to devote himself, while still leading this earthly life,
wholly to the service of God. With his own hands, said the
hunter, he had built himself a hut. Paratika grew more and
more reserved. He meditated much in the evenings, and
rarely spoke. One night I awakened to find that he had left
my side and had gone to the forest in which you dwell that
you may meditate on God, the forest men call the Abode of
the Pious. But while he thus thought of himself, he forgot us,
and forgot that we lived by his labour. Poverty visited us;
the children lacked bread; one died after another; today the
last of the three has died, and through your act. You led
Paratika astray. That you might come nearer to the true
essence of God, the three children of my body have gone
down to dust. How will you atone, O Arrogant One, when I
charge you before the judge of the quick and the dead with
the pangs their little bodies suffered, while you were feed-
ing the birds and were living far from all suffering? How will
you atone for having lured an honest man from the work
which fed him and his innocent boys, for having deluded
him with the mad thought that in solitude he would be nearer
to God than in active life among his fellows?"

Virata blenched, and his lips quivered.

"I did not know that my example would be an incitement
to others. The course I took, I meant to take alone."

"Where is your wisdom, O Sage, if you do not know what
every boy knows, that all acts are the acts of God, and that
no one can by his own will escape from action or evade responsibility? Your mind was swelled with pride when you
fancied that you could be lord of your own actions and could
teach others. What was sweet to you has become gall to me,

and your life has occasioned the death of this child."

Virata reflected for a while, and then bowed his head in assent.

"What you say is true, and I see that there is more knowledge of the truth in a single throb of pain than in all the aloofness of the sages. What I know I have learned from the unfortunate; and what I have seen has been made visible to me by the glance of those who suffer, by the eyes of the undying brother. Indeed, I have not been humble before God, as I fancied, but proud; this is borne in on me by the sorrow I now feel. It is true that he who remains inactive none the less does a deed for which he is responsible on earth; and even the solitary lives in all his brethren. Again, I beseech you to forgive me. I shall return from the forest, in the hope that Paratika will likewise return to implant new life in your womb."

He bent forward once more and touched the hem of her garment with his lips. All sense of anger faded from her mind as, bewildered, she followed with her eyes the retreating figure.

Virata spent one more night in his hut. Once again he looked at the stars, watching at sunset the appearance of their white flames in the depths of heaven, and watching them pale at dawn. Once more he summoned his birds to their feast, and caressed them. Then, taking the staff and the bowl he had brought with him years before, he made his way back to the town.

Hardly had the tidings spread that the holy man had left his lonely hermitage and was once more within the gates of the city, when the people flocked to see the rare and wondrous spectacle, although many were filled with a secret dread lest the return of this man from the divine presence might bode disaster. As if between living walls of veneration, Virata made his progress, and he endeavoured to greet the onlookers with the serene smile that usually graced his lips. But for the first time he found it impossible to smile; his eyes remained grave and his lips were closed.

At length he reached the palace. The hour of the council was over, and the king was alone. Virata entered, and the monarch stood up to embrace his visitor. But Virata prostrated himself to the earth, and touched the hem of the king's mantle in token of petition.

"Your request is granted," said the king, "before you form it in words on your lips. It is an honour to me that I am empowered to serve a pious man and to help a sage."

"Call me not a sage," answered Virata, "for I have not followed the right path. I have been wandering in a circle, and now stand as a petitioner before your throne. I wished to be free from sin, and I shunned all action; but none the less I was entangled in the net which the gods spread for mortals."

"Far be it from me to believe your words," replied the king. "How could you do wrong to the human beings whose presence you shunned; and how did you fall into sin when your life was devoted to God's service?"

"Not wittingly did I do wrong, for I fled from sin; but our feet are chained to earth, and our deeds are in bondage to the eternal laws. Inaction is itself an action. I could not elude the eyes of the undying brother on whom our actions for ever bear, be they good or be they evil, and in defiance of our own will. But I am seven times guilty, for I fled from God and refused to serve life; I was useless, for I nourished my own life merely, and did no service to any other. Now I wish to serve again."

"Your words are strange to me, Virata, and beyond my understanding. But tell me your wish that I may fulfil it."

"No longer do I desire to be free in my will. The free man

is not free, and he who is inactive does not escape sin. Only he who serves is free, he who gives his will to another, who devotes his energies to a work, and who acts without questioning. Only the middle of the deed is our work; its beginning and its end, its cause and its effect, are on the knees of the gods. Make me free from my own will, for all willing is confusion, and all service is wisdom."

"I cannot understand you. You ask me to make you free, and at one and at the same time you ask me to give you service. Then he only is free who enters the service of another, whereas that other who takes the first into his service is not free? This passes my comprehension."

"It is just as well, O King, that you cannot understand this in your heart. How could you remain a king and issue commands if you understood?"

The king's face darkened with anger.

"Is it your meaning that the ruler is a lesser thing in the sight of God than the servant?"

"No one is less than another in the sight of God, and no one is greater. He who serves, and unquestioningly surrenders his own will, has relieved himself of responsibility, and has given it back to God. But he who wills, and who fancies that wisdom can enable him to avoid what is hostile, falls into temptation and falls into sin."

The king's countenance was still darkened.

"Then one service is the same as another, and there is neither greater service nor lesser service in the eyes of God and man?"

"It may well happen that one service seems greater than another in the eyes of man, but all service is equal in the eyes of God."

The king gazed at Virata long and sombrely. Pride stirred fiercely in his soul. When he looked once more at the worn face, and the white hair surmounting the wrinkled forehead, it seemed to him that the old man must be in his dotage. To test the matter, he said mockingly:

"Would you like to be keeper of the hounds in my palace?"

Virata bowed, and kissed the step of the throne in sign of gratitude.

From that day forward the old man whom the country had once extolled with the four names of virtue was keeper of the hounds in the kennels adjoining the palace, and he dwelt with the servitors in the menial quarters. His sons were ashamed of him. They made a wide circuit when they had to pass his abode, for they wished to avoid the sight of him and would fain escape having to acknowledge kinship in the presence of others. The priests turned their backs upon him as unworthy. For a few days the common people would stand and stare when the old man who had once been the first of the king's subjects came by habited as a servant and leading the hounds in leash. But he paid no heed to these onlookers, so they soon went their ways and ceased to think of him.

Virata did faithful service from dawn to sunset. He washed the hounds' muzzles and cleansed their coats; he brought their food and made up their litter; he cleared away their droppings. Soon the beasts came to love him more than any other inmate of the palace, and this did his heart good. His old and shrivelled mouth, with which he rarely spoke, smiled as of yore at his charges' pleasure. He took delight in the passing of the years, which were many and uneventful. The king died. A new king came who knew not Virata, and who struck him once with a stick because one of the hounds growled when his majesty went by. A day came when he was forgotten of all his fellow-men.

When the tale of his years was told, when at length he died, and his body was consigned to the common burial ground of the slaves, there was no one among the folk to remember him who had once been famous throughout the land where he had been known by the four names of virtue. His sons kept out of sight, and no priest sang the song of death over his remains. The dogs, indeed, howled for two days and two nights; but then they, too, forgot Virata, whose name is not inscribed in the chronicles of the conquerors and is not to be found in the books of the sages.